BEYOND THE
CHECKPOINT

BEYOND THE CHECKPOINT

Addison M. Conley

Beyond the Checkpoint
Copyright © 2019 by Addison M. Conley.
Published by Cold Run Valley Publishing, LLC

ISBN: 978-0-9980296-2-7

Credits:
Copyedit and Proofreading: Twin Tweaks Editing, JoAnn Collins, *twintweaksediting.com*
Developmental Editor: Amber Jost
Book Design: Maureen Cutajar, Go Published, *gopublished.com*
Cover Design: Natasja Hellenthal, Beyond Book Covers, *beyondbookcovers.com*
Cover Photo (top): Rawpixelimages
Cover Photo (bottom): Addison M. Conley, Kabul, Afghanistan.

To all who served in silence.
Hold your head high.

We must not go backward.
Keep the faith and march on.

Acknowledgements

Several people have been instrumental in helping me develop my writing and inspiring me. First, I never would have made the step to publish without the vital work of the Golden Crown Literary Society and the GCLS Writing Academy. Thank you.

To several terrific authors that I've met along the way, thank you for your help and encouragement as I set upon a new endeavor with this book. The list is long, but I would like to give a rousing thanks to Caren J. Werlinger and Alison R. Solomon. They gave me valuable Indie publishing tips, and Caren kindly met me over coffee to offer her expert advice. Also, thank you, Linda North, for remaining a friend even though things got rocky in 2018.

I can't say enough great things about my fabulous beta readers: Betsy Carswell, Laure Dherbécourt, Linda North, Danielle Zion, LHK, and Anya Cavalieri. Thank you for making this book better. You pointed out things I never considered.

A million thanks to the editors for smoothing out the edges: Amber Jost (freelance editor) and JoAnn Collins (Twin Tweaks Editing). In particular, thank you, JoAnn, for being an ally and writing positive comments. No one lives in a vacuum. It's nice to hear uplifting remarks and stories from our straight allies.

To the cover artist, Natasja Hellenthal, thank you for working with me and for not freaking out with all my little changes. To the book setter, Maureen Cutajar, thank you for a beautiful design.

Thanks to my family and friends who kept me sane during several times in my life.

Lastly, thanks to the readers!!!

Take care and all the best,
Addison

Introductory Note by the Author

While a work of fiction, *Beyond the Checkpoint* is based on my experience during three deployments—twice to Afghanistan and once to Iraq. I deployed as a federal employee for the National Geospatial-Intelligence Agency and worked with military units. Like the story, the policy "Don't Ask Don't Tell" (DADT) was in place. Under DADT, a service member could be dishonorably discharged. DADT ended in 2011.

The term Joint Elite Technology Team (JETT), used in this book, is a fictional name but based on a real NSA unit. I figured JETT was easier to remember. Elsewhere, I have made every effort to simplify jargon and acronyms to provide a balance between those in the know and those with little or no military experience or knowledge of the Intelligence Community. For example, I replaced real acronyms like the JIOC and SCIF with the term Operations Center or Ops Center. Instead of JWICS, I wrote classified computer. *A glossary of terms and locations is provided in the back.*

This novel is a blend of military action, suspense, and romance. It is about the women forming a relationship as they navigate through their careers. Part of that path is through a military setting. So, if you don't know much about the military, please don't get hung up on rank. If you're military and unfamiliar with the national-level intelligence agencies, the military portion in this book may be unlike anything else you've ever experienced.

Sincerely,
Addison M. Conley

PART I

2008

Chapter 1

March 2008 – West Point, Virginia

The smell of burning rubber filled Ali's nostrils, and a sick, queasy feeling settled in, followed by heat spreading through her body. Her head spun, and her stomach churned.

"Stop! Please stop and let me out!" When he didn't respond, she shouted, "I'm going to be sick! I need fresh air!"

He radioed control through his headset, but instead of slowing down, he sped toward the curve. After fishtailing, he spun the car around, stopping next to a barrier and the viewing platform with precision. "You need to finish all the sections to pass."

Ali swallowed the bile down and jumped out of the car. "Yep. I need a few minutes to calm down."

After stumbling past the man monitoring the track, she plopped down on a nearby bench. With her head slouched between her knees, she sucked in some deep breaths. *Get a grip. Breathe. You can do this.*

Another instructor thrust a ginger ale into her hands. "Take a few sips. Slowly. We'll start you back up when the others finish."

As her fingers curled around the drink, she abruptly dropped it, then ran over to the nearby trashcan. Her body heaved as her breakfast spewed out, leaving a stale, sour taste in her mouth. Footsteps grew louder as she gripped the rim of the trashcan.

A water bottle came into view. After several seconds, he softly said, "Don't worry. It happens to a lot of people. You'll get used to it. Go ahead, rinse out your mouth."

"Thank you."

"I put another can of ginger ale on the bench. Try to drink it. It'll help."

Still trembling, she stumbled over to the bench, plopped down, and sipped the ginger ale. *Am I making a mistake? I'm preparing to enter a war zone. How crazy am I?*

Tires screeched, and the training car pulled up. Ali spilled soda on her jacket and tried to brush it off as Jack and Wendy bounced out like kids who just finished a carnival ride.

"Yahoo! That was a blast." Jack grinned. "Jesus Ali, you still look a little pale. You sure you're cut out for this?"

"Shut up, Jack!" Wendy slugged him on the arm. "She'll be fine. Give her a few." Her frown turned into a gleaming grin when she turned back to Ali. "But it was fun."

This course was the first time Ali had met Jack and Wendy, who seemed excited about their assignment of traveling throughout Afghanistan and working with the locals. But Ali's job did not list extensive travel as a requirement.

"Ready to go?" The instructor stood before her with his hands on his hips.

Ali probably looked like hell, but there was no way she was giving up. She mouthed, "Ready," as she stood, hoping he wouldn't see the slight wobble. She mustered all of her energy. "Let's rock and roll."

"Okay, I want two of your best attempts before I critique you, then we will do it again and again until it becomes second nature."

She peeled off down the stretch, pushing the speed up to eighty-five miles per hour. With the instructor's cue, she applied the brakes within the specified distance and sharply turned the wheel. The tires squealed, rubber burned, and acid crept back up into her throat, but she swallowed it down. The vehicle skidded sideways before snapping one hundred and eighty degrees. She sped up again. This time, the instructor didn't give her a heads-up. She completed the turn near the outer boundary marker and was thankful the track had extra room around the perimeter for near misses. Slowing down, she waited for his assessment.

"Not bad. Do four more." He cocked an eyebrow. "This time, tighten the turn and don't hesitate. Once you've rounded, give it the gas and go faster."

Ali interpreted his look as *get off your ass*. She wasn't backing down and took the dare. She slammed down the gas pedal.

"Two more." The instructor's voice crackled in her helmet headset.

Jack was right. It was a blast. She stopped clenching the wheel and gradually sensed how far she could push the vehicle.

"Gee, you fooled me. I give you a solid B. Now, we're going to add the other car into the mix. Remember how it's done?"

"Yeah. Match the speed of the car in front, align my side front wheel with the other car's rear wheel. Turn slightly into them while accelerating. The front vehicle will go into a spin that the other driver can't control, and I blast past him."

"You got it." He motioned for her to begin.

The maneuver sounded deceptively simple, and to her amazement, it was. They did this drill four times.

"Now he's going to chase and spin you. Let him the first time. Afterward, I want you to try to avoid and outrun him."

"And do the high-speed turns?"

"You shouldn't have a problem. Let's go!"

When the session ended, Jack and Wendy rushed up to high-five her. A strong feeling of accomplishment washed over her.

"All right folks, ready for the Shooting Gallery?" The instructor laughed. "Ali, you're up first. Yesterday was just an introduction. Take it up a notch today."

"I feel the need for speed." Jack grinned and slapped her on the back.

The Shooting Gallery was a makeshift series of alleys where they practiced scenarios of being attacked. Even though the participants playing the bad guys only shot blanks, the loud popping and rattling of rapid-fire made her pulse race, her mouth go dry, and her muscles quiver.

They piled into the SUV, and Ali drove in. The high side barriers blocked any view over the top. Other junk vehicles and a couple of buses were parked along the route. After the second turn, a car came into view, traveling at them head-on. As instructed, she put the vehicle in reverse and drove backward as the bad guys shot at them. She accelerated, hearing the instructor scream, "GO FASTER!" After miraculously maneuvering around a couple of corners, she clipped the last one before clearing the track, jolting everyone and adding a new dent to the beat-up SUV.

"Good job! Ready to go again?"

Jack and Wendy congratulated her with whoops and hollers from the back seat. The instructor flashed Ali a grin. "Do it!"

She crept down into the alley. *Much better than yesterday. It's kind of fun.* Halfway through, her muscles relaxed, then a car shot out in front while another SUV blocked the rear. Without warning, the engine died. Ali glanced at the instrument panel and turned the key but couldn't get it started. By now, the deafening sound of rapid gunfire filled the air from all directions. At last, her adrenaline kicked in. She burst out and sought cover.

"Stop!" The instructor shouted over the radio, and the gunfire tapered off. "Okay, what did you do wrong? Think about the videos and our discussion on assassinations."

"We froze for a few seconds," Ali said.

"Yes, but more than a few. And when are you most vulnerable?"

"When not moving," Wendy added.

"In real life, you'd be dead or severely wounded. Remember, you must immediately decide whether to get out and seek cover—"

"Or ram a vehicle to escape," Ali answered.

A smile lit his face. "Yes, but this is a class. We're not going to practice ramming, so I cut the engine. Now, hop in. This time, I want you jumping out as fast as possible."

After each had repeated the exercise, exhaustion began to creep in, but they still had another hour or so to go.

The instructor clapped his hands and rubbed them together. "It's time to increase the difficulty. You're going to put on body armor, strap on an empty sidearm, and keep drilling."

Jack sat in the driver's seat, and Wendy and Ali were in the back. The instructor threw in a couple of heavy equipment bags, one between them and another on the floorboard. "Trying to make it real folks."

The instructor took the front passenger seat. He was a tall guy with broad shoulders, and Ali could barely see over him. This time when the SUV stalled, Ali didn't hesitate.

"Stop! Stop! Stop! Everyone, remain in position. Nobody moves!" The firing ceased, and she froze.

"Ali," the vehicle instructor curled his finger, wiggling it several times. "Follow me."

Shit, now what's wrong?

On the other side, Wendy was halfway out with Jack's hands gripping the collar of her body armor vest.

"Jack, what the fuck is this mess?" The instructor barked.

"Wendy got stuck. I was helping her."

"No. What are you supposed to do?"

Jack didn't answer, and the instructor turned to Ali. "Do you have the answer for him?"

"Take cover and lay down suppression fire to protect you and her. She has to be responsible for herself."

"Correct, Ali." The instructor kicked the side of the SUV. The loud noise made Ali jump. "Jack, your way is the surest way to get you both killed! If they shot you, there's a good chance your body would fall onto her. You're what?" He sized Jack up and down. "About five foot ten and a hundred and seventy pounds? That combined with armor and gear means a shitload of weight lying on top of her. She'd have no chance to escape. Even if you weren't shot, you'd probably break her neck trying to pull her out. I'm sure she would appreciate your effort if the vehicle was on fire, but it's not."

The instructor rubbed his head. "Look, I know you're trying to be helpful, but it's critical that each person be responsible for themselves. Take cover and lay down suppression fire. Assist after the situation is contained." He jabbed his finger in the air. "I can't stress this enough. An object in motion is harder to hit. It doesn't matter if it's you or the vehicle. Every fraction of a second you hesitate and don't move increases your chances of getting hurt or killed. Think about that. Tomorrow at 0700, I'll review that point and take any further questions that you have. Dismissed."

Ali trudged off to her rental car, dreading the forty-five-minute drive back to the Richmond hotel. *Damn, I'm tired.*

"Ali! Someone needs to talk to you in the office."

What now? She followed the instructor into a cramped room. The dirty shade was pulled down, blocking the final rays of sunshine. A man in a crisp business suit flashed his NGA ID badge from her agency, the National Geospatial-Intelligence Agency. The strong smell of his cologne—something musk and leather—hit her as he hastily introduced himself and stuck out his hand. She shook it even though she hadn't washed the dirt and sweat off her own.

"What can I do for you, sir?"

"I was traveling from Norfolk Naval Base to headquarters, and they requested I come by and speak with you. There's an immediate need for your skills and experience."

"How immediate?" A lump formed in Ali's throat under his sharp gaze.

"We need you in Afghanistan by mid-April."

"That's much earlier than I expected. How much will I be traveling?"

He crossed his arms. "Your job requires interaction with others. Think of it this way. The opportunities to use your newly acquired skills will be plenty." The one side of his mouth curled.

Ali swallowed. The biggest killer of coalition forces was improvised explosive devices, and the enemy was getting a lot deadlier with their design, particularly with radio and cell phone controlled detonators.

"What's the assignment?"

"You'll be with JETT."

"Pardon?"

"Joint Elite Technology Team. NSA has a JETT at every major base throughout Afghanistan. It's a little different from your other NSA assignments, but you'll be fine. This team operates from the Operations Center inside the International Security Assistance Force's headquarters at Kabul. That's all I can tell you in this room."

ISAF headquarters had been attacked several months back. The images shown during an NGA briefing flashed through her mind. A suicide bomber had detonated his vehicle at a checkpoint, less than a thousand feet from the ISAF gate. The carnage was massive—mangled steel, charred blast marks everywhere, chunks of concrete ripped by debris spewed at a high velocity, and blood stains on the nearby pavement where shrapnel had cut down victims. The people closest to the bomb had been incinerated.

Kabul's ripe with targets and full of checkpoints.

"You look worried."

"Just processing the changes."

"As of two hours ago, the position hasn't been filled, but we need an answer fast. I'm going to step out of the room to grab a coffee. Want anything?"

"No, thank you."

"You've done an excellent job in training. Help us out, and I'm sure we can assist you with a select post once you return." He paused at the door. "Oh, and it's a ten-month tour instead of four. I need your answer when I return."

The door creaked shut. As the sound of his footsteps faded, she sunk into the chair and threw her head back, contemplating her choices. NGA had a shortage of experienced military candidates with extensive national-level backgrounds and expertise in geospatial applications and analysis. Civilians with joint CIA and NSA operations were pushed hard to deploy. Besides those qualifications, Ali's work on Special Forces projects put her in the crosshairs of agency recruiters.

Be honest. I also need the extra pay they're waving in front of my nose.

The door opened. He sat on the edge of the desk, one leg dangled and the other planted on the floor, and looked down at her. "So, what's your answer?"

"I'll take it."

Chapter 2

April 2008 – Al Udeid Air Base, Qatar

After the crazy connections of three separate commercial flights, every muscle in Ali's body ached. She was grimy, and a whiff of her unpleasant body odor reminded her that she had been up and traveling for over twenty-four hours. She jerked her roller bag along. One wheel had broken and wobbled, making an irritating scrapping noise.

"Alaina!"

She twisted. A tall man held a sign with her name and waved. The company logo on his bright blue button-down shirt identified him as the logistics contractor.

"Hi. I'm Joel. Welcome to Qatar. I'll make your transition as smooth as possible." He reached for her bag. "Please, let me help. You have another exhausting route ahead."

"Thank you. Do you need to see my papers?"

"No. We've got your bio and picture on file, and look around." He grinned. "Not many women with reddish-brown hair in western clothes." He handed her a small brown bag. "Hope you like a turkey club on wheat and lemonade."

"Oh my, you're my savior. And please call me Ali."

An hour later, they entered the American side of Al Udeid Military Air Base.

"This tent sleeps thirty." He handed her a paper. "That's your assigned bunk. I'll pick you up tomorrow at noon."

Inside, the cool air was like heaven. *Yes, the bottom bunk.* She flopped down and closed her eyes. *Just for a little nap...*

A noise jolted her upright. She bumped her head on the bunk above, then squinted at her luminous watch. *I slept nearly nine hours!* Rolling out, her feet hit the floor with a thud. She grabbed her toiletries, showered, then set out to explore.

"Ah, food." The smell of her favorite meal cheered her. Minutes later, she was savoring a spinach and cheese omelet and fresh kiwi, pineapple, and strawberries.

"There you are." The guy with the bright blue shirt plopped down. Potatoes and bacon were piled high on top of an omelet and a waffle.

"The schedule has been moved up."

Ali swallowed down her juice. "Okay."

She barely caught half of what he said as he explained the details with his mouth full of food. A few minutes later, she still had food left after he had emptied his plate.

"Shall we get going? We'll swing by and pick up your personal belongings, then meet the others at the gear hangar."

"Yep. All ready." Her insides didn't feel as confident as her words.

After a short drive in his truck, they pulled up to the equipment hangar. The lighting was poor inside, and the stench of sweat and a musty odor hung in the air. After adjusting to the light, she saw gear haphazardly crammed on shelves. This private firm wasn't as tidy as the military, but her agency required all government employees to go through them.

"First try on a vest." Joel pointed to various piles. "Then grab a groin plate, and throat and shoulder protectors." The others easily found body armor, but everything hung big on Ali. "Here, this one fits most women."

He tossed out small boxes onto the table. "The First Aid kit has QuikClot and all the essentials. Carry it when going outside the wire."

The prickly sensation climbed up Ali's spine. From pre-deployment class, she knew QuikClot was used to stop hemorrhaging wounds.

"Okay folks, now for the fun part: Guns." He led them to the armory.

Her breathing stilled as she held the cold metal grip of the Beretta semiautomatic combat pistol, then shoved it in the holster and strapped it on. *One week of weapons training. Nuts. Good thing I have a friend who's a cop. I owe you, Ashley.*

"Load up your clips with ammo. You'll keep everything in your gear bag on the plane."

Lots of questions popped into Ali's mind along the way to the military terminal, but she never said a word. As the only woman in the group, she didn't want to appear weak. The other guys stuck to themselves and were heading in a different direction.

"Okay folks. Hope you enjoyed your last bit of civilization. Call if your flight's been canceled." Joel waved and took off.

She passed several available seats in the crowded lounge and settled in an empty corner on the hard floor for privacy, turned on her music, and studied the others. *God, they're so young.*

The waiting room door burst open, and a female Air Force officer entered and stopped to scan the room. The officer was tall, compared to Ali's short stature, with an athletic physique. Short, sandy-blonde hair framed a tanned face. Androgynous, yet feminine. *Oh, some women are so sexy in uniform. And she certainly has an air of authority.*

The officer's gaze stopped on Ali, then she headed straight for her. Ali leaned over and fiddled with her music. *God, I hope she didn't notice me checking her out.* Although civilians couldn't be fired for being gay, the military was under the "Don't Ask Don't Tell" policy. Even false accusations could ruin someone's career.

The footsteps grew louder.

Thump.

Ali's eyes moved upwards from the duffel bag now at her feet, and into the lightest blue eyes she had ever seen.

"Ma'am." She pulled her earbuds out and stood.

"Hi. You must be Ms. Alaina Clairmont. I'm Major Lynn Stewart. NSA suggested one of us travel with you. I drew the lucky straw."

Ali's breath caught in her throat, and a slight tremor rose up her spine. *Out of all the freaking women, and you had to ogle your new supervisor!* "It's a pleasure to meet you, Major Stewart. My nickname is Ali." The major's grip was firm but not crushing.

"The pleasure is mutual. You made some of the highest training scores on record, and your ability to adapt on the fly was impressive. I know it's your first deployment, but I think you'll do well as part of the team."

"Thanks." As Ali's mind raced for more words, an announcement on their flight status blared over the speakers.

"Luckily, we snagged a C-17 instead of a C-130."

"I've never flown in a military plane."

"A C-17 is like a Mercedes Benz compared to a C-130. Real seats rather than cargo netting, and the best of all, no honey bucket."

"Honey bucket?" Ali's eyebrows knitted together.

"It's a large bucket with nothing but a curtain." Lynn's grin was enormous. "I find it hard to hold the curtain closed while squatting over the bucket and doing my business on a moving aircraft. Thankfully, the C-17 has a regular restroom with a door, flushable toilet, and sink."

"Oh." Ali rocked back and forth on her toes. "Glad to miss that."

"Do you have any questions?"

"New challenges are usually exciting, but deploying is a whole new animal. I'm nervous." Ali stuck her hands in her pockets and scrunched her shoulders. "Almost everyone in this lounge is in their twenties, and they all look like body-builder competitors. It's overwhelming."

Lynn chuckled. "We need brains as well as brawn. And don't worry, you're in good hands. Everyone on the team has deployed once or twice. This is my third. It seems they like people who run toward the fire."

"I'll be celebrating my birthday while deployed, but never expected to stay past Christmas." *Why the hell did I say that? I sound like I'm whining.* "Uh...They initially had me scheduled for a shorter deployment...I'm sorry. I know the military has it much worse with longer tours than civilians." *That's it. Dig your hole deeper.* Ali could feel the blush creep up her neck until her face was on fire.

"No worries. I wasn't offended. When's your birthday?" Lynn leaned in, "Don't worry, I won't tell a soul."

God, she even smells good—spicy and warm with a touch of cinnamon. "June 29th. I'll be thirty-six."

"I turn thirty-five on September 21st."

"Wow. The same date as Stephen King."

"Wish I could write like him."

A sergeant with a booming voice hollered, "Listen up folks. The Bagram flight has been delayed by at least three hours."

Are you kidding me? Ali's stomach growled loudly.

"Sounds like you could use something to eat." Lynn dug into her backpack and handed Ali an apple and an energy bar.

The sergeant walked up to Lynn. "Ma'am, I can show you to the officer's lounge when you're ready."

"Thank you, but that won't be necessary." A quick twitch in his face and a few seconds of silence suggested his discomfort, but he nodded and left.

"Don't you want to go? I'm sure the officer's lounge is more comfortable."

Lynn waved her hand in the air. "I get enough hobnobbing with the top brass. I can be more relaxed out here and give you some company."

"Attention," someone yelled from across the room. "Please assemble for the Kandahar flight." More than half the room stood and filed out.

"See. We've got plenty of room now." Lynn clapped and rubbed her hands. "Let's relax and talk about hobbies. What's your number-one Stephen King book?"

As they talked, Ali's anxiety drifted away. When another delay was announced, her jaw hung open.

Lynn tapped her on the arm. "Let's go grab some chow and take a walk."

"Fresh air sounds good to me."

Once they returned, Ali was yawning.

"Why don't you take a nap?"

Ali waved her hand. "I'm okay. It shouldn't be too much longer." She had barely spoken the words when it was announced the new estimated boarding time was 2100.

"Oh. My. Fucking. God. Eight hours of delays!" Ali turned to Lynn. Heat rushed up her face. "Uh, sorry for the language, ma'am. That was completely uncalled for."

Lynn's lip curled a smidgen. "Nothing I haven't heard before.

Foul language comes with the territory. Maybe you should reconsider that nap."

"Guess, you're right."

"I'll wake you in an hour or if something changes."

Ali scrunched down in the chair, propped her feet up on her bag, put in her earbuds, and closed her eyes.

—⊶⊷—

Lynn tried to read but found the newest member of JETT distracting. She tucked the novel in her backpack and studied the woman. Ali's long, thick, auburn hair, now freed from the ponytail, hung down in waves. *Gorgeous. And highly impractical for a war zone. I bet she cuts it by the end of the month.*

Lynn recalled the earlier handshake. Firm. But Ali's skin was soft and delicate. *The constant hand washing and tons of antiseptic sanitizer in the field will roughen them up.*

As she slept in the lounge chair, Ali's mouth hung slightly open. Earlier, her mouth had turned up in a nervous, yet welcoming smile. Her skin crinkled around her eyes, accentuating their rich brown hue. *It's a pity that the sun will temporarily mar your light creamy skin. I hope reality doesn't dull your smile. You're beautiful, but how will you adjust to the constant threat of bodily harm? I hope you're stronger than you look. I don't have time to babysit.*

Chapter 3

April 2008 – Qatar to Afghanistan

Stepping into the gleaming interior of the plane with its thin-cushioned seats lining the sides, Ali blinked several times. A pallet marked "blood products" was strapped down to the center aisle. A queasy feeling settled in her stomach. She redirected her attention to stowing her belongings and settled in. The heavy-duty shoulder and lap straps were another reminder this was no ordinary plane.

When the C-17's four massive turbojets roared to life, she sucked in a couple of deep breaths. Her pulse quickened with the rumble and rapid acceleration. Her fingers dug into her thighs, and her eyes pressed shut as her stomach flipped. She released her grip when the plane leveled itself in the air.

"Want to play or do you want more rest?" Lynn waved a tablet.

"I'll pass on the sleeping." Several soldiers lay on the metal plank floor. Their rolled-up jackets transformed into makeshift pillows.

"Which game? Scrabble or Monopoly? Sorry, I'm not a big video gamer. We can talk as we play."

"Monopoly."

Ali enjoyed the time with Lynn, and the flight flew by quickly.

"Battle rattle time, folks! We're twenty minutes out. Civilian!" The flight crewman pointed at Ali. "You can be stopped at any time. Have your paperwork and firearm's license handy."

She turned to Lynn. "Why are we suiting up? Isn't Bagram safe?"

"Your body armor will protect you if we take fire. Also, it's a lot easier and faster to deplane if you wear it." Lynn put her hand on Ali's shoulder. "Don't be alarmed if the pilot does a combat landing."

"What's that?"

"The pilot drops the plane into a sudden, steep descend and banks sharply once or twice before touching down. It's precautionary in case the enemy fires a missile at us."

Holy crap.

Ali's pulse raced until they had landed and were safely on their way to the housing office. It was nearly 0300 by the time billeting was assigned. Lynn went one way while a guy in a baseball cap and baggy jeans led Ali in another direction. He leaned against the side of an old, beat-up pickup truck, arms crossed. Ali jerked on the truck's tailgate handle several times. It wouldn't budge.

"It's broken," he mumbled.

Asshole. Ali heaved her gear over the gate and into the bed.

She scrunched down in the truck seat. Unable to fight off the exhaustion, her eyes fluttered shut. When the truck lurched to a halt, she bolted upright. She rubbed her eyes and peered into the darkness. A tent, enormous like one at a fairground, loomed ahead.

"I'm supposed to be in a CHU. What's this?"

"Keep your voice down. Don't want to wake your bed and breakfast buddies. There should be at least four empty cots. Use your flashlight."

"There's a separate compound for my agency." She didn't move an inch.

"Sorry, hon. I have no idea what you're talking about."

"How many does this tent hold?"

"Two hundred. Now get moving." He thumbed toward the back.

As he drove off, Ali mentally gave him the finger.

She piled on everything to make one trip and stepped inside. The dim glow of her flashlight revealed a chaotic scene. Cots full of sleeping lumps were jam-packed into every space with belongings scattered in no particular order. *What in the world?*

Weaving in and out as delicately as possible, she found an empty cot in the back. The rock-hard cloth surface had no padding. *Gee, I bet these are left over from World War I.* She rolled out her sleeping bag and stowed her gear underneath. *Wait, I didn't see anywhere to secure my gun. Dammit.* Collapsing onto the cot, she shoved her weapon between the cot and sleeping bag and fell asleep.

⚊⚊⚊

Grrrakka kkakkakk!

"Damn, it can't be morning." Ali scrunched down into the sleeping bag. What little sleep she got last night wasn't enough.

Grrrakka kkakkakk! Beep. Beep. Beep. Beep. Beep. Beep.

The unmistakable sound of a jackhammer and truck backup beeper filled her ears. Rolling over, she groaned and rubbed the sleep out of her eyes. She was facing the tent wall. Sunlight streamed through the window flap, highlighting fine dust particles drifting through the air. She could even smell the dust.

Female voices talked in hushed tones. *What language is that? No, it can't be.* Ali rolled to the other side. Several women waved and said hello in a thick accent before resuming their conversation. *Fuck, they're speaking Russian.*

Ali sprung up from the cot. She tried to strap on the weapon as if everything was natural. She collected her towel and change of clothes. Other than hello or good morning, she didn't hear a word of English as she rushed through the tent.

Upon returning from the showers, a man dressed in the standard civilian garb—khaki tactical pants and a drab, green polo shirt—stood near the door.

"Hi. They said you were at the Cadillac."

"Excuse me?"

"Sorry, I'm Ben Williams, NGA Logistics. I dropped by to take you to chow before going to the agency compound."

"Okay. Food sounds fantastic, but what is a Cadillac, besides a car company?"

"Sorry, slang for luxury bathrooms. You know…flushable toilets, shower stalls with a curtain, and a changing room. You'll have them at headquarters, but on the FOBs, you'll be lucky to have a porta potty."

Smiling, Ali said, "So, I assume a FOB isn't a remote car key."

"Forward operating base. The smaller ones are called COPs for combat outposts. You'll get to see several on your tour."

"I'm assigned to headquarters in Kabul."

"There'll always be a few side trips. Don't want you to miss your chance to visit a few garden spots."

She leaned towards him. "Why are there Russians on base?"

"They're not. Those women are from Kyrgyzstan. They work in services like the barbershop. By the way, where's your safety reflective belt? It's required when walking around, especially on Disney. The police will stop you if you're not wearing it."

"My belt's in my bag." He seemed to have a sense of humor. She replied in deadpan voice with a hint of a smile creeping into the corner of her mouth. "What's Disney? I can barely stand roller coasters, but Magic Mountain's okay."

He chuckled. "The main road through the base, and one of the few that are paved. It's named after Army Specialist Jason Disney who died at Bagram in 2002."

Ali pointed at the tent. "Why am I in there?" This time, she stared him down.

"Sorry. One of my assistants made a slip up. Don't worry. You'll be in Kabul soon enough." He smirked. "Got you a first-class ticket. Grab your gear and let's go."

—◦◦◦—

As Ali walked into the briefing room, Major Stewart approached her.

"Ms. Clairmont, I'm sorry about the tent. I can't believe they stuck you with uncleared foreign workers. I'll make sure it doesn't happen again."

"No worries, Major." Ali shrugged and breathed in Lynn's fresh shower scent.

"We leave tomorrow on the midday helo flight. Let's meet up for a late breakfast and head over to the terminal together."

"Major Stewart, Ms. Clairmont is leaving later today."

Lynn turned to the man. "Excuse me? And you are?"

"Ben Williams, NGA Logistics."

"I want Ms. Clairmont traveling with me. That's not a request."

"With all due respect to your rank ma'am, she isn't under your command until she reports in Kabul."

Lynn squared her shoulders. "NGA assigned her to my team. She travels with me."

"We canceled her helo flight, and it was immediately filled. She's scheduled for the Rhino at 1600. The last I checked, there were two empty seats, I could book one for you, if you prefer."

Lynn heard a man clear his throat behind her. She spun around and snapped to attention as the colonel in charge stood in the room.

"I'm sorry there's been a miscommunication, Major Stewart. The Rhino is NGA standard procedure. I approved her travel."

"Yes, Colonel. In that case, I would like a seat on the Rhino." Everyone immediately hushed.

The colonel looked like he'd bite off Lynn's head, then he chuckled. "Fine with me. Mr. Williams, see if you can iron out Major Stewart's new arrangements with NSA. I'm pressed for time. Let's start the meeting."

Ali sat back and soaked up the briefing, and the meeting flew by in no time.

"Major," Ben squared his shoulders, "NSA demands that you remain on the helo roster for tomorrow. You'll have to meet up in Kabul. Ms. Clairmont's gear is already in the truck." He turned to Ali. "The shoppette and coffee shop are on the way. If we leave now, you'll have an hour to relax. My assistant will drive you."

Lynn turned to Ali. "I'll go with you and buy you a coffee."

Outside the tiny Green Beans Coffeehouse, Lynn seemed preoccupied. Ali assumed it was because of the uncomfortable exchange back at the meeting.

"Where are you from, Major?"

"Sacramento, California. All of my family lives there except for an aunt in Virginia and one in Florida." Lynn's tone showed her affection for her family. "Where did you grow up?"

"Fairfax, Virginia."

"Ah, so you're used to the hectic pace of Washington, D.C."

"I wouldn't go that far. I can't stand the traffic. Fortunately, the new NGA headquarters is being built outside the Beltway."

The driver shouted, "Time to go."

"Take care, Ms. Clairmont, and I'll see you tomorrow in Kabul."

"Sure thing, Major."

Ali reasoned the major rarely deviated from protocol. While civilians were more casual, addressing folks by their proper honorific was the military way. *And she's welcome to address me anyway she wants. The woman is totally hot.* Ali grinned as she walked to the truck.

She slid into the back seat of the truck next to a young man who introduced himself as Lieutenant Paul Taylor.

His palm was sweaty. "I'm a little nervous. My buddy had a bad experience on a Rhino."

The driver followed a route away from the airfield. *Maybe there's another airstrip.* When he stopped next to a small building, Ali froze.

"The Rhino's an armored bus?" The man didn't answer her. She took another look. "And the double-cab pickup with a machine gun in the bed is the security escort? Are you kidding me?" Her last words rose in volume, and a mix of anxiety and dread settled in her stomach.

"It's time to leave." He motioned for them to get out.

"We will be like fish in a barrel if that thing breaks down!" She turned to Paul. "Sorry." The color drained from his face.

"I wasn't asking you to move. I was telling you. Now!"

They unloaded, and the driver didn't bother waiting around. A long trail of dust drifted in the air as he sped away.

Shortly after the Rhino departed, Paul tugged on his neck guard. "I'm burning up, and I can't breathe in this tin can."

Beads of sweat glistened on his face. They were required to wear their body armor vests, but Paul wore all the pieces. The groin plate and neck guard were uncomfortable. Ali's were in her backpack.

"I'm hot, too." Ali checked the overhead vents. The air was warm, and no matter how she turned the ports, only a small amount came out.

"Let's talk about fun things. It will help take our mind off the situation. Where are you from, Lieutenant?"

"Please, call me Paul. Albany, New York is my hometown."

She let him do most of the talking, as it seemed to calm him.

"What's your job, Paul? If you can say."

"ISAF headquarters was recommended to round out my career. I thought that I'd be working with NATO representatives, but I was switched at the last minute to be the aide to a full bird colonel."

"Sounds like it may have a few perks. That is, once you're out of this tin can." She smiled.

"Possibly." He leaned over. "I don't know if it's true, but apparently the colonel's been passed over for promotion. He has gone through two aides and has a rough reputation. It's going to be a challenge because I'm up for promotion to captain soon."

"Which means a lot of taking it in the chops."

"You got it."

The convoy arrived in Kabul around sunset. Ali lightly punched Paul. "Logistics straight ahead. If this guy is rude, I might just slap him and blame it on a work-related psychological breakdown. They always say us civilians aren't as disciplined as the military."

"Well, I feel like a zombie, and I'm hungry."

They both snickered at their lame jokes.

"Welcome to Camp Eggers. I'll take your gear and drop you at the chow hall."

Wow, what a pleasant change. Ali happily stripped off her body armor. The evening breeze cooled her sweaty skin.

At dinner, Paul's wicked sense of humor had her in stitches. They also filled the time chatting about travel and hiking trips. When the topic turned to games, Ali was delighted to hear Paul was a chess player.

Her watch alarm went off. "Damn. Time to go. Hey, pick us up some extra drinks, and I'll dump our trash."

"Yes, ma'am."

Passing a group of young soldiers, one heckled. "You like a little chocolate, honey? Don't you have the roles reversed?"

Ali dumped the trash and tossed the tray on the carousel with a clatter. She turned around to face them and saw Paul standing next to the table.

"Good evening, soldiers. Did I hear a derogatory comment?" After a couple of seconds of silence, Paul said, "Soldiers are not rude. I think you owe an apology to my colleague and friend." Paul gestured to Ali standing several feet away, but his eyes remained on the men. "Snap to it!" The group jumped out of their seats at attention and apologized.

"That's better." Paul leaned over and said something that she couldn't hear.

Outside, she waited until they were away from the building before asking him, "What was it you said?"

"I told them to respect all women. Also, your retired father was a tough old general that made me promise to watch out for you," he smirked.

"Wow. That was creative." Ali laughed. "I'm glad we met. We could both use a friend in this place."

"And it's not against regulations since you're with JETT and not in my chain of command. Besides, how many nerds around here like chess? You know I'm going to crush you."

"I have a few Irina Krush moves. Better watch out."

Paul stopped her before they reached the office. "It's a shame that crap still exists despite all the progress in our country and the military." He glanced around. "And while I relish being in your company, no offense, but you're a tad too old for me." His serious face broke, and he bent over heaving out coughs of laughter.

Ali's face broke into a broad smile. With her hands on her hips, she said "Okay, buddy. This old woman is going to whip your ass at headquarters. Better stay out of my way."

"Yes, ma'am." Paul nodded. "But seriously, I've got your back."

"I appreciate that." Ali stuck out her hand. "Let's shake on friendship, but watch the old lady name calling, or I'll beat you with my cane."

Chapter 4

May 2008 – Kabul, Afghanistan

Ali drummed her fingers as she scanned the available file of helicopter reconnaissance photos. *These are not the quality I expected.* The interactive map was due in six days. Embedding the right images in the digital product would provide more information to execute the raid. Her stomach growled.

"Where the hell are those guys?" She mumbled, leaning back in the desk chair and surveying the operations floor. The JETT workstations were in the back-corner row facing toward the center. She liked the location. It gave her the opportunity to see everything, and the privacy to work relatively uninterrupted.

Six weeks in Afghanistan had gone by quickly, and Ali easily fit into working with JETT. She loved the Operations Center. While the worn paint, the lack of windows, and the outside perimeter double-fence topped with concertina wire made the place look more like a prison, it had a unique vibe. All the analysts, operators, and briefers from different services and agencies melded into one cohesive unit that provided the guts of the intelligence to drive combat operations.

Whoosh.

"I'm trying to identify unusual enemy patterns by tracking their activity from reports, then geographically plotting the data with time stamps. If I'm lucky, I might be able to predict future weapons deliveries."

He crossed his eyes, stuck out his tongue sideways, and titled his head. Ali grinned and tossed a small squishy ball at him. "The final product will be an interactive map with ground and helicopter reconnaissance photos embedded and other report links. Speaking of which, I need more recon photos. You do remember how to take a picture with a camera?"

"Of course. I have my special flock of pigeons out back. Now, get going." Henderson thumbed toward the door. "The beautiful night aroma awaits you. Better take your scarf." His white teeth gleamed.

Just outside the door, Ali choked. Holding her breath, she pulled her handkerchief out of a pocket and tied it across her face. Tonight was wretched. *God knows what the hell is in the air.* The Afghans burned animal dung to heat their homes, and there was also the U.S. Army burn pit outside the city. The military swore it didn't affect public health.

The cloth over her mouth and nose did little to help, and the nights were always the worst. Between the air pollution and every fourth water bottle tasting like chemicals, she figured everyone got a dose of poison. *Guess that's why we get hazard pay.* She picked up her pace.

With minutes to spare, she hurried through the mandatory wash station and to the serving line. The young man gave her tonight's meal—some sort of stew—then heaped extra noodles onto a separate plate. They knew her well enough not to put sauce on top.

"Salamat," she said.

He slightly bowed, then lowered his face trying to hide a blush. Many of the Filipinos worked in the lower positions on base. Ali figured it was only polite to learn basic greetings, especially with the chow-hall staff.

Unable to identify the meat by taste or texture, she pushed the stew aside and took a mouthful of noodles. *Ah, that's better. Smear enough Kerrygold butter and voilà. Delicious.* She savored the simple pleasure and began reading the *Stars and Stripes.* Most of the newspaper articles were cheerful and aimed at boosting morale.

"Mind if I join you?"

Ali looked up into Lynn's blue eyes.

"Please do. What keeps you up tonight, Major?"

"The top dog called a late meeting. Seems lack of sleep is a method he uses to keep us on our toes. I had to brief them." Lynn scooped a big spoonful of the mystery stew into her mouth.

"Better watch out. I swear that stew is half rubber, and I never get the biscuits. They're like hockey pucks."

"There's nothing I can't handle. Why are you always alone when I see you at midnight chow?"

Ali swallowed. "Peace and quiet."

Lynn cocked an eyebrow. "Yes, but at least one team member could keep you company. After all, look around. Have you ever been in a more romantic school cafeteria?"

Ali chuckled. "I confess. I'm attracted to the long, folding picnic-style tables."

Lynn smiled. "They are charming. Now, please tell me the real reason? Are you having a problem with the team?"

"No, oh, no." Ali waved her hand. "I'm a bit of an introvert. I love the team, but just need some time to recharge my batteries." *Confess, you chicken.* "And if we're not swamped and everything's on schedule, they let me take an extra half hour to skype or call home. I promise I don't do it every night."

"It's important to stay connected, especially in this place."

"Yes. I helped my cousin remodel half of my sister's place, and now they're finishing it off without me."

"Now you're talking my language." Lynn snapped her fingers. "What are your skills?"

The beginning of warmth started on Ali's neck and quickly blossomed on her face. "Interior decorating. Not hardly a skill. Well, I mean...I don't have a degree or anything. I just dabble."

"Excuse me? I'd say that is a critical skill, and sometimes on-the-job experience is better than a degree. My family owns a construction business. I like to build things and worked there every summer in high school and college. But it's the final decorating touches that make a home."

"Thank you." Lynn's compliment and smile sent a zing of excitement through Ali.

"I remember you showing the team the photos of your house. It is gorgeous. You also mentioned selling it. Are you taking on another project or just want a different space?"

"My partner and I split. She left me some steep bills, and I can't afford to sell now. I'll hang onto it and sell once the market improves." Ali's hand, which was lifting a carton of milk, stopped halfway to her mouth. *Shit. Why did I say that?* Lynn continued to chew her food but was staring down at her tray. *Is she thinking about how to reprimand me? Or worse?*

"I'm sorry to hear that your relationship broke up."

After several long seconds, Lynn pushed the half-eaten dish away. The spoon rattled against the side of the bowl. Ali held her breath, fearing what was next.

Lynn wore a scowl, and her eyes narrowed. "You're right. The stew sucks. I'm going to grab another drink. Want one?"

Ali released the air from her lungs and mumbled, "Sure." As Lynn strolled over to the drink cooler, Ali covered her mouth as if to silence her thoughts. *She's my supervisor for Christ's sake.* Waves of panic spread through Ali's body as she waited.

Lynn tossed Ali another milk. "Your personal life is no one's business as far as I'm concerned. And it's not against regs since you're a civilian." Lynn took a swig of her water. "But we're deployed. Under DADT, someone could accuse a military person simply by associating with you. Don't share any more info. You don't want someone to overhear, and I don't want someone harassing an important member of the team. I've seen bad things happen on other deployments. So, please be careful." Lynn stood to leave.

"Got it. I appreciate the advice, Lynn." *Damn, I can't say anything right tonight.* "I'm sorry, ma'am. I meant no disrespect."

Lynn sat the tray down and leaned over. "Back in the states, you would outrank me in some situations. I enjoy our downtime together. It's nice to relax, but I am your superior here. Like the other topic, be careful." She started to move again but stopped. "Let's all get home safe and sound, and then you can call me whatever you want. See you at 0600 for turnover."

Ali bit her lip as she watched Lynn walk away. The major was attractive. With each encounter, Ali was more drawn to Lynn's laugh, the brightness of her eyes, and the way she surprised Ali with unexpected humor. But slipups like tonight had to be contained.

At the door, Lynn paused and glanced over her shoulder. Ali's body stiffened. *She just caught me ogling her. Again.* Ali hung her head. *Snap out of it.*

Ali's revelation a couple of days ago had surprised Lynn, but so had a lot of other things. Ali was a lot tougher than she appeared. Brains all wrapped up in a gorgeous package.

Smack.

She jumped at the sound of the folder hitting the desk.

"Why the grin, Major?"

"Nothing, sir." Lynn hopped up and stood at attention.

"Excellent reporting." The colonel beamed. "The general loved it, particularly Ms. Clairmont's work. She seems to be a good addition to your team."

Lynn breathed a sigh of relief. The hard-to-please colonel could make just about anybody tremble when he was in a foul mood. "Thank you, sir. I'll be sure to relay the message."

"Oh, and the general would like Ms. Clairmont to work with the senior civilian analyst from time to time."

"That's a completely different chain of command."

"Do you question the general?" He narrowed his eyes.

"Of course not. I'm sorry, sir." Lynn swallowed under his glare.

"Good. Why don't you take an hour or two? We need you here late tonight."

Lynn fled into the late afternoon sunshine. The smell of coffee wafted in the air, and she changed directions for the small coffee shop run by the Italians. The coffee was expensive, but spectacular.

"Hey, boss, what's up?"

Lynn craned her neck, then saw Ali in sweatpants. With her reddish hair framing her face, Ali reminded Lynn of Amy Adams. Except, Ali had brown eyes and a few more curves. Lynn still couldn't get over how Ali kept her hair so long and managed to keep it looking beautiful.

"Taking a walk before chow. What are you doing up almost three hours before your shift?"

"It's my grandma's eighty-ninth birthday. Phones are up at the rec center, and we had a lovely talk. No use trying to get back to sleep, so I hit the gym and went for a run. You know the air is a lot better during the day than at night." Ali wrinkled her nose and grinned.

"Yeah. I'm lucky that I only work nights occasionally." Not wanting to look into Ali's eyes, Lynn started walking briskly. Ali kept pace with her and chatted about her grandmother, but Lynn was only half listening.

God, she's stunning. Lynn mentally slapped herself. *Stop it.*

"You're deep in thought. Thinking of ways to torture your poor team, Major?"

"Ah...no, just a little preoccupied these days."

"I heard a rumor about you."

"Oh?"

"You like to play cards and will be making an appearance at the next Officer's Club game night. Paul invited me. Of course, provided no emergencies pop up."

Excitement and panic hit Lynn. She remembered giving Ali six hours off because of long hours anticipated for a mission at the end of the month.

"I love cards but don't always get to join. If I don't see you, have fun and give my regards to Lieutenant Taylor." Lynn tapped her watch. "I need to go."

"All right. You take care. I need to shower and do a few things. Can't be late." Ali smacked her fist into the palm of her other hand. "The boss is a real stickler for being on time."

"Yes, I hear she's a rough one. Better watch it. She can drive you crazy all-night long." Immediately realizing her double entendre, Lynn hastily added, "And you all are crazy enough on that shift." Lynn didn't wait for a response. She turned on her heels and shouted over her shoulder, "Get a move on it, Ace."

Ali shouted, "Sure thing, Major. I wouldn't want you bringing out any whips and chains."

Lynn's legs almost buckled. *Keep walking. Don't respond in any way.* Her trance broke as she returned a salute of a captain passing by. He gave her a smirk. Lynn thumbed back in Ali's direction. "I'm a hard one on my team. Have to keep them chained to the desk." She kept moving.

Chapter 5

"And so, we met again." Lynn lowered her voice and said, "Let's keep any jokes on whips and chains out of the conversation today."

Ali chuckled. "No problem, ma'am. As I recall, it was a week ago. I'll try to keep my bad jokes to once a month." She threw her arms out in a broad sweeping motion. "I love this garden and heard it's one of the best in Kabul. It soothes me."

"Yes, it is one of the best. Lucky us since it was designed to accommodate official ceremonies. Few places in Kabul have such grandeur."

"Spring is my favorite time of year."

"The scented roses of pink, yellow, and red make me forget about the war for a short time. It's a pity that there isn't more beauty throughout the city."

"I had no idea you were such a softie, Major."

Lynn bent over, and her fingers cupped a petal. She sniffed deeply. "This Damask rose is heaven. Smell." She held the petal as Ali leaned in. A shiver of delight ran through her body as a wisp of Ali's hair brushed over her forearm. Lynn swallowed and released the petal. She clasped her hands behind her back and slowly began strolling, but still, the warm tingle lingered. "I think we all would like to see more beauty and a lot less pain and suffering."

"Agreed. You're full of surprises for a hardcore military officer. Are roses your favorite?"

"A favorite of Aunte Karena. Back in 2004 when I was stationed in England, she came over for a vacation. We met up in London and spent two of our four days in Queen Mary's Gardens. It's one of the world's most beautiful rose gardens."

"Sounds like you're close to your aunt."

"Aunt Karena lives in Arlington, Virginia. I've been stationed so much in Maryland and Virginia that we've grown close." Lynn began to stroll again. "I was going for a coffee. Can I buy you one?" She longed for some good conversation, and Ali just made her feel alive.

"I'd like that."

The corner booth was empty. The smell of the coffee was grand, but the cookies were even better. Lynn bought both.

"Thanks, Major."

"You're a cookie monster. I've seen you in action. Speaking of which, I'm sorry I missed the card game. I heard you walked away a big winner."

Ali's eyes lit up. "Yes. You didn't tell me people played for goodies. I won a bag of Skittles, a handful of granola bars, and a box of cookies."

"I try to stay away from junk food. I'm not always successful. That's why I go to the gym."

Ali shrugged, and her smile dropped. "Yeah, I have a sweet tooth and a few too many pounds to prove it."

"I'm sorry. I didn't mean to imply anything negative. There's nothing wrong with your weight."

"I'm sure I'd be healthier if I lost some, and I'd look better."

"Hey, you look fantastic. Be thankful you don't have to

worry about passing any military physical fitness tests during deployment."

The corner of Ali's mouth slowly hitched up. "So, you think I look fantastic?"

What just slipped out of my mouth? Lynn rushed to respond. "You shouldn't measure yourself against others. Beauty comes in all forms." *Oh, God, that's worse. Switch subjects!* "Tell me, Ali, what drew you to be a geospatial analyst?" Lynn couldn't help but notice Ali's lips as she took a long, slow sip.

"Don't laugh. Economics may have been my major, but I was essentially a math geek who liked photography and maps."

"The intersection of the two seems to suit you well."

"I attended a job fair sponsored by the CIA after graduating college. They liked the fact that I had coursework in cartography and remote sensing. By that time, ESRI was taking off as a premiere geospatial software company."

"Huh? What's ESRI?" Lynn jokingly crossed her arms over her face.

"A California company. They are number one in the world for geospatial software and development. Anyway, it was the excitement of merging different sources to make interactive maps, rather than a simple one. Even better that someone wanted to pay me to do it." Ali's voice grew quiet. "While we can't talk classified here, you understand the power of people working together melding all data and source material."

"Yes, but you seem to pick up the technology piece quite easily. I'm not just talking about mapping software. Not everyone has that talent."

"I find it fascinating tackling new technology and presenting data and info into useful products. It's satisfying to know that I help accomplish the mission."

The way that Ali spoke about her work seemed to energize

her. Lynn admired her spirit. "I hear you're working on your master's degree, and it's not in economics."

"Geographical Information Systems. For my thesis, I'm working with metro police to analyze crime scene data."

Lynn raised her hands. "Don't go too deep into that geospatial mumbo jumbo or you'll lose me."

"Similar to one thing we do here—look for patterns in bad guys' behavior and nab them. I've rattled on long enough. What about you? Why the military?"

"I was fascinated by the Air Force. Four years of Russian between high school and college got my foot in the door at the NSA. Do you speak any other languages?"

Ali sipped her coffee and shrugged her shoulders. "I dabble here and there. Mainly for travel and to be polite. People appreciate when you make an effort. By the way, why have you done so many deployments?"

"Believe it or not, there's a shortage of specialized soldiers. And unfortunately, the wars have gone on for so long." Lynn shrugged. "I once thought that I'd do the required service and get out, but like you said, trying to make a positive difference instead of filling a database is satisfying. As the years go on, the fight seems never-ending. Still, I'm committed for at least twenty years."

Ali reached across the table, and her fingertips lightly laid on top of Lynn's hand. "I can't imagine the suffering that you've seen on multiple deployments."

Lynn withdrew and waved her hand in the air. "With fourteen years of service, it's foolish to get out now. I keep going the best I can." Lynn tapped her watch. "Fifteen minutes before your shift begins. Wouldn't want to upset the boss."

"Not until you tell me your favorite things about your hometown, Sacramento." Ali rested her chin in her hand, waiting for a reply.

Lynn finished the bite of her cookie. She couldn't help but notice Ali's soft brown eyes. Warm and inviting with a hint of reddish tone. "Besides helping with my family's construction business, I love to ride my dirt bike or go kayaking. Sacramento's got a 23-mile slice of heaven called the American River Parkway, and Yosemite's three hours away."

"You miss home. I can see it in your eyes and hear it in your voice."

Lynn peered into Ali's face and had to suppress the urge welling up inside—the desire to hug her. She hated how a simple hug, even one by a friend, could be misunderstood. But this was the life she chose. "Yeah. I'm close to my older brother, Ian. It's our fascination of building things that has kept us close, and politics, particularly, social issues. My sister and I have had our on-and-off periods."

"Family. I know how that goes." Ali's face changed, and her finger started tapping on the mug. She looked away from Lynn.

"That seemed to hit a nerve."

"I'm the one that brought up home. Guess I should share." Ali ran her finger around the rim of her coffee cup. "I have an older brother and sister. We get along, but the age difference makes it challenging at times. My younger sister's cool."

Lynn caught the hint of a smile, but it dropped. She waited for Ali to continue.

"Mom's okay, but high school wasn't a good time. My dad's drinking came into full force," Ali bit her upper lip. "He was pissed when..." Ali ran her fingers through her hair. "I became my authentic self. We never settled our differences before he died, and my mother didn't really forgive me for not making an appearance at his funeral. We get along now because she pretends those years didn't happen." Ali stared into her coffee. Her jaw tightened.

Lynn reached out and covered Ali's hand. "I'm sorry."

Ali whispered, "Thank you."

"Hey, how's it going, Ali? Good to see you, Major."

Lynn snatched her hand away as Lieutenant Paul Taylor stood over them. *God, I hope he didn't see that.*

"Terrific. You have to try the cookies. They're homemade today." Ali grinned.

"Wow. That doesn't happen but once in a blue moon." He was like a little kid excited on Christmas morning.

Lynn slid out of the booth. "I swear you two are cookie addicts."

"Guilty as charged," Ali said.

"Take my seat, Lieutenant. Ali, spend an extra fifteen minutes with your friend. And don't forget to bring cookies for the rest of the team." She winked. Again, not thinking.

Ali gave her a mock salute. "Yes, ma'am."

Lynn walked to the Operations Center. *I'm such an idiot. I just crossed the line. It can't go any further. Control!*

Chapter 6

June 2008 – Kabul, Afghanistan

The JETT's eight members all sat in the back-corner row facing toward the center of the main operations room. The room housed forty analysts, and space was at a premium. Lynn emailed turnover notes, then gathered JETT members around a tight circle for a short update between shifts. Turnover was at 0700 and 1900. With twelve-plus-hour shifts, everyone was always anxious to get out.

Tonight's turnover had been going smoothly until the Operations Center's battle captain pulled Lynn aside and waved papers in her face. Her hands rested on her hips, and she nodded. When he marched off, she blew out a huff and walked back to the group.

"Webster!" Lynn yelled. "The general wasn't happy earlier with the slides and, as you can see, neither is the battle captain."

"Yes, ma'am." Webster flinched.

In Ali's opinion, he took too many shortcuts, and his work was sloppy.

"Henderson, I want you to double-check the slides. If you're unavailable, then Ace will do it. Lastly, make sure the battle captain approves them before distribution."

"Yes, ma'am."

"Ace. Nice job on the map updates."

Ali nodded. "Roger."

"Okay." Lynn smacked her hands together and rubbed them hard. "The weather is perfect for June and volleyball. Provided everything stays calm and we remain ahead of schedule, the game is still on for tomorrow at 1700. Henderson needs one more person for the enlisted team. Anyone interested?" No one raised a hand. "Come on people. Where's your enthusiasm? Who wants to be humiliated by the Officer Corps?" Lynn jokingly balled her hands into fists and raised them in the air.

"If you take civilians, I'll play." They all turned to Ali. "What? I'm short, but I'm a good volleyball player."

"Great Ace. Take off a couple of hours early and get some good shut-eye." A huge smile swept across Lynn's face. "Then I'll see you on the court tomorrow evening for a royal beating."

"Careful. Small packages can be too hot to handle." Ali started to blush. "I have incredible stamina." *Oh my God, that's worse.* In a rush, she blurted out, "Nicole Davis was only five feet, four inches and led USC to their second consecutive NCAA National Championship in 2003."

Lynn's face went blank momentarily before warming up. "That's right, and the Californian golden girl is going to the 2008 Olympics. Aren't you stretching it a bit? Are you even five-four?"

Ali relaxed. "Close. The important thing is that you giants can't come close to my speed and reaction time." She lightly punched Henderson's bicep. "You need me."

"Sure, half-pint." He chuckled.

Lynn said, "Well, we play for fun. The guys do spike hard, but nothing like me. I'm sure you can take it." She turned and looked at everyone. "All right team. Excellent research. Let's work on presentation and not leaving out a key point. Night crew, happy hunting. Dismissed."

Chairs screeched backward on the floor and the printer sprung to life. Henderson stuck a lollipop in his mouth and grinned at Ali. She waited until the last person was out of earshot. "Can I help you with something?"

"Stamina, huh? And how hot are you? Blazing, sizzling, or steaming?"

"In your dreams." She turned to the computer. "I need details on those change requests. Please, run over to headquarters and get them for me now. They didn't come over in email."

He put his palms on the desk and leaned over, looking out at the ops floor. In a quiet voice, he said, "I'm going to ask my girlfriend to marry me."

Ali opened the computer. "Congratulations!" She liked Henderson, but the unpleasant tingle in her spine made her fear where this was going.

"The entire Operations Center loves you. You take on any job, simple or complex, and get it done without one complaint."

"Thanks. And I need that paperwork, please." Ali typed, hoping he'd take the hint.

"Don't trust Captain Stevens or the guys he hangs out with. They're stuck-up homophobic dickheads." He straightened and projected toward the others nearby. "I'll get that report. Need me to pick you up a soda, Ace?"

Her fingers had stopped typing, and her heart was racing. "No, I'm fine."

He slapped her on the back. "Okay, buddy. Be back soon."

—◦◦◦—

The next night, Ali joined the others for the volleyball tournament.

"Glad you could make it." Lynn waved. "Turns out we need a player for our side."

"Boo...Hiss...Don't join the upper crust..." The enlisted guys were all jeering at once.

Lynn cupped her hand to the side of her mouth and yelled out, "Ah, you know you've met your match." She turned to Ali. "Tonight, there's lots of teasing and polite name-calling, but all in good fun. Want to join our motley crew?"

"Lead the way."

As the game progressed, Ali grumbled to herself, "Just for fun, my ass." Both teams were out for blood. The prize—a special meal in a reserved, back section of the officer's mess hall. The cherry on top—the losers had to serve the winners before eating.

"You shouldn't have joined the brass, Ace," Henderson shouted from the enlisted side after they tied the score. "Now, to finish you off." He served.

Ali dived to pass the ball. "Crap!" Her pass was off the mark to the setter, and Lynn's spiked ball sailed wide of the boundary line.

"Oh yeah...You all are going down..." The enlisted side was going nuts as they took the lead.

Lynn shouted, "Okay, let's do it." She clapped her hands. "We can take care of these jarheads and ground pounders."

The enlisted team was on the brink of winning. Ali dove for the ball as another team member turned to make the play.

Smack. His knee collided with her face.

"God, that hurt," she choked out. Her fingers touched her face. Warm, sticky blood coated the tips.

"Oh shit. I'm sorry, Ace!" The alarm in the lieutenant's voice sounded distant.

She tried to open her eyes, but everything was spinning. Out of the chorus of concerned voices, she focused on Lynn's. A soft hand cradled her head then dabbed her face.

"Try to open your eyes." Lynn's voice soothed.

"I'm dizzy." The floodlights hurt her eyes, and she squeezed them tight again. "I feel sick to my stomach." A slight ringing competed with the voices around her, making everything seem like an eerie dream.

"The medics are on the way. Hang in there, Ace," Henderson said. "You know we've got your back."

The whirl slowed, and her nausea eased but didn't go entirely away. Ali tried again to open her eyes. She put her hand up to block the glare of the lighting. Gradually, Ali could make out Lynn's face, then the medics rushed in with a gurney.

"She's got a broken nose and a small laceration above the left eye, and she's showing signs of a concussion," Lynn told the medic.

"We'll have to take her to the trauma center for a CT and check her for an orbital fracture."

Ali grabbed Lynn's shirt. "No. I don't want to go outside the wire."

"Easy there five-foot-four monster." Lynn leaned down near her face and softly said, "It'll be okay, Ali. Trust me. We need to make sure that hard head of yours isn't cracked. Can't have any scrambled eggs on my watch."

She liked how it sounded when Lynn called her by name. She let go of Lynn's shirt but clutched Lynn's hand hard. "Go with me. I'm scared."

"I'll be with you all the way." Lynn slightly rose. "Henderson. Go get our battle rattle and meet us at the gate."

"Roger, Major."

"I'll get her bug-out bag." One of the women from Ali's barracks yelled.

Lynn's hand slid away as they loaded her into an MRAP. Ali immediately missed her warmth.

"We're in a Mine-Resistant Ambush Protected vehicle. So much better than the armored SUVs we typically drive. See, I can say that, I'm better. Do I have to go to the hospital?"

"Yes," Lynn answered, "but I'm happy you're not delirious. You do have one of the hardest heads of anyone I know. I'm going by the rules. So, chill. It's not that far away. I'm right here." Lynn's hand patted her shoulder. "Think of something pleasant."

As Lynn's gentle voice distracted her, the medic swabbed her arm. The scent of rubbing alcohol seeped in and assaulted her nose. Ali grimaced as the needle pierced the skin. The drug's efficiency was swift, and her pain began to fade. As the vehicle lurched along, she closed her eyes and daydreamed about the handsome major. She imagined them dancing under the stars on a warm summer night. Lynn dressed in a white tux with a blue tie to match her eyes, and herself in a shimmering red dress.

"What are you thinking, Ace?"

She pried her eyes open. "I feeeel soooo nicee right nowww."

"Good thing I speak slur."

"Yourrr eeyes. Soooo cuute..."

Chapter 7

Ali woke in a hospital bed, feeling woozy but much better than after the hit. She was the only one in the four-bed room. Light seeped in from the headlights of passing trucks outside. Lynn appeared to be asleep in the chair next to her.

A woman with a stethoscope draped around her neck walked towards them. Ali took in the green-colored under-shirt, and camouflage uniform under her white lab coat. *God...women in uniform.*

Lynn jostled and jumped up. "Is everything okay, doctor?"

"The CT looks clear." She peeked at Ali over her glasses. "I'm not sure how you didn't sustain an orbital fracture. Lucky hit. You have a concussion, and your face isn't going to look pretty for some time, but you will heal. If you have access to ice, wrap some in a towel and apply. It'll help with the pain and swelling. I'll release you in the care of the major, but this concussion has to be taken seriously."

The doctor handed Lynn some paperwork. "Bed rest for two days and I want her with a twenty-four-hour caregiver. Wake her every couple of hours to make sure she's coherent. If her balance or vision doesn't improve or her headaches continue, call the medics. If she vomits, bring her back."

"Work...when can I...go back?" Ali's mouth was dry.

"Probably by the third day but only if your clinic clears you. Get examined before dinner tomorrow. Also the following day, even if the caregiver doesn't see any problems. The doctor handed a bottle to Lynn. "They're not as strong as the shots. Two every six hours and only if she needs it. I want the caregiver in charge of dispersing the pills. All these instructions are in the paperwork." She patted Ali's hand. "Your base clinic will prescribe a milder medication after the two days. Okay, you can roll your gear up and be on your way."

The doctor walked off, and Lynn started to help her.

"Vertigo...not too bad...freaking...no reason."

"I don't know if you can hear yourself talk, but you're having trouble completing sentences. And yes, it was bad. Your eyes were spinning like a pinball machine after the hit. You heard what the doctor said. It's a concussion. These symptoms are serious." Lynn held out her hand. "Now come on, let's get back to base. I'd like to get you in bed."

Ali softly chuckled and whispered, "Bold...can't say that thought."

Lynn leaned over. "I didn't mean it that way," she said in a whispered shout. "You need rest. At least, you're not as delirious as earlier."

"That's me. Lost and delirious. Sorry, a slip of the tongue..." Ali snickered and rolled over into the pillow. She rolled back, and Lynn was squared off with her hands on her hips. Ali slowly calmed down. "These drugs...wowww."

"Yes. Let's get you back before you say or do something you really regret. I'm beginning to think they gave you something like laughing gas in those shots."

They rolled onto base and into the faint light of dawn. The

rising sun painted the sky a warm pinkish color against the thin layer of clouds.

"Here. Let me help you. Doctor's orders."

"I can do it myself."

"You're more alert, but I don't want to take any chances."

"Welcome back Ms. Clairmont. If you don't mind, I need a word with Major Stewart."

"Sure, Major Abbott."

Ali sat down on a bench but couldn't help to sneak a peek. Major Vicki Abbott worked directly for the general, and Lynn didn't look happy. *Is there a problem with work?* Suddenly, a weird thought shot through her brain. *Are they a couple? Stop! That's got to be the drugs.* Yet, the tinge of jealousy wouldn't go away.

Abbott left, and Lynn provided an arm to steady Ali. "Let's get some food in you. Not too much. Strict orders by the doc. I have some crackers and peanut butter."

Ali tried to turn towards the MRAP. "My bag and battle rattle are still in there."

"I've arranged for them to be delivered."

"Where am I going?" Thumbing over her shoulder, Ali said, "My barracks is that way."

"To my quarters."

Ali stopped. In a hushed voice, she said, "Are you crazy?"

"No." Lynn shook her head. "There's no one to check on you. The clinic's full, and your roommate departs for Bagram today. Major Abbott and I will watch over you."

"You room with Abbott?"

"No. The general heard about your incident. Apparently, he is a big fan of your work and ordered Abbott and me to take turns keeping an eye on you." Lynn rubbed the back of her neck. "I have the bigger room."

"Okay. Just a tad awkward." *God help me if I try to kiss you.*
After a short walk, Lynn helped her up the stairs and unlocked the bedroom door.

"Oh my." Ali glanced around. "This must be the penthouse."

"Why are you so dramatic?"

"Are you kidding me? You have a room all to yourself with a window and furniture. There are two to four in an enlisted room. We're shoved in kid-sized bunk beds. Maybe an end table if we're lucky but usually the locker is our only furniture."

"Only majors and above get a single room. The sofa's a little lumpy, and the laminate coffee table has seen better days."

"I'm crying crocodile tears." Ali fluttered her eyelashes.

"Someone's feeling better." Lynn took off her body armor and dropped it in the corner. After unstrapping her weapon, she placed it inside the locker.

Ali examined the few personal items—a slightly crumpled poster of Yosemite taped to the wall, a few photos on the coffee table, and a deck of cards. She smiled. "Maybe we should play."

"No. We need to get you in bed." Lynn blushed. "How's the headache?"

"Can't tell. My whole head hurts."

"You're completing sentences and walking okay." Lynn looked into her eyes. "Your pupils appear to be normal size." Lynn handed her two pain pills and a bottle of water. "I'll sleep on the sofa. You can have the bed."

Ali didn't complain and closed her eyes. When she woke, Lynn was gone, and Major Abbott was studying her.

Ali sat up, then closed her eyes. The spinning subsided. "I'm sick of this bed."

"I was about to wake you. It's time for your doctor call, followed by a light dinner."

"I need to go to work." Ali swung her legs over the edge.

"Nice try. How do you feel?"

Ali scraped her tongue over the sandpaper of her lips. "Hurts like hell, but I'll live. What do I look like?"

"You're a beautiful purple, blue, and black alien with an enormous honker."

"Where's Lynn?" Ali took in a sharp breath. "I mean, Major Stewart."

"She went in a couple of hours ago. Seems you're not the only stubborn one. By the way, you can call her Lynn in private. You're no longer in her chain of command. The general has gone over everyone's head. He apparently talked with your agency director. You've been removed from JETT and promoted to Special Assistant to the civilian Senior Intel Officer. You now report directly to him and the general."

"Wow. That's a crazy schedule, and I hate to leave JETT in a lurch."

Abbott laughed. "Serves you right doing a damn good job on the general's projects. Don't worry about JETT. Lynn made a passionate plea to leave you on a couple of operations. Look at the bright side. You'll work days. Well, some nights."

"Yeah, like 0500 to 1900 without stopping."

"Another plus. We will be on the same team, and I'm not your supervisor. So, call me Vicki. Oh, and we can also pack up your other things and move them here in the next couple of days."

"Huh?" Ali wobbled as she stood, and Vicki rushed to help.

"Easy there, champ."

"Why am I being moved?"

"The general wants you reassigned to the Officer's Quarters. You'll room with Lynn until an empty one opens. The

Italian first captain down the hall is leaving in two weeks or so."

"Two weeks? With Lynn?" Ali plopped back onto the bed.

"Why the worry? Does she snore?" Vicki laughed. "You can't stay with me. I traded my sofa for a recliner, and it broke. Be thankful you're out of cramped enlisted. Now, it's time for medical."

⸺◦⸺

Sweat dripped down Lynn's face and soaked her shirt. *Holy cow. I can't believe the general ordered me, in front of everyone, to take Ali as a roommate.* Running on the gym's treadmill always cleared her mind, but today, it wasn't working. *That grin is adorable. Kissing those lips would be amazing.* "Frak. Frak. Frak. I can't focus around her."

"You must be a *Battlestar Galactica* fan. Great classic TV."

She jerked her head up but didn't recognize the guy passing by. "Yeah. The second version's the best."

God, I have to watch my big mouth. That could have been someone from the Operations Center.

Slowing down from a sprint to an easy jog, her brain went back to Ali. It was getting harder to remain composed. The mere thought of being close to Ali, even just touching her arm, made Lynn's body pulse. *Oh, frak, I'm in over my head.*

Chapter 8

Ali was staring at the screen, squeezing a stress ball over and over. *Damn, another crazy shift.* She stood and threw the ball towards the waste can. It circled the rim before sinking.

"Vicki, I'm taking a break. I'll be back in an hour."

"Ali, there's no way we can work eighteen to twenty hours after the last couple of days. You've been working nonstop for six hours. It's slow now. Take lunch and go rest. Come back in three hours, and we'll switch."

"Sounds like a plan."

Instead of the chow hall, Ali stopped at the snack shop, grabbing a newspaper and granola bar before heading back to the major's quarters. *This should tide me over. I'll grab a sandwich later.*

Still engrossed in the article she was reading, Ali shoved the key in the lock and walked in. Lynn was in the center of the room, struggling with her clothes. Her pants dropped, and her arms flew up to her chest. Ali gawked. The view of firm breasts under Lynn's strong hands and her muscular six-pack abs lit Ali like a match starting a brushfire.

"I thought I—I locked it."

Ali swallowed. "And you were scheduled to be at Camp Eggers for the entire day."

"We returned early."

Snapping back to reality, Ali turned away and muttered, "I'm sorry for the intrusion." The rustle of clothes filled her ears.

"Dressed. You can turn around."

Ali walked over to Lynn who was stuffing her laptop into her satchel. "Lynn, you've been avoiding me since I moved in." Ali reached out, but then thought better, and didn't touch her. "Look, you're an attractive woman, but I'd never do anything to damage your career, and I'm not into straight women. I'll be out of your room soon."

"Another month." Lynn didn't look up. "The Italian officer's duty has been extended again. We have to bunk another month."

"Oh, shit."

Slinging her computer bag over her shoulder, Lynn moved toward the door. She stopped with her hand on the knob. In a faint voice she said, "I'm going to the rec center. I promised to help someone with his resume. He goes home next month."

"Dammit, Stewart!"

Lynn whipped around.

Aware of the thinness of the walls, Ali whispered, "I'm sorry. Why are you so damned worried? Are you that upset with sharing your room with a lesbian? Or do you think others will assume you are too? I know you have a lot at stake, but it's not my fault I'm here. We can at least be civil to one another."

Lynn appeared unsure and nervous. Her eyes blinked, and she wet her lips. Her mouth moved to speak, but nothing came out. She turned to the door again, and Ali thought she was going to bolt out of the room. Instead, Lynn dropped her bag and leaned her forehead against the door.

"Well, at least talk to me." Ali planted her hands on her hips.

Lynn flipped the lock, turned, and closed the gap between them. Soft lips took command of Ali as one hand cupped her neck and another settled on her lower back. Ali moaned as the kiss intensified with a hunger so deep that her head swirled. The slow burn of desire in her lower body blazed upwards. When Lynn's tongue entered her mouth, Ali wrapped her arm around her strong shoulders.

Beep, beep. Beep, beep. Beep, beep.

Lynn pulled away and shut off her watch alarm, then tenderly rested her palm on Ali's cheek and gave her a soft kiss on the forehead. "I'm sorry for avoiding you because," she wet her lips, "as much as I hate to admit it, I can't concentrate since you moved in."

Ali felt her heartstrings tug. Lynn stepped back and tucked her chin tightly to her chest.

"I've always kept personal matters separate from work. Now, my thoughts keep wandering back to you. If someone notices my attraction to you, my career's over."

"We worked well together before. Let's get that back on track. In private, I'd like to get to know you better. And that kiss," Ali smiled and shook her finger, "was amazing. I've been attracted to you from the beginning. I know you're under more stress..."

"DADT is unforgiving," Lynn sucked in a deep breath, "but your agency has more lenient rules than the military." Ali nodded. Lynn grasped her hand. "I'd like to kiss you again, but we have to be careful."

"I know."

Their fingers glided apart as Lynn slowly turned and walked out.

Ali ran a hand through her hair. Lynn might be gone, but Ali's fingertips and body tingled even more as the kiss and the feel of Lynn's muscular body pressed against her played over in her mind.

Chapter 9

The sound of Ali's alarm filtered into her brain. Her eyes popped open, and she grabbed the clock. "Shit, I'm late." She bolted out of bed, dressed, and ran to the general's 0600 briefing. Sneaking into the back of the room, she made it just in time to hear Major Vicki Abbott's presentation.

After the general gave the closing comments, he pointed at her. "Ms. Clairmont, is there a reason why you're hiding in the back of the room?"

Ali froze. "I'm sorry, sir."

After deafening silence, the general cracked a smile.

"Well, I hear that today is your birthday. Here's a little something." His assistant walked up to her, palm up, holding out a challenge coin bearing the ISAF insignia.

"Thank you, sir." With all the events, Ali had forgotten.

"You're welcome. On that report, please get it to me by 1500."

"Yes, sir."

As they spilled out of the room, Ali shot down the stairs and out of the building.

The report would have to wait. Lynn and Sergeant Henderson had completed a risky helicopter reconnaissance mission, and Ali and Paul were picking them up from the airport.

Paul was waiting at the armored SUV with his wide, friendly grin. He handed her a small lapis lazuli stone.

"Thanks, Paul. It's beautiful." She squeezed him tightly.

"Looks like you've been overexerting yourself again. It wouldn't be because of a certain officer, now would it?"

"The general. Let's go. We're late."

"Only by ten minutes." He chuckled and tossed the medical bag in the SUV's back seat. "Sometimes it's good to let the mind dream while the eyes take in the beauty of life." He patted Ali's shoulder. "Just don't move too close to the fire and get burned."

Ali punched his arm. "I know the military rules." She was honest with Paul from the start about her orientation. He was proper around others, but in private he was like an annoying little brother trying to coax just the right amount of information out of her.

Paul flipped on the vehicle radio and tuned to the American Forces Network, which broadcasted from Bagram. He lowered the volume enough so they could enjoy the music and still hear the operations radio. With the sun shining brightly, they joked and laughed. At one of the traffic circles outside the Green Zone, a man with a cell phone pointed in their direction.

"Ace, did you turn on the jammer?"

Fear shot through Ali. "No. I thought you did!" Looking down and seeing the green light, she relaxed her breathing. "It's on, but I don't remember." She turned off the music. "We need to concentrate."

Driving in Kabul was nerve-wracking enough. There were always attacks, and the countermeasures of a jammer only worked against radio-controlled IEDs, not on wire or pressure-plate-triggered bombs.

They reached the airport and cleared the checkpoint. Only then did she breathe a sigh of relief.

"Over there!" Ali pointed.

"Easy there. I know your drug of *handsome major* awaits you, but I worry that your energy is going to burn through the seat."

Ali swatted his arm. "I'm just happy they're okay."

"If you say so. By the way, how does she kiss?"

Ali raised her eyebrow. "Park the damn SUV, Paul."

"Yes, ma'am."

Bouncing out of the truck, Ali said to Lynn, "How was the flight? Did Henderson puke again?"

The burly sergeant said, "No. I have a cast-iron stomach. Must have been a bug last time." He patted his tummy and smirked.

"Bug, yeah sure. I made him take Dramamine," Lynn said.

The camera with a professional, high-definition telephoto lens hung around Lynn's neck. The one-and-a-half-foot lens had to be heavy.

"Where's the case?" Ali asked.

Lynn glared at Henderson. "Well, someone didn't secure it too well, and it slid out the helo door with a pricy wide-angle lens in it, too. The door gunner wasn't happy, and neither am I. Fortunately, this screwup is golden boy's first. I'd string him up if he weren't so good at his job."

"Sorry, ma'am," Henderson said.

"Did you get some good photos?" Ali asked.

"The humanitarian mission guys will be happy and so will JETT. We got different look angles of the compound of interest." Lynn winked as she bounced on her toes.

Ali hoped it was one of the bad guys on the top-ten list. She glanced at her watch. "We need to get moving. We have to pick up a classified package at Camp Phoenix, and I have to deliver a report to the general."

As they started to upload, Paul tossed Ali the keys. "Your turn to drive."

Henderson pivoted toward Ali. "No offense. I trust your analytical skills, but do you know how to handle this thing?"

"Yes. I'm qualified on defensive driving and have driven the route many times." Ali said with conviction.

Lynn slapped Ali on the shoulder. "I trust her, and we didn't get much sleep last night."

"If you say so, ma'am. Let's go. I need chow."

"Henderson, you always need chow." As the others settled in, Lynn pulled Ali back and whispered into her ear, "Happy birthday."

Paul was watching. Ali smiled at him before sliding into the driver's side. *Yes, she's a fabulous kisser.*

At Camp Phoenix, Lynn went to sign for the classified package and shouted, "This could take some time. Grab something to eat, and get a sandwich and drink for me."

When they hit the road, Lynn ate while Paul and Henderson tried to outdo each other's jokes in the back seat. The ops radio chirped with orders to divert. Ali cringed at the location, then exchanged an *oh, shit* look with Lynn.

Lynn turned and pointed at Paul and Henderson. "No questions. No talking."

Ali drove through a couple of checkpoints that only she and Lynn knew about.

Henderson mumbled, "Huh?"

"Quiet." Lynn said. "Absolutely, no questions."

Ali peeked in the rearview mirror. Their faces were twisted

in confusion. After parking, Lynn and the package disappeared into a guarded building. A few minutes later, she exited with a young man. The battle rattle hung poorly on his thin frame. Paul and Henderson were giants compared to him.

"How's our gas, Ace?"

"The tank's three-quarters full."

Lynn didn't look at her when she said, "Point 36."

Shit, I hate that place. "Yes, ma'am. Should I drop—"

"There's no time. Go."

They exited the Green Zone, driving in the opposite direction from ISAF and other U.S. facilities. Looking at Paul's and Henderson's faces in the mirror, they didn't look happy when they cleared the last checkpoint and left the city.

After about an hour, she turned off the highway. A mile down was a large compound.

The concrete chicane barriers leading up to the Afghan checkpoint forced her to drive the SUV slowly in a series of curves, like a snake sneaking up on its prey. Only Ali felt like they were the prey.

Two Afghan guards stopped them. Ali rolled her window down, just enough to offer their IDs. In broken English, the guard insisted they step out. Instantly, Ali's skin prickled with fear. This demand had never happened before.

"Out. You must. Out," the guard commanded.

Lynn said, "Stay in the vehicle!"

"Out!" The guard pointed his gun.

"Lower your guns. We are part of Operation Khorshēd," Lynn shouted to the guard as Ali waved the IDs and paperwork. He stared at them, then lowered his gun and took the papers and marched off.

"What is Operations Khorshēd?" Henderson asked.

"What did I say about questions earlier?" Lynn said.

"Sorry, ma'am."

Ali's chest tightened as she estimated the high walls on each side of them. A loud engine noise from the rear, increasing by the second, pulled her eyes to the mirrors. A deuce-and-a-half truck stopped just behind them. In front, the drop gate was down, and the two Afghan security vehicles were parked at angles. With both ends blocked, they were in a precarious position.

Ali took a couple of deep breaths, but her pulse was racing. She bounced her left leg up and down. *What's taking the fucking guards so long?* The two-and-a-half-ton monster's engine sputtered and cut. Her eyes widened, and her mouth went instantly dry.

"Are you okay?" Lynn's voice was faint to Ali's ears. "Ali, you're strangling the steering wheel."

"Yeah, I'll make it through the gate."

The guard came back, his gun lowered, and handed back the papers. "Go."

Ali grabbed the IDs and papers and tossed them at Lynn. Part of them fell to the floorboard.

"Easy." Lynn's eyebrows were scrunched. "You sure you're okay?"

"Let's just get through here."

The drop gate lifted, and one Afghan security vehicle moved out of the way. Ali carefully maneuvered around more barriers and cleared the checkpoint. *The hard part's over. I just need to make it to the secure building.*

BOOM.

Within a split second, part of what had been the Afghan security vehicle slammed next to them. Before they could react, another explosion shook them in their seats. Ali had no control of the SUV. Its engine was on fire. The run-flat tire inserts on the armored SUV automatically rolled the vehicle further from the checkpoint.

"Out! Out! Out!" Lynn shouted.

The SUV's armor protection was minimal. They had to get out before the engine fire spread. Everyone scrambled like ants.

The body armor was pulling Ali down as her legs pumped on sheer adrenaline. The sound of her pounding heart and the blood coursing through her veins seemed loud compared to the small arms fire and yelling. A burning, pinching feeling, as if someone had stuck a white-hot fire poker through her leg, caused her to falter and drop her rifle.

Remembering a row of concrete barriers, she veered left through the smoke and crouched there alone. She flinched as the pain returned. The smell in the air made her stomach curdle. It was more than the burning vehicle. It was the smell of burnt flesh.

Come on! You can do this! She removed her handgun. Her thumb crept up to the safety lever as she lifted her head and scanned around. The turning caused another sharp pain. She collapsed against the barrier. Her head stretched toward the sky. *Such a bright sunny day...*

—◁◁◁∎∿∎▷▷▷—

Lynn's breath caught when Ali ran through the smoke and stumbled. Relief flooded her when Ali made it safely behind a concrete T-wall. Ali was holding her pistol in a ready position. Her rifle was in front of the barrier, but slightly out of reach. The pistol was for close range and no match for AK-47 fire.

"Stay down!" Lynn shouted, then returned fire. An Afghan soldier lay dead, feet away. Henderson and Paul huddled behind another set of barriers and laid down heavy suppression fire. The thin young man was next to them with his head between his knees. Additional Afghan military arrived with more firepower. Lynn was grateful for the expedient backup. She glanced at Ali occasionally as the battle with the Taliban fighters continued. When the situation was contained, Lynn ran over to her. "Everything will be fine." The words rushed out of Lynn's mouth through labored breaths. Ali's skin was pale, and her hands were cold and clammy. "It's over, Ali."

Ali's voice trembled. "All in a day's work, huh?"

Henderson and Paul joined them, dragging the dazed, thin kid. "Backup is on the way. We've done a quick visual and pat down. All of us are okay." Henderson barked.

Lynn stared into Ali's face, "I'm doing you first, no arguing." She shouted to the others, "Everyone, step back and give us some privacy. Keep the Afghans away."

Lynn swiftly stripped the body armor off Ali. Her hands raced over Ali's upper torso. "I'm going to help you lie down, then I'll check your groin and lower body."

"I know. Standard procedure."

Ali's tone and slightly glazed eyes told Lynn something was wrong. Lynn squeezed her eyes shut. After feeling around Ali's pelvis, Lynn moved to her legs. She pressed on the posterior mid-thigh, and Ali flinched. There was no mistaking the dampness under the pant leg.

"Ali's been injured," Lynn shouted. Her chest grew tighter. *Don't you die on me!*

"Are you sure?" Ali's words were barely above a whisper. She tried to sit up.

"Lie still!" Lynn forced her down. Henderson came over with the medical kit and Ripshears. Within seconds, they had cut the pant leg away.

Lynn leaned over her. "It looks like a shrapnel flesh wound, but we're going to apply a QuikClot gauze."

"Not that hemostatic shit! It burns!"

Ali rattled off expletives between sniffles as the sting of the QuikClot hit her skin.

"Sorry. The worst is over now." Lynn wrapped her arm around Ali's shoulder and drew her in for a hug. "You're going to be fine."

Lynn squeezed her eyes shut. Two years ago in Iraq, a buddy died in the front seat of the Hummer after an attack. She could still hear his voice. "*I'm okay. A little pinch. It's nothing. Set up security.*" He was dead within the hour. A tiny bit of shrapnel had caused massive internal bleeding. Lynn had never forgiven herself, even though the doctors said nothing could have been done. Internal bleeding was difficult to identify. Signs, such as dizziness and pain, sometimes didn't occur for several hours.

"Hey," Ali said. Lynn opened her eyes and dropped her arm. "I expect a cake and you to sing me happy birthday later." Ali's voice was weak.

"A cookie from the chow hall will have to do." Lynn shoved back her emotions and tried to sound as upbeat as possible. She rubbed Ali's arm.

Paul jumped in. "They've got fantastic cookies at the Italian rec center."

Henderson grumbled. "For crying out loud, stop talking about food. That sandwich didn't last me. I'm starved."

Ali sniffled again.

"Hey, you're going to be fine." Lynn kissed her forehead, not caring who was around.

"Yeah. Is that why blood is on your hands?" Ali mumbled.

Lynn held up her hand. Her eyes fixated on the red splotch

covering her fingertips. "It's just a little bit. Don't worry. Everything's under control."

⫘⫘

Lynn drifted out of the debriefing. "You're next Henderson."

She walked to the restroom and went into a stall to muffle her cries. After regaining control, she hung over the sink, splashing water on her face, afraid to look at herself in the mirror. Footsteps and the *whoosh* of the opening door startled her. She swiped at the paper towel and dried her face, then rushed out. *I need to get back to my room before someone sees me.*

"Major!" Paul ran up, grinning widely and wrapped her in a bear hug and rocked her side to side. "Ali's going to be okay!" Lynn was so relieved that she almost hugged back.

"Lieutenant Taylor! Thank you for the information, but I'm not your big sister."

"Sorry, ma'am." Paul released her. "They'll transfer her back tomorrow. They said we can see her mid-morning. With luck, she should be on some bed rest for a few days and then crutches, but will make a full recovery."

"Thanks for the news. I'm exhausted. Let's get rest."

He yammered on as they walked out of the building. At the split in the path, she mumbled, "Goodbye," but he continued to walk with her. "Isn't your barracks in the other direction, Lieutenant?"

"Yes, ma'am. I just wanted to say...well, Ali's like a sister, and she's always saving my butt on my weekly reports. Today scared the crap out of me. Tomorrow, I'm going to tell her how much she means to me. Life's too short."

"You've come a long way since arriving as a newbie. You

performed exceptionally today and saved lives. See you tomorrow." Lynn turned toward her building.

He called out to her, "Sometimes performance isn't enough. Is it? This sterile place sucks the life out of us. We all need a life, Major. We all need love."

"Good night, Lieutenant. Get some rest."

Lynn swallowed back the tears and forced herself to continue.

Chapter 10

A couple of days ago, the clinic had cleared Ali to return full time to work. Hearing Operation King Viper had been moved up, she relished getting back into the thick of the action. Her excitement soon spiraled down when the general announced that a small JETT force would support the Special Forces. The small force would be led by Lynn. Now, as the ground forces neared the target, Ali struggled to maintain her professional demeanor. Her gut twisted, and she squeezed a stress ball in her hand. *Keep focused. Don't imagine the worst case scenario.*

"God blasted." Ali threw the ball in the waste can.

"Did you ever think about having someone send you one of those mini-basketballs with a hoop that hangs off the door in your next care package?" Vicki asked. "Then you can play in your bedroom without disturbing the rest of us."

Plopping down, Ali jokingly stuck out her tongue. She snapped her fingers then jumped up and called across the room, "General! Can I have a minute, please."

"What are you doing, Ali," Vicki whispered. "Walk up and ask him. Don't shout it."

"Yes, Ms. Clairmont?"

"Sir, I'd like to monitor the mission as a JETT member." She thumbed to the JETT workstations in the back of the room.

"How will that be more helpful?"

"With all due respect, sir, you have a robust team, including Major Abbott." She swung her hands out at Vicki. "I know the NSA systems, and frankly, Sergeant Henderson needs me because Corporal Webster isn't up to speed. I'm afraid he'll jeopardize the mission."

Ali turned to Vicki. *Say something! Don't sit there.*

"Ah, yes, sir." Vicki finally stood. "I concur with Ms. Clairmont. We're only as good as our weakest link."

He eyed them both. Ali was hoping he wouldn't fight her. "Very well. Hop to it."

"Thank you, sir." Ali crossed the room to the JETT stations. "Webster, you're relieved. I'm taking your place."

"Ah...but you're not—"

"Snap to it!" Henderson shouted. "She represents the general and outranks you in position and experience."

"If you need me, I'll be at the gym training for my upcoming PT test." Webster pelted his empty water bottle at the trash can and walked out.

"What do we have so far, Henderson?"

"Force is about three hours from King Viper's compound. If you don't mind, ma'am—"

"What happened to you calling me Ace? I may have been promoted, but I miss that nickname."

"If you don't mind, Ace, I wanted to grab a meal to go earlier. I hadn't done so because I was worried Webster was going to fuck up."

"Go, and grab me something too. We've got a long night ahead of us."

"Roger."

Ali logged in and reviewed the data and source reports. The sick feeling in the pit of her stomach grew. It was disturbing how the others were relying on two human sources. *What are they doing? That's not enough HUMINT.* Alliances often flipped, and the latitude of trust that Special Forces had in one particular source seemed too wishy-washy. But the op was approved at the highest level. All she could do now was monitor and pray like hell.

With the lack of windows, the air was stifling. The small thermometer at the station read almost eighty-five degrees. She hoped the AC wasn't malfunctioning again. The JETT chat screen lit up, and her attention snapped back. Lynn was checking in early.

Lynn: *Any status change?*

Ali: *No change.*

Lynn: *Where's Webster?*

Ali: *I'm taking his place. No margin for error.*

The cursor blinked but no answer. Ali mumbled, "Come on Lynn. Don't be upset. Answer, damn it."

Lynn: *I heard they're planning a cookout next month for the Air Force birthday! How's the Viper?*

Ali: *Nice. Keep on point. All quiet. Only three guards.*

King Viper was the code name given to a high-valued target located in Tagab, halfway between Bagram Air Force Base and Surobi. Evidence pinned him as the brains behind the entire network that manufactured and planted IEDs along the route from Bagram into Jalalabad. His roadside bombs had become more sophisticated. He was also a top recruiter of suicide bombers.

King Viper was a master of evading detection. It took longer to figure him out. Hopefully tonight, the months of hard work would have Viper rolled up and on his way to prison or eliminated by dusk.

Ali: *Lynn? Did you copy?*

Lynn: *Hold on.*

"Got us some BLTs. Even chow can't screw up bacon." Henderson tossed Ali a bag.

"Thanks. Hey, how many pings did we get on the computers and cell phones at Viper's compound?"

"Excuse me." He bit off a chunk of a sandwich and reached for the keyboard. She moved back. With food in his mouth, he said, "The major's got a great little device to match cell phones with users." He pointed at the report.

"How much time do they have to confiscate the technology?" She took a small bite as she watched half of his sandwich disappear into his mouth.

"Don't know. They ordered her to get it all."

Ali whipped around. "That's nearly impossible. The longer they linger, the more risk and..." She couldn't bring herself to say *chance of failure.*

He patted her shoulder. "Let's hope the Special Forces tidy things up swiftly so JETT can make a fast sweep. I'm going to grab us coffee from the conference room before things heat up."

Ali wanted this night to be over. She pushed away her worries and tried to raise contact with Lynn again.

Ali: *You there?*

Silence. Her mind began to spin as several seconds passed by. Why hadn't Lynn answered?

Ali: *What's going on?*

Lynn: *Sorry about that. Comms keep cutting out. ETA is now 0410. Guards moving around much?*

Ali: *Barely. Source reports the situation remains the same. Since your comms are on the fritz, I'll check—*

Her fingers hovered above the keys. The Operations Lead overrode all channels, and his chilling message flashed on everyone's screen.

Ops Lead: *ALCON. Double cab pickup arrived at the compound's rear exit. Three males. Weapons in bed.*

ALCON stood for *all concerned* and put everyone on alert. This compound had been under surveillance for months before making the connection to King Viper. The front and rear entry control points were guarded 24/7. Weapon deliveries became somewhat predictable, about three to four weeks apart. One occurred last week. *Why now?* Seconds passed but seemed like forever.

Ops Lead: *Two more double cab pickups. Six males. Unloading RPG-7s, assault rifles, and ammo crates.*

Ali prayed those weapons went into storage, and the extra men went to sleep, but her quivering insides told her otherwise. The JETT chat line lit up again. She struggled to breathe and control her pounding heart.

Lynn: *Guess they know we're coming. So, how do you like your burger?*
Ali: *Medium.*

Ali's eyes misted, but she held back the tears. The Special Forces and JETT were now in imminent danger.

Lynn: *And what kind of beer?*
Ali: *India Pale Ale.*

Lynn: *I look forward to seeing you soon. When we go home, I'll buy you that beer.*

Henderson set a coffee and a water in front of her. "What's wrong?"

She pointed a shaking finger to the Ops Lead messages. "Oh, dear Lord."

"Attention on deck!" The battle captain boomed as the general marched to the front of the room.

"As you were." The general scanned the group. "Bagram and J-Bad have come under attack. This mission must be completed. Do your best. Let's get back to work." He walked back to his private office.

Ali slumped into her chair. "There won't be any backup left for this mission with the country's critical hubs at Bagram and Jalalabad's FOB Fenty under attack."

Another message from the Ops Lead scrolled across the screen.

Ops Lead: *Continue. Surobi blocked, Bagram and J-Bad getting hit. AH-64 in flight.*

Special Forces: *Roger.*

"Shit," Ali pounded her hand on the desk. "One Apache attack helicopter isn't enough. King Viper's compound has nine buildings spread out in two groups. This isn't Hollywood or some video game."

The American public expected near perfection, but success was a combination of hard work and luck. Tonight, they would need a lot of luck.

"Ace, you have to keep the faith that our guys are going to be okay. I'll check with Fort Meade and see if they've got anything on their end."

She scraped her upper lip with her teeth, biting back the tears. "Thanks, Henderson."

"Anytime. One team, one fight."

Ali watched the nightmare of the crumbling operation. The soldiers were extracted and she was desperate to hold Lynn in her arms. As soon as the general released her, she sprinted across the base. She tapped on Lynn's door several times.

There was no answer.

A sound made her turn around. Lynn was plodding down the hall in a bathrobe. Ali had never seen this look on Lynn's face. It was the vacant look of loneliness, sorrow, and failure.

"Got your favorite." Ali held up a jar of Nutella, packets of cocoa, and an apple.

Lynn nodded and fiddled with the key to the point where she stopped and handed it to Ali. "I've been up for over thirty hours."

Once inside, Ali busied herself with the electric kettle and slicing the apple while Lynn dressed. Lynn slumped on the bed with her back against the wall and one leg bent.

"At one point, I thought we'd all die. If it hadn't been for that Apache gunship..."

Ali crossed the room, knelt beside the bed, and stroked Lynn's hand. "It's over now. When did you last eat?"

"Lunch yesterday...I think...oh...an energy bar, um, in the convoy."

"Do you want me to get you something at the chow hall?"

Lynn gripped Ali's hand and pulled her in. "Please, don't leave."

The teakettle whistled.

Lynn melted into her embrace.

The high-pitched whistle grew harder to ignore. "I'd better get that." Ali gingerly unwrapped from Lynn's arms and made their hot chocolate.

Other than the snap of biting into the crisp apple pieces, there was silence. Lynn probably wouldn't have eaten at all if it hadn't been for Ali's ingenuity. Remembering Lynn's fondness for everything dipped into the chocolate and hazelnut spread, Ali had traded a bottle of hand lotion for it.

Ali rose to wash the cups, but Lynn snatched her by the forearm and stopped her. The empty cups rattled in Ali's hand. Barely above a whisper, Lynn said, "Sorry. Please. Leave them for now. I need to talk."

"Sure." Ali placed the cups on the nightstand.

Lynn's strong shoulders slumped, and tears welled in her eyes.

"His name was Dustin. He was only twenty-four. His birthday was last week. I participated in one previous op with his unit, but..." Lynn stared at her hands, which twisted a tissue. "He bled out. In my arms. He's the fourth person I've seen die." She blew her nose. "I wasn't the one in charge of the overall mission, but it doesn't matter. It's the worst feeling in the world. I can't describe it."

Ali placed her hand gently on Lynn's knee. "I'm sorry. Is there anything I can do for you?"

Lynn sniffled. "You have already. Thank you for the snack."

"I guess I should let you get some rest."

"Ali, will you stay with me?"

Ali caressed the side of Lynn's face. "Sure. Let me get out of these heavy tactical pants."

"You can wear one of my T-shirts and gym shorts."

Ali worried that Lynn's current condition was more than exhaustion and sorrow. She might be in a bit of shock, but surely the medics wouldn't have released her like this. Ali lifted the covers and spooned against Lynn. Her arm slung over her side and rested on top of Lynn's. She whispered, "I think this is the best position. Are you comfortable?"

"Yes...thank you."

Ali delicately rubbed Lynn's hand until she drifted off to sleep. She couldn't take away Lynn's pain, but she'd be there when Lynn woke up.

Chapter 11

Major Vicki Abbott stood as Ali released the ball. Judging from the sound that resulted, the ball had knocked over the trash can.

"Sorry." Ali went back to typing but could sense Vicki glaring at her.

"You have a bad habit. That almost hit me. Let's take a walk, teammate."

"Maybe after lunch."

Vicki leaned over, "That wasn't a request, Ali."

They walked out back, past a group of soldiers playing cornhole. No one was at the picnic table. Ali sat on top with her feet on the bench. Vicki leaned up against the wooden pole that held up the gazebo roof.

In a low voice, Vicki said, "Ali, what the fuck is going on with you and Lynn? And skip all the bullshit. I don't give a rat's ass that you're a lesbian and if Lynn is or isn't your girlfriend. DADT is such crap."

"Excuse me, but that's a hell of an accusation."

Vicki blew out air, making a raspberry sound. "Don't play stupid. You loaned me your external hard drive so I could download music. Besides my favorites, I noticed songs from the Indigo Girls, Melissa Etheridge, and Lucie Blue Tremblay. All classic lesbian artists." She laughed. "They're all pretty awesome in concert."

Ali's head whipped around. "I never guessed."

"I'm not. My sister is. Now, let's get back to you and Lynn."

"I don't know. I hardly see her, and she's using work as an excuse."

"I think she took the op failure pretty hard." Vicki sat next to Ali.

"We talked afterward. I've never seen Lynn so fragile. Now I can't get anything out of her. She acts tough like it didn't even happen."

"Did you know she's going home to Sacramento for four weeks."

"When?"

"Next week."

Ali jumped down. "I have time coming. I'll ask for overlap—"

"Whoa. I don't think that's a good idea."

"Shutting me out is a form of avoidance, and she's more likely to open up at home than here."

"Since she didn't tell you—"

"The travel roster's open. I'd know if I checked it more frequently. After the checkpoint attack, the agency said I had some downtime."

Vicki shook her head. "I'm worried about Lynn too, but it's not a good idea."

"I have to try. I don't want to lose her."

———◦———

The day after Vicki and Ali talked, Lynn told Ali about the trip and said, "I wish you were going with me." Ali convinced herself that those words were a silent call for help. She applied for leave without Lynn knowing, and now Ali was on the last leg of the journey and would arrive in California soon.

You're hurting. We're going to get through this. I'm not going to let you go.

Chapter 12

September 2008 – Sacramento, California

The sound of the metal knocker thudding on the front door reverberated through Lynn's skull. She sat up, and a wave of dizziness pulled her back down. *Why am I sleeping on the couch?* The clock on the wall read 0845.

Panic set in as she remembered bits and pieces of last night—lots of alcohol and the friend of a friend. *What the hell did I do? I've only been home for a week.*

Dustin...

Her eyes squeezed shut, but she couldn't stop seeing his face. He lay in her arms as she comforted him, knowing there was nothing to stop the massive bleeding. His beautiful smile and deep brown, innocent eyes faded in seconds and burned a hole through her soul.

The banging grew louder. "I'm coming." Her mouth and throat were like a desert with a bitter, nasty aftertaste. *God, I promise to never do this again. Just get me through the day.* Since she hadn't installed a peephole, she hid behind the door and cracked it slightly.

"Ali? What are you doing here?"

"Do you think that only soldiers get R&R? Aren't you going to let me in?"

Panic woke Lynn faster than any cup of coffee could have. She hesitated, and then disentangled the chain. The door creaked open.

Ali flung herself into Lynn and hugged her tight. The loving gesture hastily ended, and Ali pushed her away. "You smell like beer," her eyebrows were pinched together in a deep furrow, "and something putrid."

Ali's eyes widened as she scanned the room. An open box of a half-eaten pizza and empty beer cans were on the coffee table. She stepped toward the kitchen where clutter and dirty dishes lay strewn about.

"This place is a mess and stinks." Pointing at the overflowing trash can, she said, "When was the last time you emptied it?" Her foot kicked a bottle, and she picked it up. "Wild Turkey! What the hell?"

"Yep, we closed the bar down last night." A woman's voice cut through the air.

Lynn wasn't sure whose head snapped around the fastest.

The woman wore jeans but was pulling her shirt down over her considerable breasts. Before another word was spoken, she propped her arm on Lynn's shoulder. "Who's your early-morning guest, Lynn?"

Ali's lip quivered.

Lynn flicked from the woman's grasp. "I can—"

"No need to explain. I shouldn't have stopped without calling. Obviously, you've found ample rest and relaxation." Ali ripped open the door and ran to the car.

"Ali, wait!"

Lynn caught up with her and grabbed at her arm. Although Lynn's touch was light, Ali spun around and shook away.

"Don't touch me!" Ali said through gritted teeth, then continued to march off.

"Please, Ali!" This was not the conversation Lynn wanted in her front yard. "I made a horrible mistake. I'm sorry."

Ali stopped so suddenly that Lynn almost ran into her. She twirled around and grabbed Lynn by the shirt, inches from her face.

"You're sorry? Kisses and promises all that time because of the rules? I agreed to wait, but you..." Ali's jaw tightened, and she pointed her finger into Lynn's chest. "You get home and fuck the first ho that comes along to drown away your sorrows. Gee, fucking great therapy, Lynn. Or was she always there waiting for your return?" Ali shoved her. "I wanted to build a relationship, but you obviously like to play the field at home."

"Please—" Lynn reached towards her again.

"Don't touch me!"

She watched Ali drive away, then dredged back to the house. As she passed the neighbor watering his lawn, he offered, "Sorry, looks like a tough day." She gave a shrug. The friend of a friend from the bar now stood on the porch. Lynn wished for the earth to open up and take her.

"Please, don't say anything," Lynn pleaded. "I'm sorry. I made a huge mistake, both in getting drunk and bringing you home."

A taxi pulled into the driveway.

"I'm sorry too. I like you, but this is too much drama—even for me." She bit her lip. "I'm short on cab fare. Can you spot me?"

Lynn reached in her pocket and pulled out a twenty. She closed the door as the woman dashed away.

"Ali will never forgive me, and I don't blame her. How could I be so stupid?"

She kicked the coffee table, sending pizza and beer cans flying. Flopping on the sofa, she buried her face in her hands.

The tears spilled. The harder she tried to stop them, the harder she cried.

What have I done? I love her.

Lynn had never said those words to anyone. She felt now that she may never have the chance. She curled up into a ball and sobbed.

Nothing matters anymore, none of it.

———

Ali sped onto the highway out of Sacramento, not caring where she was headed. She fought off the tears the best she could.

"I'll be damned if I let her get to me," she blurted out in the empty car. The song "I Hate Everything About You" by Three Days Grace came on the radio, and she cranked it up, singing at the top of her lungs. Lights gleamed in the rearview.

"Shit." She put on the blinker and pulled over.

The trooper took his time approaching the vehicle. After examining her license and documentation, the officer said, "Do you know why I stopped you?"

"I was speeding. I'm sorry, sir. I'll be more careful next time. May I please have my ticket?"

"Ms. Clairmont, you passed my SUV doing twenty miles over the limit." His eyes were hard, but his mouth was partially turned up as if hiding a smile. Pointing back at the vehicle, his voice became authoritarian. "You know, the big black Ford Interceptor with the contrasting white doors and golden Highway Patrol letters and decal. Oh, and the lights on top. At least you changed lanes with appropriate distance and used your blinker correctly." His radio crackled with a code. "Stay here and keep your hands on the wheel."

The air was sucked out of her lungs. In California, reckless driving came with a hefty fine and possible license suspension. *Damn it, why did I have to be so careless?*

He returned and handed back her documentation. "You have no speeding tickets over the past ten years, no prior arrests, and no outstanding warrants."

She took a breath and prayed for the best.

"Please explain to me why you're in such a hurry."

"I found my girlfriend in bed with another woman." She couldn't read the look on his face and had no idea if he was an uptight conservative or not, but he asked for the truth, and she gave it. She was tired of hiding. "We're home on short-term leave from Afghanistan."

He wrote a ticket and thrust it toward her. Although she tried to take it, he clinched it tight. "I could arrest you, but I'm giving you a break. I wrote it for fourteen miles over the limit. Slow down. It's not just your life but others that are at stake." His gaze bore into her, and Ali expected another lecture. "And Ms. Clairmont, no matter how upset you are about the girlfriend, let it go. Life is unpredictable and short."

Stunned, Ali murmured, "Thank you, sir."

He started to leave, but turned and held up his hand. "Oh, one more thing. Since you're obviously distracted while driving, you might want to save the singing for the shower and turn down the radio. Have a nice day."

Her anger turned to pain, and tears clouded her vision. She sat in the rental for a long time and let all her pent-up frustrations ooze out.

"God, how stupid am I to fall in love with such a player. Why can't I make good choices? I always go after the bad girls, and I always get burned." Her face hardened. "From now on, I'm focusing on work. To hell with relationships. I don't need the drama and bullshit."

She put the car into gear. "Fuck her. I'll tour California by myself."

Chapter 13

"You haven't talked to me for almost a week since I returned to base." Lynn's shoulders slumped.

Ali's nostrils flared.

"I'm so sorry." Lynn scanned the room then looked down at her boots.

"Look me in the face!" Ali stepped into Lynn's personal space. "What happened?"

Lynn flinched and stepped back. "I'm not sure the server room is where we should be having this conversation." She jammed her hands deep into her pockets.

"I made double sure the attendant is busy, and the noise will muffle the words. Talk!" Ali inched forward.

"I...I drank too much."

"That's the best you can do? You're all neat and professional here and—what? Your place was trash. That chick was trash. Who's the real Lynn? Is that what you want your life to be? Trash?"

"No." Lynn ran her hands through her hair and stared off to the side. Her eyes were misty. "I'm so sorry. It was a dreadful mistake. Hell, I was so drunk that I don't even know if I really slept with her."

"I need a better answer than that. Do you have an alcohol problem, an addiction to sex, or both?" Lynn's jaw dropped, and Ali threw up her hands. "You know, I don't fucking care. We're on different teams, and someone else can help you out. I'm too busy with the general's projects."

Lynn mumbled something, but the door to the server room flew open. Henderson dropped a box inside the door.

"There you are, Major. The colonel's got four people looking all over for you, and he's not in a good mood. Something's going on at J-Bad."

Lynn gave Ali another sympathetic look. "I'm sorry. I truly am."

Henderson grabbed Lynn's arm. "You'd better go now."

"You two go. I have something to check on." Ali's jaw hurt from clenching. She turned and leaned over a control panel. When the door closed, she smacked her hand on the hard metal.

Fuck her. I'm done.

Ali marched outside and took a long walk before going back to her desk.

—⟪⟫—

"Hey, Ali. How was lunch?"

She didn't look at Vicki. "Okay. Did we get any feedback on the project?"

"The general loves the threat analysis and air support pieces, but he wants an updated map with additional ingress and egress routes. I don't know why." She pointed to the screens. "Overall, it's a pretty solid package. Everything okay?"

"Yeah. What's going on at Jalalabad?"

"Don't know for sure. Someone got hurt in town, but you know there's always something going on at FOB Fenty. Only this time, Special Forces asked for Lynn by name. Looks like she might be there a couple of weeks." Vicki quietly said, "Should we be worried?"

"Special Forces are the kick-ass elite. Nothing to worry about. Do they need any help from us?" Ali displayed a report on the computer screen and started typing notes. She ignored the several seconds of silence and waited for Vicki's reply.

"No. But oddly enough, I was privy to the conversation between Lynn and the colonel. I was delivering papers to the colonel from the general, and the assistant led me into the room. It was weird. Every time the colonel spoke, Lynn argued back that it was essential for Henderson to go. I've never seen her like that. If Special Forces hadn't asked for her by name, she would have been toast. As I was leaving, he agreed on sending Henderson, then mentioned a letter of reprimand. Gee, she sure pissed him off."

Ali took a deep breath and locked the computer screen. "Let's hope nothing serious is going down."

"You sure everything is okay? You've been upset since your return. Lynn's weird too."

"Everything's fine. I'll be back in a second." Ali walked away. *Lynn you lying, cheating...* Ali choked back the thoughts and hung her head. *Admit it. A piece of me still cares.*

—◦◦◦◦◦—

Nearly a week had passed since Lynn had gone to FOB Fenty in Jalalabad, and Ali was still in a funk. Outwardly, she pretended not to care. Inwardly, grief and anger spun around faster than a hand mixer.

Paul peppered her with questions that she dodged as best she could, but she had avoided him enough. They had to talk.

Her footsteps were heavy as she trudged up the stairs to the fourth floor. The staircase was worn and laden with dust that collected faster than it could be swept away. *Sort of like my life.* Her nose wrinkled with the smell of something she searched to describe, something stale and unpleasant. Stepping into the corridor to Paul's office, the scent of lemon from the recently moped tile floor filled her. *Ah, much better.* She took a few deep breaths as she walked toward Paul's open door.

"Congratulations on your promotion Captain Taylor. I'm sorry to have missed your party."

He waved her in. "You didn't miss much. Although, I lucked out." He leaned back, smiling ear to ear, and rocked. "Camp Eggers' chow hall had wings—BBQ, Cajun, smoked, and one with a blend of sriracha sauce, butter, lime zest, and cilantro. Simply delish. Now, sit your bones down. You've been running around like crazy since you got back." Paul reached into the desk drawer and tossed out a bag of cookies. "My secret stash. I'll make some decaf. Sit and relax."

"I love these." The chocolate-hazelnut cookies reminded Ali of Lynn. The time they dipped apple slices into Nutella. She stilled her breathing and gritted her teeth as the hurt punched through her. "Is the colonel in?"

"Not today. He's at the embassy for a meeting and plans to have dinner with the ambassador. So, unless it's urgent, you'll have to settle for me." Paul gently closed the door. "We need to talk."

"Yeah, I guess we do."

Paul put his hands gently on Ali's shoulders. "Sit and tell me what the devil is going on. You've been tight-lipped too long, and it's wearing on you. It looks like you haven't slept in days."

Ali took a deep breath. "She cheated. The first day I went to her house, a half-naked woman was coming out of the bedroom with her boobs exposed."

"I'm sorry, Ali. What are you going to do?"

"Me? Fuck Lynn. I don't need her." She covered her face with her hand.

"Look, sweetie. I know you got that sailor mouth to hide the fact that you're twice as smart as most of the men on this base, but you don't fool me about your brains or your heart. You love her."

Ali put up her index finger. "Did. Not anymore."

"Did you talk to her?"

"I tried, but all she said was, 'I'm so sorry,' and, 'I got too drunk.' She sounded guilty. Paul, I can't get involved with someone that's jumping in and out of everyone's bed, and I have no tolerance for drunkenness."

He shook his head. "So, she confessed to sleeping around?"

"I saw it with my own eyes."

"You saw one episode."

"What's your point?"

"The point is you've both been through some traumatic events. I'm not defending her behavior, but Lynn hasn't been the same since the failed op." He squeezed Ali's hand. "I'm sure she regrets hurting you."

"Maybe, but I don't give a damn anymore."

"Are you certain about that?"

"Whose side are you on?"

"Ali, there's a possibility that she's acting out to hide PTSD."

The phone rang. He held up his finger as he answered. "Colonel Fitzgerald's office, Captain Taylor speaking. How may I help you?" Paul nodded and twisted his lips. "I'll be sure to give her the message, Major...roger...out."

Paul poured them a cup of decaf and laid out the cookies. "Major Abbott says the deadline has been delayed until tomorrow. And to answer your question, I'm on your side, sweetie."

"That checkpoint attack scared the shit out of me, but I didn't go shack up the minute some floozy came along. What makes you think she has PTSD? She was upset the first couple of nights after the failed op but seemed to adjust. Well, she dove into work at least."

"But pushed you away. Honey, this is our first deployment, and this is her third. You've been through one awful event, and no one died. Lynn's been through several and has seen death up close. I think she finally cracked." Paul sipped his coffee. "If so, then that could explain her actions in California. It's common for people with PTSD to be reckless and develop substance abuse. They try to hide, but sooner or later the façade comes crashing down."

"I agree she's been acting depressed and isolating herself, but she made it through the psych tests."

"Lots of people lie. It's stupid, but they think admitting they need help makes them weak. To be truthful, I don't know how much longer Lynn can continue. You know they sent her back from J-Bad this morning, right?"

"No. What happened?"

Paul bit his lip. "My confidential source said Henderson reported that Lynn barely seemed cognizant of her actions. In her off time, she was in the rec center playing video games for hours."

Ali wrinkled her brow. "She doesn't like video games."

"Apparently, she sucks at them too. Henderson went to check on her, and Lynn didn't even notice him walk into the room. I guess they have to log in at J-Bad, and the books had her there for hours instead of sleeping. Anyway, my source said Henderson told her to turn herself in for shrink sessions or he would."

"Oh my God. That doesn't sound like Lynn at all."

"Ali, I saw Lynn briefly as she was preparing to leave for a psych session at Eggers. Dark circles were under her eyes, and she didn't smile. Rumors are spreading, and the recent is they may discharge her on medical." Paul put the cup down and held Ali's hand. "Talk to her Ali. Maybe you can help."

"Or maybe I'll make it worse." Ali cringed from her own bitterness.

"Ali, if you completely cut off everyone who has ever hurt you, then what do you have left?"

"Peace."

"I think you know better than that. You'll end up a lonely shell because we're all full of shortcomings."

Paul sipped his coffee, and his gaze lingered, waiting for her to state the obvious.

She wet her lips. "You're right, Paul."

"My mother is always right, and she told me that avoidance solves nothing. Talking and forgiving is the only way to set yourself free." He patted his chest. "You won't be the same, and your relationship will change, but you can salvage the good and move on. Hopefully, that will be as a couple and not separate." He was now inches from her, and she couldn't escape his scrutiny. "You'll feel empty without going through life's checkpoints. Don't get lost, looking back and wishing things had gone better, or you had done this or that. Make it better now. Talk to her."

"You sound like a psychologist."

He chuckled. "It does run in my family. My grandfather was a psychiatrist."

"Good Lord, you've been analyzing me since day one."

"Yep." He sported a gorgeous smile. "My family taught me to be proud of my heritage," his eyes gleamed, "and how to pick good friends. I hate to see you in pain, but only you can change that."

Walking away from Paul's building, the conversation kept replaying in Ali's mind. *Have I misread Lynn so badly?* She gathered her jacket around her against the cold of the October night.

"Ali!" She jumped as Vicki grabbed her sleeve and guided her away from the main road. "Lynn's in trouble. She's a lot worse than before R&R. I've never seen her like this—ever—not even outside of work. She's really lost it."

"Oh God, I just thought she was pulling away from me, then in California..."

"Don't beat yourself up. We all misread her. Hell, I thought she simply needed a little time and would bounce back after the trip home. She had us all fooled when she passed the initial psych exams but completely fell apart at J-Bad."

"When does she get back from psych?"

"She might be back now. You should check. I have to get back to the Operations Center."

Ali sprinted the rest of the way and took the steps up two at a time. Her pulse raced as she reached the third floor. She took a deep breath before tapping on the door.

"Lynn, are you in there? Please answer." Lynn cracked the door but didn't say a word. "Please let me in. I'm sorry I've been awful to you. Please, let's talk."

"I'm leaving in two hours and need to pack."

Trembling, Ali leaned in close. "I was infuriated and upset, but I forgive you. Please forgive me. I know you're hurting." Lynn didn't answer. "Please. We'll both feel worse if it ends this way."

Lynn swung the door open and continued to pack. Everything she owned was spread out on the bed and small table. Two gorilla boxes were partially full. It was still hard to believe things had escalated this far so fast.

"I'm sorry," Ali choked out the words as she closed the door. She lightly touched Lynn's back. "I didn't know how badly the failed op affected you."

Lynn stopped folding, then slowly put her shirt in the box and turned to face Ali. Her color was ashen, and her blue eyes were circled with darkness. She wasn't the strong woman Ali knew.

"Oh God Lynn, I'm so sorry." Ali embraced her.

Lynn only returned the affection after Ali began to cry.

"I shouldn't have been a bitch to you. You said the woman meant nothing, but all I wanted to do was punish you and wallow in my anger and self-pity."

Lynn grasped her shoulders and pushed her out to arm's length. "I feel miserable about California, but you're not at fault. I've been sliding down. I tried to take care of things on my own, but I...I...I just couldn't." The tone of Lynn's voice was raw, and tears clouded her eyes. "You're better off without me anyway. I don't know if there's any way of coming back from this."

"Don't say that! You're strong and intelligent. You'll get through this."

"I don't know about this time. I can't stop...the nightmares...I can't sleep. I can't forget Dustin." Tears ran down Lynn's cheeks, and she squeezed her eyes shut. "I can't see the other faces, but I see all their suffering. It just won't go away."

Ali cupped the side of Lynn's face. "I want to help."

Lynn opened her eyes then stepped further away. "I never meant to hurt you. I wish I could take it all back. Every fuckup—"

"I could have at least given you more of a chance to explain."

"Ali, it wouldn't have mattered." Lynn rubbed her face. "I...I thought things would get better once I was away from the alcohol and back into the mission." She turned her back to Ali and hung her head. "I'm a danger to everyone here. I'm going home. Going into a full-time program." She began folding again, but her hands trembled.

The tears streamed down Ali's face. "I love you, Lynn."

Lynn paused but didn't say a word.

"Please say something. Anything."

"Ali, I'm damaged goods, and I'm not relationship material. I'm sorry, I have no more to give. You should leave now."

The words cut through Ali.

"I'll let you finish. I wish you the best with your therapy." Ali's hand was on the doorknob, but she couldn't turn it. "Please let me know how you're doing."

"I can't make any promises."

The words were spoken so softly that Ali barely heard them. She jerked the knob and ran out. The sound of her feet echoed as she rushed down the hall. She closed her door and crumpled onto the bed, burying her face in the pillow.

Chapter 14

Thanksgiving 2008 – Kabul, Afghanistan

Ali stepped out into the evening. It was a crisp forty-three degrees Fahrenheit. Off in the distance, Vicki waved goodbye to a British officer then jogged over to Ali.

"That was a lovely Thanksgiving dinner," Vicki said. "It was nice that the British team joined us."

"Especially the blond, muscular Wing Commander Oliver Hamilton."

"Yeah, he's a gentleman." Vicki walked straight ahead. A wide grin gave away her feelings.

Ali raised her eyebrows. "It seems you know him well."

"Oliver's work at the UK embassy brings him to the ISAF headquarters building a lot."

"Uh huh. I thought you'd been spending extra time at the headquarters building. Has he kissed you?"

Vicki smacked her arm. "Yes, Miss Nosy."

"And?" Ali twirled her hand.

"He gives the most toe-tingling kisses."

"That's it?"

"No sex, if that's what you mean. Some of us prefer to wait a little bit for a more romantic location. Getting caught in the barracks and sent home is not how I'd like to end my career."

"Ouch." Ali grabbed her chest, pretending to be mortally wounded. "So, what's the next step? You seem pretty enamored with him."

"His twenty-two-year service mark is in three months. He's going home after Christmas and retiring." The wicked grin was back. "I have leave coming, and he invited me to visit."

"Soooo that's what you're waiting for. Oh, you go girl."

"Get your mind out of the gutter." She winked at Ali. "But I'll consider it, should the opportunity arise." They both snickered.

Ali gazed up at the stars. It had been quiet around the city for the past two weeks. No mortar attacks, no car bombs, no IEDs blowing apart armored vehicles. She hoped it would stay that way for just a little while longer.

"Ali, I heard from Lynn the other day. They're not kicking her out—not yet—but she has to complete the six months of intensive therapy before they will even consider retaining her. She asked me to relay the info."

"That's nice."

"That's all you have to say?"

Ali swung around. "She's been gone for nearly two months, and I've emailed her so much that I feel like a stalker. I even sent her a card. What have I gotten from her? Nothing! Not one blasted word until now, and it was through you."

"Gee, I'm so sorry. You never told me."

"What use is it crying over a lost cause. Lynn made it clear on her last day—no guarantees." Ali rubbed her eyes. "I do wish her the best, but she's the one who ended it and did so with a knife through my heart."

Speakers in the distance blared with the Isha call to prayer. When Ali first arrived in Afghanistan, she didn't understand how people could tolerate the daily prayers playing over the loudspeakers, especially the one after midnight. Over time, the melodic tones had grown on her.

"Paul told me about your job offer. Are you going to take it?" Vicki asked.

"No."

"Are you crazy? Besides a pay increase, you'd be traveling to meetings around D.C. instead of the damn streets of Kabul. Most importantly, you'd be going home early and have Christmas with your family. If I were a civilian, I'd hop on it in a second."

"I'd rather be working with the operators. I kind of like you crazy guys."

"Ali, it's a team captain post in the National Counterterrorism Center. You have a chance to hit the enemy from another direction. Give it some serious consideration, please. Another opportunity like this may not come along." Vicki hugged her.

"Are you switching teams on me?"

"Don't you wish." She grabbed Ali's shoulders. In the glow of the dim overhead camp light, Ali could barely make out her solemn features. "I'm doing you a favor by hauling my ass out of bed in the middle of the night and taking your place tomorrow. Promise me you'll think about this job."

"Okay, okay. Now get to bed. 0430 comes early."

"Aye, aye, captain." Vicki mock saluted her.

Ali laughed and went off to finish her shift at the Ops Center.

—◦◦◦—

The next morning, Ali hustled over to Paul's office.

"I was told to report right away. What's so urgent that I have to skip breakfast?"

"Relax. The colonel's out of the office."

She poured herself a cup of coffee and sunk into the chair. "You could at least offer a girl some cookies."

Paul was leaning over papers on the desk. His hand hid his face.

"What's going on buddy?"

"I think you should go home." He played with a pen in one hand while still hiding his face with the other hand. "I could get you out of here by 20 December."

"I'm not taking the job. My orders say my ten-month tour ends in early February, and that's when I'll leave." Crossing her legs, she took a gulp. "Management is not the job for me. At least not right now." Paul had been trying to talk her into it for days. Apparently, he wasn't giving up. The chair squeaked loudly as he shifted. She put the cup on his desk. "Are you going to talk to me?"

Paul pivoted away from her and rocked back and forth.

"Paul, what's wrong?" When he turned, she gasped at his red, swollen eyes. *Why has he been crying?*

"I'm not very good at this." He sniffled and wiped his eyes. "The convoy to Bagram hit an IED a couple of hours ago. An interpreter, a lieutenant—"

He choked and stopped mid-sentence. A tear rolled down his cheek. Ali's heart raced.

"Ali, Vicki died. I wanted to tell you, so you didn't hear it from others."

Her breathing slowed to a near standstill, and she felt faint. Tears rolled down her cheek. "That was supposed to be me," she choked out.

"Stop it with the survivor's guilt. Vicki wouldn't want that." Paul came around to catch her and wrap her in his arms before she fell over. She could feel his body shake slightly. His voice quavered. "Once a deployer, always a deployer. You know, they'll ask you to return again. Right now, you have a chance for a break. Get the hell out of here. Go home. Get refreshed and go to work kicking ass at the National Counter-terrorism Center. Don't waste this lucky shot."

Paul's words faded, and everything was a blur. She sobbed, limp in his arms for several minutes, before she could gather herself together. Grabbing a pen off the desk, she scribbled the name of the British officer and handed it to Paul.

"Wing Commander Oliver Hamilton. Who's this?"

"It's the Brit who…" Ali sucked in a breath and forced back the emotions. "Vicki was seeing him. He's stationed out of the UK embassy but comes here frequently. She was going to take R&R after Christmas to visit him." She wiped her eyes. "I don't think I have the strength to tell him. Would you please do it for me? I know that's a lot to ask."

"Of course, I will. But sweetie, get your head around the fact that this isn't your fault. He won't blame you either. The only ones at fault are the terrorists."

She nodded and excused herself to clean up in the restroom.

The cold sting of the water only helped so much. Just as Ali got everything under control, she'd chock back up with tears. *I'll never know the person who killed you, Vicki, but I'm damn sure going to do as much as possible to stop the IED networks.*

Ali shuffled back to Paul's office.

"Get me home. I'm taking the job."

PART II

2010

Chapter 15

Memorial Day, 31 May 2010 – Northern Virginia
Two Years Later

Stephanie tossed down the dish towel and put her hand on her hip. "Ali, you're nuts to consider another deployment. Your finances are back on track. I don't get it. Why the risk-taking? Is that because of your job? Do they require you to deploy every two years?"

"You should leave it up to the men," Kevin said as he entered the kitchen, grabbed the platter of burgers and exited to the back deck.

Ali drummed her fingers on the countertop and bit the inside of her mouth. It wasn't worth the fight to argue with her older siblings' conservative views.

"Mom, you should talk some sense into her," Stephanie said.

Standing and pushing her chair in, their mother said, "Well, being a photo interpreter is an important job. I'm proud of Ali's sense of duty. If you'll excuse me, it's too gorgeous of a day to be cooped up in the house."

Ali suppressed a laugh at the old phrase that was used to describe her profession years ago. If only her family knew how integrated and complex imagery analysis had become. The screen door slammed, and Stephanie took in a breath and blew out an exaggerated huff.

"Guess that says it all. I never understood how Mom went along with all of Dad and Kevin's rigid beliefs, but when it came to your job in a male-dominated field, she never had a bad word to say. She's always been proud of your work accomplishments." Stephanie waved her hand. "I remember the old National Geographic magazines stashed in the attic. I figured they belonged to Dad, not Mom."

"Yeah. Did I ever tell you about the time she asked me about satellite pictures?"

"No."

"I couldn't answer for security reasons, and when I hesitated, Mom mentioned reading an article on NASA and the U.S. Geological Survey Landsat satellite program. I wasn't sure if I was shocked more by her knowledge of satellites as much as her knowing who and what USGS did. Whose mom strikes up a conversation on remote sensing and agricultural crop analysis?"

Through snorts of laughter, Stephanie said, "I never in a million years would have guessed you two shared the same geek fascination for geography and maps. At least, there was something you could bond over." She mixed the salad.

"Yeah." *And it's about the only thing Mom and I have in common.*

"It's good to have you here for the picnic. We missed you last year. I can't believe work sent you to a conference on a holiday weekend." Stephanie squeezed Ali's shoulder. "I need to take a few things outside. It's a warm day, and there's not a patch of shade on that deck. Be right back."

Ali pinched the bridge of her nose and sucked in a deep breath as she thought back on Memorial Day last year. Lying about the conference was easy. Visiting Vicki's grave was not, but Ali had to say goodbye in her own way. *I miss you, Vicki. Your Colorado hometown was pretty.* Ali wiped her eyes. *You'd understand about this second deployment, my friend. I need to be productive and help out in the fight.*

"You're deep in thought."

Ali jumped at the sound of Stephanie's voice. "I didn't hear you come back inside."

"Look, Sis. You know I don't always agree with Kevin or Mom. I'm just worried." Stephanie chewed on her bottom lip. "They work you ninety hours or more a week, which has to be wearing you down. It's hard on us, too. We worry about you getting hurt or killed. So, why are you going?" She rested her hand on top of Ali's, waiting for an answer.

Ali blinked several times. Her relationship with Stephanie was better than with Kevin but not free from arguments. Today, Stephanie was extremely kind.

"I miss the work. Overseas, I support all levels, and even the simplest map or image product that helps our guys move around safely makes me feel a sense of satisfaction that I don't get here." *It's the truth, just not the whole truth. I want to nail those IED bastards.* "Briefing a congressman or a group of VIPs seems like filling a black hole."

Stephanie chuckled, and Ali's mood lightened. "Yeah, the D.C. powers have to mull over every detail and argue for months or years before they take action. I guess that'd be a little detrimental in a war zone." Stephanie patted her arm. "I love you, and I'm proud of you but still think you're nuts."

"Of course, she is." Denise bounced into the room. "What's going on? Don't you goofballs smell the food outside? The burgers are almost ready."

"Ali's deploying again."

Denise smacked Ali on the shoulder as she walked by. "Certifiable crazy, but intelligent crazy. When do you go?"

"Late July."

"Okay, you're definitely off your rocker. Isn't it hotter than hell?" Denise grabbed a bowl of Stephanie's homemade candied almonds.

"I can't believe with all the danger you're talking about the weather." Stephanie grabbed the bowl from Denise. "And save some for after dinner."

"Well, talking about blood and gore isn't going to change anything. Besides, there are a lot of cute women in uniform. Maybe Ali will find a girlfriend." Denise winked.

Stephanie's face drained, and her eyes darted to the screen door. "Stop talking so loud. You'll upset—"

"You, Mom or Kevin?"

"I don't have much of a problem, but you know it bothers them." Stephanie wet her lips.

Denise said, "The optimum word there in your sentence was *much.*"

Ali sprang out of the chair. "I didn't come over to hear family arguments. Drop it, Denise."

"Sure, but it's been several months since you went out on that last disastrous date. You know there are plenty of good women out there waiting for you. I bet some cute officer in her dress uniform is waiting to sweep you off your feet."

Ali's mouth hung open. At eight years younger, Denise liked to poke. Suddenly, Kevin appeared at the back door. "Dinner's ready, and Scott and Aunt Judy are here."

As they shuffled out, Denise leaned over and whispered, "Did I hit a nerve?" Ali whipped around. Her jaw tightened. Denise put up her hands. "Okay, okay. I'll drop it."

Ali hugged her favorite aunt and Scott's wife and kids. Besides Denise, Aunt Judy and Scott and his family were the only ones who accepted her for who she was.

Scott bounced up the steps and gave Ali a one-arm bear hug. "Hey, little cuz. You should work with me more often. The customers from the last house can't stop raving about the interior. Thanks for helping me out." He announced to the party, "I've brought my famous bratwurst casserole."

As everyone piled food onto their plates, Ali hung back. She rested her elbows on the deck railing and stared at the flag, softly flapping in the breeze.

I wish you were here, Vicki. I will make a difference, even if it's small.

Chapter 16

August 2010 – Paktia Province, Afghanistan
Ali's Second Deployment

Dust billowed out and floated away as Ali sprayed down her computer with a can of air. She sneezed hard through the bandana that was serving as a mask.

"The only thing worse is being on a combat outpost," she muttered.

"Be careful what you wish for. We travel to a few every now and then. It would be a good experience for you," JETT's Sergeant Michele Miller shouted as she walked by.

Ali waved, put the computer casing on, and walked back inside. The jury-rigged door slammed and hit her backside.

God, this place is a dump. The entire building looks like it was built from scraps. Makes me wish I was back in Kabul.

"Prop it open. We need some air," Lieutenant Hernandez shouted.

Top-secret Ops Center my ass. Arguing was useless. If she didn't do it, someone else would. The Army Brigade in control of the Ops Center bent rules. Rules that would make the hair on Washington's security people catch on fire.

With the computer positioned on her plywood desk, she patted the top as it went through the boot-up routine, then blew her nose. *Damn dust.*

"Overheating again?" One of the sergeants asked.

"Yeah, I have a part coming in a couple of days."

Sipping from her water bottle, she grimaced and pushed it aside. It had gone warm hours ago and had a funny aftertaste. Someone turned up their computer speaker to full volume. The voice of Rush Limbaugh filled the room: "I'm a huge supporter of women. What I'm not is a supporter of liberalism. Feminism is what I oppose. Feminism has led women astray. I love the women's movement — especially when walking behind it."

The contractor at that computer added his own chauvinistic remarks. He nodded at Ali, laughing and bouncing on his toes.

What are you, a fucking bobblehead doll?

Lieutenant Hernandez shouted, "Tone it down. This is a politically neutral space." His grin showed where he stood, but that was nothing new to Ali.

Bobblehead said, "One more thing. We all know feminists and lesbians go hand in hand." He winked at Ali.

"Attention on deck!" Hernandez snapped to attention as the commander of the Combat Engineer Battalion entered.

Ali straightened her back. NSA's JETT was her primary customer, and all other units were secondary. Her agency occasionally directed her to work on the Engineer missions. The Engineers always showed appreciation for her work and respected her. The Army Brigade, which controlled the Ops Center, was a toss-up. Lieutenant Hernandez and a few of his cronies treated her like a private and tried to push her around. Sitting with them was like sitting in *no man's land.*

"At ease." The Engineer Battalion's commander waved his hand for them to sit and strolled in her direction.

Please have an assignment for me and get me out of this ragtag bunch of misfits.

"Good afternoon, Ms. Clairmont."

"Sir." Ali tipped her head. "What can I do for you?"

"I have a team traveling at the end of the month to Baraki Barak to inspect a construction site and school. They'll hand out gifts to the children." He smiled broadly. "I'd like to extend an offer for you to accompany them."

Her muscles tightened. *That's several hours northwest of Gardez.*

The commander handed her a photo of smiling children around a soldier.

You're here to make a difference.

"It will give you a sense of the local population and a better appreciation of our humanitarian mission."

"That sounds like a good trip, sir. Thanks for the opportunity." The checkpoint memory from two years ago flashed in her brain. *Toughen up.*

"I'd like to introduce you to Mr. Dan Galvarino."

A stocky, dark-haired man shuffled towards her and stuck out his hand. Ali eyed his pointed beard. She stifled a laugh as a vision of a gnome popped into her head and shook his hand.

"Dan's retired Army with a specialty in counter-IED cases. He's a civilian with JIEDDO and helping us out with threat assessments over the next couple of months. I'll leave you two to chat."

When Ali had been stateside, she frequently interacted with explosives experts and analysts from the Joint Improvised Explosive Device Defeat Organization. This was the first time she had met a JIEDDO analyst in Afghanistan.

"May I call you Ali?" She nodded. "I sent you an email with an attachment. Let's pull it up." He started going into every minuscule fact about the trip.

"Coming to the promotion party, Ali?" One of her teammates called out.

"After I finish with Mr. Galvarino." The words were barely out of her mouth, but he resumed discussing the tedious details.

"May I?" He pointed to the mouse.

"By all means." *God, I hope he speeds this up.* Her workstation was in the back corner of the room, and the entire row had left. *If he tries to put the moves on me, I swear I'll...*

Her concentration snapped to crystal clear sharpness. The security papers that she had electronically signed last week were displayed on the screen—a project involving top-secret, code word material.

"And here's something you might find interesting." Dan clicked on another link.

A letter with the director's seal appeared on the screen. The first line read, *Mr. Daniel Galvarino is your contact for the special project.* She read on, but the last couple of lines jumped out at her. *Mr. Galvarino is the conduit for higher-level support. For security purposes, you will not know the others involved.* Her eyes glanced down at the NGA Director's signature.

She swallowed. "So, you need help, and it involves IEDs?"

"Essentially, yes. As we go along, I'll fill you in. Anyway, when you're not busy and want to relax, I suggest putting on your headphones and watching an entertainment video. I think you'll find the actors most interesting." He pulled up her email list and clicked on a new message from the director. A video popped up with the director's face. "Just watch it when you bored, and no one's around to bug you." He pulled at his beard, intently studying her.

"I understand. Maybe you should consider this." Ali bumped him and pushed herself in front of the keyboard and typed *This trip? How important?* Ali hesitated, then typed: *I don't like extensive travel. I'll do some, but...*

He pulled the keyboard away from her and typed: *Checkpoint. Vicki Abbott.*

A chill rippled from her core to her extremities. Her thoughts raced. *What the fuck do they hope to achieve by sharing my personal info? Are they trying to test if I'm too soft for the job?* She looked away and took a drink of water. *Am I?* The dreadful flavor assaulted her taste buds. She swallowed it down in a hurry.

"Ali, I hope some of the trips have impactful results, but I can't predict that." He lowered his voice. "I will try to keep things to a minimum. If you can improve a case in any way, I just want to hear about it, especially if you think something isn't being done the right way. Do you understand?"

She nodded and leaned on the desk.

"Between the Army and being a *govie*, I've deployed eight times. It's never easy, and nothing is ever forgotten. No project or feeling is insignificant."

She clenched her jaw. "I'll do what I can."

"Ali, there's nothing wrong if you're having difficulty completing a tough assignment. Just give a shout, and I'll see what I can do. One team, one fight. It makes all the difference."

She grasped his outstretched hand. His touch was gentle, but she squeezed hard and met his gaze. "I never leave a task hanging."

"Ohhh, I don't doubt that for one minute." He grinned and squeezed back.

—⚊⚊⚊—

A week later, Ali was crammed inside an MRAP traveling to the school. Her body armor felt heavier than usual, and she couldn't get comfortable. With her shirt soaked, nothing else was being absorbed. Sweat trickled down her back.

God, it's so fucking hot in here.

The convoy stopped, and the soldier closest to the door said, "Just a minute, while we set up security."

When the guard shouted, "All clear," she scrambled out. She breathed in the cooler air while ignoring the stench from the nearby open drainage ditch.

The four MRAPs were positioned around the building perimeter in such a way as to defend as well as make an efficient retreat. She eyed the M249 SAW carried by one of the guards.

Damn, these guys don't mess around.

After settling matters with the Afghan construction supervisor, it was time to visit the existing school. Ali was shocked. From the exterior, the school resembled a group of abandoned warehouses.

Inside the courtyard, thick wooden slats covered the building's only two windows. Light blue paint was chipping off the cement walls, and larger pockmarks were here and there. She walked by a wall with deep indentations from small arms fire. The only decorations on the building were slogans, which Ali assumed were religious or political. The ground was barren and sandy.

How can this be a school? It's devoid of warmth.

They broke open the boxes and waited for the children. A woman entered, dressed in a traditional hijab, a black skirt down to her ankles, a navy-blue blouse, and a denim jacket. She motioned, and a line of young boys shuffled in wearing blue jeans and sweatpants. Some wore T-shirts with slogans in English. Their eyes tentatively scanned Ali and the soldiers.

Ali turned to the soldier helping with the boxes. "Their clothing seems unusual for a rural village outside of Kabul."

"Yes. Many of the boys at this school only have one parent. A few are orphans. Even if they have a family, they don't have much. Every now and then, we distribute clothes, but today will be the most popular since we only have toys. There's nothing like a kid's smile."

"Yes, indeed." She wanted to scoop the boys in a big hug. "Where do the donations come from?"

"Mostly churches or private citizens."

A flawlessly dressed young girl bypassed the boys and moved to the front of the line. Ali took in the white cotton blouse and a blue denim skirt with red flowers. A white bow adorned her neckline, and her hair was in pigtails with small white barrettes. She carried a large pink backpack twice as large as her torso. Ali wondered how it didn't pull her over.

The interpreter cupped his hand over Ali's ear. "The teacher is the wife of the ruler of the local governing council. The girl is their daughter and doesn't go to school here."

"Is this strictly a boy's school?"

"Schools in the countryside are usually segregated by gender. By custom, men only teach the boys after the fifth grade. Of course, Kabul is different."

The soldier added, "During the Taliban rule, females of any age weren't allowed to attend school. Women could not teach."

Ali stifled a gasp.

The interpreter gestured, and the little girl stepped forward, eyes down, face solemn. Ali gave her a small bear and candy. The little girl said thank you in Dari and finally peered into Ali's face. Her eyes grew wide, and her mouth turned from a quizzical twist into a smile as she recognized that Ali was a woman under the clunky helmet and body armor. They gazed at one another.

The girl turned to leave, and Ali held up her hand. "Wait a minute, I think there is something else in here for you." The interpreter translated while Ali rummaged through the box. The girl gingerly took the coloring book and box of crayons. Her mood brightened as she flipped through it. Ali never witnessed such a wide grin on a small child.

In a heavy accent, the teacher said, "I'm Rafia Shirzai, and this is my daughter, Jaleela. Thank you for your kindness." The woman gently pulled the girl away from the table and handed her off to a conservatively dressed younger woman.

The younger woman peered at them. While her face was ordinary, her eyes were a piercing green that shone brightly even from several feet away. Ali instantly thought of the famous National Geographic cover from years ago. Beautiful, but full of sorrow.

"Ziba is the child's nanny." The interpreter whispered in her ear again. "In Dari, her name means beautiful. She would be *a catch* as you would say in America."

After opening the last box for the few that remained in line, a somber-looking boy with the most beautiful auburn hair stepped up. Reddish freckles brushed over his nose and cheeks, and his eyes were a soft brown.

"Truck please," he said in English.

"I'll try." Ali didn't think any more were left but did her best rummaging through the box. Heartbroken, she handed him a bag of candy and a plastic dinosaur.

One of the other soldiers walked up holding a toy pickup truck and handed it over. "Last one, buddy."

"Thank you." Before leaving, he flashed them a radiant smile. "May the Force be with you."

Ali's mouth hung open. "He's seen Star Wars?"

The interpreter shrugged. "International films were

brought into the country, but the Soviets stopped imports. The Taliban were ruthless. They imposed a death penalty if anyone was caught with Western media. Some movies survived and were hidden. It's likely his parents lived in Kabul at some point. That's probably where he saw the movie and learned to speak English so well."

The teacher thanked the group and ushered the children away.

"Let's go." The soldier waved his arm and walked them toward the MRAP. "Please take my seat. It faces backward but has a good view out the window." The soldier shrugged. "Well, the best this monster has without sitting in the front."

"Thanks." She strapped in and stared through the thick metal slats. They were designed to minimize the impact of a rocket-propelled grenade. Supposedly, the slats would cause the rocket to explode a few inches outside of the reinforced glass causing the glass to fracture and absorb the shock rather than shattering and allowing the rocket inside.

Through the slats, the sights of a battered country passed before her. Young children played in the streets next to an open sewer, and trash was strewn about. The amount of rubble was staggering. When the driver slowed for the traffic, she saw an entire wall of a tall apartment building missing. Twisted metal rods and concrete dangling in thin air. Unlike Kabul, she didn't see much grass. The few trees seemed to cling precariously to the soil like the people clung to life.

American TV showed a smattering of damage. Ali doubted the average American understood the magnitude of destruction. Rubble was everywhere. Ali tried to comprehend the psychological devastation.

No one back home worries about a mortar leveling their house...the torment when a family member disappears for no reason—

forever. Americans didn't have to worry about their children being recruited as suicide bombers.

Ali slumped back and closed her eyes. *The dust will wash away, but I can never wash away what I've seen.*

Chapter 17

August 2010 – Maryland

Lynn led Deb straight to the bedroom, spun her around, then shoved her onto the bed. She crawled up on Deb and quickly unbuttoned her blouse.

"Oh God, you're an animal tonight."

Lynn's only response was to force Deb's bra up exposing erect nipples, which she ravished. Her hand slid under the skirt. She pushed the lace undies aside, then inserted two fingers. Lynn didn't hold back. She pumped at a rhythmic pace. Feeling the last waves of Deb's orgasm ripple over her fingers, Lynn withdrew and rolled over onto her back.

Deb rested her head in the crux of Lynn's arm. "What's wrong?"

"Nothing."

"Bullshit!" Deb sat up. "Okay, that was faster than what I like, but you're acting like I just gave you the plague."

"I'm sorry. I'm tired, and the drinks at the bar took it out of me."

"You had two. By the way, you were in therapy. Are you supposed to be drinking?" Lynn rolled away from her. "Yeah, I didn't think so." Deb got out of bed and started putting on her clothes.

"Please don't go."

"Why? You know, we used to have great chemistry, but this," Deb waved her hands back and forth, "was emotionless...I can get more from a sex toy."

Lynn stood and touched Deb's shoulder. "I'm sorry."

"You've said that already." She drew a deep breath and let it out. "You should really discuss intimacy with your therapist, and I'm not just talking sex." Deb rubbed her hand through her hair. "You're just...blah and don't know how to connect anymore. I don't even know who you are. Do you?"

"You know I have to be careful—"

"Don't blame it on DADT!" She stuck her index finger in Lynn's face. "Yeah, I'm sure it hurts, but for Christ's sake, we're alone. Don't hide behind that excuse." She crossed her arms and narrowed her eyes. "So, what's her name?"

"What?"

"Lynn, cut the crap. Guilt and regret are written all over your face and behavior. I shouldn't have come over tonight, but I thought you'd snap out of the doldrums, and it'd be like old times."

"Ah..."

"Pleassseeee. How long have I known you? And don't forget we have a common friend at NSA. So, what's going on? Who broke your heart? Or were you the culprit?"

"I screwed up. I'm really sorry that I took advantage of you tonight."

"And? I'm waiting. Tell me, or I leave, and I'll never talk to you again."

Lynn hung her head. "There was someone, and I royally fucked that up. She deserves better, and so do you."

"You're not over her, and trust me. Been there, done that." Deb took her keys out of her purse. "You have a private therapist, so the government doesn't know you're gay." A laugh bellowed out from Deb's throat. "Although, they've probably known for years. Anyway, get the shit off your chest. Even your friends complain about your negativity. There has to be more to life than work. When was the last time you talked with her?"

"Last week. You're right, I promise to make an appointment and see her as soon as possible."

"Oh my God! I'm not talking about your therapist. The woman whose heart you ripped apart."

Lynn cringed. "Look, Deb. I'm sorry again. Can we pretend this didn't happen?"

She huffed. "Since we have half a dozen friends in common, I'll try, but don't treat me like shit ever again. If your heart's not into it, then no more flings. I don't want to be anybody's second choice. And get some help."

When the front door slammed, Lynn fell back on the bed. She picked up her phone and texted. *I need an appointment.*

Buzz.

Lynn responded *yes* to the first available session. She had not mentioned a name to her therapist, but she had begun to talk about her relationship.

Still gripping the phone, her fingers quivered as she punched the keys.

Her name is Ali. I loved her. Taking a deep breath, she tapped the word *loved* and changed it to *love* before hitting the send button.

Chapter 18

September 2010 – Maryland

T*hud, thud, thud.*

Lynn stretched to lift the shade from the window. The sun was barely visible on the horizon. The bedside clock read 0628. "Oh, this can't be good." The pounding started again.

"I'm coming." She yelled as she threw herself out of bed.

She cracked the door and peered at the young sergeant, whose name she could never remember. He cleared his throat.

"Sorry, ma'am. I know it's Saturday, but you're needed at headquarters."

"Give me fifteen minutes."

Not waiting for a reply, she closed the door on him and hustled back upstairs to get ready.

An hour later, she was waiting alone in the director's briefing room. It was in sharp contrast to the other times she had briefed key decision-makers when every seat in the room was occupied and the entire brief was broadcast throughout the agency via secure video.

She walked up to the glass wall and glimpsed down at the agency's 24/7 Ops Center. It was a perfect bird's-eye view. Some forty feet below sat the analysts who worked swing shifts. They seemed calm. If there was a crisis this precious minute, they'd be scurrying around chaotically.

Why am I here on a Saturday? What's going on?

The wall in front of the analysts was filled floor to ceiling with massive TV monitors displaying the current news and the latest UAV feeds. She paced back and forth. Hearing the door, she snapped to attention and saluted as Admiral Kent entered. He held immense power as the Director of NSA.

"Good morning, Major Stewart. I'd like you to meet General Carr, the commander of the U.S. Army Criminal Investigation Division, and agent Master Sergeant Kyle Evans."

"Gentleman." Lynn shook their hands.

Kent motioned the assistant to start the slideshow. Lynn listened to the details about classified material being leaked and the evidence suggesting a spy ring was involved.

"Evans is a seasoned special agent with the technical skills. We need someone with NSA and cyber skills. You fit the bill, and more importantly, you have a JETT background." The gleam in Kent's eye told her there was more to this story.

"Pardon me, sir, but I'm not an investigator, and this falls outside JETT's purview." She wanted to add, *and it's illegal for us to investigate U.S. citizens without proper…*A chill ran down her spine. *This mission must have been approved at the highest level of government.*

"Beginning Monday, you'll get a three-week crash course at Quantico, tailored specifically for you. Evans will be by your side. While you're in training, we'll have experts here, brainstorming. We're looking at getting some of the software piggybacked onto an innocuous program we can push from here. That's less work for you, and your necks are not hanging out. Our target is to get you shipped out within twenty-five days."

This sounds crazy. Her muscles tensed. "Has the Army started an investigation?"

"An initial undercover investigation by General Carr's unit can't pinpoint the source, but we've narrowed things down to the Army Brigade in Paktia Province. With the leaking of top-secret JETT reports, the matter is now in our hands."

"Has code word material been stolen?"

"We can only assume the worst."

"What assets back us up?"

"Of course, there'll be a large task force back here, but you and Evans are the tip of the spear, and the only ones on the inside of the Brigade. You'll meet the Special Forces unit commander on base. He'll be your on-site supervisor."

Her hand twitched, and she moved it out of sight. After the required therapy, she had been cleared for all assignments and thought her demons were behind her. Yet, the mere mention of *Special Forces* caught her breath. If Special Forces were involved, then the mission would entail more than simple evidence gathering. This was a dangerous situation.

"Is there a problem, Major?"

"No, sir."

"Evans will be your second-in-command and in charge of technical." Kent pointed his finger at her. "I want you to run HUMINT. Time is of the essence."

"I'm sorry, sir. I don't have that background."

"Pardon me?" Kent's eyes narrowed.

Her throat went dry. She rubbed her sweaty hand on her pant leg under the table. "I've analyzed written human intelligence reports filed by others, but I've never questioned a suspicious person or recruited anyone. Surely, you need someone with that background for such an important task."

"You have excellent counterintelligence cyber skills and

will fit perfectly with Evans. The HUMINT won't be too difficult. We simply want you to cozy up to a few people and see what information you can get. Besides, you'll be busy enough with trying to make it appear that JETT is carrying on as normal." Kent leaned back and rocked in the chair.

General Carr said, "The Admiral speaks highly of you. As the JETT commander, your NSA affiliation gives you a level of autonomy. And as you pointed out, it's not JETT's mission, which is why they won't suspect you."

Lynn stiffened. "It will attract attention if you switch out JETT leadership."

Admiral Kent smiled. "Fortunately for us, the current commander's mother is undergoing an operation. Perfect opportunity to insert you. As for Evans, the paperwork will say you're a team."

There's no way I'm finessing my way out of this. She scrunched her toes in her shoes.

The admiral cocked one eyebrow. "There is one civilian working with JETT whose reports tipped us off with incidents of alleged mismanagement with some Brigade officers. Initially, the lower rank didn't take those reports seriously."

Lynn was becoming increasingly uncomfortable as they directed the briefing at her like Evans wasn't even in the room.

General Carr interjected. "The tracking software is not on that civilian's computer. Also, a technical glitch in the Brigade computers and printers prevent us from fully tracking the computer users. It has to be fixed in the field. Evans will take care of that. You'll have to be creative with distracting them."

Creative? How do they think I'm going to do that? Lynn cleared her throat. "General Carr, do you think this civilian is involved in some way?"

"We don't believe so, but everyone agrees it's prudent that

Evans installs the tracking software on as many computers and printers as possible."

Kent's arms were casually folded across his chest. "You look a little perplexed. Do you have any questions, Major?"

"No, sir."

"Very well. Please remain." Kent turned to General Carr. "I'll see you later this afternoon at Club Meade. This round of golf is on me." They shook hands.

As General Carr and Master Sergeant Evans walked out, Kent sat eyeing her with a crooked smile. The first smile of his that she had ever witnessed.

Now, it's bizzare.

"There's a potential glitch, but played the right way, it will be a plus."

"What's that, sir?"

"The civilian is a GS-14 senior analyst with a great reputation. There is a viable source that says the Brigade is pushing its weight around, trying to dictate and control, even though the analyst is not under their command."

"Has anyone tried to correct the situation?"

The admiral leaned back in his chair tapping his fingers on the table, staring at Lynn with a big grin.

Why is he toying with me?

"The current JETT commander has been staying out of the fray. The analyst's proper chain of command has spoken to the Brigade, but apparently, the Brigade has ignored them. However, I think you would be perfect for getting matters back in line and finding out what else this analyst might know. First, you must get over any awkward issues."

"I'm sorry, sir. I don't understand." Lynn was not aware of any civilian colleagues presently deployed. While she wracked her brain, the admiral continued to smirk at her.

"The woman is openly gay, which, unlike in the military, isn't punishable in the civilian workforce." He paused again. "It's 2010, Major. Congress will likely repeal DADT by the end of the year, and personally, I don't care who you choose to spend your time with or love."

Her head started aching and spinning like race cars were having a smash-up derby inside her brain. No way was she going to acknowledge his statement.

"Sir, if you are implying that this woman would sway me into breaking my oath of honor, then you are wrong."

"I'm sure she won't, but we're all human, now aren't we?" He rocked in his chair for a good minute. "DADT may fall in the future, but for God's sake, don't engage in a romantic liaison."

"Of course not." Lynn weakly mouthed.

"As a civilian, she's in a gray area and can socialize with people you cannot. Get as much information as possible without revealing the mission." He waved his hand. "Find out which of her friends have dirt on the Brigade. You can protect her from harassment to a point, but she has to stand on her own. The squabble they have is a nice distraction, so use it to your advantage."

"That would be manipulating her, sir. That would be unethical. If her reports have pointed out Brigade improprieties, then why not bring her onto the mission?"

He was now glaring at Lynn. "I have my reasons, Major. She and the rest of JETT will remain unaware of this mission. They will do their normal work, hunting down Al Qaeda. Part of your assignment is to convince everyone that you and Evans are doing normal JETT work. Are we clear?"

"Yes, sir."

"We must be able to focus our technical assets. So far, it's been like a damn needle in a haystack." He leaned over, pointed his finger, and stared her in the eyes. "Orders have changed. You will be her onsite supervisor once you hit the ground. Do everything you can to squeeze info out of her. Go up to the line, but don't cross it. Do you understand me?"

"Yes, sir."

He stalled again. "According to the official record, you both received high evaluations, but one person claimed the two of you were overly friendly in the last assignment. Fortunately for you, no one else backed up that allegation."

As his words filtered through her mind, she swallowed hard. She couldn't speak, and the sudden gleam in the admiral's eye felt like he could read her mind.

"I'm sure you and Ms. Alaina Clairmont will perform admirably again."

Even though she was sitting, Lynn felt lightheaded, then her heart beat increased.

"Do you have a question, Major? You seem to have grown quiet."

"Yes, sir. I mean, no questions, sir." To her annoyance, Admiral Kent seemed to relish in dropping the bombshell information as his lips quirked into another smile.

She concentrated on her breathing and tried to calm her heartbeat. The door abruptly opened, and an older man walked into the briefing room. He wore a neatly pressed navy suit.

"My apology for being late, sir. The Syrian incident took longer than expected."

"Major Stewart, I'd like you to meet Mr. Thomas Blair, NSA's Director of Middle East Affairs. I've given him the authority to act on my behalf on this mission."

Blair came toward her with his hand outstretched. The grip was firm, yet gentle. Something about his deep brown eyes, thick, wavy gray hair, and smile seemed familiar, but Lynn couldn't place him.

Kent smacked his hand on the table as he stood. "Do your job, Major and don't let the pretty woman distract you. Mr. Blair will finish your briefing." He didn't wait for a reply or a salute and walked off.

"Sir, I will do my best."

Kent stopped at the door and faced her. "Yes, Major. I might have asked you to bend the rules, but I'm confident you will not break them."

After the admiral's suggestion to cozy up to and betray Ali, Lynn found it difficult to concentrate on Blair's words. If Ali didn't despise Lynn now, she soon would. She fidgeted in her chair. The clock on the wall indicated Blair been talking for only ten or fifteen minutes, but to Lynn, it seemed like an hour. She couldn't wait to get out of there.

"And there is the matter of Ms. Clairmont," Blair said.

Lynn snapped to attention.

"I want to remind you of your responsibility to bring this matter to a close and keep everyone safe, including civilians."

His face was unreadable, but his eyes changed somehow and appeared sad.

"Mr. Blair, I take full responsibility for those under my command. I will not compromise anyone's safety."

He rubbed his bottom lip with his finger. "Before Ms. Clairmont's first deployment, she worked several joint projects. She is an exceptional analyst with great potential." He leaned on the table and folded his hands. "The admiral believes that you and Ms. Clairmont have a history that can be used to the advantage of this mission." Lynn could see his facial muscles clench briefly, and his eyes hardened, but his tone remained even. "I do not know Admiral Kent's level of tolerance, but I can tell you if you ruin her career, you will have made me your enemy. You don't want to do that. Keep everything in order and above board. No fraternization."

Frak, frak, frak! He just threatened me. I can't believe this is happening.

"I am also concerned about your history of PTSD, even though medical cleared you for duty last year. Do you feel up to the task?"

"Yes, sir."

Her answer was honest, but in the back of her mind, she wondered if seeing and working with Ali would spark any new anxiety.

"Very well."

He shoved a folder and pen across the table. Lynn opened it and began reading. Like every other project, the "read on" documents that gave her the clearances for the project were long, detailed, and tedious. She hurried through as best she could, but paused at the signature block that gave her permission to work on a case investigating a U.S. citizen. Below the empty lines for her and Mr. Blair were the signatures of Admiral Kent and...*Holy Toledo.*

"Any problems, Major?"

"No, sir." She signed and gave them back.

He added his signature with an expensive fountain pen. *Snap.*

With the cap on, he paused, then began tapping the pen in his hand. After several seconds, he slipped the pen into his coat pocket, but his glare remained unwavering.

"I'm counting on you, Major. Don't disappoint me."

"Yes, sir."

The uncomfortable silence that followed made Lynn want to crawl under the table.

Chapter 19

October 2010 – Paktia Province, Afghanistan

Ali's jaw dropped when the JETT commander walked into the conference room with an unexpected guest. After the announcement that Lynn was taking over, Ali zoned out. When they were dismissed, she shot out of her chair.

After a power walk for nearly an hour, her calves burned and her throat was bone dry.

I should have brought a water bottle.

Her tongue flicked away the salt from her upper lip. She marched on until she reached the ring road. With her hands on her hips, she looked out at the perimeter's double fence topped with concertina wire. Sunlight glinted off one of the watchtowers and momentarily blinded her.

Damn, I forgot my wraparound sunglasses.

At this point, she should have turned back. Instead, she straightened her spine, pushed her shoulders back, and crossed the road towards the fence. Truck tires crunched behind her.

"Get in. It's dangerous outside of a vehicle."

Ali halted at Lynn's voice. She marched over to the truck and almost ripped off the door handle. "Half of the enlisted from my tent quad are in the guard towers this time of day.

Unlike the cramped office, the expanse of the sandy landscape and the solitude calms me down. Besides, it's such a delightful day," she said sarcastically. She jumped into the passenger seat and slammed the door.

"That's not the point. There's no place to hide. A sniper could easily pick you off, and where are your sunglasses? They're more than a fashion statement."

"Really? I thought every sexy model was into shatterproof polycarbonate lenses." Ali fluttered her eyelashes then crossed her arms. She propped her lug sole boots on the dashboard. "This isn't going to work, Lynn."

Lynn drove back to the middle of the base and parked at the rear of the repair yard. They sat in silence.

A low rumble grew louder, and a heavy equipment transporter passed by, carrying a twisted MRAP. Ali's breath caught as Vicki's face flashed in her mind. She forced herself to take a deep breath. The smell of diesel stung her nose and filled her lungs.

"Look, Ali," Lynn spoke in a gentle voice. "I didn't ask for this assignment, and I'm sorry things didn't work out before. We're here now, and we have our orders. Let's get along and do this for all of our fallen buddies."

Lynn's elbow was propped on the windowsill. Her head turned away, and then rested in her hand.

Dustin. Give her a break. Ali said in a calmer tone, "I tried to contact you several times, but only once did you respond, and it was curt and cold. I was worried about you."

"My therapy went well, and I'm fit for duty. That's all you needed to know."

"Jesus, Lynn. You could have at least answered an email or two. Maybe you had someone else to comfort you through the therapy." Ali regretted the words, but they spilled out, and there was no way of taking them back.

Lynn's jaw tightened. "Again, I'm sorry for what happened. Mentioning Sacramento is intentionally throwing salt on a wound. We're both professional. If you spit nails at me all the time, it's going to be rough. Let's call a truce because we have to work together."

Lynn took a banana out of her pack and offered it to Ali.

"No, thank you." Ali closed her eyes.

"Suit yourself." Lynn slowly savored the fruit.

After a few minutes, Ali sat up and gave Lynn a scowl. "Why are we out here? Do you think giving me the silent authoritarian treatment is going to make me change my mind about you?"

"Nope." Lynn drew the word out and took a drink of water.

After another five minutes or so, Ali blew up. "I'll work with you and put my best foot forward, but I don't have to like it. Start the damn truck and take me back or I'm going to walk!"

Ali reached for the door handle. Before she found it, the door popped open. Startled, she found a solemn face inches from her own. The man wore the stripes of an Army senior non-commissioned officer, level E-8.

"Ali, meet the new JETT second-in-command, Master Sergeant Kyle Evans. Ms. Ali Clairmont is one of the best analysts on the team, but watch out for her wicked streak of stubbornness."

"Ms. Clairmont. I hope you are all you're cracked up to be, according to your file."

He shut her door and leaned onto the windowsill. The warmth of an android and the accent of an ivy leaguer unsettled her as much as Lynn's criticism.

"Miller is JETT's second-in-command, and I—"

Lynn cut Ali off. "You received orders from your agency that you will now report everything—every report, every map, every image, every note, every conversation—to JETT leadership. We are JETT's new leadership. No disrespect to Miller, but Evans is my NCOIC. In case you forgot, that means he's in charge when I'm not around. Understood?"

Yeah, loud and clear. You're in charge of everything but the special project. Whatever the hell that turns out to be.

Dan had told her to be on the lookout for any mishandling of classified material. So far, other than ignorance, arrogance, and misogyny, Ali hadn't found anything concrete with the Brigade. Lynn's taking over the JETT was a distraction that would have to be handled delicately.

Evans cocked his head to one side. Gesturing his upturned palm toward Lynn, he said, "You should answer the major, Ms. Clairmont."

"I understand you're my new supervisor perfectly, but I'm not going to sacrifice quality or bend over if someone tries to push me around." She glared at Evans.

"You've always been ethical. I expect no less now," Lynn said. "It appears to me that security is lax on base. I'll be tightening the entire JETT procedures to prevent any accidental classified spillage under my watch."

"JETT's not the problem and neither am I. The Brigade—"

"I can't control the Brigade since they're under a different chain of command, but hopefully, they will treat our interactions with the highest standards. Help me out. Do you know of anyone who is sloppy or that I should be concerned about?"

Ali propped her feet back on the dashboard and brushed the dust off her boots.

Lynn softly said. "I sense something's going on."

Ali shrugged. "Same age-old story. A few bad apples spoil the whole bunch." She folded her hands on one knee and drew it to her chest. "Lieutenant Hernandez and a few of the guys, including a couple contractors, try to intimidate me all the time. Hernandez took me out back one day, screaming in my face—and I mean at the top of his lungs—that if I didn't like him or the Army, then I should go home." Ali laughed with a tinge of bitterness. "He just can't get it through his head that I'm in a different chain of command. Hell, he doesn't understand basic technical issues like my workstation is on the NGA network and not even connected to the Army. The bottom line is I don't trust him. His misogynistic, asshole personality doesn't help."

"Their computers aren't even at the same classification as NGA and JETT," Evans said.

"Precisely! He's technically an idiot. I've tried to explain until I'm blue in the face. And speaking of that, the only way I can transfer secret reports is by dumping it onto a disc and handing it to them. That's because almost all of my reports contain imagery products that are too large to email. They don't understand file size."

Lynn's face was hard. "The Brigade controls the physical space of the Ops Center, but you're a high-level civilian representing your agency working with JETT. We'll put a stop to that. Are they harassing you in other ways?"

"It's subtle things, usually bully comments when I'm alone. But one big thing that pisses me off..." She sunk into the seat and crossed her ankles. "They're all-source analysts—research dudes gathering bits and pieces from others. They are not subject matter experts in imagery or signal intelligence. Okay, they have some training in our disciplines, but it's a week or two at best. At times, it can be downright dangerous."

Lynn's head snapped around. "What do you mean?"

"It's stupid arrogance. Like I have basic NSA training, but I don't tell you how to do your job that you've spent years perfecting. They frequently ignore my expertise, and I've caught them annotating unclassified imagery with wrong information." Her hand went up. "Which I have reported. They just don't know what the hell they're doing. They figure anyone can read a map, so why not any old image. And just so you know," she held her index finger up, "most of the Google map images are one to three years old. They have no clue how to work with classified remote sensing and imagery."

"Geez. What a mess. Part of your job is teaching. Have you—"

"Lynn, I've helped the young soldiers where I can, but most are inexperienced. When Hernandez and this one sergeant come along, they clam up." She threw up her hands. "To make it worse, those two dump projects on me, then send the Brigade team members off to do guard or chow hall duty. I'm left swamped, and the Brigade team doesn't get a chance to improve. It's annoying and frustrating."

"Is Hernandez the main obstacle?" Evans asked.

"He's backed up by a captain and a major. Trust me. They're uniform blind. They don't want to go against another soldier. I'd bet a truckload of chocolate that Hernandez is filling them full of lies about me, but honestly, I think the main reason is they're jealous."

Lynn scrunched her eyebrows. "Jealous?"

"If you examine the statistics over the past six months, you'll see the Special Forces and Engineers have had a boat-load of success. The Brigade lacks in that department. So, it's like a macho turf war. They want to appear to be the toughest guys at the top of the heap, and they detest me working with other units because they want to control me."

"Holy crap," Lynn said under her breath.

"Don't get me wrong. There are good people with sharp skills in the Brigade, but a few Brigade leaders are weak and on a power trip. That brings everyone down. Unfortunately for us, they just happen to be in the Ops Center. Honestly, I've worked with many fine military personnel over the years and have never seen such a screwed-up unit."

Lynn shook her head. "We have a job to do, and we need you and everyone on JETT to operate at the highest level. I'm going to move your workstation to our side of the room. That should immediately cut down on some of the abuse."

"We'll set things straight." Evans hopped into the back seat. "Shall we go have a bit of lunch before we shake things up?"

His stare went back and forth between them. The smirk on his face made Ali's stomach lurch.

"Sounds like a divine idea. Is the chow decent around here, Ms. Clairmont?"

"Yes. Occasionally, they serve MREs if supplies run low."

"Ah, delicious field rations." Evans smacked his hands together.

Ali turned around. Evans cocked his head to one side as they peered at each other. *His jet-black hair, dark eyes, and light skin really do make him look like an android.* She repositioned her body forward as Lynn drove.

Chapter 20

The private pointed to the fridge. "Help yourself to water or an energy drink. Colonel Peterson will be here in about fifteen minutes." He left them alone.

There was a *whoosh* sound at the closing of the door, and a fan came on.

Evans said, "Sweet. I didn't know they had soundproof rooms overseas. Leave it to Special Forces to get all the bells and whistles. By the way, you pushed Ali's buttons. Is she strong enough to hold up?"

"Don't let her façade fool you. She's a highly dedicated professional with an experienced background. If she smells wrongdoing, then she's onto something." Lynn cleared her throat. "Ali's problem is she wants to make things right instantaneously. In the process, she can become irritated."

"In my experience, too much emotion leads to disaster."

"Her heart is in the right place. I will calm her down, get her concentration back, then find out what she knows."

"But headquarters also wants to use her as a distraction."

"She won't be much good if she gets kicked out of the country. Trust me. I'll calm her down a notch or two. And by the way, what a brilliant hard persona you displayed. That will make her think you're all business. Keep her focused and push her more towards me, but don't go too far. Don't let her see your soft side."

"I have a soft side?"

"Yeah, you smile once a month." Lynn jokingly punched his shoulder. "Your fiancée seems nice. I enjoyed her humor at the picnic."

"I got lucky."

He seemed to be good at his job, yet Lynn found it odd that they had no contacts in common. She knew a lot of people, including upper management at three cryptologic centers outside of Fort Meade headquarters.

"Lynn, this is an important assignment. We need to be totally in tune. Was she your girlfriend? That's what I heard."

Lynn gave her best neutral look. "No."

"You never slept with her?"

Lynn didn't blink and held his gaze for several seconds. "I'm not sure where you're going with this—"

"General Carr believed that Admiral Kent picked you because of the 2008 assignment. Everyone seems to think she will be more pliable with you. I personally don't care if you're gay or not. I just feel it's best if you and I have no secrets between us."

Lynn clenched jaw. The sound of the door swishing open caused them both to turn. A tall man entered and pushed it closed. They saluted upon seeing his eagle rank insignia.

"I'm Colonel William Peterson, good to finally meet you both. First, my covert investigator role remains only in this room. Clear?"

They both nodded.

"My unit is one of JETT's customers. They cannot visit JETT in the Brigade Operations Center without causing alarm, and to be honest, you don't need to know who they are right now. I will run the ops from here. For communications between us, use the encrypted email account. You can also use Jabber, but I personally hate that damn chat app." He held up his index finger. "Remember, everything you write is cataloged and sent straight to the top. For conversations between you two, the truck has been outfitted with software that constantly checks for bugs, and Evans will maintain it and ensure no one has tried to plant anything while it's unattended. Any questions so far?"

"No, sir," Lynn said. Evans shook his head.

Peterson handed a small bag to Evans. "That's the last of the hardware to hack into the Brigade's computers. The more we can do remotely, the better. Headquarters said you're still working on a secure connection back to Meade. How far are you?"

Evans was rummaging through the bag and took out a dull silver metal square about the size of a jewelry box. "I'm connected to headquarters but haven't sent any sensitive messages." His finger tapped on the little box he was holding, "This is what I needed to scramble the signal. Now only headquarters can read it. I've already installed the software to double-check if someone tries to break into us."

Peterson nodded. "Don't forget, Admiral Kent or Mr. Blair could jump in anytime. Hopefully, you have what you need at this point, but just in case you need additional equipment and can't make it to our compound, we have a drop zone." He spread out a map of the FOB and explained the details.

The meeting was winding down until Peterson said, "Now regarding Ms. Clairmont. I don't want to scare her off," he pointed to Lynn, "but I am aware you two have worked well together on a previous deployment. Keep it going. We need to get some bugs into the computers of her contacts."

Frak, frak, frak. How were they going to do that? And did NSA brief everyone on our past? Frak!

"Lastly, you will attend early Catholic Mass this Sunday. Drop by here on the way back to the other side. We'll have some goodies."

"Pardon me, sir. I'm not Catholic," Lynn said.

"Not everyone is, especially the Brigade leadership." He winked. "Evans will fill you in. Going to Mass provides an excuse for leaving your office and coming to this side of the base when you have no reason. Got it?"

"Yes, sir."

He turned to the computer. "Well, that wraps it up, unless you'd like to add anything, Admiral."

Lynn hadn't realized the admiral was listening in. Kent's voice bellowed over the speaker. "I think that will do. We are depending on you two. Let's shut down this illegal operation."

Lynn was nervous and shifted in the chair. "Sir, we're single-threaded, and anything could happen to us. What if who we're tracking discovers us before we figure them out?"

"I think you know the answer, Major. Let's not have any tragic endings here." The admiral's words ended the meeting.

A wave of queasiness swept through Lynn. After Peterson departed, she said, "Evans, I think someone would go for Ali first. How are we going to protect her and do the mission?"

"Sorry, Major. I'm the tech whiz. It's out of my realm, but maybe I should rephrase my earlier comment: Rekindling a romance might be the only way to wrap this up swiftly and protect her. I can provide cover and help you find an isolated location so you won't get caught."

"Stop insinuating."

"To put you at ease, I'd be a little more discreet, but we don't have much time. Think about it. Besides, the alternative—as in hurt or dead—could be a lot worse. By the way, you might also order her to practice at the firing range with another JETT member. We all need to be up to par." He stood and said over his shoulder, "Let's go, I have to get the hardware installed."

"You seem to forget you're second in command."

"Whatever."

Lynn grabbed his arm. "Is something else going on here? As you pointed out, there should be no secrets between us."

"Come on. My job is infinitely harder, and we're wasting time."

Lynn ran her fingers through her hair and followed Evans out of the soundproof room.

Chapter 21

Sergeant Cramer grabbed Ali's arm. "Do you know the junior enlisted who got kicked out last month?"

"Yeah." Ali kicked a rock. "What a way to go. Overall, he's a good kid. He should have known better with all the warnings and paperwork, but you know the mind of a nineteen-year-old. They think they are invincible. I wonder if he understood how harsh his sentence would be. Those are the rules—no alcohol in a war zone. Zero tolerance, and it's illegal in Afghanistan."

Cramer whispered, "The booze is coming through Captain Dalton."

"Are you sure, Jill? He's a bit weird, but damn, they'd lock him up for years and throw away the key if they caught him."

"That's not the half of it. He's involved in more than liquor."

Ali narrowed her eyes. "Let's take the long way to the Shoppette. We can talk more freely in the open once we move away from these buildings. I don't want someone overhearing us."

Jill Cramer was the same rank as her partner, Michele Miller. Jill was in the Engineers, and Michele and Ali were members of the JETT.

After a group of soldiers passed, Jill said, "Captain Dalton is a frequent rider on my team's humanitarian missions. Other teams monitor and inspect the construction of new police facilities. I know Dalton's an intel officer, but four times, he's passed up trips to the police headquarters. Instead, he's gone with my team to school or medical facilities. He's visited some two or three times and always has a meeting with the Afghans."

Ali cringed. "When an intel officer meets with Afghan officials, I usually hear about it. The info is on things like the Taliban influencing or threatening locals. I don't recall any recent reporting."

"I've noticed that he meets with the same Afghan guy and sometimes with the man and his wife. That's not the worst part." Even though they were in a clearing, Cramer scanned the area. "He brings a bag or briefcase. It's not the official double-locked gear."

"That's serious. Sounds like he's hiding something."

"Yes, but none of the officers question him or inspect the contents since he's on Brigade orders. I asked once and was told we don't have the need to know."

"Who is signing Dalton's orders?"

"Major Ratcliffe."

"There's something strange about both of them. Can't put my finger on it. Have you reported the issue further up the chain?"

"I've told Dan."

Ali exhaled with relief, but she couldn't let Cramer know. She had to maintain Dan's cover. "Dan's not the proper channel for reporting security violations."

Then the thought struck Ali. Dan's expertise was his knowledge of explosives: from how they were manufactured to finding the persons and organizations involved in IED attacks. She grabbed Cramer's arm, "Wait a minute. Do you think Dalton's involved in bomb manufacturing?"

"No. It's just that Dan has connections at the Pentagon."

"How do you know that?"

"Remember my friend that visited last month? She recognized him. He's a retired command sergeant major. There is no higher grade of rank for enlisted, except the Sergeant Major of the Army. She says he has clout, and she works in an office that supports the Secretary of Defense."

Ali caught the waver in Cramer's voice. "What else is going on?"

"Dalton threatened me." Cramer kicked the toe of her boot in the sand. "You know Michele and I have been so careful with DADT. He told me to back off. Said he would out us to my chain of command and promised to make Michele's life hell. Ali, I'm scared." Tears were gathering in her eyes. "I trust Dan, and he says he will help. I only told you because it's wearing me down."

Ali wanted to give her a hug but restrained herself. "Did you tell Dan about the threats?"

"No, only about the improper procedures and my suspicions."

"I understand your fear. Stay strong." She quickly rubbed Jill's arm. "I trust Dan, too."

⚬⚬⚬

That evening, Ali spotted Dan around the burn barrel. It was the only method they had of destroying classified papers since the shredder had broken. Several people were milling about.

"Hey Dan, how's it going today? Got any anything for me?"

"Hi, Ali. I was planning on dropping off an assignment tonight on Major Stewart's desk." Dan kept feeding the barrel.

"Good. I like working projects for you guys."

"Well, we appreciate you doing both a classified and unclassified package. You've helped the unit tremendously. I have another roll-up report I'll email to you. Good stuff for your weekly status report back to headquarters."

"Thanks. I love reading about the capture of bad guys and their weapons. I get satisfaction knowing I've helped. Even if it's just getting you guys from point A to Z safely."

"You make my job easier, and all the soldiers appreciate it."

"Hey, why are you out here at the burn barrel? Who's relegated you to this lowly job?"

"I like making sure classified is destroyed, but I also pissed off Major Ratcliffe. He gave me everyone's classified. I've already been out here for about an hour."

"Wow. How'd you do that?"

"You're awful inquisitive today." Dan narrowed his eyes, then cracked a smile seconds later.

Two other people who had been chatting nearby tossed their cigarette butts in the trashcan and walked back inside.

With no one else close by, Dan said, "Got anything for me today?"

"Cramer and I talked about Major Ratcliffe." Ali turned up her nose. "He's a spooky guy. Never smiles or says much. According to Cramer, he and Captain Dalton are evil twins."

"Dalton brings back minor shit that could easily be collected sitting behind a desk. At least, that's all he reports." Dan threw up his hands, "Ratcliffe is Dalton's field supervisor. Something's not right. We're looking into them but haven't made a solid connection."

"Dan, I know what Cramer has told you."

"It's being taken care of. Keep your eyes and ears open, but be careful. I'm not entirely convinced there aren't others."

"Good evening, Lieutenant Hernandez!" Ali called out to warn Dan and reached into the bag to help.

Hernandez walked around Dan, then towered over Ali. He barked, "What are you doing out here Clairmont? You have no business with the Engineers."

"Oh, I beg to differ, Lieutenant. We have several projects that Ms. Clairmont is working on." Dan piped up.

Hernandez ignored him and said to Ali, "Stop by my desk and brief me, Clairmont."

Dan twisted the proverbial knife into Hernandez. "Oh, but she can't do that. It's top secret. You have the clearance, but the projects are strictly need to know. Oh," Dan held up his index finger, "and I believe the new JETT leadership made it clear that Ali's support has to go through Major Stewart."

The lieutenant glared at Dan before turning back to Ali. "I expect you to inform me of what you can, simply out of professional courtesy." He turned and walked away.

"Shit, Dan! You have a set of balls!"

He winked. "Like brass."

"You know he reports every tidbit up the chain. I think he even takes notes on how each of us uses the porta potty." She laughed.

"Okay Ali, no one else knows this. So, keep it quiet. The Brigade is being disbanded after this deployment. What's interesting is the Army is going out of its way to send each member to an entirely different unit. In other words, this bullshit rodeo is about to end one way or another. I hope to clean out the barn before they leave because there is a lot of manure. I haven't figured it all out yet, but I can smell it. So, anything else going on with Cramer that I need to report right away?"

Just as Ali was about to tell Dan about Dalton's threats, Hernandez came back around. Dan dumped the rest of the papers in the pit and squirted some lighter fluid in the barrel, which shot flames into the air.

"Almost done, Lieutenant," Dan said.

"Finish up and get back to work."

They ignored Hernandez as he walked off in a pretentious huff, hands folded behind his back.

"So, how's life under the new JETT leadership?"

"Okay."

"Just okay?" Dan grinned.

"What's that supposed to mean?"

"Well, Evans is a little strange, but the new major is cute and seems to know her shit. I hear you used to work with her."

Ali focused her eyes on the flames. "Yeah."

"Are there tantalizing details you're leaving out?"

Ali shot him a look. A helicopter flew overhead. In addition to the noise, dust swirled in the air.

"What's your point?"

"I served twenty-two years in the Army, and I've been out on deployment most of the past six years as a civilian. I never married—didn't want the bullshit."

"Sounds good to me."

"Yeah, but the truth is I screwed up a few relationships. Listen. Life goes by fast. It's not a game, Ali. Life doesn't have an autosave. You can't go back and do things over. You need to move beyond life's checkpoints to progress."

Ali's pulse hitched. "You spend too much time playing video games."

He laughed. "Guilty as charged. But seriously, think. Life is tough. Don't pass up a chance to make things better."

"She's my direct supervisor."

"On paper, but not on the project. Besides, making things better could be just strengthening a friendship," Dan chuckled and winked, "or a roll in the hay. We're all human."

Hernandez rounded the corner again, leaned against the building and lit a cigarette.

"I'll touch base with you later. But take it from an old man, end everything on a positive note. Don't hang onto bitterness."

Dan stirred the pit and put the lid on.

Chapter 22

Over the headset, Lynn said, "I won't lie. We're going to one of the more dangerous combat outposts."

Ali arched her eyebrow, and smartass words popped into her brain. *Yeah, the machine gun under the fuselage and four uploaded air-to-ground missiles are a sure clue.* But she merely said, "We've got a job to do. Let's roll."

Some ten hours later, the new equipment, including a mobile satellite dish, and the software were installed and glitches corrected.

"Just in time. It looks like we've got an hour before the helo arrives." Ali wiped the grime off her face with her bandana.

"They're not coming tonight."

"What?" Ali blinked her eyes. "Dan's going to Kabul and Bagram for a week. I had to discuss a project with him."

"Email him."

This complicates things. And what am I going to use for night clothes?

"Ladies, follow me." The platoon captain led them past the shower huts. "Thanks to solar panels, we have warm water, but the stalls are first come, first serve and on a short timer. That's why some of the female soldiers choose to shave their head. Life on the front."

Next, he led them down into an underground storage room. "Since the last mortar attack, we're triple stacked in sleeping accommodations, and right now even officers are sharing with enlisted."

They stepped into a dimly lit room with bedding between two storage shelves.

"Since the locked briefcase must always stay with you, we've rearranged supplies to make this a sleeping room."

"Thank you, Captain," Lynn said.

He waved his hand around. "There are a couple of thick foam mats and several blankets. The pillows are small but should do. Sorry, it's cramped, but it's all we can spare. The best part is it's warm. Breakfast is from 0630 to 0830." He grinned. "We pass out top-of-the-line MREs. Choice meals run out fast. Do you need anything?"

"We're good. Thank you."

He pointed to the plywood door. "There's a latch. Best to lock it in case someone forgets. You don't want someone coming in here for supplies when you're sleeping or changing clothes."

After locking up, Lynn unrolled her sleeping back on top of the makeshift bed. "If you want, we can split up, but we'd be a lot warmer sleeping next to one another." Ali stood frozen with her arms crossed. Lynn took a deep breath and let it out. "Ali, I need rest and so do you. Get over it. They've given us the best they've got."

Turning towards the wall, Lynn stripped down and put on gym shorts and a T-shirt, then crawled under the blankets and pulled her sleeping bag up to her chin. "Are you going to sleep standing up?" Ali hastily crawled under. Lynn propped herself up on an elbow. "Wait. Don't you have other clothes? Where's your sleeping bag?"

"I only have this tactical uniform, and I've worn it for two days. Sorry if I stink." Ali laid her arm over her eyes. "I'll be okay."

"Now, I understand why the captain gave us extra blankets. You should—"

"Evans said we were flying back tonight, and I...I only grabbed my personal day bag."

Lynn flung her head back. "You should always bring your bug-out bag with at least three days of MREs, clothes, and a sleeping bag."

"I know. I made a mistake." Ali twisted her lips. "On the plus side, I have a tablet with games and contraband."

"Contraband?"

"Lesbian romance novels." Ali grinned as Lynn's eyes widened.

"Jesus, Ali. You're okay on a U.S. base, but when you leave for home, delete the material and reload it later," Lynn said in low, annoyed tone.

"Why?"

"I can't believe you asked that question. You were briefed before deploying." Lynn got up, grabbed her bag, and tossed Ali a T-shirt and sweatpants.

"I know most of the Muslim countries consider any media with sexual content as pornographic—"

"Afghanistan never checks because you fly in and out through U.S.-controlled Bagram Air Base." She went back to whispering. "In Qatar, all civilians transfer from the U.S. military through Qatari customs. They have strict Shari'a Law and randomly check magazines, movies, and computer files." Lynn shook her head. "Homosexuality is illegal and punishable by lashings and/or imprisonment. And by lashings, we're talking ripping into the skin on the back, blood, and scarring. Having a lesbian book puts you in their crosshairs."

Ali's mouth gaped. "I didn't know it was that bad. I just thought it'd be a fine."

Lynn put her arm around her and drew her near. "They might not be as harsh on you as a Westerner, but don't take the chance."

"I'm sorry."

Lynn leaned back and closed her eyes. "It's okay for now. Just don't forget to delete it before you fly into Qatar. You can reload it when you get to Europe. We've both been under a lot of pressure. Let's get some sleep."

The next day, they passed the time by tweaking the computer systems and providing additional training. The computer chimed, and Ali clicked on the email. She hung her head.

"What's wrong?"

"We have to wait another day for the helo pickup."

"That's okay Ms. Clairmont." A young sergeant popped his head up over from the computer. "It's Saturday. For those of us off duty, we play games after dinner and trade goodies from our care packages. It'd be fantastic for you to join us. New blood." He smacked his hands together. "Unless you're too chicken." He chuckled. "My name's Todd."

Ali shook his hand. His hair—what was left from the crew cut—was light blond, and contrasted against his dark brown eyes.

When he left, Lynn leaned in and whispered, "With your long auburn hair, you have a lot of these young guys and a few gals stealing looks."

"It's in a ponytail."

"Even sexier."

Ali swatted her arm. "Behave. They're too young."

"Grrrr...they'd like a cougar."

"Someone's going to hear you." Ali smiled at how relaxed Lynn appeared. *I wish I'd see that more often.*

At dinnertime, they sat around joking as the meals were passed out. Empty equipment boxes of different sizes were the tables, and chairs were well-worn and a mismatch of camp chairs and metal folding chairs. They pampered Ali by giving her one of the few padded chairs.

"Please take my chicken meal. You'll regret it if you eat the pork one. It's yuck." Todd grinned at her from across the makeshift table.

"Thank you for your hospitality." Ali took a bite. "Yum. This is really tasty."

"It's the best and has 1,200 calories to keep you going. And the lemon poppy pound cake is awesome." Todd gestured, bringing his thumb and forefinger together, kissing them, and separating them like an Italian chef.

"Wow. You're welcome to have my dessert."

"Thanks. Do you have a boyfriend at home? I mean...it'd be nice to write to you or something every now and then."

Ali almost choked on her water while Lynn smirked at her.

"Yeah, and he's the jealous type." Ali nodded. "Sorry about that."

"Listen up folks," the lieutenant yelled. "Poker's going to be on that end, and Risk is on this end." He handed Lynn and Ali some snacks. "We chipped in for you to make bets. But, it's all for fun."

While Lynn played cards, Ali plotted global domination strategy against the five other gamers. With her bandana loaded with peanuts, beef jerky, and cheese-flavored crackers, Ali was determined.

Halfway through, Lynn pulled up a chair and sat slightly behind Ali. "What's going on?"

Ali leaned back. "Those two players are trying to dominate North America. The five bonus armies and only three points of entrance to defend made it a tempting target, I intend to gobble up Asia."

Lynn threw up her hands. "Okay. That was crystal clear."

Ali laughed, then whipped around toward Todd. "Hey." She threw a cheese cracker at him. "I know what you're doing. You're trying to distract me, but it's not going to work."

He tossed out half of a candy bar. "How about we form an alliance and whip these guys?"

"Ah, chocolate! I accept the bribe." They high-fived one another and chuckled.

Lynn cupped her hand over Ali's ear. "Be careful, or you'll be married before dawn." Snickering, she strutted back to the poker table.

BOOM.

A loud explosion was followed by the crackle of small arms fire. Everyone grabbed their weapons. The lights flickered out. Ali was pulled to her feet and pushed into a ditch behind the tent. The firefight echoed all around.

"Don't move!" Todd pressed his forehead to hers and dashed out.

Her heart was pounding, and she was breathing too fast. *Slow down before you hyperventilate.* Soldiers darted around her, carrying ammo and weapons as she huddled down. She had no idea where Lynn was.

BOOM. BOOM.

She flinched, and her body shook. *Don't be a wimp.* She readied her weapon just in case. *Damn Beretta with its stupid safety. I wish I had a Sig Sauer.*

Things gradually quieted down, then she heard several soldiers shout, "All Clear." Ali closed her eyes. *God, please don't let Lynn be hurt.* A foul smell assaulted her senses, and a hand was on her shoulder.

"It's over. You okay?"

Ali slowly opened her eyes and scrunched her nose. She looked Lynn up and down. "What the hell happened to you?"

"I was carrying an ammo crate between firefights. When I ran past the latrines, a mortar hit. I miraculously went un-scathed, but it splattered everywhere, then I slipped."

Ali snickered. "I've always admired your gleaming white beautiful smile, but the brown splotches don't add to your debonair style. Why are you stripped? Not that I mind the boy shorts and sports bra."

"They checked me out, and trust me, my tactical clothes need to be burned. Now, let's make sure you're okay."

"I am, and unlike you, I don't have on decent underwear that passes for shorts." Ali couldn't help herself. "I wear black bikinis."

———

A tall female sergeant thrust a bottle of lavender shampoo, body wash and a set of bath gloves into Lynn's hands.

"They're yours. Keep 'em. We're giving you a leisurely ten-minute shower time. You'll need it." Pointing to a bench with a folded uniform, she said, "There are only eighteen women on base, but we pulled together a set that should fit you. I salvaged your tapes and rank insignia, but it took a bit of scrubbing."

"Thank you. I know it's tough getting supplies out here. I'll do all I can to send you some goodies. Any favorites?"

The sergeant laughed. "Anything." She snapped her fin-gers. "I love chocolate, but you know what trades well? Those hand warmer packets."

"I'll do my best."

Lynn managed to get clean and scurried back to the storage room. Not knowing if Ali was awake, she quietly snuck in and found her reading. The glow of the tablet lit Ali's face and caught Lynn's breath. The cute reading glasses made Ali look innocent and sweet. *I know there's a lioness underneath who knows how to stalk and kill.*

"You certainly smell better," Ali said without looking up. "Why are you staring at me?"

"Ah...sorry. You look so...academic." *Did her lip curl slightly?* Lynn stripped. *Academic...yeah, hot for teacher.* "The glasses and all. I just don't see you wearing them in the Ops Center."

Ali glanced at Lynn over her glasses. "By the way, nice undies. The boy shorts project strength, but the undies show more skin. More of your feminine side."

I'm going to have a heart attack if she keeps this up. Lynn slipped on her nightshirt and settled under the covers. "Why are you reading? Aren't you tired?"

"It relaxes me."

She's definitely trying to hide a grin.

Ali turned to Lynn. "Speaking of academic, did you know there's a study that fiction readers scored higher in empathy toward others than nonfiction?"

"Huh? That came out of nowhere. What's that supposed to mean? Do you consider me less empathetic?"

"No. It was just an interesting study." She gave Lynn a gentle squeeze on her arm. "Reading lets your softer side shine through. It'd help with your blood pressure."

"Uh-huh. And your glasses and comment show your geek side." *Right now, my blood pressure is going through the roof. I'll burst if you touch me again.* "What are you reading?"

"A sci-fi called *Face of the Enemy*. The characters are students in an interstellar military academy with a war about to break out. The author has woven social aspects of prejudice and justice into the plot with one of the protagonists hiding a big secret that could threaten their budding romance. The romance is sweet and doesn't overpower the sci-fi. I highly recommend it."

"Romance, huh. What's your favorite book?"

"Too many to name." Ali rested the tablet on her chest. "It's sad that reading LesFic is a normal part of my life back home, but it's illegal in this part of the world. I probably should have told you about the eBooks. I'm sorry."

"No, but you are taking a chance. Can I see your tablet?"

"With the eBook app, you can organize novels in several ways." Ali clicked on the main menu and handed it over. "I have my most recent up front. Feel free to browse."

Lynn perused the menu and made her selection. As her eyes settled on the page, she read to herself: *Taking a firm grip on her hips, she made soft swirls around her clit with her tongue before sucking forcefully.* Lynn handed the tablet back to Ali. "It's one way to entertain yourself." The passage had instantly jump-started her libido. She rolled over to the wall, hiding her flushed face.

Through giggles, Ali said, "*Falling for Love: A West Virginia Romance* by Addison M. Conley. A good story with just the right amount of sex. I'll loan you the tablet if you want."

"Keep it down, or someone's going to hear you."

Ali continued to laugh, and Lynn rolled back halfway on top of her and covered her mouth. The softness of Ali's lips on her hand started a tingle rippling through her body. Ali's deep chocolate-brown eyes turned from mirth to desire. Lynn settled on her back. Staring at the ceiling. *I want to kiss her so bad.*

Ali propped her face on a cocked elbow and stared down at Lynn with a wicked grin. "You're a lesbian." Ali held up the tablet. "Why do you have trouble reading a few sensual scenes?"

"You mean erotica."

"A few sex scenes within a novel is not erotica. I don't usually buy erotica." She wiggled her eyebrows and said in a low growl, "Well, I do have a few books. But your problem is you're too vanilla. You barely touched me in Kabul and certainly nothing that I'd consider sex."

"I can't believe this is happening. First, you barely talk to me, then apologize and decide we can be friends. Now, you tease me in bed. What's next?"

Ali leaned in, and Lynn could feel her breath and smell the scent of her skin. The tingling amplified in her core.

"Lynn, I understand how hard you've worked for your career. But we're in the middle of fucking Taliban country on a dinky fifty-man platoon combat base. We're in a locked room sleeping on a pad on the floor." Ali moved her lips to Lynn's ear. "I dare you to speak truthfully. What do I mean to you?"

Lynn swallowed. *Control.* "You've always been more than a friend."

"You have a funny way of showing it. Today was close. We could have died any minute."

Over the past two years, no one had come close to Lynn's heart like Ali. She was the only one Lynn truly wanted. *Rules be damned.* Lynn tenderly kissed Ali.

"I care for you deeply, but we shouldn't go further. We need to get some sleep."

The scream, *No way! She's not doing this to me again,* roared in Ali's head. Ali rolled on Lynn, pinned her arms above her head, and kissed her. Lynn barely struggled, then fell into a rhythm.

Ali broke contact but kept her face close, brushing her lips against Lynn. She loosened her grip and caressed the palms of Lynn's hands with her fingertips while her mouth moved to Lynn's neck, kissing and sucking. Her leg glided steadily, rubbing between Lynn's thighs through the thin shorts.

"Ali." Lynn's voice was barely audible.

"Shush."

Ali drew Lynn in for another hot kiss. Their tongues danced gently as Ali's hand slid down to the hem of Lynn's shorts, slowly tracing figure eights over the area below her belly button. Lynn moaned as Ali's hand moved underneath her underwear. Ali teased with gentle swirls, then entered Lynn delicately. As she picked up the pace, Lynn moaned.

At climax, Ali enjoyed the way Lynn's muscles spasmed around her fingers while her heart pounded and body quivered. When Lynn's glazed-over eyes became more focused out of their lustful daze, Ali said, "Please, make love to me."

Lynn caressed Ali's cheek. Letting her hand trail down her neck, shoulder, and arm. She rolled Ali over onto her back, scrunched up the T-shirt, and took a minute to admire her full breasts. "So beautiful," she whispered.

Slowly and delicately, Lynn circled one of Ali's nipples, first with her fingertip then her tongue. She teased and flicked the bud before finally taking it into her mouth and sucking hard while her other hand cradled Ali's other breast. With Ali's breathing deepening, she dipped between Ali's legs, lightly exploring. Her fingers moved faster and sunk into Ali's core as she ravished her breasts.

Ali's sighs were soft, and her hand massaged Lynn's head, urging her to suck harder. "Don't stop." Lynn did so anyway, smiling into Ali's face.

"Stop teasing. More, please," Ali said. She pushed Lynn's head to the other breast and gasped. Lynn increased the stimulation, pleased at Ali's response. When Ali became too loud, Lynn's other hand covered her mouth. Soon, Ali arched in waves of pleasure until she lay limp.

—◦◦◦◦◦—

Rolling over, Lynn stared at the ceiling, listening to their ragged breathing. She never wanted this to be their first time, but Ali was right. They could die at any minute. After a moment of peace, guilt seeped in and gnawed at Lynn. *Why can't I tell her about the op? She's going to be upset when she finds out.*

Ali slid her finger down Lynn's temple to her lips. "Why did we wait so long?"

Lynn pulled her near and lightly kissed her forehead. "We need to get some sleep." She grasped Ali's hand and kissed her palm. "Always know that I've only wanted the best for you. I would never intentionally do you any harm."

"Then don't leave me heartbroken. Let's explore a relationship after this deployment."

Lynn hesitated. "That might be possible. Get some rest now. I need you sharp and hitting the ground tomorrow."

Ali curled up on her side and closed her eyes, but not before slipping her hand into Lynn's.

Chapter 23

The wind outside loosened the tent ventilation flap, and it whipped back and forth. More of the fine dust seeped through. Lynn fastened it quickly. *Damn storm. Glad, we got off the combat outpost before this hit.*

Her watch chimed a two-minute warning. With her scarf wrapped around her face, she slipped on her desert goggles and stepped outside.

Beep. Beep.

She leaned into the gusts and trudged towards the sound of the truck horn. Grains of sand pelted her as she walked, stinging the small amount of exposed skin. Judging the surrounding area, visibility appeared to be about a hundred feet. She yanked open the truck door and jumped in next to Evans.

"There is no logical reason to be out in this storm. Did anyone question you?"

Evans calmly said, "Of course they did. I told them that you insisted on picking up supplies that came in a couple of days ago at the airport and wanted to visit church afterward, and that while you're okay on your own, I felt better driving you." He smirked as he cautiously began to drive well below the speed limit. "I also may have painted you a little batshit crazy. As for the sandstorm, this is nothing! A real haboob has less than a foot of visibility and shuts everything down. Luckily, they occur in the summer, and we'll miss that excitement."

"Are you making progress?"

"I should ask you the same question. Did you get anywhere with Ali?"

"Why did you tell her it was a one-day job?"

"You know that enduring hardship in close quarters often brings people closer together. Is she at least talking to you?"

"Yes, but she had no sleeping bag. We were lucky the unit had blankets."

"And what happened?"

"I think we re-established our friendship."

"A few kisses or make-out session wouldn't hurt to sweeten her up."

"I told you to drop the subject! Let me worry about her. You take care of the technical part! What happened while I was gone? Did you get the software installed? What about the imaging?"

"I finished the day you left. Task Force and Colonel Peterson are monitoring. The Brigade has five laptops approved for outside use. Two are authorized for secret read-only info, and the other three are for unclassified data. All require prior approval of the Army Corps—"

"I'm aware of basic security protocol." Lynn rubbed the bridge of her nose. "Tell me something I don't know."

"Last month, a national guardsman working for DIA returned home, claiming someone had used his computer without authorization. After a thorough out-processing interview, DIA had a repairman come in, but he actually swapped out key components to send back to investigators. The Department of Defense Cyber Crime Center and our guys have been working together. They found some encrypted files and sections of the hard drive that were wiped clean. The interesting part is that no one has been able to crack the encryption, and they haven't been able to recover the wiped files."

Lynn's eyes grew wide. "The best in cyber forensics can't figure it out? It would take one sharp, tech-savvy criminal to achieve that level of expertise. Have headquarters scour the backgrounds of all Brigade soldiers with specialty training."

"Already done. They'll have an answer for us in a couple of days." Evans shifted gears as the sand swirled around them.

"Good call." She smacked Evans's shoulder. "Now, please slow down a bit."

—⁂—

Three days passed and still nothing tangible. Lynn stepped out of the Operations Center and returned with a coffee in her hand.

"I'm hurt, Major. You didn't think of your second in command when you grabbed your cup of joe?"

"Sorry, Master Sergeant. You have two legs. Get your own."

Evans closed his station down and leaned against the post next to Lynn's computer. "I think I'll do that on the way to the counter-IED unit. They requested we stop by. We should get started, or I won't be able to get a drink."

"Well, we certainly wouldn't want that tragedy to happen. I think I'll drive today." Lynn held out her hand for the keys.

A half-cocked smile showed on Evans's face. *Gee, no sourpuss face today. Maybe he* is *human.*

Farther down the road, he said, "It's a beautiful day, Major."

"Cut the sugar, Evans. What have you got?"

"Task Force identified two people with specialized computer training. One is in security in charge of computer reimagining, no surprise there, but the other is Captain Dalton. He works closely with Major Ratcliffe, who has access to the top-secret computers in the Brigade headquarters that interface with the laptops. Ratcliffe's job gives him a perfect reason to have an office there and in this building."

"What about outside meetings?"

"The log was encrypted, and I couldn't crack it. Headquarters is handling it. And guess who controls it?"

"My bet would be Ratcliffe."

Evans gleamed at her from the passenger seat. "Yes indeed. Turns out that Dalton's training is far above normal. He has a master's in cybersecurity and coding."

"Why isn't he an NSA officer?"

"Dalton was slated to go work for NSA, but that didn't happen after he punched out his commanding officer six years ago."

"Why wasn't he court-martialed?"

"The commanding officer dropped the charges. There was some speculation that Dalton had smut on the guy." Evans made a drumroll sound on the dashboard with his hands. "Also, it seems that pretty boy Dalton was passed over for promotion in his last review. If he doesn't make it this next cycle, he's out."

"There's a motive, but it sounds too smooth. Why is Dalton still around if he's a bad apple?"

"Well, his father was retired General James Dalton. Died last year."

Lynn flinched. "And I bet the Brigade's colonel came up the ranks with the general."

"Bingo. Now, dear major. What is our next plan? Without an electronic fingerprint, we've got nothing substantial on these guys."

"I've arranged for us to borrow a Brigade secret laptop. We need to upload a new lab program that propagates tracking bugs to the other laptops. Apparently, our buddies at Langley are now willing to share."

"Excellent. I love new toys." He grinned and twiddled his long slender fingers.

"Easy, boy genius and stop with the Mr. Burns imitation. It freaks me out."

"Who's Mr. Burns?" His face was blank.

Lynn shook her head, "Never mind. Anyway, the hard part's beginning."

"And what's that?"

"It's your turn to cozy up for information to the woman in computer re-imaging."

"I've already been flirting with her."

"You've been flirting?"

"Relax. It's innocent, and I'm just doing it for the mission. Now, what about Ms. Clairmont?"

"Don't worry about her. Mind your tech issues."

"Have you had a little rendezvous?"

"Stop!"

Lynn pulled over to the side of the road and stomped on the breaks. The truck jerked to a stop, and she spun towards Evans. "I care about Ali deeply. Your needling me is annoying the piss out of me, and," she pointed her finger, "it's none of your business." She wet her chapped lips. The chalky taste of dust and something unknown didn't help the roiling in her stomach.

He studied her intently. "My apology for implying otherwise. I didn't mean any disrespect. I can see that you love her."

I'm about ready to wring your neck. Frak. I bet he's reporting on me as much as I'm reporting on Ali. She plastered on a smile. "Ah, Evans. You know soldiers, especially enlisted, don't talk like you." She let the words sink in. His facial expression didn't change, but his body stiffened.

"I'm a little different, but that's my techie side."

Lynn waggled her finger. *Stay calm.* "Nope. It's your ultra-spook side. So, I'll stay out of your business, and you stay out of my business. I'll handle Ali. Got it?"

"Loud and clear, Major."

"You know, if you threw in some humor and varied your voice inflection a bit more, you wouldn't come across as some hybrid between Borg and Cylon." He blinked a few times, and a genuine look of confusion clouded his face. She sighed. "You know for a techie, it's hard to believe you've never watched *Star Trek* or *Battlestar Galactica*."

She put the truck in gear and headed out.

Chapter 24

"You're quiet." Ali touched Lynn's arm.

"Just thinking about crazy feedback from Fort Meade on the daily report I have to file." Lynn shifted gears. "And I think the truck needs some maintenance."

"Thanks for inviting me. The gym and shoppette are nicer on this side of the base."

"Yes."

They had grown closer, but guilt filled Lynn. The tech side was not yielding enough evidence. She twice requested that Ali be read into the op, and both times, the request was denied. Instead, Admiral Kent ordered her to increase interactions and butter up Ali to the max.

"Lynn, I want to apologize for the night at the combat outpost. I shouldn't have taken it further. I'm sorry I jeopardized your career."

"It was mutual. I think we're working well together. From now on though, we need to think of the mission first. After this deployment, maybe we can be more, but for now, let's leave sex out of the equation."

Ali dropped her hand and faced the side window.

Frak. I was cold. Lynn pulled the truck over. "Ali, look at me." The knife twisted deeper into Lynn's stomach when Ali turned. Her face looked devastated. "Come here." Lynn wrapped an arm around her. "DADT's going to fall sooner or later." She kissed Ali's forehead. "I care for you deeply, but the military is a slow beast to change." Lynn cupped her face. "That's all I can give now. Please be patient. Let's get through this deployment alive and not court-martialed."

"Agree, but I don't want a future where I'm the lover in the shadows." Ali had a bittersweet smile. "Think about us seriously." She raised her finger. "And don't ever rip my heart out again."

"I promise. Right now, let's get to the gym and do a little shopping." Lynn combated her inner demons. One screaming what a jerk she was and the other crying. She swallowed and pushed it all away for the mission.

After an hour at the gym, they showered and walked around the shoppette. Lynn bought a book of crossword puzzles while Ali got a new shirt, and they each purchased a slushy drink and walked to the garden. It wasn't much, a fifty-foot by one-hundred-foot lot with grass, but it was the only greenery on base.

The flags of the U.S., Afghanistan, and each of the services on base fluttered in the wind on tall flagpoles. Red rosebushes next to a small memorial contrasted against the dust and rock elsewhere on base.

"This pales in comparison to the garden at ISAF headquarters. I miss our times meandering through the roses."

"Yeah, that place was gorgeous." Lynn bit her lip. She missed those moments, too. Life rushed by, but those moments with Ali among the roses always remained fresh in Lynn's mind. She motioned to a bench. "You said something the other day that started me thinking. Something about Captain Dalton."

Ali let out a sigh. "You mean the arrogant, pompous ass."

Lynn crossed her ankles and leaned back. "He's a bit odd."

"Odd doesn't even begin to describe him unless you mean he has a Darth Vader personality."

A couple of people walked by but didn't stay. "He's gone a lot from the Operations Center. Do you know where he goes?"

"Why are you this interested? He's not under your command."

Thinking quick, Lynn said, "I think it's prudent to limit his access to JETT reports. You've been here longer than me and see a side of him that he doesn't dare show to another officer. So, what's your opinion?"

"This Brigade has a lot of hidden garbage."

"Such as?"

"Haven't you noticed they bicker with Special Forces all the time? It's harmful and plain un-American." Ali scooted closer. "The month before you arrived, they refused medevac if Special Forces didn't divulge their plans with the Brigade before execution."

"Are you sure they threatened to withhold medical services to wounded soldiers?" Lynn was aware of the overall complaint but not the details.

"Yes. They were trying to strong-arm Special Forces into giving up their plans."

"Did you report this? What did your agency say?" Ali gave her an odd look and turned away.

"The colonel told him that I misunderstood the words spoken by the briefer. With all the ops going on, he said they had limited air support, and that medical helicopters were in high demand." She turned back toward Lynn. "He said that under such conditions," Ali made air quotes, "medevac helos could be unavailable if they were dispatched elsewhere. That is the only reason why he supposedly advised Special Forces to inform him of their movements."

"Sounds reasonable."

Ali grabbed Lynn's hand. "Yes, Lynn, but that's not what was said." In a whispered shout, she said, "Major Ratcliffe leveled a threat against Special Forces in the colonel's name. I swear it. And others were talking about it too. Ask the other JETT members. And do you know why Special Forces won't reveal their operations to the Brigade ahead of execution?"

"No."

"The Brigade trains the Afghan Army. Special Forces thinks someone's been leaking info to the Afghans."

Lynn's mouth hung open. "I believe you."

"Yeah, so be happy we're on a different computer network than the Brigade. They can't get any info from us unless we release it to them."

Lynn's mind spun, and her stomach clenched. *With what Evans had said the other day, it sounded as if the spy or spies had found a way to tap into the computers.*

"This is horrible. JETT is going to have to be more cautious. I'll have to consider more options to keep us safe." *Pushing Ali too hard might backfire.* Lynn decided to wait before prodding her for the names of her sources. "Let's get going."

Ali filled her in on a few more details on the walk to the truck. Lynn needed more info and decided to slowly drive the long route back to the Ops Center.

"There's another story that's repulsive and could have cost lives."

Lynn swallowed. "Tell me more."

"Before I arrived, the gate to the Afghan Special Forces enclave on another base was welded shut in the middle of the night. The base is under the Brigade's command."

Lynn was familiar with the report and feigned ignorance. "Who would do such a thing?"

"I was told the Brigade, but they denied it. After the gate was opened, the command refused to allow the Afghans into the chow hall for a week. They forced them to eat MREs, but the Afghans were low on supplies." Ali balled her hands into fists. "And the disgusting battalion gave them MREs with pork! Lynn, the Afghan Special Forces have American advisors, which we both know are deep covert soldiers. Somehow, the battalion got away without punishment, and the higher-ups in the Brigade pushed it under the rug."

The pork comment was never in the official report. "Was the incident reported?"

"It was. Another reason why the Special Forces guys don't talk to the Brigade unless it's an emergency. But that's not the most interesting part."

Ali's hand was now on Lynn's shoulder.

"Which is?" Lynn said in the calmest voice possible.

"Dalton was in charge of the intel company on base. He was moved here one week after the Special Forces filed a complaint against the Brigade. Coincidence? Perhaps. But I wouldn't put it past him to be involved."

Lynn popped the clutch while trying to shift gears. She couldn't recall Dalton being in the official report.

"Ali, these are grave allegations. Who told you this?" Lynn didn't mean to blurt it out and softened her voice. "I'm not trying to get you or your friend into trouble. I'll be honest. I've had concerns about Dalton all along. I don't want him accessing top-secret JETT reports."

Lynn reached over and squeezed Ali's hand. "I trust your judgment, but I'd feel a lot better if I knew who told you the info. No offense but a person's experience and years of service add credibility." *If Ali had full access to the mission, this charade today would be unnecessary. Who or what agency is against Ali obtaining the special clearances?*

"My friend isn't a young sergeant." Ali scooted down in her seat. "It's two people. Dan and Sergeant Cramer have both complained about him. Cramer's had more run-ins."

Lynn squinted her eyes. "Dan's excellent reputation as a retired E9 gives him clout. Who's Cramer?"

Ali propped her lug boots on the dashboard, and Lynn worried she was going to clam up. "Please talk to me. This sounds serious. I can help. And we need to protect JETT if Dalton is a bad guy."

"Let's go to the lookout. There's probably no one there this time of day."

They drove the rest of the way in silence. Lynn barely had the truck in park when Ali jumped out and sat on the hood. The lookout was only a small hill. It wasn't much, compared to the rest of the flat, desolate land, but it was elevated enough for them to see most of the base.

"What's up?" Lynn could see the muscle in Ali's jaw tighten.

"When you invited me today, I planned on telling you. It's just hard."

Lynn didn't like the sound of this. "Go on."

"Sergeant Jill Cramer is Miller's wife."

"What!? Sergeant Michele Miller of JETT?"

"Calm down."

Lynn kicked the dirt. "What the frak, Ali?"

"They had a private commitment ceremony in Massachusetts back in 2005 that they kept secret. They didn't want to get kicked out of the military." Ali turned to Lynn. "This is the first time they've been assigned together since Fort Devens. The Army has no problem letting straight married couples deploy and sleep together."

Lynn rubbed her face. "DADT is still in place. They're taking a hell of a risk. Since Miller's performance has been exemplary, I have no problem looking the other way if their relationship doesn't interfere with the mission."

"I know you're not happy but—"

"Let's chalk up the violations. There's us, and now my third in command and her wife. Okay, despite all that," Lynn threw her hands in the air, "is Dalton just a condescending jerk or has he done something? Is someone else doing something they shouldn't? Ali, it's your duty to inform me." *Calm down or she'll freeze on you.* Lynn put her arm around Ali. "If you're in trouble, I'll try to help the best I can, but don't make it worse by hiding information. The hole will only get deeper."

Ali bit her lip, took a deep breath through her nose and exhaled and sharply said, "Dalton's blackmailing Cramer."

"How?"

Ali filled in Lynn on Dalton's improper security handling of a laptop and meeting Afghan locals without another military person present.

"Ali, those are security violations and should have been reported!" Lynn's face was hard.

"She did report them."

"How long has this been going on?"

"I'm not sure. When Cramer persisted, he brought up her marriage to Miller and threatened to out her to the colonel."

"You said Cramer reported it. To whom?"

"Dan." Ali turned away when she said his name.

"He's a civilian and has no authority in this particular situation."

Ali shrugged. "Dan's connected and has some folks checking into it." She walked away.

It was not proper protocol reporting to a civilian not in the chain of command, no matter how well he was connected.

Maybe this was why Ali is being kept out of the loop. Dan and Cramer's involvement needed to be reported, but Lynn made a snap decision to play dumb if Miller and Cramer's relationship ever surfaced.

Lynn walked up to Ali who had her arms crossed. She ignored Lynn and stared out at the vast expansiveness of sand and stone.

Get her to talk more. "Ali, how did you find out about Cramer and Miller if they have been discreet?"

"We met in the chow hall." She turned and was biting her lip. "One day, I left my tablet for a few minutes to go back for a drink. Cramer accidentally bumped it and, in the process, saw my LesFic eBooks."

Lynn's eyebrows shot up. "You have to engage the lock screen on your devices! I've seen your phone and tablet in the designated drop-off storage bins outside the Operations Center. Anyone could pick yours up by accident."

"Relax. I now press the button before laying them down to lock instantly, and I changed the screen lock from a two-minute timer to ten seconds in case I forget."

"So, Cramer and Miller eventually confided in you?"

"Days later, they told me their love story. They're like you—dedicated to the max to serving."

"This is a lot to take in Ali. I'm going to restrict Dalton's access to reports. I'll give him some excuse. For now, let's keep this conversation between us. I need to figure out what to do, and I don't want Miller living in fear. Okay?"

Ali nodded.

"All right. Keep your eyes and ears open and let me know if you suspect any more possible security violations. I want to keep JETT clean."

Evans and headquarters had been tracking Dalton for about a week, and this new information helped. *Why did Ali not come forward until now, and why did she go to Dan? This sure doesn't look good.*

Lynn drove Ali back to the Operations Center. "I have a few things to take care of."

"Okay." Ali didn't close the door right away. "I shouldn't have said anything today, but my gut is telling me something's terribly wrong."

"You did the right thing. I'll see you later."

As Lynn drove away, she saw Ali in the mirror. She hadn't moved.

"Frak. Frak. Frak. I can't let her down."

Lynn drove back to her tent and ran up the steps. Her tent mates should be working. *Make sure.* "Hello. Anyone around?"

She plopped onto her bed. The enormous tent was divided into individual rooms separated by plywood walls with a twin bed and a wobbly nightstand made of scrap wood. It was basic compared to ISAF Kabul headquarters, but heaven compared to combat outposts. *Right now, I wish I had been assigned to a COP instead of this NSA fraking mess.*

After resting for a few minutes, she cleaned up with facial wipes. Staring into the tiny mirror taped to a board, she looked older than her mid-thirties. "Get a grip and get back to work," she mumbled. The report would be lengthy and painful but had to be done.

To clear her head, she decided to leave the truck and walk, grabbing a take-out dinner and shuffling to her desk. After nodding to Ali and the rest of the team, she passed the 1800 briefing preparations over to Evans and settled down to the computer with a thick paper file next to her. As she typed her report, she would glance down and pretend to be engrossed in the data, occasionally taking bites of her sandwich.

"Aren't you calling it quits?" Ali asked. Apprehension was written on her face.

"I have to finish this boring monthly report. Nothing special, but you know they'll bust my chops if I don't. You all head out. Miller, why don't you wrap it up and walk Ali back. We can handle things for a few more hours." Lynn motioned to two junior members of the team sitting at the far end from her.

"Are you sure?" Miller asked.

Lynn shooed them away. "Go. Tomorrow's another day. It's quiet, and everyone's doing an outstanding job." She leaned back and crossed her legs, smiling. "No need to worry. I have things under control."

Ali nodded slightly, and Lynn wanted to wrap her arms around her. *Someday, this will all end. I hope she's still talking to me.*

An hour later, Lynn finished the report for NSA headquarters and reviewed the details on the screen. There was no mention of sex with Ali last week. Bare bones were in about Cramer, but Lynn did not discuss her marriage to Miller. *Frak. You're damned if you do, and damned if you don't.* She punched the "Send" button.

Glancing at the clock, it was three hours until midnight but only just after lunch back on the U.S. East Coast. Rubbing her face and yawning, she had just stood to stretch when an icon signifying an encrypted Jabber text from Fort Meade popped up on the screen. It had only been twenty minutes. Her pulse rose, and her hand briefly hovered over the keys before typing in her password. The screen unlocked, displaying the mission message and the electronic signature of Admiral Kent. She hit the "Accept" button.

Admiral: *Dan Galvarino interviewed four days ago at Bagram. Very informative. His agency is cooperating. Get introduced to*

Cramer somehow. And STEP IT UP. We need Evans's technical, and your human intel as proof. Otherwise, the case is weak. This has to wrap ASAP!"

Lynn: *Is Dan involved with Dalton? I feel he's hiding something, but Ali trusts him.*

Admiral: *No.*

Bolting upright, the near instantaneous response surprised her.

Lynn: *When is Dan coming back? If you're sure he's not involved, could he be helpful?*

Several long seconds passed while the cursor blinked, and she was beginning to wonder if there was a malfunction. Suddenly, the message popped up.

Admiral: *There was a hit-and-run last night. He died. Murder investigation underway.*

Every nerve in Lynn's body fired. This sounded more elaborate than a few rogue Brigade officers.

Lynn: *Is our cover blown?*

Admiral: *Standby.*

She leaned back, rubbed her forehead, and took in a breath, fighting back the emotions. *Why is Kent's answer taking so long?* She stared at all the exposed wires running along the ceiling and rocked in her chair. *Like my life, twisted.* Ping. An official email from Kent sat in her inbox with "Security Forms" in the subject line and an attachment in the body.

She clicked on the various agreement buttons before the system allowed her to view the full document. It gave her access to yet another special program. As far as she knew, clearances were never granted without someone in the know physically present. Hastily, she read and electronically signed, then sent it back. Another Jabber chat window flashed with a different warning. She hit the "Accept" button.

Admiral: *Dan Galvarino was CIA, and they didn't tell us that Ms. Clairmont was one of his sources until yesterday.*

Stunned, she reread the message. Ali was involved with the CIA. *What the frak is going on?*

Lynn: *What about Evans? Is he really an Army CID investigator? I need the truth to be successful.*

Admiral: *Evans is also CIA but works with CID.*

Lynn: *WHY WASN'T I TOLD?*

She stared at the screen, half waiting for the administrative order to punish her.

Admiral: *Don't use caps on me again! I will ignore it for now. For whatever reason, CIA wanted Evans's and Galvarino's affiliation hidden. Forget it. You need to concentrate.*

"Frak, I might as well go all in," she mumbled over her mug before taking a swig, setting it down, and banging on the keyboard.

Lynn: *This has been a dangerous mission from the start. I am happy to serve my country, to assist in stopping the breach of security, bring justice for Dan, and protect Ali. But, you throwing my former relationship with Ali in my face was a threat to ensure I'd take the assignment. You insinuated, and Evans continues to suggest, that I use that relationship to control Ali. She should have been brought in from the start. Why wasn't she?*

Lynn pulled out a deck of cards, shuffled over and over, thinking this text was the one that probably would get her in trouble. She doubted the admiral would pull her out, but she had to know.

One sergeant yelled across the room, "I know it's late, ma'am, and I'd love to play, but we're still at work."

She forced a laugh and reshuffled the cards. *They've used us all along. Damn you Kent, answer!* Her fingers flew back to the keyboard as Admiral Kent's reply displayed.

Admiral: *Evans was placed for technical. Your past work for me at headquarters and your service record showed dedication to duty and exceptional skills, and it was agreed that no one knows JETT operations better than you. Yes, I thought you'd be good at squeezing info out of Ms. Clairmont, but a genuine concern about her safety was expressed from the start. NGA refused to pull her out. We didn't know why. With CIA's revelation, now we know. It was also suggested you were the best choice to protect her without raising suspicion. As for your "friendship," nothing more needs to be said. As for Evans, tell me if it happens again. I will take care of it! He is only there for technical!*

Lynn tilted her head. *Someone else wants me in this job?* She stared at the latter part of the message. Kent did not say the precise words but clearly gave her a huge "don't tell" warning. Lynn wondered if Kent's support would change if she were faced with a written allegation. Another message flashed, snapping her back to the moment.

Admiral: *I agree that Ms. Clairmont should be told. We're waiting on all the other agencies to concur. I will get back to you soon. Remain silent about Galvarino's murder and the mission until I give the word. And let me worry about CIA playing its own game. Understood?*

She had the urge to ask more questions but thought better of it.

Lynn: *Roger.*

Admiral: *Since you're calling Mr. Galvarino and Ms. Clairmont by their first names, I hope you're not getting soft. Get some rest.*

Lynn lowered her head in her hands. She still couldn't believe everything that was happening. After 9/11, all agencies were supposed to coordinate. *This is a fraked up mess.*

Chapter 25

Thomas Blair wanted to see Admiral Kent immediately after Major Stewart's report came in but had to wait for a couple of hours. Now he sat stoically in front of his old friend and boss, pretending to appear unfazed by their argument. In all their years of working together, they had never had such sharp differences.

"Fortunately for us, the Brigade does not take Ms. Clairmont seriously. We have to act," Kent said.

Thomas Blair wanted to stretch his neck and pop his knuckles and even scream but remained calm as always. "With all due respect, I have to disagree. Ms. Clairmont is not trained, and CIA wants to send in a replacement for Mr. Galvarino."

"We're running out of time and will lose the momentum if we wait."

Blair uncrossed his legs and leaned forward. He wet his lips and could feel his facial muscles twitching and his heart racing. "That will piss CIA off."

"Let it," the Admiral growled.

"Sir, inserting her into a trip to monitor and bait Captain Dalton is too risky."

"Her risk increased the very moment CIA recruited her to gather info for Dan Galvarino and kept their operation from us for months! We have no more time Thomas! There are no other options!" Kent lowered his voice. "I'm sorry, but Dalton will be suspicious of any last-minute replacements. We will have enough trouble inserting new security guards. We have to do this."

Blair rubbed his eyes. "She's only an analyst that provides imagery and other geospatial products. We should come up with some excuse and insist NGA pull her out."

"If we send her home now, we lose our insight. We need her!"

He knew Kent far too well. This operation would be pushed through no matter what. "At least, explain the full extent of the operation and the risks involved. Give her the courtesy to accept or decline the job." Blair faced the window and silently prayed for the best.

Kent tapped his fingers on the mug as steam rose from the hot coffee. "Why are you so engrossed in the career of a young analyst? If I didn't know better, I'd say you're fond of Ms. Clairmont."

"I'm fond of her work." Blair leaned back in the chair, straightened his tie, and brushed his pant leg. The smell of strong coffee waving in the air and Kent's gunmetal stare caused his stomach to flip.

"You're nervous, Thomas. I've never seen you like this." Kent narrowed his eyes.

Blair swallowed, and wet his lips. "The stakes are high."

Kent kept watching him while rubbing his finger on his lower lip. After several long seconds, Kent said, "I'm authorizing the sting operation, period! No further discussions. You'll supervise from the ground. I believe we can have you in the air within four hours." Blair's jaw dropped, and Kent chuckled. "Didn't expect that, huh?" Kent rocked in his chair and put his hands behind his head.

Blair nodded.

"Double check with my secretary that your clothing measurements and shoe size are still accurate in the computer. Be back within two hours to pick up your bag and stop by the armory. And Thomas," Kent softly said.

"Yes, sir." Blair stood and awaited further instructions.

"We all have secrets and have made sacrifices." Kent picked up a picture of his son killed in Fallujah, Iraq. Putting the picture down, his facial expression shifted to his well-known battle-hardened expression. "Bury your feelings, and do your duty."

Thomas Blair's chest and throat constricted at the gravity of Kent's words. Despite his expert ability to hide behind a poker face, he could feel the flutter of his eyelashes, blinking several times. He cleared his throat. "I'll do my best. You know I always have."

"That I do."

Blair's stride toward the door wasn't at his usual brisk pace. After all these years, his emotionless business side had cracked. He paused with his hand on the doorknob. "Thank you, sir. I won't jeopardize the mission."

"You're welcome, Thomas."

Chapter 26

Lynn shuffled her feet down the hall towards the Brigade commander's office. *What if he's involved with the classified leaks?* At the door, she took a deep breath and exhaled before knocking.

"Come in."

She saluted and stood at crisp attention. "You wanted to see me, sir."

"Sit down, Major Stewart."

He eyeballed her for a few seconds with intense scrutiny.

"Major, I know you've only been here a couple of months, but unfortunately, I have to inform you of a problem on your team."

"Colonel, I've seen nothing but positive performance and the prior team commander left good evaluations."

"Not their technical performance."

"I don't understand. Why am I here, sir? JETT is a top-notch team."

"Ms. Clairmont, Staff Sergeant Miller, along with another female in the Engineers, have been reported as lesbians."

The words sliced right through Lynn. She tried to steady her breathing. "I see. And how do we know these allegations are legitimate?" Lynn waved a hand. "Perhaps, someone is settling a score." She didn't know how the words came out without trembling. Her heart thumped, and she could feel the muscles in her body tighten.

"Two officers, one NCO, and two contractors have signed an affidavit. I sent the reports to Bagram and to Ms. Clairmont's agency."

"Sir, we are talking about career women who have dedicated their lives to our country. Sergeant Miller has sixteen years of exemplary service. As for Ms. Clairmont, I worked with her before and personally can attest that her work is exceptional. She is a civilian."

He raised his hand for her to stop. "It's my obligation as the Brigade commander to make sure military law is obeyed by everyone." He stressed the last three words. "A decision has been reached, and I intend to waste no time in cleaning up this fiasco. Tomorrow, we will convene. You will say nothing in the meantime. Am I clear?"

"Yes, sir."

"Dismissed."

She forced her trembling muscles to stand, then saluted and walked out. Further from the building, she mumbled to herself, "Dammit. Goddammit." With her head down, she lengthened her stride. Boots crunching under the gravel. *Everything is falling apart. I feel like I'm in the middle of a derecho.*

She reported the meeting to Fort Meade and waited for a reply. She had no clue what was about to unfold. Over the next twenty-four hours, she tried to maintain a composed appearance. She might have fooled everyone else, but Ali kept glancing her way. Burying her face inches from the computer, drinking cup after cup of coffee, Lynn's mind twisted and meandered, trying to come up with options to divert the massacre that was about to happen. *Maybe it would be better if Ali went home. She'd be out of danger. Or would she?*

It was now less than an hour before the colonel would pull the trigger on the meeting, announcing the decision. Lynn hastily opened her email and Jabber chat. Nothing. She envisioned herself picking up the computer and throwing it across the room. Instead, she tapped her foot and kept toggling between screens.

Admiral Kent's secure icon popped up, and Lynn's throat went dry.

Admiral: *Ms. Clairmont's agency has left it up to the Brigade commander on whether she stays or is sent home. Corps won't reveal the decision on the others. Do whatever it takes to keep them on base.*

Lynn: *Yes, sir, but Ali has to be told the truth.*

Admiral: *Other agencies have now signed off. Report to the Special Forces compound after the Brigade meeting and bring Ms. Clairmont. Colonel Peterson will read her onto the program and issue her clearances. That is, if you manage to keep her on base.*

⊷⦚⦚⦚⊶

Ali locked gazes for a split-second with Lynn as she walked by. *God, she looks like shit. I don't buy her excuse that she has insomnia. Something's going on.*

A young sergeant tapped Ali on the shoulder. "Can you please help me? I'm having trouble displaying the new statistics page for tracking IED attacks. I'm not sure if it's a technical glitch again or if I'm doing something wrong. The major gave me five minutes to print it out."

"Sure." She punched the keys to close her computer and helped the sergeant, then marched to the main conference room. Miller and Cramer sat outside in the hallway. *Oh, fuck.*

Michele was resting her elbows on her knees. Jill was leaning up against the wall, arms folded with a grim expression on her face.

"Hey, Ali. Guess you're here for the same meeting with the colonel," Jill said in a flat voice.

"The colonel?"

Michele eyes were red-rimmed.

"Ladies, the colonel wishes to see you now."

Oh, God, Dalton must have talked. Or did Lynn? No, she wouldn't do that. Would she?

"Come on, Ali." Jill lightly touched her arm, then put her palm in the middle of Michele's back. "One team, one fight."

They were ushered in. The colonel, Major Ratcliffe, Lieutenant Hernandez, and Lynn were seated on one side. A staffer sat in the corner with a notepad.

After Miller and Cramer saluted, the colonel motioned, "Please sit."

Ali said, "What's this about?"

The colonel gave her a look and motioned to the seat again. His face was emotionless. Ratcliffe and Hernandez stared at them while Lynn hung her head and chewed on her bottom lip. Ali maintained a fixed stare at Lynn, but she wouldn't look up. The colonel shuffled some papers while silence filled the room.

"Ladies, a complaint has been leveled, charging that you are involved in homosexual activity. Five individuals have signed an affidavit, including two officers present at the table."

Ali's pulse dropped, and a sick feeling roiled through her body. She had no doubt Ratcliffe and Hernandez were the officers on the paperwork, but why hadn't Lynn done anything to stop this senseless onslaught?

The colonel went on. "The paperwork was sent to Bagram and to NGA. They have examined the evidence, and a decision has been reached." He seemed to have a gleam in his eye as he paused. "Major Ratcliffe is Sergeant Cramer's commander, and Major Stewart is in charge of you two." He suddenly pushed the closed manila envelope down the table. The whoosh was the only sound around. The envelope stopped in front of Lynn. "Major Stewart will read the verdict."

You son of a bitch! Ali gave Lynn an equally harsh scowl.

Lynn's face was pale as she scanned the paperwork. She read Miller's and Cramer's verdicts in a level voice but paused a couple of times to take a sip of water. Miller and Cramer were not being discharged, but they would be split up and reassigned.

When asked if they denied the charges, Miller said, "Sir, I love my country and the Army and have dedicated my life to both, but I will not deny my love for Jill." She reached out and intertwined her fingers in a sign of defiance.

Cramer said, "Whom I love should have no impact on my ability to serve, but I will abide by the order."

"Ms. Clairmont, were you aware of their relationship? How do you plead on the accusations against you?"

Ali scrunched her toes in her shoes and clenched her jaw, trying to think of what to say.

The colonel wrote a note in the file. Without looking up, he said, "Obviously, your silence speaks volumes."

Ali stood up swiftly causing the chair to scuff the floor, making an unpleasant sound, and he stopped. She leaned across the table and glared at him. Out of the corner of her eye, Lynn's hand rose slightly to tell her to calm down.

She pointed her finger down, jabbing the table. "Miller's and Cramer's performance is of the highest standard, and you're treating them like criminals. As for me, I am not involved with anyone. You do not know my sexual orientation, and it is none of your business whether I am celibate, straight, gay, or whatever. And for the record, I have observed plenty of heterosexuals engaged in infidelity and haven't heard one word about that." Her eyes locked on Hernandez. Lynn was shaking her head slightly and mouthed the word 'sit,' but Ali remained standing.

"You may be a civilian, but NGA has left the decision up to me," the colonel said through gritted teeth.

Hernandez said, "Ms. Clairmont has been helpful to others outside of her team in the Operations Center, but she is also a disruption. I have warned her numerous times about causing discontent with political conversations."

Ali laughed. "Yes, military regulations require a neutral workplace. Is that why you allow your friends to listen to the Rush Limbaugh radio program on their computers? I don't remember you asking them to curb their political comments or their off-color jokes. They sling mud when news of DADT comes across the screen. I don't see you correcting them."

Lynn stood abruptly. "Enough! Sit down, Ms. Clairmont."

Ali froze then sat. She was clenching her jaw so tight that it hurt.

Lynn remained standing. "Sir. I mentioned before that Ms. Clairmont's work is exceptional." Lynn was gripping her pen tight. "I need her to stay. In fact, NSA has ordered me to put Ms. Clairmont on the project that Sergeant Evans and I are working on. She has skills we need. I promise to counsel her. This won't happen again."

The colonel tapped his finger for several seconds. "Very well. Ms. Clairmont can stay, but if I hear any more disrespectful comments, I will have both of your hides. Also, she may be a civilian, but I want her counseled on the dangers that homosexuality pose to the military. There may be talk

within certain elements in Congress of more lenient regulations, but right now," his voice rose, "DADT is still the law. I
need soldiers focused on work."

"Yes, sir." Lynn nodded. "Ms. Clairmont, I believe an apology is due."

*This Brigade is led by a bunch of spineless, homophobic, cheap-shot
individuals...But there are still good, hardworking soldiers that
needed my help.* Ali forced out the words, "Please accept my
apology, Colonel."

Ali could tell Hernandez was suppressing a grin. He finally
said, "I disagree. I think Ms. Clairmont's presence here is a
bad influence on the troops."

Ratcliffe said, "I concur. Please reconsider, Colonel."

"Sir, again Ms. Clairmont is crucial to the new JETT project. She has confided to me that her sister is a lesbian," Lynn
turned back to the officers, "and was brutally attacked in
college. Ms. Clairmont formed a gay-straight alliance. As you
can see, she's rather sensitive, and the homophobic slurs have
obviously set her on edge."

Hernandez narrowed his eyes at Lynn.

"In fact, the joking and political conversations are out of
hand. I've heard several complaints from my team as well as
others that it is distracting, and it verifies Ms. Clairmont's
claim that several in the Operations Center are involved."

Lynn looked at Hernandez then back at the colonel. "Before
this meeting, I was hoping to discuss more productive ways of
handling differing opinions and toning down the rhetoric with
Lieutenant Hernandez."

The colonel's mouth hung open, and Lynn kept going. "Sir,
please let me counsel her. We can give her light duty. I
promise this won't happen again. A replacement at this stage
would set us back." Lynn focused on Ali again. Her eyes were

pleading, and her voice was soft. "Ms. Clairmont, I think a more sincere apology is in order."

Why has Lynn concocted this story about my sister? Ali studied Lynn's face, but she only slightly nodded. *Say something. They're all waiting.*

"Yes, Colonel. I'm sorry for my outburst. I want nothing more than to do my job, and do it well." Looking at Hernandez, Ali launched into an Oscar-winning performance. "I'm sorry, but the comments of your staff have brought on flashbacks." She took a deep breath, squeezed her eyes as if she was going to cry and buried her head in her hand. She faked a sniffle and mumbled through her hand. "The attackers said they were trying to make my sister straight."

The room was silent, and Ali chanced a glance. The vein in the colonel's neck was no longer bulging, and his facial features softened.

"I'm sorry for your pain, Ms. Clairmont, but I will not tolerate your insubordinate language in the future. Major, I want Ms. Clairmont confined to her quarters for the next forty-eight hours unless she is in your office receiving counseling or running menial errands as punishment. She can eat MRE's at the picnic table outside the tents. We can discuss the harassment allegations later."

"Yes, sir. Also, I believe Ms. Clairmont would benefit from going to church with me. In fact, we could go a couple of times throughout the week. I've been busy but meaning to get on a regular schedule."

Ali's brain screamed, *Church? What the hell is going on?* The words almost popped out of her mouth. Instead, she took out a tissue and dabbed her eyes.

The colonel's nodded. "Hmm, interesting idea. Give it a try. This meeting is adjourned. Major Stewart, I want a word with you in my office."

As they filed out of the room, Lynn lingered. "Sergeant, please take Ms. Clairmont to my office."

Chapter 27

"It's chow time, Sergeant. I can handle it from here." Lynn thumbed towards the door.

Ali took off her Operations Center access badge, tossed it on the desk, and said, "Guess I won't be needing that for the next forty-eight hours. Jesus Christ, how can you remain so uncaring in the face of such injustice?"

"Uncaring? Ali, I was blindsided." Lynn locked the door.

"You are the perfect case of denial. Oh, you're excellent at the job, but do you have to be such a loyal lapdog?"

The ugliness of anger rose and spread. Lynn stared Ali down. Rooted in her spot, Lynn clenched her fists. The epitome of calm, no one had ever ruffled her, but Ali touched every corner of her inner self and evoked all kinds of emotion.

Ali blinked first and nervously shifted from one foot to the other. Lynn relaxed her stance.

"I hope you don't think I was the one who turned Miller and Cramer in. I'd never do that. It was Ratcliffe and Hernandez on that affidavit."

"I'm sorry." Ali's voice dropped. "What's going on? Why the crazy story about my sister?"

Lynn gently grasped her shoulders and whispered, "I had to come up with something because I need you here. There are bigger fish to fry, and it's a dangerous situation. Control yourself. You're better than they are, but if you continue mouthing off, you'll only dig a hole for them to bury you."

"Dangerous? Bigger fish? What's happening?"

"I can't explain now but soon." Lynn released her, picked up the badge and pressed it into Ali's chest. "Put it on. We need to go back, file the classified weekly, and make sure your station is secured."

"It is."

"Humor me." Lynn motioned Ali to go first. "And be careful of your words. They're looking for any excuse to get rid of you."

As they walked into the Operations Center, Lieutenant Hernandez's subtle smirk spread into a full grin, and he kicked back in his chair. After a few minutes of gloating, he strolled over.

Lynn quickly said, "We've got one more report, then I'll put her on admin leave."

"I want my soldiers to be able to use her station when she is gone," Hernandez said in an authoritative voice.

Ali stood, and Lynn stepped in between, with her back toward Hernandez, and mouthed the words, "Stay calm."

Stepping around Lynn, Ali said, "I'm sorry, Lieutenant. As I've explained a thousand times, my NGA computer is not connected to your network and is not the property of the Army."

Lynn breathed a sigh of relief that Ali had answered calmly. She turned towards Hernandez, but before she could chime in, Ali said, "Furthermore, it would be a violation of security for me to let you use this equipment since you are not part of my agency."

Lynn gently grabbed Ali's arm and pulled her back. "I'm afraid Ms. Clairmont is correct, Lieutenant. Now if you'll excuse us, we need to finish this report."

Ali sat and booted up the computer, but Hernandez didn't budge. God, he was ticking Lynn off. She pulled up a chair next to Ali and watched the screen. Without acknowledging his continued presence, she said, "Lieutenant, we're under a deadline and need to get this done without any distractions. We should be done within ten minutes."

Hernandez backed down and walked away. Once he was out of earshot, Lynn pointed to the screen and quietly said, "We need an excuse to go to the other side of the base. You don't happen to have one, do you?"

Ali continued to type and said, "Not a church night, Major?" The corners of her mouth slightly curled into a smile as she turned to Lynn. "By the way, what denomination is going to rescue me from homosexuality?"

"Please don't be difficult."

Ali attached the files, hit send, and switched to the unclassified computer. She whispered, "Fortunately for us, our excuse has finished downloading." She stood and detached a hard drive from the unclassified system. In a voice loud enough to be heard, Ali said, "The weekly summary is out, and I'm sure the UAV unit on the other side of base would appreciate getting their data brick a day early. Can you drive me?"

"Let's go."

Mid-way through the trip, Lynn pulled over and shut off the vehicle. She rested her arm on the seat back. "I know you're hurt and angry. I totally get that. Ali, I have no idea what the colonel put into the report he sent up the chain." Lynn leaned closer. "I did defend Miller and Cramer's spotless service records even though it was a hopeless situation."

Ali sat with her arms crossed. When Lynn reached out and touched her shoulder, she didn't flinch or brush Lynn aside.

"Ali, the work of the entire team has saved lives. You and Miller have made a difference. And while I don't know Cramer, I've heard good things about her. Don't forget that. Don't let the bullies around here beat you down to their level."

Ali faced her with moist eyes. "They were the only friends I had around here where I didn't have to play good little girl and the pronoun game. I am too afraid to be myself around others." Ali took out a tissue and blew her nose. "When are you going to tell me about the reason for the made-up story?"

"Soon."

"I'm surprised those guys bought that ridiculous crap." Ali laughed. "Especially about church, but I found it most entertaining."

"I had to think of something."

"Your reputation of not cursing—which is rare for a soldier—probably helped."

After the hard drive was delivered, Lynn swung by the Special Forces camp. "Please come inside."

Ali scrunched her eyes. "I don't have the clearances."

"You do now."

—◦◦◦◦◦◦—

Goosebumps formed on Ali's skin when Lynn and Colonel Peterson led her into a soundproof room. *This is anything but normal. What is Lynn involved in? Does this have something to do with Dan?*

Following his instructions, she inserted her ID card into the reader and logged into the computer. An entirely different system popped up, prompting her to change her password. *Wow. I've never seen an organization set up access that fast.*

"Now please go to your email. You'll find new security forms."

The official paperwork was temporarily assigning her to a multi-agency operation where she would be reporting to NSA. She moved to the next email with a video attachment. This one was from Admiral David W. Kent, the director of NSA. Her breath hitched as she pressed the play button.

The admiral came on the screen. "Ms. Clairmont. You have been given an assignment of vital importance to our nation. Your leadership on the base will be Colonel Peterson and Major Stewart. They will provide you with the paperwork and all the details. I thank you for your dedication and service to the country."

She read the security paperwork, and Peterson verbally stressed certain parts. After signing, she stared at the multiple agency and organization seals below the signature block. Curiosity and disbelief coursed through her body. Peterson casually strolled to a mini-fridge and brought them each a bottle of water.

"May I call you Ali?" He said.

"Yes." Ali thought he was too calm for everything going down.

"Thanks to Dan's, Cramer's, and your work, we have Captain Dalton, and Major Ratcliffe under closer scrutiny. I hope you can tell us that someone else besides Sergeant Cramer was tracking their activity? She's not much use since she's moving."

"No one else. Cramer gave me what she could, and I reported every incident that I witnessed." Ali leaned on the table. She turned to Lynn. "Tell me, Major Stewart. What was in your report about the job at the combat outpost?"

Lynn slumped back. Ali almost regretted the words, but she was still upset. *Dan wasn't the only one holding back. Lynn was involved. Why didn't she tell me? Was her affection an act all along?*

Peterson said, "I'll leave you two alone while I catch up with headquarters. You can tell her about Dan."

After the door sealed, Ali snapped, "What about Dan? And what's your role in all of this?"

Lynn sat motionless staring at the floor.

"You've brought me this far. Answer my questions." The muscles of Ali's stomach tightened. "Lynn?"

Slowly Lynn scooted the chair to her side and embraced her. Ali could feel the tension in her body. In her ear, Lynn whispered, "I'm sorry. Dan's dead."

Chapter 28

Peterson returned with Evans, and another soldier ushered Ali away.

"I can tell she cried, but she seems to be in control now. Do you think she's stable?" Evans said.

"Sometimes you lack compassion." Lynn took some deep breaths.

"All right folks. Let's not bicker. We need to focus."

Lynn stiffened at Colonel Peterson's voice. "Yes, sir."

Minutes later, the door opened, and Thomas Blair walked in. Her eyes went wide. A senior executive in a war zone spoke volumes for his rank, and the trust Admiral Kent had in him.

"Mr. Blair, good to see you again." Peterson reached out his hand with a broad smile.

Blair clapped him affectionately on the shoulder while shaking his hand. "How's your father doing?"

A flash of sadness shone on Peterson's face. "Thank you for asking, sir. He's in the final stages. Doesn't know anyone, but he's being cared for. I want to thank you for the video of the ceremony honoring the work of the NPIC team. It was a joy for my family to see what role our father played in the Corona Program."

"My pleasure." Blair tipped his head toward them. "Major Stewart. Master Sergeant Evans. Let's get to work."

Blair's face was now back to neutral and all business. She made a mental note to look up the terms NPIC and Corona. Peterson said, "As ordered, Ms. Clairmont has been brought on board. We have her finishing paperwork now."

Blair smile disappeared. Lynn had felt the room was hot and stuffy before, but now a surge of heat rushed through her body. *Is something wrong?*

Spinning the dials on his briefcase, Blair removed a double-wrapped package. "We're running out of time. Admiral Kent informed me that the info passed to the Afghan military is making its way into Russian hands." He tore open the package, and a pile of stapled packets came sliding at them down the table. They each grabbed one from the scattering on-slaught. "These are the profiles of the Afghans who may be involved. Evans, cross-check the after-action reports on all trips with this list. I want to know anyone in the Brigade who had an opportunity to meet with these men," his index finger shot up, "and three women. Cramer has been interviewed twice. Her info is helpful, but most of it was in previous reports. Major, work with Ms. Clairmont."

"Yes, sir."

"And one more important thing. My work here is also as a liaison with key Afghan officials who are assisting us. There is no need for Ms. Clairmont to know about my role in this operation. She is only to work with you three. Is that clear?"

They all mumbled their concurrence.

"Now, Major. We need to send Ms. Clairmont on a human-itarian trip. One that includes Captain Dalton."

"Sir, that's highly dangerous." Lynn didn't mean the words to sound as harsh as they did, especially to a superior. Surprisingly,

Blair didn't immediately respond. He wet his lips and took a deep breath. A wave of concern washed over his features that Lynn found unsettling and baffling.

"Are you questioning Admiral Kent's judgment?"

"No, sir."

"I'm aware of the risks, but there appears to be no other way." He clenched his jaw and brushed his pant leg several times. "At the very least, we need to explore the opportunity. Ms. Clairmont is dedicated. I'm sure she will agree once a reasonable plan is laid out. The best place to start is with that list of bios. Show her. In the meantime, work with Peterson to come up with a simple plan that is as safe as possible while achieving the objective."

"Yes, sir."

"A security team of undercover guards has already been assembled. They will fly into the base as soon as Peterson gives the ready signal. You have two weeks to come up with a plan." Blair was looking straight at her as if Peterson and Evans weren't in the room.

"Why two weeks?" Lynn adjusted the collar of her uniform. *That's too fast for such a complex mission.*

"We're running out of time." Blair's mouth twitched a touch, and his lips pursed. "The Secretary of State visits Kabul in two weeks and is scheduled to fly onto Moscow. It's more than politics that I'm worried about. A soldier suspected of being associated with Dalton committed suicide at Bagram." He wet his lips. "The CIA took possession of his belongings, including a journal that had information and a picture of you. It's only a matter of time before they come for the entire team."

Lynn sat too stunned for words. For a few seconds, she only heard the sound of the fan from the air handling unit. Blair rested his elbow on the table and rubbed his forehead with his hand. "Believe me. I want no harm to come to anyone. This is the best chance we have. I don't think Dalton suspects her. The security team is tops. We can't force her to do it, but I know enough about Ali to know that she will want to help."

He never calls anyone by their first name. And he called her Ali, not Alaina! What the frak. There's something more in his eyes. What?

Blair stood and closed his briefcase. "I need to make a quick trip to Jalalabad. They appear to have someone there who is connected and talking. After that, I'll be in Kabul for a couple of days. I want sound options when I return. Everyone in and out quickly and brought home safely. Notify me immediately if there are any urgent developments."

Evans and Peterson followed him out the door. *Focus.* Lynn opened the computer, toggled the switch for the unclassified side, and googled Blair's name. One official bio popped up but no other news-related articles. She scanned the page, and her eyes stopped at the words "The National Photographic Interpretation Center" followed by the acronym NPIC.

According to the article, Blair had worked there before joining the NSA. She surfed on the acronym NPIC and Corona. The CIA public website contained some interesting documents on the declassified satellite program Corona and the role of the photo interpreters who worked at NPIC. She almost choked on her water. *NPIC was a CIA office that became part of the National Geospatial-Intelligence Agency.* Her hand covered her gaping mouth. *That's Ali's agency.*

Hearing the whoosh of the door, Lynn closed the screen and jumped up. "Hey, Ali."

Unfortunately, Evans was on her heels. "The guest," his eyebrows quickly hitched, "has departed."

"Lynn, I hope you have more interesting information to tell me about this mission because I spent the last hour reading boring papers." Ali plopped in the opposite chair. "So, what's going on, and who's the guest? I want to catch whoever's responsible for killing Dan."

Lynn handed Ali the bios of the Afghans. "Do you recognize any of these faces or names? Maybe someone in the Brigade has spoken about them."

Ali flipped through the pages. Her body stilled, then she jumped up and leaned across the table, holding out the paper and jabbing her finger at the photo. "I know her."

"From where?" Lynn's heart raced.

"Before you arrived, I visited a government school, not one connected with a mosque. The female teacher was the wife of the ruler of the local governing council. At least that's what the interpreter said. We handed out candy and toys."

Lynn grabbed the page. "Rafia Shirzai, a teacher and administrator, and her husband, Arman, government worker, assignment unlisted. Ali, do you remember the location of the school?"

"Baraki Barak," Ali said without hesitation.

"Are you sure?"

"Yes. It was a joint project with the Engineers in Logar Province."

Evans smacked Lynn on the arm. "Baraki Barak is halfway to Kabul. Log in, Major. Call up the spreadsheet."

Lynn switched to the classified side. "Dalton's been there three times." Her fingers flew across the keyboard. "The woman and her husband are also connected to a clinic in Ahmed Khel, and Dalton's been there six times. What the frak? And Dalton and Ratcliffe are scheduled for another trip."

"Perfecto. That's our chance." Evans clapped her on the back.

In a low voice, Lynn said, "No. It's too dangerous. I won't allow it."

"We can't miss our opportunity." Evans scolded. "She can do it."

"Do what, Lynn? Evans is dancing around like a teenager invited to the prom, and the look on your face went from serious to scared shitless in an instant."

Evans didn't waste time. "We must send you in covertly to monitor the situation. This could be our chance to get them both."

"It's in three days. Bl—" Lynn stopped herself, "won't be back. Resources are spread thin. The security around the Engineers isn't enough. Things can go bad in a heartbeat if someone else is in on this."

Evans interjected. "Yes, but—"

Ali jumped out of her seat. "Hey, guys! I'm in the room. Talk to me like an adult, please." She crossed her arms. "What undercover mission? Who wants me to go?" With each syllable, Ali's voice raised. "Look. Don't keep me in the dark any longer. I'm pissed at you two enough. We have to catch Dan's killer!"

"Quiet." Lynn put up her hand.

Ali rolled her eyes and put her hands on her hips. "Is your mind gone? We're in a soundproof room. Now, tell me what the fuck is going on, or I walk!"

Lynn couldn't hold back the details any longer. "Headquarters says the Russians are getting reports. They want us to set up a sting op with you as the monitor."

"Ah, you mean the bait." Ali crossed her arms.

"Well, it's a perfect opportunity to distract them." Evans leered. "They will be busy ogling your sexy figure. You are rather appealing."

"Evans!" Lynn's voice shrieked. "Sit!"

"Yes. Like a good boy." Ali snapped her fingers twice and pointed to the chair. "Both of you listen to me. Dalton and Ratcliffe are probably suspicious of you taking over JETT at the last minute. I've been dealing with these arrogant guys a lot longer, and they're dismissive of me. Since Cramer was forced to leave, they probably think they can do what they want."

Evans pointed his finger. "Precisely. We need to get the security team here to protect you and grab Dalton and Ratcliffe."

"Okay, Evans." Ali's arms were crossed, and her mouth was in a deep scowl. "What extra security? CIA? Dish or I don't go."

He shrugged. "Trust me. They know their shit."

"No!" Lynn smacked her hand on the table and rushed up to Ali, grabbing her by the shoulders. "It's too soon to plan an op, and it's too isolated on the Chamkani-Gardez Highway."

"Don't get soft just because it's me. That pisses me off." Ali pushed her hands away.

Lynn rubbed her eyes. "Ali, please. It's sixty klicks from Gardez and only thirty minutes from the Pakistan border. Ambushes happen all the time. It's way too dangerous for an untrained person. Let's check the list for another date and location. There has to be another way."

"I can make my own decision."

Ali's eyes showed unwavering determination. Lynn fell into the chair and squeezed her eyes shut for a moment. Most of the scenarios didn't end well. Her voice cracked. "Please don't do this."

Ali ran her slim fingers through her reddish-brown hair. "Frankly, I don't think you have many options."

I'll never forgive myself if something happens. "Okay," Lynn conceded. "But only if headquarters approves. First, let's run it by Colonel Peterson. Ali, think this over. We'll be right back." Lynn followed Evans out the door.

After a few steps, Lynn grabbed Evans, spun him around, and pulled him inches from her face. Through gritted teeth, she warned him in a low voice, "No one gets hurt under my watch. I'll go to the admiral and shoot it down if we can't formulate an airtight plan within 24 hours." She released him. "Now get Peterson."

She watched him walk away, then turned on her heel. With her hand on the door handle, she swallowed and said a silent prayer. *Please change your mind.*

"Ali, I'm sorry how this has unfolded."

"Stop!" Ali paced back and forth. "Did you set me up to come onto you?"

"NO! I do care about you."

"As a friend with benefits? After all, that seems to be your MO."

"No. I...I love you."

Ali stopped pacing and faced Lynn with wide eyes. "Kind of two years too late. You could have told me when I first said it to you."

Lynn ran her hands through her hair. "I was messed up and had nothing to offer you. Please don't agree to this. I couldn't live if something happened to you. This can't possibly be pulled off safely with only two days' planning. I'll tell Peterson when he gets here that it's a no go."

"This may be the best opportunity to catch whoever killed Dan. I don't want someone else getting hurt. As for the classified, you damn well know that thieves take more the bolder they get. We've got to stop this."

The door opened, and Evans shot through. "It's a go."

Panic hit Lynn. "What the frak are you talking about? Where's Peterson?"

"He immediately contacted the admiral who approved."

Lynn lost control and grabbed Evans by the lapels and shook him. "You, asshole!"

"Lynn, stop! Have you lost your mind?"

Evans's jaw tightened. "We have to work together for now. After this is over, I will pay you back, Major. I'm going to get some rest. I suggest you two do as well. Headquarters and Special Forces are now handling the preparations." He wiped his lip with the back of his hand. "Check your email." He walked backwards to slip out the door as if expecting another attack.

Lynn hung her head. "I'm sorry. I'm exhausted."

"Just calm down. There must be a reason for Evans's last words. Open your email."

Admiral Kent had indeed signed off. They were to report tomorrow at 0600 for an update. The operation was going down in 72 hours.

Chapter 29

The Sting Operation

Chink. Chink.

Lynn jingled a set of keys over and over in her hand. Dustin's face flashed before her eyes. She blinked rapidly but didn't take her eyes off the video screens. *Stay strong. We've got to get Ali home in one piece.*

Chink. Chink.

Evans cupped his hand over hers and said, "Stop it. It's irritating, and I can't think."

After putting the keys in her pocket, she wiped her brow. *Why am I sweating so much?* She stood up, then leaned over and grabbed the table.

"You okay?" Evans and the other four Special Forces guys were watching her.

"Yeah. I'm going for a walk before the op begins. I won't leave the compound, and I'll be back soon."

Blair blocked her way. "A word with you, please."

Breathing in the cold outside air helped the dizziness. Blair motioned to his armored SUV, then opened the door and waited for her to get inside. The driver and a bodyguard with a Heckler & Koch MP5 submachine gun eyed her.

The SUV felt like an airtight, stuffy coffin. The smell of

leather cleaner hung in the air and caused her stomach to flip. Blair slid in. She focused straight ahead and took a deep breath before daring to glance into his stone face.

"Leave us," he flicked his wrist at the driver and guard.

"Sir, Colonel Peterson contacted Admiral Kent after you left for Jalalabad. We meant no disrespect."

Blair held up his hand for her to stop, then peered out the window before turning with a glare that could melt glaciers. She thought he would finally scream. She waited for him as several long seconds of silence ticked by.

"As you might recall from my greeting with Colonel Peterson, I once worked at NPIC. Leaving out the boring details, essentially the same agency as the one that employees Ms. Clairmont." The steady tone of his voice didn't match the rest of his face, which had grown red with anger. "I still have friends at NGA." He was grinding his teeth now. "I also have a connection with Ms. Clairmont's family."

What the frak does that mean?

He held up his finger again, then brushed imaginary lint off his pants. Lynn wanted to reach out and smack his hand away but softened when he turned. His face and eyes were full of sorrow.

"Major, I have a personal stake in Ms. Clairmont's welfare. And since you're her lover, I'm sure you do as well." Within seconds, his face hardened again. "This sting op has more risks than I can count. I'm disappointed you could not present a better option to the admiral."

Evans's lies made her boil. "I understand, Mr. Blair. We're less than an hour before they reach the compound."

"Major, we may have our differences, but today, we all will do our best to ensure everyone comes home safely, hopefully with the spy captured. Afterward, I want all the details on how

this op was planned and executed in your after-action report."
He opened the door. "Let's get back inside. We have a job to
do."

"Yes, sir."

It wouldn't matter that Evans jumped rank to push this
operation, Lynn was Evans's commander and had to take full
responsibility. That meant taking the heat, and likely a disci-
plinary letter in her file, once the op finished.

Back inside, she sunk into her seat next to the Special
Forces analysts monitoring the situation and slipped on her
audio headset.

"Listen up, folks," Colonel Peterson's voice boomed over
their headsets. "Ms. Clairmont and Captain Dalton are in one
MRAP with four guards. Major Ratcliffe's in another. The
other two MRAPs are transporting medics who are not privy
to the operation. All the guards are undercover Special Forces
with body cams. The MRAPs also have hidden cameras."

Lynn could hear Peterson pacing right behind them.

"You all should have studied the picture of the Afghan
teacher and her husband. Now, the laptop Dalton was given
only had unclassified data. We made a forensic image before
he picked it up. Ratcliffe did not check out a computer.
Catching either with classified information in their possession
or copied onto the laptop would seal the deal. Catching them
passing anything classified to the Afghan couple would be the
cherry on the top. So, be on the lookout."

Blair said, "To add an extra incentive, we set Ms.
Clairmont up with fake NSA documents. After the medical
clinic, the convoy is supposed to stop at a combat post where
Ms. Clairmont is to deliver the documents. She will pretend to
break all the rules. So, don't be alarmed when you see the
security bag is unlocked, and she talks about losing the key.

That's part of the plan. Also, she will leave the bag unattended. Filming Dalton's reaction will help, but if we're lucky, he might try to steal something."

"Thirty minutes to approximate showtime, sir," the Special Forces lead analyst announced.

Thank God, the hidden cameras and mics are state of the art. Lynn took a few more deep breaths. *Calm down. Breathe.* She didn't care if this assignment got her a promotion or thrown out. No one could get hurt. *Dustin...blood...* "What if it's another connection, not this woman, and we've got it all wrong?" *Frak, I said that out loud. Control yourself.* She turned to her right. Blair's eyes bore into her.

"We sit back and wait, Major." He moved up next to her and patted her hand. "And pray that today is not a day for sacrifice."

———◆———

Ali hoped her nervousness simply came off as naivety. "I remember an earlier trip. It was wonderful to see the children smile." *Oh, no. Did I just tip him off?* "Anyway, after hearing about the vaccination program, headquarters thought it'd be a great opportunity."

"Polio and measles are still common. Do you know what you've gotten yourself into?" Dalton said with no emotion in his voice.

"Seeing a clinic will give me an experience I can't get behind a desk. The mapping data is needed from the sensors on the hull of the MRAP, and the package, you know...has to be delivered afterward." Her eyes darted to the bag holding the fake classified. She mumbled, "Oh shit. It's unlocked." She rummaged around in her pocket. "I can't find the key." She acted as frazzled as possible.

The MRAP lurched to a stop.

"Are you ready, Ms. Clairmont?"

Ali bit her lip and pointed to the bag. "It's only for a short time. Do you think it will be okay?"

If it had been an actual classified bag, they would both be at fault for leaving it unattended. Ali worried for a second that Dalton wouldn't buy this charade. But this was what headquarters wanted her to do.

"Of course. One of the guards will be posted outside and make sure no Afghans enter." He smiled and motioned to exit, clenching the briefcase with the laptop.

"That's a large briefcase."

"I have to interview some administrators. It requires lots of paperwork."

After entering the clinic, the smell of antiseptic and something sickening—*the foul stench of stool*—hit her immediately. A healthcare worker greeted them with a smile. A strand of straight black hair peeked out from under her cap. She had a lazy eye with the eyelid dropping almost shut over the lovely dark brown iris. She directed them to wash up, and handed them protective gowns, gloves, and masks.

Dalton didn't put on the protective dress. "You'll see that the tour is pretty cramped. They aren't crazy about having men here who aren't medical staff." He looked toward the snap of Ali's glove. He plastered a smile up to his ears. "I need to get to that other business. See you later."

He waltzed out the door. Ali started to follow but was grabbed by the female guard accompanying her who whispered, "Don't worry. We've got him and Ratcliffe under surveillance. Let's look for the woman."

The healthcare woman said to the group, "Respiratory and diarrheal diseases take the lives of many children. We try to keep things sanitized as best as possible, but there aren't enough cleaning supplies. The smell tends to linger."

An Afghan woman wearing a traditional dress with a colorful headscarf appeared to be the same build as the woman they were looking for. But when she turned, Ali saw she was not the teacher.

"I have to be blunt," she said in an American accent. "I've volunteered here for almost a year and don't care for military inspections, but I know we don't get humanitarian funding without them. After a quick tour, I expect you to keep out of the way while we administer care. Even better, there are other buildings on the compound. Got it?" She quickly put on the protective clothing. "Let's go."

Every space was packed with people or supplies. Children slept upright or in their mother's arms as there was barely room to walk. Unlike those at the school, these children were malnourished and sick.

"That end of the hall is off limits. We've got several cases of measles. As you can see, we need every dime and penny we can get. Now, please go back that direction and stay out of our way."

Ali shook her head. They had not seen the Afghan woman yet. Outside, they walked in the direction of the supply building. Ali stopped in her tracks. Her hand flew to her mouth. A child about the age of five dangled in her father's arms. Burns on the legs were so severe that the skin had sloughed off in spots. Ali turned away.

"You okay?" A man with soft brown eyes came up and asked. His name tag identified him as a doctor.

Her guard replied, "She's fine. We were just leaving."

Ali shook off the guard's hand. "What happened to the child?"

The doctor swallowed and pursed his lips. "There's nothing we can do. I'm sending them to the building where patients are near death. The father says she fell into cooking oil, but that's not what happened."

"What do you mean?"

The man sucked his lip into his mouth before looking into Ali's eyes and answering. "The burn marks were even on both legs. Some of the Afghans punish their children by dipping them into hot water or oil. This was too hot. She won't survive."

"Oh my, God." The words barely come out of Ali's mouth. Suffering children crushed her.

"I don't know how important you are, but we need an increase in funding." His eyes pleaded. "This country has been at war for over thirty years, and a large segment of the population is in dire poverty and uneducated. Abuse is widespread, especially in rural areas. We see it in all different age groups. Beyond the physical cases, we try to treat mental issues and educate. Progress is slow."

Ali held up her hand to the guard then squeezed her eyes shut for a few seconds and took some deep breaths. She wiped her eyes with the back of her hand.

⚞⚟

Lynn couldn't take her eyes off the screens. The feed from the hidden cameras and mics was excellent quality.

When Ali turned away from the burned child, Evans said, "She's too soft, but that should be to our advantage. Shows she cares deeply about the women and children. Makes her role believable."

"Quiet. No unnecessary comments," Lynn said without looking in his direction.

"Well, I'll be damned." Peterson pointed to another screen. A car arrived, and the Afghan couple got out and greeted Ratcliffe. Rafia left the two men and walked towards the mosque. Ratcliffe pulled a small object out of his pocket. "Zoom in," Blair ordered. "Where's the audio?" One of the analysts clicked the computer mouse, and the conversation filled the room.

Ratcliffe said, "We weren't able to get you everything you asked for. You can check the thumb drive later." He handed the drive to Arman and said, "We're having trouble with Pakistan."

"I understand." Arman put his hand over his heart and nodded, and Ratcliffe walked away.

Lynn bumped Blair on the shoulder and pointed to another screen. The woman entered a mosque, and Dalton followed.

Blair said, "Don't roll up Ratcliffe and the Afghan until Dalton is out of view. And switch the audio for God's sake."

Evans leaned back in the chair, hands behind his head. "Women and men have separate mosque entrances and don't mingle. Either they've found a clever way, or we're chasing ghosts with these two."

An operator shouted. "He's left the mosque!"

Dalton reentered the MRAP. He shuffled through Ali's bag but didn't take anything, then exited and went back to the mosque.

"Why didn't he take anything?" Evans said.

"Clever shyster." Blair leaned in. "By examining the contents, he's judging the level of classified that Ms. Clairmont is trusted with. The next step is to butter her up over several weeks and establish a level of camaraderie. Ultimately, he would look for a way to take advantage of her or find something of blackmail value. Classic handler behavior." He pounded his fist on the desk. "But we're going to catch him, and everyone is coming home safe and sound."

Lynn rubbed her neck. *Come on, Ali. Identify the woman and get back here safely.*

—◦◦◦—

The guard grabbed Ali's elbow to move her along. "Time to go. They're going to move on arresting them."

Halfway across the courtyard, Ali glanced across the street. "Stop! Dalton's already handed it over. Come on!" She tugged the guard in the other direction.

"What are you talking about? The mosque is surrounded, and Dalton and the woman are inside."

Ali pointed to a woman. "She has a briefcase and looks like the family servant, Ziba."

The guard spoke into her headset. "Send two guns across the street. Clairmont says the servant has the briefcase...Copy that." She turned to Ali. "You're right. Dalton and Rafia came out of the mosque and are being detained."

—◦◦◦—

Lynn and Blair were glued to the screen showing Ali's movements while other analysts watched the guards moving in on Ratcliffe and Dalton.

"What the frak are they doing?" Lynn threw down a pen and pointed to the screen. "They crossed the street into an area with multi-story buildings. They're easy pickings in that narrow alley." She turned to Peterson. "Stop them. It's too dangerous with only one guard." Every nerve in Lynn's body was on edge.

"I agree. Tell the guard to stop."

The audio operator replied, "I can't. For some reason, our comms aren't getting through. We can hear them, but they can't hear us."

"Fix it!" Lynn yelled. The hair stood on the back of her neck, and unpleasant goosebumps spread over her body. Blair rubbed his head and moved away. He leaned against the wall with his arms crossed. His face was ashen.

—◦◦◦◦—

"Ziba," Ali called.

The young woman opened the door to a car and tossed in the briefcase.

"Ziba! We know what's going on. Please don't do this." Ali pleaded.

"Stop!" Ali's guard had her gun drawn.

A man exited the car pointing a machine gun, and two more Afghans came out of a doorway with guns drawn. Ali cursed under her breath. Over the sound of her pounding heart, she heard another MRAP.

Two more American guards rushed in with their M-16s drawn. The one standing next to Ali said something in Dari that sounded harsh, and the Afghan man said something back at a more rapid pace. No one put their guns down. Ali was frozen with fear. *One wrong move and everything is going to hell.*

The guard who spoke Dari said, "Ms. Clairmont, can you positively identify this woman."

"She is Ziba, the nanny and servant of Rafia Shirzai."

"That's good."

The guard spoke more Dari and waved the tip of his gun. The Afghan man finally lowered his gun and motioned to

Ziba. She grabbed the briefcase and walked it over to the American as another MRAP rumbled up.

"Ms. Clairmont. Get to the MRAP. Don't say anything until we're back at base."

Ali quickly moved but stopped at the rear door to look back. One guard carried the briefcase towards the convoy while the other guards were walking backward with their guns still pointed at Ziba and the Afghans. Ali took a seat, and a soldier handed her a water.

"You'll feel better."

"Where's Dalton and Ratcliffe?"

"In another MRAP. It's over. We'll get you back on base soon."

Chapter 30

Tomorrow before dawn, they would leave for Kabul and then home for more interviews. Until then, a guard trailed Ali wherever she went.

"I'm going to dinner," she shouted over the plywood wall. Outside, the setting sun painted rosy shades over the mountains. It was about the only thing she'd miss. Her chest ached. She rubbed her forehead and the bridge of her nose and tightly squeezed her eyes shut. She couldn't shake the feeling of being violated. *Why couldn't they tell me from the beginning?*

In the chow hall, the smell of sweet peppers, onions, and sausage drifted in the air. Probably not the wisest thing to eat before bed, but it was one of her favorites. *Definitely not as hot as the curry chicken.* The chefs here were some of the best and cooked a variety of American dishes. It was especially delicious when they had fresh ingredients.

"May I please have the broccoli and cheddar soup and celery and carrots as well."

"Yes, miss."

The Sri Lankan server smiled, and Ali slightly pressed her palms together, in front of her chest, and slightly bowed her head. The expression of gratitude went a long way. Most of the soldiers didn't seem to understand that and just pointed.

In the sitting area, a small group that she and Dan used to sit with were off to the right. Turning on her heels, she headed in the other direction and found an empty section. *OMG, this soup is wonderful.*

"Congratulations. I didn't expect the mission to go this smoothly." Evans strolled up, sat his tray down, and popped the top on an energy drink.

Ali snapped the celery stick in two and slowly swirled a piece in her broccoli and cheddar soup. She took her time, crunching and savoring, then sipped her apple juice. *I'm not going to let spooky Evans ruin this.* He buttered his bread, looking at her with a sadistic smile.

"Evans, you of all people should know the chow hall is not the place to discuss this." *And wipe that mocking grin off your face, Mr. Tech Weirdo. Damn, what was the name of that old movie? The one with a Baldwin brother having secret surveillance cameras and mics in people's apartments. He looks just like that guy.* "And, I don't remember inviting you to dinner."

"No one's around, and I don't intend to mention anything I shouldn't. However, I must say that the major played you well." He took a bite of his sandwich. The corners of his mouth still held a sneer.

"What the hell is that supposed to mean? She did her job. Yes, I was upset that I was not told at the beginning, but she was following orders."

"Was she?"

They both paused when a worker walked by.

"Say your piece and go on your merry way."

"Was she following orders when taking you as a lover?" He took a spoonful of tomato soup.

Ali wanted to flip over her tray and spill her dinner all over Evans's tidy uniform but calmly said, "I have no idea what you're talking about."

"Oh dear, Ms. Clairmont. It's no secret that you two were an item on your first deployment. Why do you think Washington picked the major in the first place? They wanted her to cozy up to you and regain your trust, but sleeping with you was her idea. That was the fastest way to use you, and it worked. A magnificent one, I might add."

Ali talked herself off the ledge of causing a scene in the dining facility. "You're a prick, Evans. Get out of my face and don't spread any untrue rumors."

"Why? Don't want to see your girlfriend get punished?" He leaned toward her. "There was no family emergency with the prior JETT commander. Oh, and by the way," he raised his finger and showed his gleaming teeth, "it should be lieutenant colonel soon. I hear that was a big motivation for agreeing to take the case. Although, I'm sure getting in your pants was also a plus." He leaned back, and his eyes roamed and focused on her chest. "You do have a nice body."

The chair fell over as Ali jumped up. "Get out!" Several soldiers, rows away, turned to look at the commotion, and she signaled that she could handle the situation. Her face felt hot. *Get out before I wring your fucking neck.* "I think it's time for you to leave."

Evans picked up his tray. "I'm sorry. I was insensitive." He lowered his voice. "I know that you're a lesbian, but I have a soft spot for beautiful women."

I bet you do. Asshole.

"You are truly stunning. I couldn't let you go without telling you about how Major Stewart bragged that it was so easy to convince you. I wanted you to know the real story. Her motivation was greed to get promoted and get a choice assignment. Sadly, you meant nothing to her. Your motivation was truly for love of country. I hope you can go on with your life. I'm sorry things didn't work out as you expected."

"I'll give you credit for one thing. You know how to lay it on thick." Ali's voice was only loud enough for him to hear.

She leered at him walking away. The guard rounded the corner, and the two nearly collided.

"I go to the bathroom for a minute, and he shows up. What did he want?"

"Don't worry. He had nothing of importance to say. Seems to be a habit with him." Ali took her tray to the waste bin.

She pushed open the door and turned up her collar. Leaning into the bite of the cold wind, she trudged ahead, her feet wobbling on the larger clumps of gravel.

A rumble of a convoy caught her attention. Ali ran in front, not flinching at the blare of the horn and shouts from the occupants. *That should put some distance between the guard and me.*

With Evans's words lingering in Ali's mind like a thousand bee stings, she headed to Lynn's. Ali told herself that Evans had to be lying, but she had to hear it from Lynn herself.

—◆◆◆—

Lynn picked up the promotion papers. She only filled them out at the insistence of Admiral Kent. Yet, she was sure Blair was going to bury her by the end. *Powerful guys like that don't forget people like me. Yep, I pissed in his cornflakes, and I'm toast.*

The door flew open with a bang as it smacked against the makeshift nightstand, and Lynn spilled her drink on herself and the papers. She tossed the papers down and whirled around. "Ali, what are you doing here? Are you okay?"

"Sorry. I just ran into Evans at chow." One arm rested on her hip, and her eyes moved from Lynn to the bed.

Lynn's eyes momentarily cast down towards the pile. The visual scene—belongings stacked on the bed—was so similar to their departure from the last deployment. She swallowed down the painful memory.

"I guess this op should be a nice feather in your cap." Ali's voice was low.

"Yes. We both did well."

"You're up for promotion." Ali pointed to the application.

The guard bolted in. "No talking. Orders were that you were to remain apart until Washington could conduct interviews. Ms. Clairmont, I'm going to ignore that you showed up in the major's quarters. The flight to Bagram is at 0500. Not much opportunity for packing and sleep." She tugged on Ali's sleeve. "Let's go. And please watch the convoys. You nearly gave me a heart attack."

Lynn stepped closer to her. "Ali, I know this has been a tough assignment. We can talk when this is all over."

Ali wet her lips and swallowed. "Guess I'll leave you now."

She walked out without saying goodbye, and Lynn started to follow, but the guard stopped her.

"Better finish packing." The guard shut Lynn's door.

Chapter 31

December 2010 – Maryland

Lynn tossed her coat and keys on the foyer table and kicked off her shoes. Nothing felt right anymore. Even the two weeks around the Thanksgiving holiday with her family felt like going through the motions.

After heating up leftovers, she grabbed a bottle of wine and headed for the living room. She sunk into her recliner and channel surfed. "Ah, a Leonardo DiCaprio and Russell Crowe movie." Clicking on the info tab, she read the blurb. "*Body of Lies*...a CIA agent hunts down a powerful terrorist leader while being caught between the unclear intentions of his American supervisors..."

She punched the off button and threw the remote onto the coffee table. It clattered across the surface and the battery compartment lid popped off.

Kent's last words echoed in her brain. "Be proud. We couldn't have done it without you two being the tip of the spear." *Yeah, thanks, Kent. I'll never forget those closing remarks.* Lynn rubbed her head. *And the anger on Ali's face back in Afghanistan when she said, 'Ah, you mean bait.' We honorably served our country but were nothing more than pawns.*

NSA had told her and Ali the bare minimum when the

mission concluded. Captain Dalton was charged with espionage but wasn't talking. Ratcliffe was fully cooperating, and the thumb drive he gave to Arman Shirzai only contained a list of school and medical supplies stuck in Pakistan. Five others had been arrested on espionage and murder charges.

There had been an enormous corps of investigators and computer forensics behind the scenes, and she and Ali were told to step back, let the proper authorities handle matters, and wait for the time to testify. *I want nothing more to do with covert operations. I can serve on other projects.*

Lynn pulled up messages on her smartphone and reread the only text Ali had sent. *Hi, I've been swamped at work and busy with the family. I hope you're doing well! Best wishes, Ali.* It didn't sound like Ali was having difficulty fitting back into work and life.

Lynn swiped the screen and hit the photos button. Her favorite was one she had snapped on a Nikon Coolpix at the combat outpost during the game night before the mortar attack. Ali was pointing to the goodies in her bandana like Vanna White on TV.

"I miss you, Ali. I wish you'd answer my calls and emails."

Lynn put her phone in her pocket, grabbed the bottle, and shuffled back to the kitchen. She poured the wine down the drain and stood at the sink for several seconds, looking out the window.

"I can't do this alone."

She snatched her wallet from her pocket but couldn't find what she was looking for. "Fraking mess!" She turned the wallet upside down, shaking everything out. As her fingers spread the pile out, the therapist's business card settled on top. She picked it up and twirled it in her fingers, then made the call.

Chapter 32

December 2010 – NGA Headquarters, Springfield, Virginia

Ali stood in the lunch-counter line as some guy hashed out a grievance with the cashier. She stared at her food on the tray. *Guess this is the last meal before the firing squad.*

A weird feeling, like she just didn't belong anymore, had haunted her since being home. The neat, orderly world she had left was predictable, boring, and was about as mentally stimulating as watching reality TV reruns. She never said this to anyone, especially the agency therapist during mandatory post-deployment screening. The culture of the business was to look picture-perfect.

Home wasn't a relief. Her family's attempts to drag her to family dinners and engage her in small talk were annoying. Denise had even tried to fix her up with some chick.

Ali gazed at the chocolates shaped like Santa and Rudolph the Red-Nosed Reindeer. *Christ, how am I going to survive Christmas? I'm not shopping. I'll give cards with a check.*

"Hi, Ali."

"Nathan! Wow, it's been ages." Ali plastered on the fake smile that had become all too easy to pull off. "How's Charlottesville? Tired of working with the Army so soon?"

"Had to come up for a couple of days." Although close to

her age, time hadn't been kind to him. He was nearly bald and had a small beer belly. "Shall we have lunch together?"

"Sure." They found a small empty table in the bustling atrium.

"Do you like working here, Ali? I mean, the campus is gorgeous, but headquarters is massive. Everyone's so formal, and the traffic in the area is maddening."

She shrugged. "It's the people that make the job. I could work anywhere really if the team is decent." *At least that's the way it used to be. Everything is dull nowadays.*

"How was deployment?"

Chewing her food meticulously, Ali thought for a split second about telling the truth. "Just another day at the office." *He's not a deployer. He wouldn't understand.* "Tell me about your family and Charlottesville." Nathan started spinning his fork in the mashed potatoes. *Shit, I hope he's not going through a divorce.*

He dropped the fork and put on a smile that seemed forced. "Teenagers. Youngest is thirteen and wants to be an artist, the oldest is nineteen and attends the University of Virginia, and the twins are fifteen, and live and breathe sports."

"Wow, UVA is one of the best in the country. Impressive."

Now his smile was broad. "She's always been the studious one."

"How does she feel about being so close to home?"

The sparkle in his eyes dimmed. "I'm sorry, but I need to get going. It's been wonderful to see you." Nathan came around and met her halfway for a hug and lingered a bit. "I wish you all the best Ali."

"Ditto." She watched him dump his trash. He glanced over his shoulder and waved.

She checked the time and groaned. With minutes to spare, she trudged up the stairs to the sixth floor.

As she entered the agency's executive suite, NGA Deputy Director Andrews stepped out with a wide grin and held the door for her. She smiled back while dreading what was inevitably coming. He motioned to the sofa and asked her about her holiday.

"Thanksgiving was full of kids running around. I have two nieces and three nephews."

"Super."

Ali had only met Mr. Andrews a couple of times during official duties. Others said he was a fair man. This was her first time in his office. She tried to calm herself as he offered her a cup of coffee or tea.

"Ali, your willingness to put yourself in the line of fire during the sting operation was beyond the call of duty and appreciated. Everyone agrees it would have dragged on longer without your help."

"Thank you, sir." She accepted the china cup and took a sip, not even remembering what she had asked for. *Ah, Earl Grey.* Ali wondered why Andrews was stalling. Surely, sooner or later, the agency would punish her, even if it was only a verbal reprimand. Apparently, now was the time. Why else had they called her to Mr. Andrew's office?

"I know you've expressed interest in the ongoing investigation, but the initial mission was way beyond the agency's charter. We only allowed you to continue because CIA felt you were in a short-term position to help. We had no idea how dangerous things would get." He crossed his legs. "Mr. Dan Galvarino was respected throughout the community and will be missed."

Clenching her jaw and holding her breath, she nodded and turned towards the window. The sky was gray as a cold front blew through.

Not wanting to give the impression of being fragile, she

straightened her spine. "Dan was a dear friend. I can honor him by dedicating myself to our community work."

"Further assistance won't be needed until Captain Dalton's court-martial sometime in late 2011."

When is he going to get around to the point? "Yes, sir."

"Good. We've been pleased with your overall coordination with the military, NSA, and CIA, but it's time to move on. And while you've gained a lot of management skills, your forte has always been analysis and software." She nodded. "Regarding you and Major Stewart..." he stammered.

Now, we get to the heart of the matter. "Sir, as I told the military—"

He waved his hand. "All the military mess is drama. We're not concerned about your personal life. Although, it should be outside of working hours." He got up to refill his cup and seemed a bit embarrassed.

He's read my file and my response to all of the military investigations. "I'm sorry, sir. I know a war zone is considered working 24/7. It won't happen again. It was entirely my fault. I've told the military that our relationship is over." *Dammit, why did I say relationship?*

"It's a minor issue in our opinion. To ease your mind, I've been told the matter is leaning in favor of Major Stewart and should be settled soon." He cleared his throat. "Your account as to what happened seems to have satisfied them. However, that's not why I called you." He sat back down, and his eyes bored into her. Over the rim of the cup, he said, "Would you be open to working away from headquarters and far away from your family and Major Stewart?" After taking a sip, he sat patiently, waiting for a reply.

Blinking several times, she said, "Far? What are you proposing?"

"The Australians want us to expand our footprint at the Defence Imagery and Geospatial Organisation in Canberra. They are specifically asking for a senior analyst with a strong scientific background who has experience in the field." He put down the cup. "I won't fib. Your name came up in a long list, and we didn't want to throw you into the fire so quickly. However, we have a problem." He wet his lips. "It seems there are only two NGA employees with experience working with the Aussies on their technology upgrades. You're one."

Nathan. Ali swallowed.

Amazing how the agency seemed to overlook little rule breaks when they were the ones in trouble. Ali took a long sip of the tea. *This could be a good break from the family, and a hell of a lot more challenging than the work routine around here.*

"How long is the assignment for?"

"At least a year, beginning in February. Possibly longer. We would fly you back for Dalton's court-martial and give you two weeks of personal leave. I'll be frank. The other person has turned us down citing hardship on his family. To be fair, you need to think about the impact on your family and any relationship that you have."

A slight blush ran up his cheeks as he turned away to sip his beverage. For a man in his late sixties, he seemed to be doing the best he could.

"We need a timely reply. Otherwise, we will be forced to select you or the other gentlemen."

There was a knock on the door, and Andrews excused himself.

Sitting alone in his large office, she ticked off the pros and cons.

Lynn. I don't know where the hell we stand, and it's for damn sure, I'm not going back in the closet. Maybe we weren't meant to be after all...My family will be upset but will get over it...I need a new work environment to challenge me...Think of the adventure. I've always wanted to explore Australia's nature preserves and its cosmopolitan cities. It sounds exciting...Oh, my Australian friends mentioned the Sydney Gay and Lesbian Mardi Gras is in late February. Who knows? Maybe I'll meet someone...This could be really good for me. A genuine smile lit her lips.

"Sorry about that." Andrews softly closed the door. "As I was saying, we're crunched for time and have to make a decision in the next 48 hours."

"I'll take the assignment."

Andrews's eyebrows shot up. "Don't you want to think about this and discuss the move with your family?"

"Sir, this is an opportunity to expand my horizons by working with our coalition partners. I have the skills, and I'm available to go immediately." She extended her hand.

They vigorously shook hands. "Wonderful. We can start the paperwork tomorrow."

"Yes. Thank you, sir."

Nothing in life is perfect, but a change of scenery in a non-war zone may be just what I need to feel alive again and back on my feet.

Chapter 33

December 2010 – NSA Headquarters, Fort Meade, Maryland

Sinking down in a cushiony chair in the foyer of the NSA director's suite, the bacon and eggs Lynn consumed earlier now gave her heartburn. *Why has Admiral Kent called this meeting?*

The room was warm and stuffy, and the volume of the TV playing in the background was irritating. Every office in headquarters had to have one or two screens on one of the major news channels. Overseas, most chow halls had the TV tuned to the Armed Forces Network. It seemed she could never escape the constant barrage of news.

Someone entered the foyer and turned up the volume. "Yesterday, the House voted 250 to 175 to repeal the 'Don't Ask, Don't Tell' policy, sending the issue to the Senate. Efforts to overturn the 17-year-old law, banning gays from openly serving in the military, now has the backing of three key Republicans. Senator Olympia Snowe of Maine said she would vote to repeal the law, joining fellow Maine Senator Susan Collins, and Senators Lisa Murkowski of Alaska, and Scott Brown of Massachusetts..."

With DADT on the verge of falling, Lynn felt cheated. *If only the circumstances and the timing were different, then I would have had the opportunity to have a family.* She rubbed her lip and tightened her jaw. The lack of closure with Ali only added to the pain. *Why hasn't Ali returned any of my calls or emails? Stop. Shake it off.*

"Major, Admiral Kent will see you now."

"Thank you, ma'am."

She saluted Kent, then fear crept into her body at the sight of Blair's rigid posture.

"Sit, Major." A lump formed in her throat at the sound of Kent's harsh tone. "I'll get to the point. We've been discussing your eligibility for promotion."

Blair was sitting back with one hand over his mouth and methodically twirling a pen with the other. He didn't take his eyes off of Kent.

"I'm honored to be considered."

"Unfortunately, Master Sergeant Evans filed a complaint."

The muscles of her body constricted, and the slight pulsing in her temples now throbbed. Lynn expected opposition from Blair but not Evans.

"He claims you slept with Ms. Clairmont." He took a deep breath and let it out. "If you recall, I told you at the beginning of the op to go up to the line but never cross it."

Evans, you malicious, sack of shit. Taking a deep breath, she carefully considered her words.

Kent folded his hands on the table. "We talked to Ms. Clairmont."

Lynn's soul screamed to fight, but her body gave up. *Shit, who cares if I slump into my chair. My career's over.* Ali was the most honest person Lynn had ever met. She could see a situation where an investigator put the screws to Ali. *And Blair's got it out for me.*

Lynn was shaking inside. "And what did Ms. Clairmont say?"

"That she made advances toward you, and you resisted."

Lynn couldn't believe her ears. Kent didn't give her a chance to reply.

"A panel has been convened to review Evans's accusation. Their decision will determine whether your package goes before the promotion board or if charges are brought. Mr. Blair and I have been summoned to provide testimony. And while you succeeded in the mission," the admiral waved his hand in the air, "I've had to think long and hard. Evans's allegation is serious. We go before the panel this afternoon."

Blair had dropped the pen and was brushing his trousers, then looked at her for the first time. He softened his posture but didn't say a word. *His face looks disappointed. Or is it pity?*

Kent tapped his finger on the table. "At the beginning, I was willing to give you the benefit of the doubt because I trusted your integrity. I expected you to put duty above everything and not act on your affection for Ms. Clairmont. Having this brought into the open and scrutinized is an annoyance."

Here it comes. Lynn clenched her jaw waiting for the hammer to fall.

"Mr. Blair had specific concerns, but he has fully convinced me that you should be promoted to lieutenant colonel."

Wow. "Thank you, Mr. Blair."

He nodded, then brushed his pant legs again.

The admiral cleared his throat. "Rather than finish your term at Fort Meade, I'm suggesting South Korea. That's what's currently available, and it would be a good fit for your career." Kent shoved paperwork her way. "Read the fine print carefully. The panel meets at 1400. The room number is on the sticky note. Bring the papers and don't be late."

Blair said, "You're a good officer, Major Stewart. You completed the mission and kept everyone safe. I'm sure this will be behind you after today. Don't waste this opportunity. Serving in the military and government service are far more satisfying than getting out and becoming a contractor. The choice is yours."

Back in her office, Lynn scoured through the papers from the admiral. Her mouth hung open. Signing meant lying. Lynn's signature was giving her solemn oath that she had turned down Ali's sexual advances. Not signing meant a discharge.

She tried to call Ali, but there was no answer. *Maybe, she's in a meeting.* She called Paul Taylor. Since the 2008 deployment, he had left the service and was a contractor at NSA. With luck, maybe he could tell her how Ali was doing.

"Hi, Paul. Have you heard from Ali lately?"

"Yeah...ah...Have you checked your email?"

Her stomach dropped. "An hour ago, but I didn't see anything. It's been a little busy here."

There were several seconds of silence. "Check your personal email. I'll send you my cell number. You can call if you want to talk. I'm leaving early today." He hesitated again before saying, "I'm sorry, Lynn."

Lynn switched to the unclassified system for internet research. A warning appeared along with terms of agreement. Accepting the terms meant she was subject to monitoring, but she didn't care at this point. She needed to know what was going on. Click.

Dear Lynn,

I'm sorry I haven't spoken to you. The military warned me not to contact you about Evans's accusation. They said if we talked before your review board, it would appear that I was conspiring with you. I hear the board meets today. Hopefully, everything turns out okay. You deserve this promotion. No one has worked harder than you. Your devotion to duty and integrity is second to none.

This isn't easy for either of us. Lynn, I care tremendously for you, but our careers are on opposite trajectories. I was given the opportunity for an assignment in Australia, and for several reasons, taking it was the right thing to do.

I planned to leave after New Year's, but things have changed. I'm now at Dulles, waiting to depart for L.A. where I'll catch the flight to Sydney. I hate goodbyes, and I'm sorry I didn't tell you in person. Take care of yourself.

Love Always,
Ali

Lynn's breathing was shallow. Her eyes filled with tears as she reread the message. The door opened, she hit the logoff button, spun around, and ducked her head in the adjoining file cabinet.

"You okay?"

The last thing she wanted to do was have a conversation with her office mate. "Yeah. I have some things to do." She kept her head down and aimlessly rummaged through the cabinet until her colleague was absorbed in his computer. Taking a breath, she shut the cabinet drawer and grabbed the paperwork and her hat and coat. "I won't be back the rest of the day. Have a safe drive home."

Rather than taking the tunnel between buildings, Lynn walked outside. The wind was bitter cold. The sky was gray and threatening to snow. She wanted to feel something other than the deep agony of losing Ali.

Publicly, Lynn appeared picture-perfect with a string of successful projects. She couldn't remember when she worked less than twelve hours a day. Other than her breakdown in 2008, she always completed a job above and beyond what was asked. *And it's all been at a terrible cost to my personal life.*

Lynn stepped inside and headed to the cafeteria. She sat in the back corner away from others, passing the time until the panel convened. The alarm on her watch jolted her back to reality. She swigged the rest of her coffee, which was now cold.

Walking numbly through the corridors, she barely got to the room on time. Her body might have been sitting in the chair attentively, but fear tumbled inside her head while the panel members discussed the validity of the charges.

"Major Stewart. Major!"

Lynn snapped out of her haze. "Yes, sir."

"You've heard our discussion and the admiral's recommendation, but it seems you haven't signed the paper."

A young lieutenant placed the signature page in front of Lynn. She stared at it.

"Well, Major. Is there a problem?"

"No, sir." Lynn signed. "Everything occurred exactly as Ms. Clairmont stated. I thank you for the opportunity to continue to serve."

"Do you have anything further to add before our final deliberations?"

"No, sir."

"Dismissed."

She saluted and marched to the hall to wait for the final decision. *How ironic? On the cusp of DADT's defeat, I just might be one of the last ones kicked out.*

Within an hour, the admiral walked out smiling. "Looks like your promotion package will move forward. Are you going to take my recommendation on Korea or do you have another suggestion?"

Lynn plastered on a hollow smile and shook his hand. "Korea will be fine, sir." Kent walked off, but Blair remained. "You are a good officer. I wish you luck." Blair patted her shoulder. "I think you deserve a long weekend. I'll put in the paperwork. Take off, Major. That's an order."

"Thank you, sir."

He took some steps then turned back around. "Thank you for your exemplary service." His voice was soft and almost remorseful. "Hopefully, this dark period of our country's history will be over soon."

Lynn drove home on autopilot. The loud click of her condo's deadbolt sounded like a prison lock. She dropped everything and crumpled to the floor, knees drawn to her chest, and sobbed.

PART III

2014-2018

Chapter 34

A li tossed her handbag next to the desk and plopped down at her computer. Staying up late to watch a movie had been a mistake. Lavender wafted to her before the steaming mug of black tea was set in front of her. She grinned at the President's Daily Briefing Team emblem on the extra-large mug. A chocolate croissant appeared in front of her.

"Good morning, Ms. Mentor. Looks like you could use a little more energy."

Ali shook her finger at Carla. "I knew you'd make it. What cabinet member do you support?"

"John Brennan."

"*Wahoo!*" Ali high-fived her. "Oh, he's tough. But it's a large PDB team. You'll learn a lot."

"Yeah, if I ever get past research and actually get a chance to brief him."

"You will."

After completing her assignment in Australia, Ali had returned to her old division with new vigor. When asked to teach briefing techniques to a few students, she jumped at the chance. Carla was one of the best, and the only one to be accepted on the President's Daily Briefing Team.

"Thanks for all the help. I couldn't have done it without you."

"It was your hard work and accomplishments. I just gave you a little shove. I'm so happy for you. Next, I want to see you brief President Obama."

The phone rang, and Ali's eyes shot to the caller ID. "Sorry, I have to take this."

"Talk to you later." Carla waved.

Ali answered on the fourth ring.

"Hello...Yes...I'll be there."

Staring at the treat in front of her, Ali didn't feel hungry anymore. Her muscles were already beginning to tremble. She clutched the mug and walked out.

Chapter 35

An hour after the call, Ali waited in the cold reception lounge. Security always seemed to schedule the polygraph on a symbolic or inconvenient day. Twice it occurred before a holiday and once on her birthday. Today was Friday. *What a way to start a weekend. And before lunch!*

For the most part, she managed to tune out the TV playing in the corner until she heard the words "Don't Ask, Don't Tell." The announcer mentioned the station would have a special story tomorrow at six. The third anniversary of the official end of DADT. A picture of Stephen King splashed on the screen, reminding viewers to tune in to the *All-day 67th Birthday Movie Marathon* on Sunday.

Ali swallowed her sadness along with a sip of her tea. Sunday, the twenty-first of September was also Lynn's forty-first birthday.

She scanned the room for the remote. Not finding one, she climbed one of the plush chairs, stretching to reach the off button. Punching at it, she nearly toppled over, and then jumped down. But the silence did nothing to hide her expression of loss. Ali bowed her head and pinched her nose. *If I had only given her another chance.*

She pulled a tissue from her handbag and dabbed her watery eyes until they were dry. Like every other time, Ali had chosen the easy way out. Running and hiding had been her only option as a child. As an adult, it was a crutch she still clung to.

She couldn't use that crutch today. The polygraph always dredged up the horrible truth. No one could help her, not even Lynn. The tightness in her chest suddenly made it difficult to breathe. *Calm down. Breathe. In. Out.* Reaching for her tea, she knocked it over.

"Shit."

Ali scrambled to her knees and hurried to sop up the tea as it seeped everywhere.

"Ms. Clairmont, we're ready for you now." A man with a crewcut opened the glass door between the lounge and security offices. "Don't worry about that. I can have someone clean it up."

Ali collected the PDB mug—empty and now chipped—and her handbag. She forced her body upright and forward, attempting to display a smile.

"Thank you."

—⟋⟍⟋⟍—

The examination room was more sterile than the lounge. The walls were annoyingly bright white, and the fluorescent lights beamed down like in an auto mechanic's garage. The focus of the room was an imposing chair. The tubes that would be strapped to her chest and stomach lay stretched out. Waiting for her were a blood pressure cuff and something that resembled a whoopee cushion. The esoteric apparatus tracked blood pressure, pulse, respiration, muscle movement or twitch, and the skin's electrodermal response. And of course, video to record everything.

Looks like an alien abduction system.

The test was designed to measure anxiety levels and physical reactions when the test subject was asked questions. The tester would repeat the questions about espionage, loyalty to the country, and other subjects, over and over in a monotone voice. Each set of answers would be scrutinized for variations and anomalies.

"I'd like to remind you that it's important for you to sit completely still and look straight ahead." He sat at a desk to her right, barely out of her peripheral vision.

Stupid test. I bet if they could get away with it, they stick a probe inside me.

He went through a series of questions. "Let's have a break." He turned off the machine, and the needles stopped. "Is something going on today? You seem to have problems." He leaned against the wall, looking down on her.

"No." *And here we go with the insinuations.*

These sidebar comments were not part of the polygraph. One way or another, the test had gotten to every single person she knew.

Stop leering at me, jerk.

"I reviewed all your data and was amazed you came out during the last test."

Reviewing is part of your job. Why are you mentioning this?

The memory of five years ago—snot dripping from her nose as she confessed to being a lesbian—sent a shudder inward. Knowing all of it was on audio and visual made it more horrifying and humiliating.

He cocked his head from side to side as if there was food stuck on her face. "Have you ever hooked up with someone you shouldn't? Someone who might be into illegal things?"

"No." *Asshole. And you're probably a homophobe.*

"Okay, let's go again." He started the test and asked her the same set of required questions.

The standard questions went on and on...Have you ever spied against the government? Have you ever stolen any secrets? Do you have an allegiance to a foreign government? Have you ever advocated the overthrow of the American government?

He stopped the test. Silence hung in the air. He came around and leaned over with his hands on his knees. "Something appears to have upset you. Anything you'd like to tell me? Are you feeling guilty about something? You know Alaina, there really is no need to worry unless you've done something wrong."

I've done nothing wrong. Unhook me.

She looked down at the floor. Anywhere, but in his face.

Ali knew this strong-arm tactic and resolved to remain composed against the accusations, insinuations, and lies. It was like good cop, bad cop, but with one maniacal tester.

"Okay. Let's start the test again." He hurled the standard test questions at her again.

After what seemed an eternity, he stopped and made more comments that deviated from the standard. She knew he was trying to get under her skin, but it felt like a personal assault with a tone she hated. With each comment, Ali sunk deeper into her dark state.

"Alaina, have you done something wrong? Maybe it was as simple as taking home a ream of paper. Have you stolen anything?"

She looked from the tester's eyes to the floor. She could not fend off the assault of feelings and voices deep within. They consumed her...

"Did you steal my beer?"
"No."
"You lying little bitch." The spittle from his mouth
flew into her face.

"Have you ever traded sex for secrets?" The tester was
leaning into her face.
"No."
"Do you have any friends that would ever persuade you to do
something illegal? Maybe you should tell me about your friends."
The ugly voice of her father kept creeping into her mind...

"Who's your friend, Alaina?"
Their kiss stopped.
He laughed as her girlfriend ran from the room.
"Never figured you for a pussy-licking cunt."
Denise skipped into the room. "Daddy, you're
home." *She wrapped her arms around him.*
"Yes, my little daisy. Go play. . ." *He turned back*
to Ali. *"Take care of your sister, or I'll take care of*
you." *He seized his crotch.*

The man snapped his fingers. "What are you thinking
about? We've got a long way before quitting time. How did
your deployments go?"
"Fine."
"I didn't hear you."
"Fine."
"Is there anything that's not in the paperwork?" He
reached for a folder on the desk, making a spectacle of
shuffling through papers. "What about your relationship with
Major Lynn Stewart?"

Her voice was barely above a whisper as she mumbled, "She was in charge of JETT. It's all in the paperwork." In her mind, she screamed, *asshole.*

"You've earned many achievements and awards. With such a stellar background, this should be a breeze for you. Why is today such an issue? Aren't you proud of your work? Or are you trying to hide something?"

"No."

"No to what question? Talk to me, Alaina." He smacked his hand on the desk.

The voice of her father, drunk and mean, roared inside her head. Her mother never kept her safe...

"It was just a small argument, nothing. Go lie down, Eddie."

"Don't tell me what to do, woman! Alaina, sit down. Now!" He looked around. "Where's Denise?"

"She's with friends. Please, Eddie. You've been drinking."

He shoved her mother toward the door. "Go pick her up."

After the click of the deadbolt, he backed Ali into a corner, "I've told you and told you. I don't tolerate this teenager backtalk." He pointed his finger in Ali's face. "You think you're so much better than anyone with your grades. And you want to go to college. What a waste. You're a piece of shit."

Smack.

"You're a carpet-munching whore. You're nothing, and you always will be nothing."

Smack.

"Guess you like the punishment." He pushed her down, her cheek pressed against the floor. She felt his full weight crush on top of her. . .

"You're positive that nothing is wrong?"

Ali shook her head. After all these years, she could still feel the tightness of her swollen face.

"Maybe something about one of your deployments. Did you always go by the book or did you ever break the rules? What about the investigation in the second deployment?"

A tear rolled down her cheek.

"Okay. Let's take a break. Restroom and water fountain are to the left down the hall. When you get back, we're going through the same questions. Think about things. Tell me what's bothering you, then we're going to start again."

His fingers scarcely touched her sides as he unhooked the hoses. Still, she squeezed her eyes tight.

She could feel his glare upon her as she moved to the door. When she turned the doorknob, he put his hand on the door. "I want you to think long and hard about what responses you've given. Cooperating is so much better than punishment."

Punishment. Her father punished her for everything...

She ran for the door.

He lunged and stopped her. "Guess you like the punishment." He pushed her down, her cheek pressed against the floor. She felt his full weight crush on top of her. . .

He released his hand. She yanked the door open. A torrent of tears ran down her face as she inched towards safety. The sound of his footsteps as he trailed her down the hall made her pick up speed. He was close.

"What are you feeling right now?"

"I wish I were dead." She slammed the bathroom door shut and locked it. With her back to the door, she slid to the floor. She drew her knees to her chest and sobbed into them.

He banged on the door. Others came. Their voices faded.

The thumping ceased. Minutes later, it began again. "Ali, it's Dr. Martin. Please let me know you're okay." More thumping. "If you don't respond, we're going to have to force the door open."

Ali recognized the voice of the agency psychologist who had done her last post-deployment assessment.

"I'm okay."

"Good. We need to go downstairs and have a talk."

Ali blew her nose on toilet paper and splashed water on her face. She had no choice. If she stood any hope of keeping her job, she had to bare her soul to the agency psychologist, wait for their assessment, and retake the polygraph. They'd also require her private therapist to submit an evaluation.

⊸❧⊷

Five hours after the polygraph began, Ali walked out of the building with her head down. The cold, cleansing rain soaked her clothes. She crawled inside the refuge of her car and collapsed on the steering wheel.

Her father had been dead almost twenty-four years, but she could not eradicate what he had done. There had been triggers and reactions before, but nothing like today.

Her mother and older siblings didn't like to talk about his drinking or her sexuality. Ali felt utterly alone and abandoned.

If not for her younger sister Denise, Ali would have thought it was all in her mind.

"I hate you, you son of a bitch!" She pounded her fists several times against the steering wheel. "I've tried so fucking hard to put you out of my mind, and you keep haunting me."

The sky opened up, and the rain beat down and stifled her sobs.

Chapter 36

September 2014 – Northern Virginia

Ali reached for her phone and only succeeded in knocking it on the floor. Yawning, she stretched and picked it up.

"Hello."

"Did I wake you?"

"Hey, Paul. Yeah, don't you sleep in on the weekend?"

"Maybe until eight, but it's nearly ten. That's not like you. Are you sick?"

"No. What's up? Got any plans this weekend?" There was a moment of silence. *Oh, shit, he's coming to dinner tonight with his fiancée.*

"You forgot." He chuckled. "Well, I'm sorry to say that we can't make it. Jada's parents crashed our plans."

"Oh. Okay."

"Don't sound so heartbroken." His bellowing laugh made her feel better. "Besides, I found a couple to stand in for us."

"Huh?"

"Trust me. Besides, it sounds like you need some cheering up. Your guests will arrive at six."

"Who are they?"

"I want you to be pleasantly surprised, and they love your BBQ. I have to get back to work. Enjoy the dinner party tonight."

Ali popped out of bed and went straight to the kitchen. She had just enough time to get her boneless country-style ribs seasoned and in the slow cooker. *It's a new day, and I shouldn't be alone. A little company will do me good.* As dinner cooked, she played *Mjoll the Lioness in the Skyrim Special Edition.* Hearing the doorbell, she closed the game, tossed the controllers in the storage bin, then smoothed her clothes.

"Surprise!"

"Oh my God. I can't believe it." She exchanged hugs with her old 2010 deployment buddies, Michele Miller and Jill Cramer.

"Hey girl, how's it going?" Jill grinned wildly.

"Come in." Ali pointed to the sofa. "Make yourselves comfortable." She breathed in the scent of the flowers. "This bouquet is amazing. I love Stargazer lilies."

Michele said, "I had to stop by Fort Meade headquarters on our way to Georgia and saw Paul at a meeting. We were going to call you, then he told us about the busted dinner plans. So, we hatched a plan to surprise you."

"I'm so happy you did."

Paul had been such a dear friend since 2008. Last year, Michele was at Fort Meade for three months of training, and Ali introduced them. Out of all the odd coincidences, it turned out that Michele grew up in the same suburb of Albany, NY as Paul. The only reason they had never run into one another in high school was because of the age difference.

"What's going on in Georgia? Jill, I thought your mom retired and moved to Florida."

"She did." Jill tilted her head at Michele.

"I've been reassigned to Fort Gordon. Jill quit her job and is going to find one down there."

Ali's eyebrows shot up. "Georgia doesn't recognize same-sex marriage, and it's not a gay-friendly place outside of Atlanta. How's the atmosphere on base? I heard conservatives are pushing back and looking for any religiously based excuse to be a thorn in everyone's side."

Jill threw up her hands. "Believe me, anything is better than being back in the military and fighting to be stationed together."

"You don't regret getting out?"

"Hell no. I never thought I'd leave, but Michele's NSA job is definitely the better position. And if I can't find a job, then maybe I'll be a stay at home wifey."

"Ha!" Michele jabbed her finger in Jill's middle. "Over my dead body."

Jill put her arm around her wife and kissed her. Ali loved how the Army's 2010 decision to separate them hadn't dulled their love for one another.

Ali put the food on the table, Jill set glasses of water out, and Michele uncorked and poured the Cabernet. The conversation around dinner was light until the end.

"It's been ages since I've talked with Lynn, but I had to contact her about a project recently." Michele swirled her wine then looked at Ali over the rim.

Ali rose and gathered the plates.

"Ali, the damn dishwasher can wait. Please, let's talk."

Ali sank into the chair and crossed her legs and arms. "What did she say?"

"That you ran into one another at *National Women's Music Festival* in July."

Ali could feel the anger rising up. "Yeah. Weirder than you and Paul being from the same hometown." She flicked her wrist. "What are the chances? Out of all the fucking places, she flies from South Korea to vacation in Wisconsin while I just happen to be there. We ended up barely fifty feet apart. Unbelievable!"

"You've said it's over and she's in a relationship. Why's it still bothering you?"

"Honey, careful," Jill whispered to Michele.

"No, Jill. I think Michele might be right," Ali propped her head in her hand and played with her napkin, "Seeing them all kissy-kissy was..." Ali waded up the napkin. "At one point, the chick had her tongue so far down Lynn's throat that I thought I'd have to come in and administer CPR. And her hand kept cupping Lynn's ass."

"So, why did you watch?"

"I'll turn the question around. Why did she mention it?" Ali tucked a stray strand of hair behind her ear, then crossed her arms.

"Ali, you're my friend, and I'm concerned. Listen to your own voice. You still sound upset."

Ali closed her eyes and took a few deep breaths. "During our deployments, Lynn said she didn't date colleagues and that being outside and away from the base was the only time she was comfortable. Well, I guess since DADT's fallen, she's pretty damn comfortable."

"Don't let memories hold you back. You were the one who went to Australia at the spur of the moment. What was Lynn supposed to do?"

Ali blurted out, "After Evans made his allegation, there were other questions the military asked me. They had claimed to have gathered evidence of Lynn at parties with multiple women. They even read a list of names and asked me if I knew any of the women. And," Ali held up a shaky finger, "if I had ever known Lynn to have a threesome. Do you know how much that hurt?"

"Oh Ali, I'm so sorry." Michele grabbed Ali's hand.

"You know the military background investigators sometimes come up with crap to see what the reaction might be." Jill leaned back in her chair. "Someone with a grudge could have told some crazy story. Obviously, they didn't find anything solid because the Air Force promoted her."

"Yeah, but she's such a workaholic. I thought Lynn would be in a rocker before she would change and come out."

"So true, but she's not the only workaholic," Jill smirked.

"Point taken, but you know it comes with the job. Oh, please don't tell Paul. You guys are the only ones I've told."

"We won't say a word," Jill said and bumped her wife's arm. "It's getting late, we should hit the road."

"No way! You're spending the night. It's pouring."

Jill said, "If you don't mind."

"But we need to leave at the crack of dawn," Michele added.

"No problem. I don't get to see enough of you guys, and my spare bedroom is roomy."

"Terrific. Thanks, Ali."

"So, have you been dating?" Jill waggled her eyebrows. "Ouch!" She turned to her wife. "What was that for?"

"You tell me not to talk about Lynn and you nosey-in on her dating."

Jill shrugged and smiled. "I just don't want Ali to be alone."

Ali threw her head back and laughed. "You two are hopeless snoops, but I love you. I know Paul can't keep his big mouth shut and talks to Michele all the time." She flicked her hand. "I go to a women's dinner group once a month and a dance every so often. I've met a couple of interesting prospects, but no, Miss Nosey, I haven't met anyone who has swept me away." Ali got up and picked up another bottle. Waving it in the air, she said, "Since you're spending the night, let's have a second bottle. Oh, I also have the movie *Gravity*. Have you seen it?"

"That's a good one. I saw it last year, but Michele hasn't seen it."

Michele rolled her eyes. "You know Jill goes for anything sci-fi."

Jill walked over to the TV and waved a DVD in the air. A giant smile lit her face. "Looks a lot better than *Gravity*, but it won't play on an American DVD player." Jill slid the cabinet open. "Oh, you have two players."

"A work colleague gave me her used player and some European DVDs." Ali took a healthy swig of wine.

"A love prospect? I'm sure the cuddling during this was fun."

"Jill, leave her alone."

"No. Just a friend. We never watched them together."

"If you are watching *Lip Service* alone, then you need to get laid. Tell me. Is it the British and Scottish accents or is it a fascination with Frankie? There are some differences, but she kind of looks like Lynn, except Frankie's hair's straight."

Ali felt her face flush. "Put in the damn sci-fi movie."

Chapter 37

October 2014 – Osan Air Base, South Korea

"I'm sorry ma'am, but we had to bounce you for the VIP. We'll get you on the next one. Sorry, it'll be a couple of hours."

"Thank you, Airman." *Frak, I hope I don't miss my connection.*

"Ma'am, I see you have a Battlestar Galactica book. I'm a fan. My love of the original TV series rubbed off on me from my parents."

Lynn wasn't old enough to be his parent, but she felt like it.

"Yes. You have a good day, Airman."

The music in the background switched to oldies from the 1950s. "Earth Angel" began playing. She only knew the song because it was one of her grandmother's favorites.

Glancing over her itinerary, she noticed one meeting with no subject was tacked on at the last minute. From the attendees, Lynn suspected it was to discuss a new assignment. The Air Force had already taken the unusual step of extending her tour. *But why four days of meetings? Why can't this be done via video telecommunications?*

She tossed the paperwork back into her briefcase. No use in second-guessing the powers that be. Despite the meetings, the extra leave at the trip's end would give her time to clear her head after the breakup with her girlfriend. The two had been together for almost two years, but it wasn't working. After stretching, she opened her laptop to research easy-care perennial plants and flowers. Rose rosette disease had wiped out her aunt's beloved roses, and Lynn had promised to sketch out some ideas for a new garden.

Lynn paused and closed her eyes. A vision of Ali among the roses, her head tilted and a mischievous smile and brown chestnut eyes peeking out from auburn hair, made Lynn swallow. Nearly six years after that first deployment, and she still couldn't forget the way she felt when strolling through the garden with Ali. The aura of tranquility mixed with lust when she had held that rose petal for Ali to smell. The scent of the roses still lingered in her mind. Whenever Lynn caught a whiff of scented roses on a woman's perfume, she always turned and hoped to see Ali.

That didn't end well either. Stop daydreaming and plan the garden.

After searching for nearly an hour and making a list of choices, Lynn started looking for professional designers. She knew her aunt couldn't afford that, but Lynn decided to pay for the service as a gift.

Her fingers stilled on the keyboard, and her heart practically stopped. There was a picture of a gorgeous redhead with a man. Their arms draped over each other's shoulders. Lynn's gut twisted into a pretzel. *Is Ali married? No, she can't be. Maybe she's bi.* Lynn felt like her breakfast was going to come up. *Stop, you jealous idiot.*

She took a breath and read on, "Ms. Clairmont helps with her cousin's home renovation business and has won local gardening awards." *Oh, thank God.*

Staring at Ali's picture, the raw emotions came roaring back. Ali was intelligent, honest, and oh-so damn sexy from

Chapter 38

January 2015 – NGA Headquarters, Springfield, Virginia

A fter the busy holiday season, 2015 had started off as a good year. Ali had passed the second polygraph a week ago without a meltdown, and yesterday, she had been nominated for an award on a work project.

Strolling down the division hallway, she heard, "Ali, can I please have a word with you."

"Yes, sir."

"Please sit down." The division chief's face was blank as he motioned to the chair.

Without looking up, Dave Curtis flatly said, "Your Branch Chief doesn't want to let you go."

Are they moving me? Is something wrong?

After letting her dangle for a few seconds, he cracked a smile. "We need you to slide over as the temporary senior analyst next month."

"Excuse me? What about Dory?"

"She will be out for a couple of weeks, then returning on limited hours. Her job is too important to leave open. So, do you accept?"

"Sure." She hoped the waver in her voice was not detectable.

"Ali, your papers have gotten a lot of attention, and you're one of our best briefers. Since your commitment to the briefing class has ended, I need you to step up and work with the division junior analysts, especially with their writing skills. And who knows? If all goes well, there may be a promotion around the corner. Go back and talk to Dory. You have two weeks to learn from her before stepping into her shoes."

"Yes, sir. Thank you."

He chuckled and held out his hand. "Please, it's Dave."

Feeling elated, Ali walked out with a bit of a bounce in her step. As she rounded the corner, a young woman was with Dory. The dazed analyst walked away, and the edits on her paper seemed to bleed off the page.

"How can I help you?" Dory peered over her glasses.

Ali moved closer. "Division wants me to...ah...fill in for you." *The words stammering from my mouth probably aren't a good impression.* Ali rubbed her palms on her pant legs.

"Does that make you nervous?" Dory asked.

"No."

Hell, yes, I'm nervous, but I'll never admit it. Dory held three master's degrees and had a good forty years of experience between the military and the agency. No one knew for sure what Dory's job was in the military, but rumors had it that she was involved in PSYOPs.

Directors had come and gone at NGA and its predecessor agencies, and Dory was on a first name basis with many of them. In fact, the rumor was that being on Dory's shit list was one of the worst places to be in the entire Intelligence Community.

"I...ah...have two weeks to shadow you and learn the basics."

"Well, we had better start first thing tomorrow."

"Yes." Ali licked her lips. "Are you okay with this?"

"With your appointment?"

Ali nodded.

"I should hope so. I was the one who recommended you. Don't look so dumbfounded. Sure, you have a lot to learn, but have you looked around? We're short on experienced people. Your attention to detail and research are tops." Dory loudly tapped her index finger on the table. "And note—Dave demands concise projects on schedule, and he always does his best to keep us out of the political crossfire. Seek his opinion often."

"Sounds good."

"See you tomorrow at six sharp." Dory turned to her computer and started typing.

Ali waved and began to walk away.

"Oh, one more thing." Ali turned, but Dory didn't skip a beat at the keyboard. She said, "Wear some practical shoes and comfortable clothes tomorrow. You're going to go to every meeting with me. I'm going to cram as much as possible in that head of yours, and soon, it will be spinning like Regan's in the Exorcist."

Dory stopped her typing, and folded her hands. Her mouth formed a crocked grin. "Now, should you accept this assignment, the offer will self-destruct in a few weeks." Her low voice was worthy of an Emmy. "Should you be caught messing up, this senior intelligence officer will disavow any and all knowledge of your activities. Good luck!" She cackled like an evil witch. "Check your email because I'm sending you some documents and will be quizzing you tomorrow." Her smile lingered.

"Thanks, Dory."

"Oh, you'll thank me for taking back the avalanche of work when I return. However, I have been on their case for an assistant. Make us proud, and I might insist that you get that position." Warmth as well as mischief shown in Dory's eyes.

Ali strolled back and spent the next couple of hours poring over the documents. As it neared the time to leave, she swiveled around in her chair. Snow was falling. The flakes were huge and glorious as they floated to the ground. Traffic would be a mess, but nothing could put a damper on Ali's mood.

Chapter 39

The video conference with the Brits went over schedule and did not run as smoothly as usual. With the bluster of the new president, who knew how much longer the British would be sharing their intelligence. Now, she was running late for a two-thirty meeting suddenly called by the division chief.

She pivoted sharply around the corner and almost knocked a woman over. "Sorry," Ali mouthed and kept on.

Her footsteps made uneven thuds on the thin industrial carpet, but she refused to let her slight limp slow her down. Her stride had never been the same after taking a fall downhill skiing last winter. *Good grief, am I ever going to make it out of here on time?*

She punched in the code and entered. One of the branch chiefs motioned to an empty seat, and she squeezed past the crowd. Even the side filing cabinets were doubling as seating. Ali became the fulltime senior analyst last year after Dory was promoted. The day was always long and seemed to be filled with endless meetings.

"Thanks for saving me a seat."

"You're welcome."

Ali focused on the division chief sitting about ten feet away, and her heart stopped. Next to him in a blue silk blouse, the same shade as her eyes, was Lynn. Except for some crow's feet and laugh lines, Lynn's face hadn't changed much. Her naturally sandy blonde hair was longer, right above the collar and more styled in waves.

Ali opened her notebook, wrote the date, and doodled. Never in a million years did she expect to be working with Lynn again, especially in the third largest government building in the Washington D.C. area.

The assistant dimmed the lights to get everyone's attention, and Division Chief Dave Curtis rose. "Our deputy division chief slot has been empty for several months. The director has selected a candidate through the inter-agency Joint Duty Assignment." He gestured at Lynn, "Effective immediately, Lynn Stewart from Cyber Command will be the new deputy division chief. Lynn, please introduce yourself."

Ali closed her notebook.

"Good afternoon..."

People milled around to welcome Lynn afterward, but Ali jumped up and rushed out the door. When she reached her desk, she threw her notebook in the drawer, powered off the computer, and marched to the garage.

—⸿⸿∩⸿⸿—

Inching down Shirley Highway toward Washington D.C., Ali slapped the steering wheel with her hand. Besides her knee, her whole body ached today.

"Damn you, Lynn! Fucking damn you! Why do you keep coming back into my life?" Tears pooled. She wiped them away, but it was no use. More came, and she couldn't stop the mascara from running.

"Fantastic. I look like a bad Johnny Depp pirate." The older man in the car next to her gawked. "I might as well continue to talk to myself since I look certifiably crazy."

She turned on the radio, and WTOP announced that traffic into D.C. was being forced off at King Street because of a bad accident. Creeping off the exit ramp, she could see emergency vehicles and police around a jackknifed tractor trailer and two vehicles. The ambulance slowly driving away with flashing lights and no sound was ominous.

Her cell rang. She took a deep breath and punched the Bluetooth answer button.

Tracy's voice shrieked, "Where are you? You're late! Are you even showing?"

Ali ground her teeth before answering. "It is President's Day weekend."

"Stop right there. You promised. One, you wouldn't work as much, and two, that you'd spend more time with me!"

"I'm not the one scheduling dinner ten minutes from my office. I can't set my own hours like you."

"Look, Ali. Do you even want a girlfriend? No, don't even answer that question!" Tracy's voice screamed, "You're probably screwing someone else at work."

Ali's response was a quiet voice. "You've falsely accused me of dating someone else before. I'm through with the accusations and the way you treat me. Good luck, Ice Queen. You can have your castle all to yourself. I'll get my things when it's convenient for me." Ali cut off the call. *Not exactly how I anticipated ending things, but it was an overdue train wreck.*

They had had a few arguments over the past year, but nothing like the raging firestorms lately. Ali was steadily growing uncomfortable with Tracy's increasing alcohol consumption and controlling behavior.

"No more!" She banged her hand on the steering wheel again.

Her stomach growled as she passed the Village of Shirlington, which had some of the best restaurants. She cut through a nearby neighborhood, thinking it would be faster, but accidentally turned down a dead-end street. A 'For Sale by Owner' caught her attention. Her eyes studied the property. It was in terrible shape and stuck out among the surrounding immaculate houses.

Buying so soon would be a rash decision, but after partnering with her cousin, their renovation projects had always made a profit, especially the last two.

"I need to stretch my legs anyway," She mumbled to herself.

She rubbed her knee and limped up to the doorway. As her hand reached up to knock, the door opened.

A frail man said, "Can I help you?"

"Hi. I saw your sign. Any chance I could take a quick peek?"

The old man had a grim look and hesitated. A woman stepped behind him and said, "We were about to leave, but Dad, let's give her ten minutes to walk through." He stepped aside and mustered a weak smile.

The house smelled stale with lingering cigarette smoke as if the windows hadn't been opened in years, and the carpet was heavily stained. The furniture, out of the eighties, was encased in see-through plastic covers. The fireplace hearth was separating and crumbling. Ali moved into the kitchen and tripped on the cracked linoleum flooring but caught herself before falling. The pine cabinets and appliances dated from at least the sixties.

The kitchen back door opened to a deck that needed sanding and staining. The backyard was in decent shape.

"The pond is Dad's pride and joy." The woman pointed to the corner of the lot. "He put in a new pump last year."

Ali gawked. The garden pond had to be at least sixteen feet long.

The woman thrust an information sheet into Ali's hand. "We're asking two hundred and ninety-five thousand cash. We need to close fast." The old man grimaced at his daughter's cold words. "After Sunday, we're not taking any more bids. Act fast if you're interested. You need to go now."

"How many bids do you have?" Ali had to ask as they walked to the front door.

"Several." The woman said curtly.

"Thank you for your time."

Back in the car, Ali ran a search, then dialed her cousin.

"Hey, Crazster. What's up?"

"Scott, I've found a three-bedroom split-level with a basement, attached garage, and a garden pond."

"Which needs more work, the interior or exterior?"

"Both are a disaster, and there are possible foundation issues. They want all bids in by Sunday."

"Whoa! No way."

"It's less than two miles from Shirlington."

"That's an ideal location, but even with my magnificent carpenter skills and your artsy-fartsy designs, you have got to be out of your freaking mind. It may be a good deal, but I'm not interested in investing in something that needs that much work. It would stretch my resources and time."

Ali chewed on her lip. "I want to buy it for myself. I have the cash and an extra two hundred thousand for reno. The time can be stretched out over six months or longer. Please Scott. I need your help in fixing it up."

"Oh, you know Miss Fancy Pants won't stand for a dump.

Are you sure your brain isn't fried? And where's this going to leave you if you blow all your cash reserve?"

"I need my own space again. Fixing up a place gives me a feeling of accomplishment."

He laughed. "Are you still with her?"

"No. Please, Scott. I've googled the numbers on comps and an empty lot. It's worth the risk. Are you with me?" Ali could hear him fretting. "Pretty please with sugar on it."

"You're my favorite cuz, Alaina. I don't know how much time I can give you, but I'll help. Are you sure this is the right decision?"

"Stop worrying about me."

"Habit."

Scott cleared his throat, "By the way, where are you sleeping if Tracy's out of the picture?" After she didn't answer, he said, "Spend the night with us. It's close to your job. If you get here early enough, you can help Brooke with her AP Calculus. It's her only non-A." He chuckled. "God knows she didn't get her smarts from me. She surpassed me long ago."

"Sure. Thanks, Scott."

Ali texted her real estate broker. *Need bid with an escalation clause by Sunday. Property will be my home. Broke up with Tracy.*

The reply read, *It's a holiday weekend. Good thing you're a dear friend. Email me the details, and I'll get it done. Congrats on dumping uptight Ms. Prissy.*

Ali tore open a granola bar with her teeth and turned the car around. "Today's a new beginning. Let's have some music." Punching in her favorite station at the stop sign, she took a drink of water. "Hell, yeah!"

She sang, "Wo-o-o-o-oh, wo-o-o-o-o-oh..." along to the lyrics of "Best Day of My Life" by American Authors while drumming her fingers on the steering wheel. The song finished. "Yep, moving on and never looking back."

Chapter 40

April 2017 – Northern Virginia

"**B**oy are you lucky," Scott smirked. "I know. It's a great buy. Cost me a bit more with the escalation clause, but it's worth it." Ali motioned at the mess. "It's a challenge, but the bones of the house are solid."

"Yes, on the house, but what I meant is, I snagged someone to help with the reno on the weekends." Scott was all smug, grinning and waggling his eyebrows. "I think she's a lesbian, and she lives two streets over. Joe who worked on that Springfield property, you remember last year, introduced us."

"No fixing me up!"

"I wouldn't dream of it." Biting his lip did nothing to hide the silly grin. "Besides, my crew is busy for the next two months, and beyond demo, you can't do shit. You even require supervision with that."

"Hey, I'm good at painting and design, and I'm an award-winning landscape designer."

"You mean flower garden design with the garden club?" His wicked grin lit up his eyes, and Ali lovingly punched him on his muscled shoulder. "Ah, Crazster. I love ya, but there is a lot of work here that you can't do. You need help with your bum knee, and my schedule is packed." He stuck his hands in his pockets and rocked on his toes. "Be on your best behavior because she's dropping by in fifteen."

"Dammit, Scott."

"Think positive. She's cute, and you might get lucky."

"I'm not dating! And it would be awkward with her living in the neighborhood." Ali leaned on the banister, which started to give way. Scott caught her as it snapped and crashed. Her eyes wide, she stared at the pile of wood below. "Okay. I need help. How do you know she does good work?"

"She inherited the house from her aunt and has been living in it while renovating it top to bottom. Joe swears by her. The best part—she's does wood working even though she's a desk jockey like you through the week."

"Where does she work?"

"Don't know, but judging from the lower level bedroom she turned into a library, she's some sort of important professional. She had a history and an electrical engineering book on the coffee table by the window."

Ali rubbed her chin. "And what were you doing in her library? Having tea and crumpets?"

"Joe told her I was a carpenter, and she gave me a tour. Made the bookshelves herself out of walnut. Simple but a thing of beauty. Oh, and she did her own kitchen cabinets. I'm telling you, she's the real deal and seems kindhearted. Not like the wackos you usually manage to attract."

Ali walked into the kitchen. "Does she know I can't pay top dollar? Or did you neglect to mention that."

"I told her you had a breakup and were getting back on your feet."

Ali flung her head back. "Oh my God, how much did you reveal?"

"That's it. Besides, it gives you an advantage."

"Yeah and makes me look like a damsel in distress looking for a sugar mama."

Scott bit his lip. "Oh, the only project she has left on her house is landscaping. I told her you might exchange that for her skills."

"Ohhhh...You're so dead, dude."

"Come on. It won't hurt you to make friends with your neighbor. And you know it was over for months with Tracy." He laughed and went about taking measurements.

—◦◦◦◦—

Scott grinned as he opened the door. "Please come in. My cousin's in the backyard, enjoying the sunshine while sketching some designs."

The smell hit Lynn immediately. Though the windows were open, the musty smell mixed with smoke was strong. There was a hole in the wall into the kitchen. The fireplace hearth was falling apart. If this were any indication of the rest of the house, it would be a lot of time and hard work.

"You didn't mention this was a total gut job."

"It's a challenge, but that's what makes it fun. And my cousin is excellent at interior and landscape design but struggles with the other."

Lynn could see Scott was a charmer a mile away. He didn't say his cousin was a lesbian, but she got the feeling Scott was trying to play matchmaker. The blue sports car parked in front of his truck prominently displayed the HRC "=" sticker in the rear window and probably belonged to Scott's cousin. Also, knowing Joe's fat mouth, he probably outed Lynn to Scott.

They stepped into the kitchen and past the old pine cabinets. "Does this Chambers gas range still work?"

"Ah, I don't know. Too afraid to turn it on. Is it an antique?"

"Sure is. Model C series from the late 1960s. Looks in decent shape."

Lynn crouched down and had her head in the main compartment and ignored the kitchen screen door slamming.

"Lynn, I'd like you to meet my cousin, Alaina."

She backed out of the oven and turned to meet the homeowner. Ali's beautiful face was before her. She had forgotten Alaina was her formal first name. Seeing Ali brought back a rush of warm feelings, but when Ali's mouth turned into a scowl, Lynn's heart sank.

As they stared at each other in silence, Scott's head whipped back and forth. "You two know one another?"

Ali backed up and spun out the door.

"Ali, wait!" Lynn pleaded.

"Please leave," Ali shouted over her shoulder.

Lynn ran after her. "Please, Ali! Please talk to me."

Ali walked to the shed and proceeded to arrange garden tools. "I'm busy, so make it quick."

Lynn's brain fumbled for a reply and finally blurted out, "I never had feelings for anyone the way I did for you."

"Excuse me?" Ali's sharp tone cut like a knife.

"I chose my career. I was a scared chicken shit. I should have told you how I felt from the beginning. If I had it to do over again, I'd choose you."

"You'd choose me, huh. Aren't you forgetting a few things? One, your girlfriend. Two, I haven't been exactly waiting around for your return. Three, you're my fucking boss again!"

"Cynthia and I broke up some time ago." Lynn felt the old scars of regret and shame. "The mistakes I made were awful, and I can't take them back, but I've had plenty of time to think and shape up my life. You probably don't want anything to do with me, but I hope you can forgive me. I'd at least like to be your friend."

"Friends? Do I have to repeat myself? You're my boss!"

Lynn put her hands back behind her head and rubbed her hair several times. "I think about you all the time. I intended to contact you once I got settled, and never imagined they would assign me to your division. It was sheer coincidence."

"Coincidence or not, seeing you at work will be difficult enough. There's no way you're helping on my house." She stood with her hands on her hips. "I admire your knowledge and how you execute and handle tough intelligence problems, but outside of work, your life is a disaster. Please leave."

Lynn swallowed. "I'm sorry, Ali. Please believe me."

"At NGA, I'll work with you and be polite, but that's it. I don't want any contact outside of work."

Lynn turned and walked away. *The best thing in my life, and I fucked it up.*

—⁓⁓⁓—

Sitting on the bench next to the pond, Ali mindlessly stared at the cost analysis paperwork for the reno.

"You okay?" Scott asked.

"Yep."

"Got more than one word to say."

"No."

"It's unlike you to keep things from me. I'm your straight male cousin, but aren't I your best buddy?"

Ali didn't look up or say another word.

"Okay, Crazster. I have to check on the other job. Call me if you want."

The tears welled in her eyes, but she was hell-bent on not letting him see her lose it. "Sure."

As she watched the setting sun, her thin jacket no longer kept out the chill.

Chapter 41

April 2017 – NGA Headquarters, Springfield, Virginia

A li tapped on the door and stepped into Dory's new office. "Welcome back. Do you have a few minutes?"

"For you? Always." Dory motioned around the room. "You'll have to excuse the boxes. I've been too busy to unpack."

After carefully mulling over what she wanted to say, the words wouldn't come out. She took the time to move a small box out of the seat across from Dory's desk. "Nice office."

"Hmmm. The shades of white and gray aren't extremely cheery, but it will do. I can't believe my trip turned into three months. You think we've got problems here, you should spend time with our colleagues out in the field. There are many days that I hate being at this level of management—too much political 'grin and bear it.' Why the long face?"

"The new deputy division chief."

"The retired lieutenant colonel." Dory stopped twiddling her thumbs. "Ohhh..." Her eyes widened. "She's the one?"

"Yeah."

"Oh. My. God. I'd argue to take you with me, but I'm afraid you've made a name for yourself. They're not going to let you move for the foreseeable future. Sorry. As for your personal life, Tracy is a rough ride, but gives you a good excuse. You'd never cheat."

Dory was laying it on thick. Ali drew in a deep breath and let it go. "We broke up."

"At last." Dory's mouth turned into a rueful smile as she poured hot tea into cups. "Hope it wasn't too painful." The look said to Ali the words she knew that Dory would never speak—*I told you so.*

"No. I was going to end it but hadn't made my move yet."

"And what about the new deputy? Maybe Lynn has changed since leaving the military?"

Ali's head whipped up. "She's my boss! Again!"

Dory took another sip. "Yes. So, why let something from years ago bother you if it's not a problem? You must work together, and you're both adults. Seek common ground, apologize, and move on."

"I'm not the one who needs to apologize!"

Dory held up one finger and paused. Instead of chastising Ali, she rummaged through a box and retrieved a bag of cookies. Ali declined the offer. Dory took a couple. After taking a bite, she said, "It's the thought that counts. I'm sure Lynn carries much of the blame, but it does take two to tango. Be the bigger person. Go smooth things over. I hate to point out the obvious, but holding onto bitterness is unbecoming, and others will notice if your positive personality turns sour. They will gossip. Lastly, your work will suffer if you don't dump the negativity."

Ali bit her lip and threw her head back, then leaned onto Dory's desk. "There's something else."

Dory rocked in her chair. "Yesss. Go on."

"I bought a house while you were away on TDY. For myself."

"And that's a problem why?"

"My cousin's friend found this handywoman that lived around the corner. Care to guess who she is?"

Dory's hand flew to cover her mouth, and she giggled. After getting the laughter under control, she leaned back. "Well, that takes the cake. You had better find a way to be civil or your life will end up utter hell for the next year."

"I need her help at the house," Ali stared at her feet, "but I'm not sure how we'll get along. One minute, I want to punch her lights out, and the next, I want to kiss her." The volume of Ali's voice trailed off at the last words.

"She is rather dashing. And if she's the professional you described, then she will point out the conflict of interest and remove herself."

Ali nodded.

"Look Ali. Regardless, patch things up. For now, you have to work with her. If you become more than friends," Dory waved her hand, "you can worry about which one needs to move on to another office. And always keep your private life outside of work, and not like what happened last week."

"What happened last week?"

Dory scrunched her eyes tight and shook her head. "Let's just say that one high-level person should have his butt fired. Apparently, he doesn't care if cameras are in the parking garage."

"You're kidding?"

"And it wasn't with his fiancée."

It dawned on her who Dory was talking about. "That's why she threw the engagement ring at him and told him off in the coffee shop! News of their fight spread like wildfire."

"Pretend I didn't tell you that story and don't spread their names around. My point is, do your job and maintain decorum. If you lose control of your heart, don't lose control of your brain and act irrationally in the office. And for God's sake, lose the negativity." Dory pointed at the clock on the side wall. "Time is marching on. I have an appointment coming in at five. You'd better hurry because it is with the new illustrious Ms. Lynn Stewart."

Ali jumped out of the chair. "Thanks for the advice."

"Anytime."

Chapter 42

May 2017 – Northern Virginia

The strong smell of coffee urged Ali to get up. Her eyes fluttered open to the exposed ceiling joists, and the two new beams that would support the weight of the new layout of the upstairs living area.

Get moving.

As she swung her feet out from under the covers, the cool basement air sprung her to life. She dashed to the bathroom.

From the toilet, her living quarters sprawled before her—a bed, a single nightstand, a rollaway clothes rack, and loads of boxes packed with her possessions. In the far corner, a dinky makeshift kitchen with a coffee maker and toaster on a small table next to a small refrigerator and utility sink. She was thankful Scott's crew got the basics done so she could move into the basement, but there was still so much to be done.

"I need this basement studded and drywalled first, starting with the bathroom. This is driving me nuts. Where's the towel?"

She flung her hands to shake off the water, then jumped into worn jeans and a sweatshirt, slipped on her work boots, and shuffled over to the automatic coffee maker. With a mug of steaming brew in her hand, she traversed the old pine stairs and took stock of what needed to be done.

Yesterday, Scott looked like the grim reaper when he dropped off the tools necessary to demolish the non-load-bearing walls marked with a big X. She had helped him with this type of work a zillion times but had never worked alone.

Gazing down at the sledgehammer, reciprocating saw, and circular saw, she remembered his words, "Look Crazster. I tease you a lot, but you know what you're doing." He shook his finger in her face. "But even pros screw up a time or two. Don't cut off a damn finger."

Thud, thud, thud.

"Geez, I haven't even started yet, and he's checking up on me."

Thud, thud, thud.

"Coming!"

She stretched, and popped her knuckles before swinging the door wide.

"What are you doing here? It's seven thirty."

"Seven fifty, and I get it. You hate me. You have a right to, and we'll probably never be friends again. A day hasn't gone by that I haven't felt guilty for my mistakes, but you need help now. Scott can't spare anyone." Lynn motioned to the truck. "He sent me with this load of supplies. If you want me to leave after I unload, then fine, but please let me help you. I could work on a different part of the house, and we wouldn't have to see one another."

"That's still fraternizing." Ali crossed her arms tightly.

"Not anymore. I spoke with the director and explained that it would be best if they moved me because of personal reasons between us."

Ali's hands flew to her hips, and her face scrunched up. "You had no right!"

"Look, I didn't go into details. The words 'personal reasons' were enough. He's friends with Admiral Kent. And yes, disclosing a conflict of interest is required and the right thing to do."

Ali attempted to shut the door, but Lynn jammed her boot into the opening.

"Please, Ali. I'm not asking to start a relationship again. We don't have to become friends if you don't want to. Let me work for forgiveness. I'll help for free on weekends. It's the least I can do for you. Besides, your cousin will be pissed if I bring the truck back full. He needs it empty for a job after lunch."

Ali sucked in a deep breath and stepped aside. "Fine. Unload then help me with demolition. It'll work faster with the two of us. Tomorrow, be here no earlier than eight thirty."

"You got it."

For the next two weekends, they worked with only small talk. Lynn still had hope.

Zip. Zip. She screwed the subfloor sheathing to the floor joists.

Ali walked in and leaned up against the door, watching her. "Good thing Scotty sent three workers this week. I didn't think things would be that tough."

"Yes. And thankfully, there were no surprises to add to the timeline."

"Did you watch *The Walking Dead* last night?"

Zip. Zip. "Yes. It was different."

"I sometimes hide my eyes at the squirmy stuff, but I like to see how the different characters react to stress." Ali shrugged. "Sort of like a release valve for my own steam."

"That makes sense." Lynn chuckled. "I just never would have guessed you'd be into zombie shows." She reached into her tool belt but came up empty. "Can you hand me the box of screws over there?"

"I think it's interesting how they all need each other to survive." Ali handed her the box, and their fingers touched.

"Thank you." Lynn continued to work even though the touch had sent a tingle down her spine.

"You're almost done."

"Yes, about another hour. It helps that this is the only room that needed the subfloor replaced."

"Want to grab a quick bite of dinner when you finish?"

The piece of sheathing slipped out of Lynn's hand. She snatched her finger away before it got pinched. "Sounds good. I'm hungry."

Ali thumbed over her shoulder. "Okay. I'm going to sit out by the pond."

Lynn took a moment and smiled. The offer was the first solid step towards reconstructing their friendship. Happy, she whistled a tune as she maneuvered another piece into place.

A shrill, piercing scream came from the backyard. She dropped the heavy-duty screwdriver and ran to the kitchen door only to see Ali racing toward her. Lynn barely got out of the way as Ali came blasting through.

"What's wrong? Are you hurt?" Her hand was on Ali's shoulder, and her eyes skimmed her body looking for an injury.

Ali sputtered out, "Big snake," between labored breaths.

"Did you get bit?" Lynn sunk to her knees looking at Ali's legs for any indication that her skin had been penetrated.

"No, but it was big. It's coiled in the grass near the pond."

"Calm your breaths. Do you have a square point shovel?"

"Shed. Right side. Hanging up on the pegboard." Ali's eyes were wide. "You're going after it?"

"Yes."

"Let me get my camera." Ali whipped around and disappeared.

One minute, she's wailing and running into the house, and another, she wants to capture the moment in a picture.

Carrying the shovel out of the shed, Lynn saw Ali creeping toward the pond with eyes cast downward, scanning over the grass. Lynn wanted to shout, *Watch out. It's next to you,* but that would be too cruel. A few snorts through Lynn's nose gave away her humor at Ali's expense.

"Did it move?" Ali was still scanning.

Lynn couldn't hide the smile, and more laughter escaped. Ali gave her a scowl. "It's not funny."

"You know most snakes are non-venomous and people misidentify them all the time." Lynn's words were only met by a deeper frown. "Okay, Ali. Let's go see what kind of snake is sunbathing on your lawn."

With Ali tiptoeing behind her, Lynn approached the pond.

"That's your snake?"

Ali nodded and furiously took pictures a good ten feet back.

Lynn tossed the shovel aside and picked up a nearby stick. Pinning the snake behind the head, she picked it up and held it out toward Ali. "It's an Eastern Black Rat Snake. Non-venomous and a beneficial species to have around. Come closer, and you can see it has round eyes and no triangular head." The snake wiggled about, clearly irritated.

"Put that thing down."

Lynn laughed loudly. "It's a two-foot-long, harmless baby. I'm going to put it back."

"What! Are you crazy?"

"Ali, calm down. They're harmless and eat rodents." The snake's body was now moving vigorously.

"I don't have rats. Maybe mice occasionally."

"They're tearing down an old apartment building along Four Mile Run. It was an old building, and rats scatter into the surrounding area when their nests are disturbed. This guy is saving the neighborhood from being infested."

Ali shook her finger. "You should put him down before he bites you."

"He can't get to me the way I'm holding him, and I know how to handle him. You sure you don't want to touch him while I have a good grip on his head?" Lynn wanted to laugh again upon seeing the grimace on Ali's face. "Are you going to take some pictures or just stand there?"

Ali snapped a few shots. "They don't bite if they're non-venomous?"

"Oh, they can bite when irritated."

"How are you going to put him down without getting bit?"

"Watch." Lynn gently put the snake back in the grass pointing toward the trees, released her grip and swiftly stepped back. The snake slithered away as Ali snapped more photos.

"The boys used to dare me to catch snakes when I was a kid. I went to the library and learned everything I could. The bite from non-venomous ones will hurt, but they won't kill you. Do you know what a venomous Copperhead looks like?"

"Yeah, but not up close."

"It's the one you have to worry about around here." Lynn pointed to the stacked firewood. "They like wood piles."

Ali shook her upper body with an over dramatized effect. "Call me a fraidy cat, but snakes give me the creeps."

"But you like to hike?"

"I know Virginia has over thirty species of snakes, but hopefully they don't want to see me just as much as I don't want to see them. Enough of the snake talk. Please wash your hands."

Lynn held out her hands and scrunched her fingers like a monster, then stepped toward Ali.

"Don't you dare touch me."

Lynn growled and lunged. Ali sprinted away with Lynn on her heels. By the time they reached the deck, Lynn was bent over laughing.

Ali turned on the nearby hose. "Rinse your hands."

"Yes ma'am." Lynn rubbed underneath the cool water. "Is that good enough?" She squinted to look up at Ali.

"No."

Lynn's eyes snapped shut as cool water sprayed on her face and soaked her shirt. "Oh, that's war." She grabbed the end and forced it in Ali's direction.

"No fair. You're stronger."

Ali dropped her grip and ran. Lynn chased her until the hose wouldn't stretch anymore. Laughing at each other in the middle of the yard, Ali stepped forward and slipped. Lynn moved in to finish her off.

Ali raised her hands up to protect her face. "I give up. You win."

Lynn dropped the hose and ran up to turn it off. Despite the fact they were soaking wet in a breezy afternoon, she felt elated.

"Oh my." Ali brushed her pants, but it was useless.

"Oops, sorry about your muddy jeans."

"I started it. All in good fun." Ali's grin was wide. "I'll grab us some towels and fresh T-shirts and sweatpants. Scott left a pair the other day that should fit you. I washed them. And we probably should order delivery. How about your favorite Greek restaurant? I'll buy."

"Ah, bribing me with food works every time."

Lynn watched the sway of Ali's hips as she walked away, and the sensation of warmth spread through her.

They shared more laughs through the evening as they ate on the back deck. Their friendship was getting back on track. Deep inside, Lynn hoped for more.

"Thanks for everything, Lynn."

"You're welcome. It's getting late." She rose and pushed in her chair. "I'll see you tomorrow morning."

"Oh, I forgot to tell you. My niece's birthday party is tomorrow." She pulled a key off her ring. "Here. Let yourself in."

The fact that Ali trusted her with the key put another smile on Lynn's lips.

Ali snapped her fingers. "The party should be done by two. Wanna play hooky and blow off the house tomorrow? We could hike around Lake Accotink."

Lynn leaned her hand on the doorway above Ali's head and smiled broadly. "I'd love to."

Chapter 43

May 2017 – Lake Accotink, Springfield, Virginia

They stopped at a cluster of wild blue phlox that flourished along a small stream. The sun filtered down through the canopy of deciduous trees, allowing just the right amount of sunlight for the fragrant flowers to grow. The nearby stream gurgling over rocks was the only sound.

Lynn watched Ali crouch on her knees and snap some pictures. *You're gorgeous among the flowers.*

"I often come out here on days off. Most people do the hour power hike, but they miss a lot. I take my time. Isn't it gorgeous?"

"Yes, and the scent is lovely as well." Lynn cleared her throat. "What about those snakes?"

"I've seen a couple. One was lying across the trail. I didn't finish that day."

They walked to a hilltop with a vantage point of the lake. A few people were enjoying the day in canoes. The silence was peaceful.

"We'll have to rent a canoe next time."

Ali nodded and wrapped her hand around Lynn's. "I'm sorry that things have not always worked out in the past. Let's put that aside and focus on the positive. Today is beautiful. Let's finish our hike."

Ali squeezed her hand, then climbed down the hill toward the trail. Ali's pace had significantly increased and her arms pumped. She seemed to be lost in thought as she stopped at a bench.

"You need a rest?" Lynn held out a water bottle.

"No. I need to say something. Please forgive me. I've gone a little overboard with punishing you. Can we do a reset? I miss our friendship. I miss us."

"I forgive you. Yes, I'd like a reset." *I forgive you because part of me has never stopped loving you.*

Chapter 44

Ali let out a sigh as Lynn finished the last section of the upstairs master bedroom. "Wow. I don't know how you did this on your own. Yeah, you have the lifter, but these sheets are heavy. The work is exhausting. And I can't believe the amount of dust." Ali quickly cleaned up the mess with a shop-vac.

After Ali finished, Lynn peeled away her dust mask. "The final sanding is the last chance to get the whole job right. Any taping flaws will be glaringly apparent afterward. But I think we did an excellent job. Thanks for helping me."

Ali's mouth twisted into a grin. "I did like watching your muscles as you carried those sheets, but then I felt too guilty and worried about you getting hurt." Ali ran her fingers along the wall. "You do have the art of taping, spackling, and sanding down pat. Thanks for teaching me even though I know I tested your patience."

Lynn cracked a smile. "Don't be so hard on yourself. It takes time, and you were a good student." She moved to the bay window, looking out over the backyard and setting sun. "That's a beautiful view. You picked a good house, Ali."

Ali joined her. They stood in silence, admiring the sunset.

Various shades of pink and golden yellows mixed through the wispy clouds. After several minutes, Ali said, "It's almost eight-thirty, and we haven't eaten. Guess we know how to spend a rousing Saturday night. How about pizza?"

"Oh yeah, with pepperoni and extra cheese please."

Ali shook her head. "You should eat healthier."

"You can add your veggies, but just a few." Lynn cocked her head.

"Okay, I'll agree to pepperoni, but I want feta cheese, spinach, and mushrooms."

"I like feta—adds some tang and saltiness. But mushrooms? Nope."

Ali placed her fingers on Lynn's lips to silence her and didn't remove them immediately. A bolt of excitement shot through Lynn's system.

Their eyes lingered for a moment before Ali said, "You get pepperoni only if I get mushrooms." She removed her fingers and Lynn immediately missed her touch.

"Deal. Or we could get two pizzas." Lynn bit her lip but couldn't hide the grin.

Ali smacked her on the arm. "Oh, you colossal foodaholic."

"Makes great leftovers, and you owe me." Lynn bounced on her toes. "We finished tonight. Now the bedrooms are ready for painting."

"Aren't you coming tomorrow? I need help with the yard."

Without thinking, Lynn said, "Yeah sure, if you promise we quit early, dress up, and have dinner out on the town."

The pizza tonight was only the fourth time they'd shared a meal. All had been take-out or delivery after working in the house. Lynn felt panic as Ali hadn't said a word. *Have I messed it all up by suggesting a date?*

"That sounds lovely, but I want to take it slow."

"Absolutely. Just dinner and talk," Lynn quickly added. *God, this will be our first formal date.* "How about Zaytinya in D.C.? Excellent Mediterranean food. My treat. It's one of my favorites. You can buy next time. And nice jeans and a blouse are fine." Lynn hoped there would be a next time. As Ali called for pizza delivery, Lynn called Zaytinya and was delighted to snag a seven o'clock reservation.

Date night, Washington D.C. and Arlington, Virginia

The night at Zaytinya was heavenly, and so was the kiss at the end of the night. It was wonderful to hear Ali laughed again. Lynn was optimistic and excited, but cautious about tonight.

It's our second official date! Excitement bubbled up. Lynn tamped it down and knocked on the door.

"Hi, I'm ready."

Lynn watched as she locked up.

"Is there something wrong?"

"No. You look beautiful, Ali."

"I'm dressed in capris and a polo shirt."

"The cream-colored capris and cobalt blue shirt...You always look striking even in work clothes."

"Thank you."

To hell with caution. Gently, Lynn placed her hand on Ali's lower back and pressed their bodies together. Once more, she slowly kissed those tender lips she'd be dreaming about. She wasn't sure if the sweet taste of strawberry was Ali's lips or the lip balm, but she couldn't get enough.

"Wow."

"I'm sorry. I know you wanted to go slow."

With a stroke as light as a feather, Ali ran her fingertips down Lynn's jaw. "The kiss after our dinner date was lovely. This was sizzling. I'm not complaining." Lynn went to kiss her again, but Ali pulled away. "Except, I did want to see this concert. Let's go. I'll make it up to you later." Ali winked and grabbed her by the hand.

The air was warm with the scent of vanilla from the Sweetbay Magnolia mingling with the aromas from the outdoor café. They ate their food while dangling their feet in the fountain.

"Now I know why you wanted to get here early. This is a fantastic view."

"Mm-hmm. The garden fills up fast. Want a bite of my lemongrass chicken soft taco?" Ali broke off a piece and leaned into Lynn's shoulder, holding it inches from Lynn's mouth.

As Lynn's lips closed around the bite, the tips of Ali's fingers brushed her lips.

Lynn nodded. "Yum." Kicking her feet in the water didn't help cool the fire erupting inside. "The black bean burger's delicious too." Lynn broke off a piece of the burger and held it out to Ali.

Ali raked the bite off gently with her teeth. The gesture made Lynn swallow, and from the looks of it, Ali enjoyed the tease.

"Half of my cupcake?" Ali held it close.

Lynn examined the delicate fingers hold the cupcake. *If we weren't in public, I'd take a big bite of you.* By now, her body was buzzing from the intimate act of affection.

"Thank you."

"You have icing on your face."

"Is that so?" Lynn turned, and Ali wiped her thumb on the corner of Lynn's mouth.

"Ladies and Gentleman, Welcome to *Jazz in the Garden* at the National Gallery of Art... Tonight, we have the amazing Tony Craddock Jr. & Cold Front." The crowd erupted. Lynn found it challenging to keep her eyes on the show. She was more interested in continuing the dance of seduction and feeling the goose bumps up and down her body. The desire to kiss Ali senseless was overwhelming.

The concert flew by, and they rode home in Lynn's car. At Ali's house, Lynn intended to hop out and escort Ali to the front door. All along, she hoped Ali would invite her in. Before her hand was off the ignition, Ali leaned over and gripped her forearm.

"Thank you for joining me. I had a fantastic time."

"My pleasure."

"Now about those sizzling kisses. Do you have strength for another?"

Looking into Ali's brown eyes, Lynn took her mouth, relishing in her soft lips and delighting when Ali allowed her tongue inside. One kiss turned into another.

Lynn separated and pressed her forehead against Ali's. "I've never stopped caring for you. I'll never hurt you again. I promise."

"I believe you."

"Ali, I don't want to mess it up. I'll let you decide when to take it further." She intertwined her fingers with Ali's.

"I've thought about us constantly over the past few days. We've certainly had rough patches, but don't you think we've wasted enough time? It's been nine years." Ali kissed the back of Lynn's hand. "To hell with slow. I want you to spend the night. I know my basement is only partially finished and isn't the most romantic."

Lynn laughed. "Watch out. I happen to know who did that job."

"Yes, and I'd like her in my bed tonight." Ali's finger moved down and tugged on the waistband of Lynn's jeans.

"Waking up to you will be bliss."

Ali led her into the house and down to the bedroom. She threw a light scarf over the bedside lamp, creating a soft glow. Tender and slow, they undressed one another. Their hands and lips teasing just enough of each other's skin to spread the flame of desire. With their bodies pressed together, warm and soft, Lynn couldn't get enough of the scent of Ali. Her hair smelled like a mix of vanilla and cocoa butter. Her skin like jasmine petals.

As the kissing became more passionate, Lynn guided Ali towards the bed.

Breathless, Ali broke off. "I'd like to lay in your arms for a few minutes."

Lynn wanted Ali, but on Ali's terms. The back of Lynn's hand skimmed down Ali's cheek, over her lips. She drew Ali's body to hers tightly and kissed her. "I'm all yours."

She eased Ali onto the bed, cradling her. Ali's head rested on her chest with her auburn hair spilling around her. Her soft lips were so close to Lynn's breast.

Ali rose to face Lynn, and her brown eyes were warm and commanding. "I want to explore your beautiful body."

Fingertips ever so slightly traced circles over Lynn's heart, coming close to her nipple before skimming down to her stomach. The tease made Lynn's nipples rock hard.

Lynn's pulse ticked up, and she ran her fingers through Ali's hair. "So silky. Oh..." Ali's hand brushed over one nipple, and her mouth kissed the other. Lynn sucked in a deep breath. "Please, Ali."

Ali smiled and positioned herself on top of Lynn. Her teeth raking in a nipple, alternating with her swirling tongue. Lynn grasped the sheet in a tight knot as Ali lavished her breasts. The tingling between her legs intensified. As she was about to plead, Ali planted kisses over her stomach.

Once more, those lovely brown eyes glanced up into Lynn's. Their eyes locked briefly. Ali smiled then crawled down to Lynn's thighs and nestled in. Her hands explored and caressed, only occasionally brushing over Lynn's swelling clit.

The teasing was erotic, but Lynn needed Ali, now.

"Ali...OH..."

Ali swiped her tongue upwards in a long slow motion over Lynn's clit then flicked the tip several times before taking her fully into her mouth. Ali's hand moved up caressing Lynn's breasts as she teased Lynn further with every movement of her lips and tongue.

Throwing her head back, Lynn moaned. She could hear and feel the pounding of her heart. The rising and falling of her chest matched the acceleration. "God, please don't stop." Ripples of pleasure rolled over Lynn as her muscles clenched and relaxed over and over.

Ali increased the rhythm, nipping and sucking, until bursts of light flickered under Lynn's half-closed eyelids. Her body blazed like a firestorm, she gasped for air as if she couldn't breathe. Urgent need, mixed with intensity, pushed Lynn further than she had ever been. Her body clenched once more, and her heart thumped wildly. Ali rested her head on Lynn's belly as her body calmed.

Soon, Ali inched up beside her, resting on her bent elbow and looking down into Lynn's face. She kissed the tip of Lynn's nose.

"You're gorgeous. I like your strong, take-charge personality, but in bed, I marvel that you trust me to let me have my way with you." Ali smiled wickedly as her fingertips traced a line from Lynn's sternum to her stomach.

"I love you, Ali. I always have."

Ali tenderly kissed her. "I've longed to hear those words. I love you, too, and want us to be together. We don't have to live in the shadows anymore."

"I promise to be there for us." Lynn twirled a strand of Ali's hair in her fingers. "No more hiding. How about being my date for the work dinner party next month."

"Hmmm. Let me see." Ali tapped her finger on her lips. She giggled. "Absolutely."

Lynn hugged her tight. Ali's giggle tickled against her chest. She kissed Ali deeply, then nuzzled the side of Ali's face. Taking a deep breath, Lynn let the fragrance of Jasmine petals fill her. Ali moaned as Lynn delicately nibbled and kissed.

Half lying on Ali with her upper thigh between Ali's legs, Lynn rubbed her leg slightly up and down as her mouth moved to Ali's throat, then back to her mouth with hunger. Through labored breaths, she stopped and looked into Ali's eyes. "Tell me if you are uncomfortable with anything or if you want something."

Ali's eyes glistened and her lips curved into a smile as her finger caressed Lynn's neck. "Have you ever known me to not speak my mind?"

Lynn tilted her head. "No. So, my lady, what would you like your knight to do?" She kissed the halo of Ali's neck.

"Stop teasing me."

Lynn smiled and laid kisses along Ali's neck and collarbone, and delicately sucked in the skin every now and then. Her heart beat harder as her mouth reached Ali's breasts and her hand glided past Ali's stomach, slipping between Ali's legs. Lynn gently rubbed Ali's sensitive skin before sliding in two fingers. She stroked while kissing and sucking Ali's taut nipples.

She liked the way Ali arched her back and pressed harder into her hand. Nails raked along Lynn's shoulder blade, then fingers clenched her hair. Ali's writhing, and the rising buzz in her own body, drove Lynn on. When Lynn's mouth moved lower, Ali whimpered with delight. Keeping up the pace with her fingers, her tongue flicked Ali's clit, then sucked it into her mouth. Ali arched up, pressing even tighter into her.

"I want your tongue inside me and everywhere."

Lynn nuzzled between Ali's legs, moving in and out with every subtle cry of pleasure from Ali's throat. Each reaction gave Lynn joy. She varied her pace, teasing and tormenting, then giving all until Ali's body relaxed beneath her. She moved up to admire Ali's gorgeous auburn hair falling over her face. Ali's eyelids fluttered. Her eyes were dazed and pleased. Ali's hand wrapped behind Lynn's neck and drew her in for a long kiss.

They lay in one another's arms, and Lynn had never felt so comfortable and at peace as she did now.

Chapter 45

Ali rushed to the front of the house and propped the door open wide. "How much does that thing weigh?" she asked as Lynn maneuvered the appliance into the kitchen.

"Fifty-four pounds. It's more bulky than heavy."

Ali watched every muscle flex in Lynn's strong arms and shoulders as Lynn anchored the microwave into the mounting brackets and hooked it up to the receptacle in the cupboard above.

Lynn casually propped her hand on the counter. Her blue eyes gleamed. "I've never seen someone get so excited over a microwave."

"Well, I've never had such a cute handywoman. You should wear sleeveless T-shirts more often." Ali smacked her on the butt as she walked by.

"Hey." Lynn grabbed Ali and drew her in. "Better watch out. If you treat this handywoman too harshly, I might leave the kitchen cabinets half done."

"If you don't finish, then I won't pay you." Ali waggled her eyebrows. "And you know my payments are always rich."

"Hmmm…I think you're behind on payments over the past couple of months. Better catch up or I might leave."

"Is that so?"

Ali ran her fingers through Lynn's hair and took command of her lips. Tongues explored. When Lynn's hand caressed her back and moved lower, Ali moaned. As Lynn's lips moved to her neck, Ali's cell rang. She let it go to voice mail, but it rang again.

"That ring tone is my sister. I'd better take it since she's called twice."

"I'll remember where we left off."

Ali winked and answered in a chipper voice. "Hi, Denise. What's up?" She slumped against the counter and wrapped one hand around her forehead and eyes. "Okay...How...All right...Call me when we need to go over arrangements...Bye...Love you, too."

It took a few seconds for Ali to realize that Lynn's hand was on her shoulder.

Lynn's words, "Ali, what's wrong?" finally reached her brain. Ali's throat constricted, and she could barely swallow. She gazed up into Lynn's pleading blue eyes, but her vision blurred from the gathering tears.

"My mom died."

"Oh honey, I wish I could make the pain disappear." Lynn wrapped her tightly and stroked her hair. Ali clung to Lynn, and the pain and tears flowed.

"I think I need to lie down."

⟶⟶

Ali sat up. She was alone. She wiped her eyes with a new tissue and shuffled to the bathroom.

After washing, she stared in the mirror, watching the drops slide down her face and listening to the plink, plink sound as they hit the water surface. Nothing ever seemed to wash away the sadness deep inside.

Ali opened the medicine cabinet and grabbed the bottle of Advil. *Fuck, it's empty.* She hurled it in the trashcan and leaned over the vanity.

How do you explain love and contempt for your mother? She had said those words before to the therapist. They rang loud in her head now. Her mother could be caring one minute, then overlook...

Ali crossed her arms over her chest and compressed her body. She squeezed her eyes tight. Her fingers dug into her shoulders. She could hear her mother's voice from years ago, "Oh, Ali. You know he didn't mean it. He's had too many tonight. It will be better tomorrow."

Excuses, excuses, excuses. I'm not sure she'd believe me anyway.

All of Ali's life, her mother would cut her off or make some excuse whenever Ali tried to discuss her abusive father. Carol Clairmont only saw a tiny bit of what went on. While he was alive, there were the threats to ensure Ali's silence. After he died, her mother sunk into oblivion. Inside Ali, the hurt pooled and festered until it ruptured like an abscess, bleeding and leaking puss. And every time, Ali would hide the pain and suffer alone.

Last week, Ali mentioned meeting Lynn. Her mom stood up, waved her hand and said, "I don't want to be part of your lifestyle," then walked away.

Ali uncrossed her arms, opened her eyes, and slammed the mirrored door of the medicine cabinet shut.

"Hey, are you okay? I'm sorry, but you didn't answer when I tapped on the door and called out." Lynn's arms cradled her from behind. She spun her around and lifted her chin. "It's going to be okay. I'm here when you want to talk."

"What's there to talk about?" Ali looked down.

Lynn took her hand. "Tell me what's wrong. Your family lives within an hour's drive, but you've only said a few things about Denise, and that your mom and two older siblings pretend you're not a lesbian."

After wetting her lips, Ali said, "We had a strained relationship even before I came out. Things were a little better after my dad died." Her eyelashes fluttered, and her hand covered Lynn's. "He was not like your dad. I don't have many good things to say about him." Ali could hear the disdain in her words. The tears welled up, and she flung herself into Lynn's arms. "I'm sorry. It's painful to talk about."

"Let's go sit and relax. You need a good meal." Lynn's voice was soothing.

"The kitchen isn't finished."

"We'll make do. Besides, we've got the microwave. And you know my ability to heat leftovers is legendary."

The corner of Ali's mouth quirked up. "Yep. I remember the time you burned something in Afghanistan and folks ate outside rather than endure the stench."

Lynn threw her hands up to her heart and gave a mock display of being mortally wounded. "I was distracted, but I promise to do good by you, my fair maiden." She sunk to one knee batting her eyelashes. "Besides, we've got some serious problems if I mess up soup. Oh, I also picked up a baguette and brie." Lynn started to stand and grimaced.

"Okay. You can dispense with the funny stuff now."

"Yes, but can you give me a hand."

"You're serious?"

"Afraid so. My back gets me every now and then."

"God, I hope you didn't hurt yourself lifting that microwave."

"A couple of ibuprofens, and I'll be fine."

"I'm out of Advil, but there might be some in the basement."

They ate their meal outside—partially cloudy with a refreshing breeze. Afterward, they watched an episode of *Orange Is the New Black* and ate popcorn.

"Thank you for dinner and for not burning anything, especially the popcorn." Ali tried to keep a straight face but broke out into a snicker. "It was fun and just what I needed."

"Do you have any idea when the funeral might be? I'd like to be there for you."

Ali bit her lip knowing that Lynn's presence would cause questions, but she was sick of bending to her family's wishes. "It would mean a lot to me to have you there."

Chapter 46

Ali was silent as Lynn drove them to Ali's older sister's house to receive friends and family after the funeral.

"Ready for this?" Ali grasped her hand in a strong grip. "Don't be surprised if you're bombarded with questions. My family can be polite in public, but watch out if they corner you." Ali half smiled and wiped her eyes with a tissue.

"I can handle it." Ali kissed her lightly on the lips. Lynn enjoyed the feel of Ali's soft skin. She brushed the back of her hand down Ali's cheek.

The gathering was somber at first but grew happy and boisterous as funny stories were shared. Lynn had never seen this much food. Every person showed up with a huge dish. Lynn walked out to the back deck before another one of Ali's relatives shoved food in her hand. She searched for Ali in the crowd and finally saw her off in the corner with her older brother.

She discreetly watched from a distance. Ali's face was contorted, and it appeared that Kevin would cut her off every time she tried to speak. Lynn wanted to desperately go over and stick up for Ali. They soon calmed down, and Kevin hugged Ali.

"Here's another iced tea for you."

Lynn didn't need more but politely accepted the drink from Ali's younger sister, Denise. "Thanks."

"Are you my sister's lover?"

Lynn coughed. "Congratulations. You take the prize for speed and directness."

"Why thank you, Ms. Stewart. Don't let Kevin and Stephanie's slick gentle tongues fool you. They hide a lot of bullshit behind the prim and proper façade." Denise smirked. "And your answer to my question is...?"

"That is a personal matter that is none of your business. However, I am her girlfriend." Lynn's eyes darted around as she took another drink.

Denise stepped closer. "Sorry. I'll tone it down since you're worried," she pointed around the yard with the drink in her hand, "which you have a right to be. Some of these people are uncomfortable with my sister's life. I learned early on to keep my mouth shut, especially around our dad."

Something told Lynn not to ask, but she wanted to understand. "Oh, how so?"

"Well, if you are my sister's girlfriend, then she's probably already told you he was a drunk, a proselytizing hypocrite, and a misogynistic creep." Denise's face was hard.

"Did he harm any of you or worse?"

"He was hell on Ali." Denise's jaw was tight. "He usually made sure bruises never showed, and he never missed an opportunity to tell Ali what a failure she was."

"Did he mistreat you?"

Denise shrugged her shoulders. "He mainly ignored me. I was the accident. The runt who was eight years younger than Ali, thirteen from Stephanie and fifteen from Kevin." Her eyes narrowed. "Kevin and Stephanie moved out before dad's drinking hit rock bottom." She let out a huff. "Ali got the brunt of his wrath, but she doesn't like to talk about it. I was only ten when he died, but I saw enough. I understood far more than anyone thought."

"I'm sorry. She said your dad was not a good man but didn't elaborate."

"Of course, Kevin and Stephanie always said Ali exaggerates. I think they were like Mom—always minimizing. Kevin lives in his own pretentious little world. You know the kind where families have one mommy, one daddy, and nothing bad ever happens if you play by good Christian rules. Just so you know, I don't have a stick up my ass."

"It's good you don't have a problem with your sister being a lesbian. She needs family support."

A broad grin spread across Denise's face. "So, what's the story with you two? She says you've known one another for years."

"We met at work, and I've been helping her with the house renovations."

"No more juicy details?"

"I don't kiss and tell, and I think your sister has been through enough lately."

"Mom's death or the bitch Tracy?"

For a second time, Lynn choked on her drink. "Look. I'm not sure Ali would appreciate you—"

"Revealing her secrets." Denise twirled the ice in the glass, making an irritating clinking sound.

"Hey. Is this girl-talk or can I join in?"

Denise whirled around. "Sweetie, can you bring us a plate of appetizers?"

He tilted his head and said, "Guess that's my cue."

As her husband turned to walk away, Denise reached out and patted him on the shoulder. She winked at Lynn. "I'm all for equal rights. If it wasn't for this uptight crowd, I might have squeezed his butt." She flicked her wrist. "Anyway, Kevin and Stephanie took after Mom and buried the truth, but don't let Ali do that to herself."

Too surprised at Denise's bluntness to say anything, Lynn nodded.

Ali joined them on the deck. "Hey sis, I think it's time that I punch out." The two embraced.

Lynn couldn't help but notice that Ali's posture toward Denise was more relaxed than with her two other siblings. The hugs also seemed to last longer.

"Now that I'm not traveling so much for work, let's have dinner in the next week." Denise's smile widened. "I'd love to chat more with your girlfriend. It would be fun."

"Sounds great. I'll text you." Ali grabbed Lynn's hand. "We need to say goodbye to Stephanie."

Denise bounced on her toes. "I'll go with you and rescue you if she tries to trap you in a long conversation."

After all the goodbyes, they headed for home. Ali was quiet and gazed out the window. Halfway through the trip, Lynn reached over and clasped Ali's hand.

"Thank you, Lynn. I'm sorry if anyone made you feel uncomfortable."

Lynn rubbed the back of her hand. "I was happy to be there for you."

"Denise is my easy-going sister." Ali took a deep breath and let it out. "She has good humor, but she can be a bit intrusive."

"She's chatty and pleasant."

Ali chuckled. "That's a polite way to put it. Denise is straight but not narrow-minded. She will be scrutinizing you to see if you measure up to date her big sister, but she means well." Ali's look softened. "Did she tell you a little about our dysfunctional family?"

Lynn nodded. "I'm sorry, Ali." She pulled the truck over. "Come here."

Ali snuggled into Lynn and rested her hand on Lynn's leg. "You may find this hard to hear. As much as I loved my mom, I'm happy to no longer hear her alternate reality of our family life."

"I understand." Lynn tucked a strand of hair behind Ali's ear. "You don't have to let that past define you. You've moved on. You deserve happiness."

Chapter 47

October 2017 – Northern Virginia

Lynn brushed Ali's cheek with the back of her hand. "Are you sure you want to go through with this so soon after your mom's funeral? Maybe you should postpone the surgery after matters are settled with your mom's estate."

"They recommended surgery over a year ago. I'm scheduled, and I'd like to be done with it. The physical therapy only helped a little."

"Good afternoon, Ali."

"Hello, Dr. Timmons. I'd like you to meet," Ali reached over and held Lynn's hand, "my partner, Lynn Stewart. I've put her on the HIPAA paperwork."

"Pleased to meet you, Lynn." He nodded and sat at the desk, opened his laptop, then absent-mindedly clicked a pen in his right hand. "The surgery is scheduled for next Thursday, but there's a bit of a problem."

His pursed lips bothered Lynn.

"I don't understand." Ali brow furrowed.

"As I said before, the chances of needing a blood transfusion during orthopedic surgery are low but higher than other procedures. And there is a present shortage in the blood bank." He dropped the pen and straightened his tie.

"To be safe, we still need a blood deposit."

"Didn't my siblings come in for testing?"

"I'm sorry. They are incompatible," he softly said.

"What about other relatives?"

He leaned back in his chair. The pen was back in his hand. Lynn found the clicking irritating.

"Your blood type is B negative, which is rare. Only two percent of the population has that type. The hospital has requested blood to meet your needs."

"Okay. How long will that take? As I said before, I have a lot of aunts and uncles on both sides."

He bit his lower lip and took a deep breath. After several seconds of silence, he leaned forward and folded his hands. "Your sister Denise has blood type A, and your older siblings have blood type O."

"Yes."

The information hit Lynn like a hard blow to the stomach, but from the look on Ali's face, she didn't understand. The doctor wet his lips.

Ali's voice raised. "What's going on?"

Holy shit! Lynn leaned over and put her arm around Ali. She rubbed Ali's shoulder.

In a panicked tone, Ali said, "Do I have cancer or something?"

"No."

A knock sounded on the door, and the office assistant walked in. "Here is a paper copy of the hospital archives you requested. I was surprised. Many of the records over thirty years old were destroyed to save space. You're lucky they still exist."

"Thank you." He forced a smile at Lynn and Ali. "Please give me a minute." He scanned through several pages of each file then cleared his throat. "Your mother was type O, and Mr. Clairmont was type A. I'm sorry Ali, but it's impossible for Mr. Clairmont to be your father."

The color drained from Ali's face, and she fell into Lynn's arms. Lynn whispered in her ear, "I'm here for you. It's going to be okay."

The doctor retrieved a drink. "This juice might help."

Lynn could see Ali's hand slightly shake as she brought the drink to her lips.

"Would you like to lie down?" The doctor's voice was soothing.

"No. I'll be all right. I need to wrap my head around this. How positive are you that he's not my dad?"

"One hundred percent. It's genetically impossible. I know this information must be shocking to you, which is another reason for postponing your surgery. We will try to find a blood type match as quickly as possible. In the meantime, it will give you time to absorb the information we've discussed."

Ali gripped Lynn's hand. "Take me home, please."

⊷⊶

The clock read nearly six p.m., Ali rolled out of bed and groggily shuffled down the hall, yawning. A wonderful smell wafted in the air, she abruptly stopped. *Brownies.*

Lynn kissed her forehead and lips, then pulled her into a warm embrace.

"I was about to wake you. I fixed a chicken casserole. We missed lunch."

Ali swallowed. "Smells great."

"Honey, it might be a good idea to talk to a therapist."

Ali bit her bottom lip. "Yep. Sounds like a good idea given the fact my mother lied to me for years, didn't protect me, and the man I thought was my father made me feel as if I caused all the problems. Just a tad above the normal shit storm everyone deals with."

Lynn leaned her forehead against Ali's. "You need to focus on the fact that you're an amazing person who has accomplished a lot in your life. Now sit while I serve."

"I wonder if my older sister and brother know anything. Someone must have suspected. I bet Aunt Judy knows. What if my father was one of the guys at my mom's funeral or at the wake?" A wave of uneasiness rolled through her.

"Calm down. There's plenty of time to figure things out. For now, let's eat."

Lynn spooned out the casserole onto plates. Glasses of water, rolls, butter, and the brownies were already on the table. While Lynn ate, Ali stared at the brownies.

"Sorry, Ali. I've always followed the rules. There's no marijuana in them."

Ali gave a weak smile. "Lame joke."

"I know my cooking is not the best, but I do a pretty good casserole."

Ali mumbled, "It's the brownies." She reached out for Lynn's hand. "It's not your fault. Thank you for taking care of me and loving me." After squeezing Lynn's hand, she took a few bites. "We used to vacation at Lake Anna when I was young. Mom would always bake brownies in the cabin." She wiped her eyes. "That was long before Edward started drinking heavily. Long before he started abusing me. At least now, I understand why he took his anger out on me."

"You were a kid. It wasn't your fault. Not only was he in the wrong, but your mom should have stopped the abuse and moved out or kicked him out." Lynn smoothed her hair. "How old were you when things started going wrong?"

"He always yelled, and it got worse over the years. I was thirteen when he first hit me. Stephanie and Kevin had already moved out of the house. The yelling and abuse grew worse every year of high school. I always thought it was because I was gay. I came out my junior year, and the shit really hit the fan."

"Sounds like Edward didn't find out he wasn't your father until you were older."

Ali scrunched her brows. "I think you're right."

"There's plenty of time to dig for facts. You've only had a bowl of cereal all day. Please, eat something, honey."

"I love you." Ali kissed Lynn's hand.

Chapter 48

Ali was sitting on her Aunt Judy's front porch swing. It was another delightful day in October, partly cloudy and sixty-six degrees, but she was too nervous to enjoy it. She kept scrunching her toes in her shoes, and contemplating the questions she wanted to ask. When the screen door slammed, Ali jumped.

"How'd the doctor's visit go the other day? Scotty says you're going to have surgery." Aunt Judy handed her an iced tea.

"Fine, but I decided to put it off. I have too much going on right now."

"You sounded a little upset on the phone. Is there something wrong?" She watched Ali out of the corner of her eye. "Got problems with your new girl, Lynn? She seems pretty nice. Scotty raves about her and not just about her carpentry skills. You need to bring her over for dinner."

"No, we're fine. Thanks though. No one likes to admit I'm a lesbian, not even Mom when she was alive, but it never seemed to bother you." Ali smiled. "That means a lot to me."

"If she makes you happy, then that's what counts. We were taught not to advertise our business, but that was a different time."

Despite the racing of her heart and mind, she softly said, "I need to know some important things about Mom."

Aunt Judy lowered her drink. "Oh, like what?"

"My father. I know he's not Edward."

Ali could see the worry lines forming on Judy's face, then she looked out over the lawn and took another drink.

"What makes you think that?"

"I have a rare blood type. One that makes it impossible for Edward to be my father. Mom has passed, and I can't ask her. Do you know anything?"

Judy rubbed her temples. "I understand the curiosity, but what good would it do now? Think about your brother and sisters."

"What about me? Don't I deserve the truth? I think my siblings can hold their own." The silence dragged on until Ali pleaded. "Please don't treat me like Mom by dismissing my feelings."

Judy let out a sigh. "I'm sorry, dear. I don't know much."

"That's okay, just tell me what you do know." Ali wrapped her arm around her aunt.

Judy put her tea on the end table. "Well, your mom," she swallowed, "used to have one of those classified jobs. Like your job. Only back then, it was illegal for her to say where she worked." Judy leaned in and whispered into Ali's ear. "She worked for the CIA."

Ali's grip loosened around her aunt's shoulder. "When? I thought her only job was the bakery."

"Carol worked the classified job from 1961 until she became pregnant with you. She quit right before Christmas 1971. When Edward lost his job again, she got a job at the bakery. You were in school then."

"Are you sure about this?"

Nodding, Judy said, "Oh, yes." Her voice dropped to a whisper again. "The building had no windows, a tall fence around it, and guards at the gate. I sometimes dropped her off." Judy's eyes widened. "The guards carried guns."

"What did she do?" She couldn't visualize her mother other than the bakery woman.

"Secretary, I think. Most women back then didn't have many opportunities. Your family was lucky she got the job. The pay was excellent, and your family needed money with Edward's work on and off." Judy patted Ali's hand. "Just before anyone knew Carol was pregnant, she said her position was eliminated for budgetary reasons. Years later, she told me the truth."

Ali dropped her arm from her aunt's shoulders and steadied herself on the swing. "Go on. I need to know."

"She had an affair with a married man and was certain you were his child. Things were more complicated then, and Carol made the choice not to leave Edward." Judy lowered her head. She wiped her eyes before turning back to Ali. "Of course, that was long before Edward started drinking and hitting your mom." She took a deep breath and let it out. "I'm sorry. It took me some time to figure it out. The marks didn't always show, and I didn't notice until it was too late. Your mom was so ashamed of what she had done that she took the punishment Edward dished out." Judy waded up the napkin in her lap. "Your mother was a wonderful woman, but she changed after Edward started drinking. The life seemed to go out of her, and she just lived day to day."

Ali wondered if Judy knew Edward also abused her but was hesitant to go there. "Does anyone else know about the job or that Edward is not my dad?"

"I don't believe so. Edward didn't know about the man

until you were older. You were about twelve when he found out about the money."

"Money!"

"Shush." Judy grabbed her arm. "Let's move inside."

Ali followed her aunt into the living room. She felt a little lightheaded.

"Oh, child. You look so sad. Maybe we should stop here."

"No, I want to know. I need to know. What if there are medical conditions that I could inherit?"

Judy nodded. "I never met the man. I don't even know his name. But apparently, he was a gentleman enough to pay monthly child support. Anyway, Edward discovered the money." Judy rubbed Ali's hand. "But you know, your real father kept on paying Carol. Edward didn't object and took control of it until he died."

Ali's mouth gaped. She wet her lips. "I never had any college loans. Did my real father pay for my education?"

"Carol said he paid extra. She didn't elaborate."

Ali was overwhelmed that her dad had not abandoned her and had paid for her support. *But why hasn't he contacted me?*

"Oh, my. I think this is all too much for you. Some things might be better left in the past."

"Please, Aunt Judy. I have to know." Ali leaned closer. "I'd like to know who my real father is or was." Ali swallowed. "My agency, NGA...well we..." Her voice quavered. "We work with CIA. Can you give me any more details? You said you drove Mom to work sometimes. Do you recall where?"

"It's not there anymore. It was torn down two or three years ago."

Ali's breathing slowed while her heart rate climbed. "There was a building at the corner of First and M Streets."

Judy snapped her fingers. "That's it. It was a stone's throw from where the baseball stadium is now. That area is so nice with all the new businesses and restaurants." Judy patted her hand. "I'm sorry dear. That's all I know."

There was a knock at the door. Judy went to see who was there. Ali took some breaths. She wiped her hands on her pants. *My God, this can't be.*

"Ali, honey, it's Lynn."

"Hi, I'm done at the hardware store and thought I'd do some grocery shopping. Need anything?"

"Aunt Judy, do you mind if I talk to Lynn alone for a minute?"

"Sure, I'll be in the kitchen. Call if you need me."

Ali whispered, "You're not going to believe what she told me. I'm still trying to take it all in."

Lynn sat next to her. "You look a little shell-shocked."

"I'd like to go home. I think I've had enough surprises for one day."

Chapter 49

Ali closed her eyes and hung her head partially out the window like a puppy dog, sucking in the fresh air. "Lynn, pull over." Ali pointed to the park.

"Tell me what's wrong, sweetie." Lynn draped her arm over Ali.

"As I said, you're not going to believe this. I'm not even sure I do." She told Lynn about her dad knowing about her and explained the support payments.

"Sounds like your dad's a decent guy."

The emotions swirled in Ali again. "Lynn...he..."

"Hey, hey. Relax. Breathe. I'm right here." Lynn massaged her neck.

Ali took in Lynn's warmth. "We all worked for NPIC."

"I thought you always worked for NGA. What's NPIC? I've heard that acronym before, but I'm not sure where."

Ali rubbed her temples. "I work for the part of NGA that used to be under the control of CIA's National Photographic Interpretation Center. After a major reorganization back in 1996, Congress realigned us with the Department of Defense." Ali twisted to face Lynn. "It's beyond wacko insane. We all worked the same type of job, in the same building at different times." Ali shook her head. "They demolished the old D.C. building after we moved the agency to Virginia."

"Wow."

"Yeah, tell me about it." Ali's hands flew up. "What if my dad got me hired? What if he works at the agency now or I've worked on one of his projects? Lynn that's a conflict of interest."

"Hold on. First, he cared enough to help. Maybe he did give you a recommendation for the job. Nothing wrong with that. Second, he'd be in his seventies or eighties and probably retired." Lynn's brow furrowed, and she bit her lip. She hoped he was retired and not deceased.

"What are the chances? It's crazy, right?"

"Honey, what do you want out of this?"

Ali leaned in and rested her head in the crook of Lynn's arm. "I want to know who he is, if I look like him, if I have aunts and uncles, cousins, and what his parents were like, and if I have other brothers and sisters." Ali finally took a breath. "I want to hear his story, and why he never visited me."

Lynn kissed the top of her head. "Who has your mom's financial records? That might give you a clue."

"There are tons of boxes in Stephanie's attic. She volunteered to sort them from personal items. We were supposed to meet in a couple of weeks." Ali slapped her hand on her forehead. "Shit, I hope she didn't throw anything out. We only have to keep seven years of papers since the initial estate forms were filed."

"Put your mind at ease. Start looking through the papers now. I bet she will welcome you taking over the task."

Ali nodded. "Sounds like the best place to start."

"What about your friend at work?"

"Yeah, Dory knows a lot of people and knows tons of stories. NPIC was a fraction of the size NGA is now." She took in a breath and blew it out. "But things were so compartmented back then, and people from other divisions only talked to one another if it was necessary."

"It won't hurt to ask." Lynn wrapped her arms around her tightly. "Now, do you feel better?"

"Yes, but still a little scared."

"Things would be too boring if we didn't have challenges. And I know a gorgeous woman with dogged determination."

Chapter 50

"Your mother was how old?" Dory rocked in her chair.
"She would have been seventy-seven next month."

"I'm sorry, Ali. I never knew your mother. I'm twelve years younger than your mom, and I went into the military right after college. Lucky for you, I do know the agency historian. We're working on a display to honor agency women for next year's Family Day. No guarantees, but maybe he knows something."

Ali grinned. "Thanks. That'd mean the world to me."

"Dear. I hate to be macabre, but there's a high probability your father is deceased or retired and no longer living in the area."

Ali slumped in the chair. "Yes, but I'll keep digging and find as much as possible. I'm starting with my mother's papers and personal items. If nothing else, I'd like to find a picture of him."

"Sounds like a plan. My friend Sam started his career in NPIC's library in 1968. He's considered the foremost authority on imagery intelligence." Dory picked up the phone and punched the speaker button.

"Hello, Dory."

"How's my favorite NGA local historian?" Dory said with glee.

He chuckled. "Ah, my favorite analyst turned manager, and the only one left that seems to have any common sense. What can I do for you, my dear? You're not trying to get out of Family Day are you?"

"Absolutely, not."

"Good because between you and me, we cover almost a century of knowledge. Now, how can I help you?"

"Nothing earth-shattering. Do I have to have a good reason to talk to an old friend?"

"No, except you're always so busy. You usually make a lunch date when you want to have a friendly chit-chat, and your arrival and departure are timed to perfection. It's ten fifteen in the morning. Something's off."

"Geez, got me on that one. Listen, Sam. I can't give you any details, but I promised a friend to gather a bit of information. I know I can count on your discretion."

"Of course. I'll be happy to assist if it's unclassified info and releasable to the public."

"Did you know or ever hear of a Carol Clairmont who worked as a secretary in Building 213?"

"Yes. By the time I met her, she wasn't a secretary. She had moved on to an experiment." He laughed. "Well, that's what some of the old geezers at the time called it. Director Lundahl started a research team of all women with the intent of eventually training them to be photo interpreters. Mrs. Clairmont held the title of research assistant and was assigned to the department following the development of Soviet missiles."

"Holy cow."

"Yes, indeed. She was highly regarded. I even saw her on a light table more than once. She was lucky to have been assigned to a team of men who weren't chauvinists. I was going to start digging up official pictures next month for our women's history display, but I could start sooner. I do believe we have a couple of Carol."

"That would be wonderful, Sam," Dory enthusiastically said.

"You know, it was always upsetting to me that some of the men didn't even think women should be working back then, especially if they had children. Mrs. Clairmont had two little ones and finally quit when the third one was on the way. I was sad to see that she had passed away recently. God, rest her soul. She was such a nice woman and worked so hard."

"Thank you, Sam. Goodbye. Let's have lunch soon." Dory's voice was choked with emotion.

"Bye, Dory."

Dory hung up the phone, took a tissue and held out the box to Ali.

"Oh my, God." Ali's hands were shaking and a few tears ran down her cheeks. "I had no idea. It doesn't even sound like the woman I grew up with."

Dory blew her nose, then chuckled. "Well, we are in the business of protecting secrets. How did your mother feel about your deployments?"

"You know, that was one thing I couldn't figure out. She seemed to live the whole Ozzie and Harriet way of life, except when it came to my job. She was supportive." Ali stood. "Thank you so much, Dory."

"You're very welcome. Now go forth and conquer the day. Focus on the positive, do good deeds, and spread cheer."

Northern Virginia

For almost a week, Ali had rummaged through the boxes of her mother's personal belongings. Thus far, the tedious task yielded nothing.

When she arrived at her sister's house tonight, Stephanie asked her why she was in such a hurry. Ali stuck to her story. She wasn't ready to reveal they were only half-siblings. When Stephanie asked about the large envelope in her hand, Ali mumbled some excuse. Minutes later as Ali climbed the steps to the attic, she couldn't remember what she had said.

She sat on the floor in the middle of her sister's attic with her legs crossed and the large envelope on her lap. She swallowed and peeled it open and removed the photographs. The smiling woman reminded Ali of the mother she used to know before Edward's abuse.

A note stuck between the photos fell to the floor.

Hi, Ali,

 I hope this helps in some way in your search for the truth. Sam listed the names of the men in the photos—all public info approved for the Family Day event. I did do a little investigative work myself. Unfortunately, all are deceased but one, and he left the agency in 1966, long before your mother became pregnant. I wish you luck.

 Dory

Ali stuffed the photos and note back in the envelop and set them aside. After a deep breath, she mumbled, "Time to get started."

The boxes against the wall were not organized. Kevin and Stephanie had thrown things in to get them out of their mother's house quickly. Ali rushed forward and grabbed one. "Maybe, my luck will change today."

When she opened the lid, she saw her mother's employment papers with the NPIC emblem centered at the top of each page. Taking a stack, she scanned through them—personnel action forms, letters of recognition and congratulatory memos, and training certificates.

"Dammit!" Nothing jumped out at her. Unclassified with little information and so inconspicuous that she would never have known what it meant if it hadn't been for the emblem. "Keep going. There has to be something in here."

Ali pulled one photo out of her mother at a typewriter and a man smiling behind her and "1964" written on the back. "Yep, men were in absolute control. Glad, it's changed for the better." She lifted the lid on the next box. Her heart stopped.

"What the hell?"

Ali fumbled her cell phone out of her pocket and punched in Lynn's number. "Honey, you're not going to believe this."

"What did you find?"

"I just pulled out a duplicate of a declassified U-2 image from October 14, 1962. Analysis of the U-2 was proof the Soviets were installing missiles in Cuba. Two days after these images were snapped, NPIC used them to brief President Kennedy." Ali paced back and forth as she talked. "The fortieth anniversary of the Cuban Missile Crisis was celebrated in October 2002 at my agency. This is—wow—so unbelievable."

"Stop! Take a break. You're talking too fast and lost me in the alphabet soup and history. What the frak does the Cuban Missile Crisis have to do with your parents?"

"I didn't think of it before, but Mom started working at NPIC a year before the Cuban Missile Crisis. She probably was involved!"

"Okay. Please, calm down. You're breaking my eardrum, and your sister might hear you."

"Oh, sorry. Anyway, what's really exciting is the duplicate declassified U-2 images were only given out at the fortieth anniversary ceremony to agency employees and distinguished guests. I was there and received one. My Mom would not have received one unless my dad was at the same ceremony. God, this still freaks me out that we all three worked for the same agency."

"This is great news. When are you leaving? It's getting late."

"Sorry, I'm going to stay longer. Don't wait up for me."

"Okay. Love you."

"I love you, too. Oh, Lynn?"

"Yes?"

"You're the best thing that ever happened to me. Even through our ups and downs, my heart was always with you. When I get home, I'm going to show you how much you mean to me."

"I can't wait to kiss your beautiful face. One hour. No more or you'll be too tired tomorrow." Lynn laughed. "But if you take your time showing me how much I mean to you, then we are both going to be exhausted."

"Oh...just a little longer. Bye, sweetheart."

Ali found a few more mementos and one letter of recognition dated April 20, 1971. The letter read:

Dear Mrs. Clairmont,

    It is my pleasure to inform you that the recommendation for an Outstanding Performance Rating submitted by your supervisor is approved.

    You are commended for the manner in which you have been

performing the assigned responsibilities of your position. The excellent quality and quantity of your work as a Research Assistant is highly significant to the success of the National Photographic Interpretation Center. Your dedication and effort will further benefit the mission of this center by providing inspiration to other employees.

A copy of this letter will be made a permanent part of your Official Personnel Folder. I extend sincere congratulations for your achievement and wish you continued success in your career.

Sincerely,
Mr. Arthur C. Lundahl
Director of the National Photographic Interpretation Center

A note scribbled below the signature read:

Happy tenth anniversary at NPIC, Carol. You've been a true asset to the team, and I know you'll make an excellent photo interpreter.
Best Regards,
Art

"Holy moly! I heard how he frequently showed up at people's desks to chat, but this is amazing!" Ali shook the letter in her hand as she did a little dance.

"Ali, it's almost nine. What in the world are you doing?" Stephanie was standing behind her.

Ali froze. She dropped the letter in the box and turned to face her sister. "I didn't hear you come up. Sorry for being noisy."

"When you didn't quit at eight, I thought I'd check to see if you were still alive. Clearly, something has you tickled."

Ali saw the 1964 black and white photo out of the corner of her eye. "I found this photo of Mom. I didn't know she typed.

Did you? Gee, the clothes they used to wear." Ali giggled for effect.

"I heard she worked briefly as a secretary. Dad didn't like her driving into the city." Stephanie smiled. "Great photo. Mom's cute, but the hairstyle." She laughed and hugged Ali. With her hand on the doorknob, Stephanie said, "See you another night. I'm going to bed."

"Goodnight."

As soon as Stephanie shut the door, Ali went back to rifling through the box. More boring papers. She was ready to give up and go home when she spotted a color photo sticking out from underneath some papers. Her mother was wearing a casual dress and with a radiant smile. Ali moved the papers aside. A man was standing next to her mother and rested his hand casually around Carol's shoulder. A lump formed in her throat. He had features similar to Ali's, including wavy reddish-brown hair.

"Who are you, mystery man?" She whispered.

—◦◦◦◦◦—

Lynn rolled over. "Hi sweetie. Sorry, I feel asleep."

Ali crawled on the bed and softly wrapped her arms around Lynn. "I love you." She gave Lynn a kiss on the neck, then a warm, slow kiss on the lips.

"Ummm...I love you, too."

"I know we need sleep, but," Ali held up her index finger, "first I have to tell you what I found." Ali handed Lynn the folder. "There's a letter from Art Lundahl and a color photo. I think my dad's in the photo."

"Who's Art Lundahl?"

"Damn you NSA wienies. You don't know anything about

imagery. How in the world do they ever let you on a Joint Duty Assignment? They need to ship you back to Fort Meade. Lundahl was one of CIA's best, the founder of NPIC, and the father of imagery intelligence." Ali handed her the picture. "I'm going to brush my teeth. Be back in a jiffy."

Lynn studied the photo and immediately recognized Ali's mother in the center. To her right was a man with hair similar to Ali's, and the same lopsided grin. Somehow, he looked familiar.

Ali crawled into bed. "I think the guy is my dad. Do you think I'm crazy?"

Lynn kissed her tenderly. "Yum. Beautiful crazy. Yes, I think you're onto something, but you rock the hair much better."

"When I saw his face, most of my anger softened. I hope he's still alive." Ali cuddled next to Lynn's side. "I can't believe I found him so fast. Tomorrow at work, I'll search the global address book and see if he's still working. Maybe I'll get lucky."

"You know his name?"

Ali yawned and adjusted her pillow. "Yeah. It's on the back of the photo. Thomas Blair."

Chapter 51

"Good morning. Can I help you?"

Lynn didn't recognize the secretary, and the woman was way too chipper for this time of day. "Good morning. I need to see Mr. Blair."

"And you are?"

"Lynn Stewart."

"He usually doesn't begin appointments before eight. What time is your meeting?" The secretary put on oversized glasses with a purple frame and squinted at the computer. "I don't see your name on his schedule."

"I don't have one, but I'll wait all day if I have to."

The woman focused at Lynn's badge clipped to her blazer. "Well, Ms. Stewart, that could be a long time. He's in with the director most of the day, and I don't see that number giving you access to those meetings."

Lynn pinched the bridge of her nose. "Look, I'm sorry ma'am. I've been up most of the night. Please ring Mr. Blair. Tell him Lynn Stewart from the 2010 Paktia investigation is here, and that I must speak with him. It's urgent."

Lynn turned as two tall, beefy men dressed in dark navy suits appeared. "Is there a problem, Clarice?"

"I'm not sure. Please stand-by."

The secretary picked up the phone receiver. "Hello, Mr. Blair. I'm sorry to disturb you. There's a Ms. Lynn Stewart here that insists on seeing you...No, she doesn't have an appointment, sir." The secretary hung up. "Gentlemen, please escort her out."

Lynn couldn't believe Blair refused to see her. "What did he say?"

"As I said, Mr. Blair does not see anyone without an appointment."

The one guard grabbed Lynn's arm while the other one spoke into the radio. "Additional assistance needed in Mr. Blair's suite."

"Cancel that order! Release Ms. Stewart."

The secretary bolted out of her chair and knocked over a stack of papers. "Sir. I'm sorry, but you hung up after asking if she had an appointment."

"I'm sorry, Clarice." Blair turned to Lynn. "This is entirely my fault." He held open his office door for Lynn. "After you, Ms. Stewart."

Lynn's frustration boiled over once he closed the door. "You have an entire hidden life. No more coverups. Why couldn't you have been a part of her life?"

He wet his lips and swallowed. "Even though I didn't raise Ali, I couldn't be prouder. She's a fine woman and an exceptional analyst."

"Is the job all you care about? You missed a life with a wonderful daughter."

"I wish I had been more of a father." His brown eyes misted over.

Lynn came to his office angry, but seeing him so vulnerable stabbed at her heart.

"I'm sorry. That was uncalled for." She ran her hand through her hair.

"No need for apologies. I deserved that."

"I just don't understand how you could work in such close proximity and not tell her. And in 2010, you said something to me about having close family connections. Why didn't you say something? Why didn't you pull her out? It was too dangerous. We're lucky the sting operation didn't end up with someone killed."

"Admiral Kent insisted we present her with the opportunity." Blair swallowed. "We would have lost valuable time, and it would have been a conflict of interest if I'd stepped in and removed her. Not to mention that Kent wouldn't have allowed it." Blair motioned to some comfy wing-back chairs.

"She found a color picture of you and her mom, and connected the dots with the looks. Your name is on the back. You can't put off talking to her. You owe it to her."

"You're right." Blair's face was contorted like he was fighting back emotions. "I thought I was doing the best thing by staying out of her life. How is she? Sounds like you two are back together."

Lynn shifted in the chair. "I love her and don't want to see her hurt. Please talk to her as soon as possible."

There was a tap on the door, and the secretary poked her head inside. "I'm terribly sorry to interrupt, but Ms. Ali Clairmont is on the phone for you, sir."

Blair locked eyes with Lynn. "Everyone's in Global now. I used to have an alias." He swallowed. "Clarice, please ask her to hold. I'll be a few minutes. And please apologize for the wait."

"Yes, sir."

He brushed imaginary lint from his slacks, except this time, his hands were shaking. Lynn reached out and touched his knee.

"Ali only wants the truth. Speak from the heart and every-thing will be fine." She thumbed towards the door. "I should get going. Traffic's a killer this time of day."

He nodded. Tears had welled up in his eyes.

Chapter 52

October 2017 – Northern Virginia

Lynn threw her keys on the kitchen counter and plopped into a chair. While she had told Ali about taking the day off, she didn't say why.

"What in the world was I thinking?"

The house was quiet. She suspected that wouldn't last. It was likely that Ali would not finish her workday after talking to her father.

"Might as well make myself useful," Lynn mumbled and began to cook.

Ali walked in the door less than an hour later. Lynn was relieved when she ran up and hugged her tight.

"Hey, sweetie. Your eyes are all puffy. I didn't think you got that emotional over my Shephard's pie."

Nuzzled into Lynn's ear, Ali whispered, "I talked to my dad." She kissed Lynn's cheek, then let go and lightly punched Lynn in the arm. "Why didn't you tell me last night?"

"I thought it was him, but—"

"Bullshit. You knew it was him." Ali wiped her face with her hand.

Lynn shifted from one foot to the other. "Okay. I panicked. You were so happy. I didn't know what to say. My immediate reaction was to drive up there and wring his fucking neck."

"Not his *fraking* neck?" Ali put her arms around Lynn. "I was mad for a little while, but I know your intentions were good. By the way, I hope you're making a large Shepard's pie."

"Yes. I know you love the leftovers."

"I do, but I also invited him to dinner."

"Wow. I would not have guessed that speed in a zillion years. Are you sure about tonight?"

"I don't know if I'll ever be ready, but there are questions I want answers to. My emotions are all over the place. The more I put it off, the more I'll spin."

"I understand." Lynn rocked her and smoothed her hair.

"I told him a little about Edward over the phone."

Lynn positioned her to look into her face. "That's incredibly brave."

"I'm tired of everyone refusing to talk. I want it out in the open. I don't want to be ignored. It was so horrible that later in life, I questioned my memory. If it wasn't for the few times talking to Denise and the therapist, I would have lost my mind."

Lynn kissed Ali's forehead. "Go on. Take a shower and rest. I'll finish dinner preps."

——⊸⊸◦⊶⊶——

As Lynn led Thomas Blair inside, Ali took a deep breath. Earlier, she felt more confident. Now, she wondered if rushing into a meeting was a mistake. At times, her life felt like a Rubik's Cube with bits and pieces twisting and turning in an attempt to fall into place.

Their eyes met, and he stepped forward. Ali stiffened and

extended her hand. "Thank you for coming Mr. Blair. I've asked Lynn to stay. She's my partner. I want her by my side."

"Of course. Thank you for having me."

He sat in the chair next to the sofa, and Ali scooted tighter against Lynn. She examined the man in the finely tailored suit, crisply ironed, with the blue geometric tie.

"Why did you stay away?"

"Ali, I didn't know that Edward abused you or your mother. I would have taken you both away if I had." His eyes pleaded. "And your mother's inactions...her not protecting you...she...she doesn't sound like the woman I knew. I'm so sorry."

"You never answered my question."

"Carol asked me to stay away, and I abided by her wishes. I was trying to do the right thing."

"Why would she do that?" Ali gripped Lynn's knee tight to hide a slight tremor.

"I never meant for you to pay for my sins." Eyes brimming with tears, he removed a white linen handkerchief and dabbed them. Softly, he said, "Please forgive me. You're my only child. My wife and I couldn't have children."

New tears rushed into Ali's eyes. "I forgive you, but do you know how much you've hurt me?" *We're both hurting. Give him a chance while he's still alive.* Ali softened her tone. "Please tell me about those years."

"I've prayed so many times for God to forgive me. The truth is I fell madly in love with your mother." The smile faded. "My marriage was okay, but we had fallen out of love early on." He brushed his pants. "I was unhappy and working lots of overtime to be out of the house. I was thinking of divorce, then I met your mom."

He shook his head and sniffled. For a man of such power, he seemed so vulnerable in this moment.

"My mother was obviously smitten with you to risk her marriage. Tell me about the good times."

"We lived by the seat of our pants. We'd steal away for an hour or two once a week. Longer if we were lucky. We would often walk down by the monuments, talking, enjoying dinner together, or..." Thomas cleared his throat, and his eyes darted away before looking back at Ali. "I want you to understand, I loved your mother." His hand started to tremble, and he covered part of his face.

"If you loved her, why did she stay with Edward?"

He stood and shuffled over to the window, not saying a word. Ali felt rotten. Her mother taking the other half of the story to the grave only added to Ali's pain. It wasn't his fault, and insinuating otherwise was not going to resolve anything.

He finally said, "Looking back, people may think it was to protect my career, but it was really about you and your siblings. Yes, Carol and I ignored all the consequences in our blissful adventures. We lied and told our spouses we had to work late all the time." He blew his nose. "When Carol got pregnant, I was both elated and terrified. My wife was sterile, and I was excited about becoming a father. At the same time, I was petrified we would be punished for unethical conduct."

He turned, and his face shone utter despair as if he aged several years in the past five minutes.

"The sad truth is the world was extremely misogynistic during that time. Much worse than today. Carol would have been scorned and fired immediately. Because of my stature and accomplishments and simply being male, they probably would have slapped my hands and forgotten about it the next day."

He rubbed his forehead and paced back and forth. "The punishment toward your mother wouldn't have stopped at work. Edward would have divorced Carol, and that would not have been the end. The law would have instantly let him take everything—all the kids, including you, and every penny." He stopped. His eyes focused on Ali. "Edward could have banished your mother for life from seeing her own children. The world was so harsh back then."

A new sadness cursed through Ali. *I missed so much. What if this man had raised me and not Edward?*

Thomas crossed the room and sat back down, leaning his elbows on his knees. "Your mother asked me to stay away so she could be with her children. She loved being a mom. Without her children, the light of life would have gone completely out of her. So, we broke up." His voice cracked. "When you were born, I was delighted you were healthy. You were beautiful. It was painful, but I honored Carol's decision. And she honored mine by sending a picture and note every now and then."

"What about your wife? How did she deal with this?"

He folded his hands, and his face turned pale. "I didn't tell her at first, but she eventually found out. When you first started school, she discovered an antique box with your pictures, notes, and the cancelled checks. Up until that point, I was able to hide the financial transactions because it was my family money that enabled us to live a comfortable life. The checks to your mother came from those assets."

"Did you split up?"

"No. It took me by surprise, but she agreed with the child care payments and believed they were my moral obligation. By that time, I never would have left her. She had been diagnosed with multiple sclerosis. Over the years, we both softened and her illness brought us closer together. She died ten years ago. I never remarried."

Ali could barely see through her tears. He reached for her hand, and she didn't resist. Lynn handed them more tissues and took some for herself.

"As I said, your mother never mentioned Edward's vices or the abuse. Was there ever a time when it wasn't bad?"

"I have some early memories before he started drinking. You gave my mom monthly payments. Why?"

"I was responsible for bringing you into this world. It was the least I could do."

"She probably used it for all of us."

"I'm sure she did. The only time I insisted on control was when you enrolled in college. I paid the university and landlord directly. I would have withheld payment if you didn't take school seriously." His smile returned, and his eyes lightened. "But you rarely made mistakes. I was proud of how hard you worked to earn your grades and pay for your own books."

"Thank you. I'm grateful for not having a college loan." Ali wiped her hand down her face. "Did you get me the job at NPIC and later help with my promotions at NGA?"

"No! Well, not illegally if that's what you're implying." His brow furrowed. "As you recall, you went to a job fair at your university. Several members of the Intelligence Community were there."

"Oh my, God. You were there!"

The crooked smile popped on his face. "I took your application, but I already knew your grade point average and all about your extracurricular activities: student government, debate team, volleyball team, and an excellent scholar. I simply made sure your resume got to a few supervisors, but it was your achievements that easily set you apart from the others and got you the job. Of course, as you know, you had to pass the polygraph to get a real assignment."

"Things were so different. It was so boring in the beginning. They basically kept me in a corner reading training manuals and military equipment identification books." She raised her brows. "Then it was like an avalanche after I passed the poly. By the way, the poly has never been easy for me."

Thomas's face quirked, and he tilted his head. "Why?"

"Every time the tester played good cop/bad cop or needled me during breaks, it would remind me of Edward taunting me. He often called me useless and an ungrateful brat and worse..." Ali's anger bubbled up. "I would have taken more slaps over Edward's emotional abuse any day. He was always accusing me of everything. I was worthless in his eyes."

"I'm so sorry, Ali."

"Oh, honey," Lynn wrapped her arms around Ali. "Let it out and let it go. He can't hurt you anymore."

She cried as Lynn soothed her. When she calmed down, she heard Thomas blow his nose several times.

"You have a remarkable partner. I was worried during that second deployment."

Ali turned back to Thomas. "Didn't you cross the line by being involved in the operation since you knew I was your daughter?"

"Admiral Kent made me the lead. He hinted about our relationship when he sent me forward. I should have recused myself, but I wanted to be near you." Thomas glanced between them. "I never knew he suggested to Lynn to use her feelings to manipulate you."

"Ali, honey. We've talked about this. I—"

"It's in the past. I know you didn't do anything to hurt me. I love you." Ali hugged Lynn. "I have for a very long time. It took me time to realize how lucky I was. I could have lost you at any time over my selfishness."

Ali released Lynn and shifted in her seat. "Thomas, when did you first know I was gay?"

"Do you realize you called me Thomas? Sounds so much better than Mr. Blair."

The corner of his eyes crinkled, and he smiled. "It was around the time you started coming out at work. Ali, your sexuality doesn't define who you are. I look at you and see an accomplished, stunning, strong woman who happens to be my daughter." His eyes shone brightly. "I look at the two of you and see a loving couple. I may have had some difficulty understanding early on, but I never would have shunned you."

"Thank you. Those words mean a lot to me." Ali squeezed his hand, then stood and leaned in to hug him.

"Thank you for seeing me so soon. This day turned out better than I hoped. I wasn't sure you would forgive this old man."

"You're not old."

"I know one thing that's not old. It's my nose. What's that delicious smell?"

Lynn popped off the sofa. "Shepard's pie. I almost forgot. Let me check it, and I'll be right back."

"Ali, I don't want to anger you. This may be too soon to suggest, but I'm a firm believer in counseling. Talking to a psychologist could help you a lot. The agency offers it all the time to returning deployers, and it pains me to see so few accept."

"No need to worry. I've been seeing one on and off privately for several years. It took me a while to find someone I felt comfortable with."

"Good."

Lynn bounced back in the room. "Dinner's done."

Thomas immediately rose. "I'll help set the table."

During the meal, they shared happy stories. Ali perked up when Thomas mentioned a brother, two sisters, and nieces and nephews living in New York, Pennsylvania, and Ohio.

"I'd like to see some pictures sometime and hear more stories. Will you join us for dinner again?"

He patted her hand. "That would be my pleasure."

After Lynn served dessert, Thomas said, "There is one more story," he fluttered his hand in the air, "a little sad, but I think you should know." He paused, and his jaw tightened, but his eyes remained bright. "Your mom allowed me to name you. Alaina was my youngest sister, and Ali was her nickname. She died during high school."

"Oh my, God. How?"

"I'm sorry. I didn't mean to make you cry again." He reached out for Ali's hand. "It was a car accident."

Lynn handed everyone tissues and rubbed Ali's shoulder.

"Thomas, the tears at this point are a way of releasing pent-up pain and an enormous relief rather than anger. Lynn and I have learned the hard way that holding bitterness only denied ourselves happiness." She turned and kissed Lynn gently on the lips.

"I agree." The clock on the wall chimed nine p.m.. "I'm usually in bed by now, but I'm so happy you called. Every fiber in my body feels relief and joy."

"Don't be a stranger. I'd like to see more of you and get to know you better."

"Likewise." His eyes started tearing up again. "Well, I'd best be on my way."

After putting on his jacket, Thomas stepped forward and embraced Ali. She returned the emotional act with a tight grip. "Hugs never felt this good before. Thank you."

Chapter 53

Lynn busied herself by cleaning the house. Ali was talking with her sisters, and it was taking longer than Lynn expected. At the sound of the door, Lynn turned to see Ali. Her eyes were red. Her clenched jaw and furrowed brow revealed an anger Lynn didn't often see.

"What happened?"

"It was interesting and informative." Ali's eyebrows flicked up. "I knew Denise wouldn't freak. Initially, Stephanie was still as a mouse and walked out on the deck, leaving us sitting in the kitchen. Then she took a walk, leaving pies in the oven. She was gone until we cleaned up." She crossed her arms. "When she returned, everything careened off the emotional cliff."

Ali yanked the kitchen chair back, scraping it across the tile. She slouched back, folded her arms across her chest, and clenched her jaw. Lynn filled a glass of water and placed it on the table.

"Thank you." Ali took a swig and set the glass back down hard. "I thought yesterday with Kevin would be the worst. He left for college when I was eleven and never returned home. And he always acts so," Ali threw up her hands, "straitlaced.

But he listened and believed me. Stephanie," Ali's voice cracked, "shocked me today. She knew about my abuse but kept quiet all these years! Can you fucking believe that?" Ali smacked her hand on the table and almost knocked the water over.

Lynn was momentarily speechless. While Stephanie wasn't as liberal as Denise, she seemed to be kind to Ali.

"Apparently, Mom confided some to her and even talked about leaving Edward." She sucked in her bottom lip and reached out for Lynn's hand.

Lynn leaned over and placed a delicate kiss on the corner of Ali's mouth. "I'm sorry."

"Anyway, Stephanie was always Daddy's girl and didn't believe Mom at first. Today she revealed that she's been seeing a therapist for the past five years dealing with her marriage, and the guilt that she saw Edward..."

Ali squeezed her eyes shut. A tear leaked out of one corner. "Stephanie..." Ali's mouth turned and twisted. "She saw Edward hit me when I was sixteen." The tears streamed down her cheek. "He was screaming I was a 'pussy-licking whore.' I remember as if it were yesterday but didn't know Stephanie witnessed the attack. And to hear Stephanie say those words and know she didn't do anything just cut me to pieces."

"Oh my, God." Lynn embraced Ali. "It's all over, honey. Cry. Let it out."

"I'll get snot on your shirt."

Lynn reached out and grabbed some tissues. "I don't give a frak but take these." She rocked Ali. "Let it out. I'm here for you. I always will be."

Ali wiped her face. "Anyway, I guess the realization that I was a lesbian, and her father physically abused me, sent Stephanie into denial and into her own little make-believe

world. The psychologist gave Stephanie the standard forgiveness speech about how she'd never feel peace until she
faced me, which she did today." Ali squeezed Lynn's hand.
"Stephanie doesn't like to display tears in front of anyone, but
today was different. She had a total meltdown."

Lynn took Ali's hand in hers. "That's good, right?"

"Yeah, except a part of me is so damned pissed at her." Ali's
voice turned sharp. "She was twenty-one and a college graduate.
She could have stopped it, but she didn't!" Ali wadded the tissue
and threw it in the trashcan. "You know, I think it would have
been years before she said anything, if ever. She thought it was
an isolated incident, and he was only angry because he found out
I was a lesbian." The last sentence was said through gritted teeth.

"People make mistakes all the time. At least she was trying to
deal with it through the therapist." Lynn could see the mix of
sadness and anger. "Don't let the negative consume you, honey."

"It was the way she said things after the tears. Stephanie
had the gall to say, 'So many things made sense since he
wasn't your dad.'" Ali picked up the dish towel folded on the
table and threw it across the room. "It got worse. She then
said something about '*Her dad* would not have done such
horrible things if he hadn't been wounded by our mother's
actions.' Can you believe that shit?"

"Sounds like she didn't think before she spoke."

"She followed that up with, 'Alcohol does terrible things to
people,' then started loading the fucking dishwasher. Those
are the exact same goddamn words Mom would say whenever
I tried to talk with her. They even said that to the police over
his two DUIs!" Ali pounded her fist on the table. "Dammit!
Lots of people have problems with alcohol. It doesn't make a
person an abuser or pedophile."

Lynn's gaze shifted from focusing on Ali's crossed arms

and angry face to looking behind her through the screen door. Stephanie was there, standing like a stone statue. Her face was pale, and her eyes puffy from crying. Ali wasn't aware of Stephanie's presence.

"You're right. I've been meek and mistreated you. Neither Mom nor I protected you like we should have." Stephanie softly said.

Ali's head whipped around. "You have a lot of nerve!"

"Easy, honey," Lynn whispered.

Stephanie slowly opened the door and gingerly walked in. "I'm partially the reason for your pain. I turned a blind eye. I didn't want to believe that monster was my dad." Stephanie's head was bowed. "I only saw him hit you that once, and I wanted so desperately to believe that it wasn't true. I should have known better, but I was still young, too. I should have stopped him, but I was also scared. He was so drunk. The pain and guilt will be with me forever. Please forgive me."

By now, Denise had quietly come through the door. "Ali, Stephanie and I had a long talk after you left." Her mouth formed a half-smile. "Well, I sort of did most of the talking in a voice that shook the earth. But after I shut up, she admitted this to me." Denise put her hand on Stephanie's shoulder. "I believe her. That doesn't excuse what happened, but we need to heal. No matter what comes our way, we're still sisters."

Stephanie pleaded, "I love you, Ali, and I am so sorry for my pathetic response. From now on, I promise not to shut you down when you want to talk."

Ali leaned her elbows on the table and rested her head.

"Please, Ali. Say something," Stephanie pleaded.

Ali rose and stepped towards Stephanie, looking her in the eye. "I forgive you, but I have to confess that it's going to take me a long time to feel close to you again."

Stephanie sniffled. "I understand. I'd feel the same way if I were in your shoes."

"I'll give it my best if you will, too."

Ali hugged her sisters. When she broke contact, she walked over to Lynn, wrapped her arms around Lynn's neck.

"I love you." Ali's mouth took possession of Lynn. Her tongue slipped in, gently at first, then with intensity. They had never kissed in front of Ali's family, but Lynn melted into Ali's embrace. The taste of Ali's strawberry lip balm and soft lips were too irresistible. She was breathless when Ali withdrew.

Ali draped her arm over Lynn and turned back to her sisters. "Lynn and I have been through a lot together and had our share of mistakes, but we love each other. Part of the deal in healing our family is you recognize Lynn as my partner. No more hush, hush, and denial. Either you accept Lynn or we part ways, because I'm tired of being treated as if I'm damaged goods."

"Absolutely," Denise said as she elbowed Stephanie, whose mouth hung open.

"Of course, I've been a little old-fashioned, but I like Lynn."

"Oh yeah, forgot to mention it. Lynn moved in last week and will be renting her house. Bottom line: I don't want to hear one bad word if we hold hands or kiss at a family event. Well, not a French kiss, but everyone else shows affection to their partners. I want the same."

Denise put a hand on her hip and said, "That's never been my problem. What do you have to say Stephanie?"

"Ah...I...I see your point." She licked her lips. "You should be treated equally. And for the record, I think Lynn seems good for you. In all honesty, she's the best girlfriend you've ever had."

"Partner not girlfriend."

Stephanie smiled. "Lynn is welcome as your partner to family events."

"And between the three of us, we can shut Kevin down if he complains." Denise punched her fist in the air.

"Surprisingly, he was easy to talk to yesterday, and he promised to treat Lynn better."

"Wow. I knew I felt the earth move." Denise giggled.

Chapter 54

May 2018 – Eastern Shore, Maryland

Ali sunk into the sofa. "This beach house is an amazing rental. Why so big? I could fit a boat in the living room." She made a sweeping motion with her arm. "And a gigantic deck facing the ocean with an outdoor fireplace. Wow."

"You deserve something special for our anniversary." Lynn kissed the tip of Ali's nose.

"Anniversary? We've only be living together for about eight months."

"Don't you remember Lake Accotink? That was May last year. You asked me for a reset, and don't forget last month."

Ali blinked a couple of times. "Sorry, what did we do last month?"

"We met ten years ago last month."

Grabbing the back of Ali's neck, Lynn pulled her in. She sucked on Ali's lower lip, grazing it with her teeth before diving in for a full kiss. Her body tingled more as her tongue met Ali's. Her hand skimmed down Ali's neck to her chest, circling a nipple, sending sensational bursts of pleasure to her lower body.

"I think we've got enough time before the art fair," she whispered while her hand slipped under Ali's T-shirt.

"Sounds like an offer I can't refuse."

After one more kiss, Lynn cupped Ali's chin and looked deep into her eyes. "I love it when your eyes get so smoky."

"Less talking, more action."

Lynn retook Ali's mouth with a relentless need, and her hand stroked the muscles of Ali's stomach while her mouth moved to Ali's neck.

"Ah..."

"Like that?" Lynn dipped below Ali's waist band. "Your clothes are loose, but I think it'd be much better if they came off."

Ali sucked in a deep breath as Lynn's finger glided lower. Lynn withdrew suddenly.

"Tease."

"No. Just a prelude." Lynn stood and held out her hand. "I want you in the bedroom now to savor every inch of you."

Ali popped up off the sofa and into Lynn's arms. They stumbled towards the bedroom while kissing and groping.

Lynn planted kisses over Ali as she peeled off each garment. "So, beautiful," she mumbled, then took a mouthful of Ali's plump breast while tracing the curves of her hips. Lynn pushed her onto the bed and crawled on top.

"Uh-uh." Ali pushed her shoulder. "I want you naked."

Lynn jumped up, whipped her shirt and sports bra off in one swoop. Ali sat on the edge of the bed as Lynn wiggled out of her jeans and boy shorts.

Ali leaned back and curled her finger with a sultry come-hither look, then slowly crept backwards and spread herself. Lynn's heart beat faster as she positioned over Ali.

She caressed and kissed from Ali's neck to her inner thighs as she breathed in the scent of her lover. "Your skin's so soft."

Her eyes glanced up to watch Ali's face as her fingers gently moved into the tender folds, exploring and, with each stroke, inching closer and closer to Ali's clit. Over the roar of her own beating heart and breathing, Lynn listened to Ali's soft cries. She slipped two fingers in, and her tongue flicked Ali's clit. Ali arched her back as Lynn's fingers glided faster and faster. Lynn's tongue circled and flicked until Ali cried, "Please."

Lynn smiled again then her mouth took all of Ali in, sucking and nipping until Ali twitched below her. When she felt Ali was depleted of energy, Lynn moved up and laid next to her, gently caressing her breasts. Her body buzzing.

After a few minutes, Ali rolled her over and positioned her leg between Lynn's hips, moving against her slick sex, while her thumb rubbed over Lynn's taut nipple. "Slow and steady or..."

"Quick, please." Lynn gasped.

Ali nestled between her legs. Lynn drew a sharp breath as Ali gripped her ass and that nimble tongue began long loving strokes.

"Oh, dear." Lynn fists tightly clenched the sheets.

As Ali alternated between long strokes with the flat of her tongue and flicking rapidly with the tip, Lynn lifted her hips to meet every move. Ali thrust inside Lynn then back to the clit. Bright bursts of light flashed behind Lynn's eyelids as she crested each wave. A hand moved to Ali's head. Her fingers firmly gripped the scalp and loosened over and over as Ali licked until Lynn's whole body exploded in an intense orgasm. Her chest heaved and her heart beat wildly as she gasped for air.

They laid there in bliss for some time, their fingertips gently tracing loving circles over each other's skin.

Lynn finally chanced a look at the clock. "We should shower and go to the art fair."

"What's the rush?"

"If we go now, we'll catch the last two hours. I really want to see it."

"I was the one that wanted to go."

Lynn smoothed Ali's hair and kissed the top of her head. "I read about one of your favorite artists. I think she might be here."

"Who?"

"Ah...can't remember the name." Lynn scooted out from underneath Ali and moved towards the bathroom. "Come on. I'll make the shower worth your effort."

After showering, Lynn dressed while Ali put on makeup. She rushed to make the bed and snatched up the discarded garments from around the room. She threw them in a laundry bag, and tossed it in the closet.

"Why are you cleaning the room? We'll only mess up the bed later."

Lynn shrugged her shoulders and tapped her watch. "Almost three p.m. and time to go. You don't want to miss this one. I heard this year is super."

She put her hand on the small of Ali's back and guided her out the room.

Ali let out a sigh. "What a day. Fantastic sex, art, dinner, and a stroll through the town. I'm tired. Maybe we should watch a movie in bed."

"No. The night is young." Lynn pulled her towards the deck.

"My feet are sore."

"Let's walk along the beach, then relax in front of the outdoor fire. Come on. You're always telling me how much the beach walk revitalizes you."

"True. Any chance of a foot rub afterward."

Lynn grinned and tugged harder.

As the cool surf washed over their ankles and sand squished between their toes, Ali relished being cradled in Lynn's arms. They had come so far. Even after every low, they bounced back stronger and wiser.

"The water and fresh air reinvigorated me, but I'm getting cold. Lynn, thank you for surprising me with this trip. I love you."

Lynn rubbed her shoulder and kissed her. "Love you too, and you're welcome. How's your knee?"

"It keeps getting better. I wish I had done the surgery sooner. I'm going to miss this—the ocean, the sound of the waves lapping on the shore, the walks with you in the surf...Maybe we should move to the ocean when we retire."

Even in the moonlight, Ali could see Lynn's eyes glisten with joy.

"I like the sound of that. Us, together in retirement. Now let's get back before you turn into a popsicle. I can feel you starting to shiver."

Rounding the corner, Ali grabbed Lynn's arm. "Someone's on the deck, and the fire's roaring."

"No worries. I paid someone." Lynn kissed Ali's hand. "There's chilled sparkling champagne, non-alcoholic of course, and snacks waiting for us. As I said, you deserve to be treated special."

"I am so lucky to have such a thoughtful partner." Ali squeezed Lynn tight.

"Welcome back, ladies," a man called out. He motioned to the deck loveseat.

"Happy tenth, sweetie." Lynn kissed her mouth, then leaned her forehead against Ali's. "I could kiss you all night. Let's relax, and I'll make it up to you once he leaves."

They snuggled into the loveseat, and the gentleman poured their drinks and disappeared inside.

"You pamper me too much."

"I enjoy the return on my investment." Lynn leaned in and brushed her lips against Ali's then traced Ali's bottom lip with her tongue. Lynn sat back and licked her lips.

"You're teasing again."

"I wanted to get the taste of you and the champagne from your lips. There's plenty of time to make out later." Lynn waggled her eyebrows. "That is, if you're not too tired."

"The ocean helped wake me up, but you have revved up my engine."

Ali grabbed Lynn's jacket and pulled her in. Her mouth captured Lynn's. She started gently, then took her with a wild thirst, nipping Lynn's ear before moving to her neck.

"Oh, my. You know I have trouble resisting you."

"Then don't." Ali sucked in the tender skin on Lynn's throat.

Lynn pressed her hand against Ali's shoulder. "I want you, sweetie. But the server's still here."

Ali pulled back. "Dismiss him, and let's make love in front of the fire."

"Sounds wonderful except I don't want to give a show to someone who might walk by on the beach."

"That's what blankets are for. Be adventurous."

"Tempting, but you know I'm the modest one."

The server reappeared with a plate of smoked salmon, cucumber slices, cheese, and crackers.

Lynn rubbed her hands together. "My favorite. Looks amazing. Thank you." She piled food onto a plate. Ali watched her in disbelief.

"Enjoy, ladies. I'll be leaving now."

Lynn waved and leaned back with a full plate. She shoved a large piece in her mouth.

Ali sipped her champagne and eyed Lynn. "You're still hungry? Dinner wasn't that long ago."

"Yep. Oh no, it looks like he forgot something."

Before Ali could get a word, Lynn rushed into the house and returned, placing a bowl next to the food platter.

"What's in the fancy bowl?"

Lynn poured more champagne into their flute glasses. "Caviar dip." She popped a cracker in her mouth.

"Caviar dip in a foil-wrapped bowl?"

Ali cocked an eyebrow, and Lynn stopped munching half-way through.

"Ah...I made it yesterday when you were in the shower."

Ali wrapped her arm around Lynn and whispered in her ear, "But now that the server's gone, maybe we should have fun and snack later." She twirled a strand of Lynn's hair with her finger. "Finish your cracker and make love to me."

"Have some. The crackers have a little parmesan, and the dip is awesome." Lynn crammed another cracker in her mouth.

Ali dropped her arm. "You're turning me down for food?"

"I'm not turning you down. I'm hungry." She took Ali's hand. "The night is young. Let's enjoy the fire. Look." She waved her hand. "The outdoor fireplace is situated so we can also see the ocean. Now, please have some dip. I bought it, especially for you."

"I thought you made it?" Ali cocked her head.

Lynn stopped chewing and crammed another cracker in her mouth. "It's a little of both. I combined the two."

"Okay, goofy. Stop talking with crackers in your mouth."

Ali ripped off the foil. She blinked and picked up the bowl.

The reflection of the white sparkles of a diamond ring contrasted against the dip as she rotated the bowl.

Lynn got on one knee. "Ali, I love you and want to spend the rest of my life with you. I pledge to work hard to make you happy and to always be by your side. Will you marry me?"

"Wow. I never expected this."

"Marry me."

Ali leaned in, brushing her hand down Lynn's face. "I'll marry you on one condition."

"Okay." Lynn cleared her throat. "What's the condition?"

"You give me at least a year of engagement. We had enough drama this past year, and there are still people to meet in your family and the Blair family. We don't have to have a fancy ceremony, but I want as many of our friends and family to join us as possible."

"But you'll marry me?"

"Yes. Are you going to remain on one knee all night long?" Ali cracked a devilish smile. "Or do you need help getting up?"

Lynn jumped up, throwing her hands in the air and dancing around. "Yes! She said, 'Yes!'"

"Is there someone you're shouting to?"

Lynn cupped her hands and yelled, "I'm the happiest woman in the world! She said, 'Yes!'"

In the light of the blazing fire and glow of the moon, Ali saw movement. Footsteps echoed from every direction as family and friends descended onto the deck. Ali put her hand to her mouth.

"Oh, my God."

"Are you okay?" Lynn squinted, looking concerned.

"Yes!" Ali wrapped her arms around Lynn's neck. Her body shook.

Lynn whispered in her ear. "You sure?"

The softness of Lynn's lips tickled Ali's ear. "I can't believe you pulled this off. I love you, Lynn Stewart."

Lynn picked her up and spun her around, yelling, "Yahoo!"

Ali was punch-drunk from the surprise and from the spinning. Her siblings and Thomas Blair were the first to congratulate the couple. Thomas wrapped his arms around a woman with long, gray wavy hair and a woman about Ali's age.

"Ali, this is your Aunt Sara and her daughter Jane from Ohio."

There was no need for words, only hugs. Laughter and smiles mixed with tears of joy. As others congratulated them, Ali figured the deck had to be filled with at least forty people. Their work colleagues were in the back of the crowd. Dory and Paul enthusiastically waved.

Next, a man stepped forward. He was helping a frail old woman. Lynn squeezed Ali's shoulder but didn't say a word. Her face was beaming.

"Hello Ali, I'm Lynn's brother Ian, and this is our Aunt Louise."

Ali hugged them. She was careful with Louise, who suffered from Parkinson's disease. With a slight tremor, Louise held Ali's hand.

"I prefer Florida." Even Louise's voice trembled. "It's so cold here, but I wanted to see my darling niece." She smiled at Lynn, never releasing Ali's hand. Slowly she turned to Ali. "Do you plan on having children? I heard artificial insemination is more effective and reasonably priced nowadays."

Ali's jaw dropped. "We haven't thought about that."

"Well, you should. Lynn talks about you so much. All good. I'm sure you'd be lovely mommies."

The words were heartwarming, but becoming a parent in her mid-forties was a bit daunting. Ali could tell Ian was hiding a laugh. Scotty was further away but with his hand over his mouth, snickering. Ali turned to Lynn.

"Uhm...We'll think about it, but...ah..."

"Aunt Louise." Ian rubbed her shoulder while she still held Ali's hand. He kissed the top of her head. "That's a splendid idea. Now let's give others a chance to say their congratulations." She nodded, and he carefully helped her to the side.

Aunt Judy was next. She rocked Ali back and forth. "I'm so happy for you." She hugged Lynn. "Take good care of our girl."

"I will."

Scotty bounced on his toes. "And you thought I was too bold when I got you a hot woman to help you fix up your house. Looks like she fixed a lot of things. I'm happy for you." He kissed Ali on the cheek and bear hugged them both.

The rest of the friends and family made quick congratulatory greetings.

"Oh, listen up, everyone!" Ali cocked an eyebrow. "Lynn, there is another condition on our marriage." She twirled her fingers through Lynn's hair. "A black tux rocking that curly blonde hair. Got it?"

"Yes, ma'am, but only if you wear your wavy auburn hair cascading down your back." Lynn caressed Ali's hand and kissed her palm.

Scotty yelled, "Lynn, you forgot to say plenty of cleavage showing and backless." He dipped a cracker and stuffed it in his mouth.

Ali waved him off.

"Oh crap." Lynn darted over to Scott.

"What's wrong, babe?"

"With all the excitement, I forgot to put the ring on your finger."

In a frenzy, Lynn yelled at Scott, "Stop. Where's the ring?"

"Huh?" he mumbled around a mouth full of crackers and dip.

Lynn grabbed the bowl from him. Her smile dropped as she turned it around several times. Her fingers dug in. Silence grew.

She threw her head back, looking up at the stars. Ali's stomach dropped. Lynn lowered her face and removed the ring from the dip. She rushed back to Ali.

"Oh, no. Not like that. It's got caviar on it."

Lynn grabbed a glass of water and poured the water over her hand and the ring. After drying it off with her shirt, she proudly held it out.

Ali broke out into a bout of chuckles but managed to say, "I was always attracted to your good looks and sincerity, but it's your endless charm and debonair style that hooked me."

Lynn slipped the ring on Ali's finger. It fit perfectly.

Scott cupped his hands over his mouth. "Kiss! Kiss! Kiss!" Soon, he had everyone chanting.

"Give me the best French kiss ever," Ali shouted.

Lynn smiled. "With pleasure."

Glossary of Terms

Al Qaeda Militant Sunni Islamist multi-national organization founded by Osama bin Laden. In 1999, the United Nations Security Council adopts Resolution 1267 linking Al Qaeda and the Taliban (Afghan political group) as terrorist organizations.

Battle Rattle Slang for body armor.

Chow Hall Slang for dining.

CIA Central Intelligence Agency

CID The United States Army Criminal Investigation Division

COP Combat Outpost

DIA Defense Intelligence Agency

ESRI The Environmental Systems Research Institute is a world leader, developer, and supplier of software, web Geographical Information Systems (GIS) and geodatabase management applications.

FOB Forward Operating Base

Geospatial Data that relates to the physical world or is associated with a particular location.

Green Zone Security zone in the heart of Kabul that includes ISAF Headquarters, the U.S. Embassy, key Afghan buildings, and International Embassies.

Helo Slang for helicopter.

HUMINT Human Intelligence

IED Improvised Explosive Device

IC Intelligence Community. Agencies and departments (military and civilian) that gather intelligence information on foreign entities.

ISAF International Security Assistance Force

JETT Fictious term that stands for Joint Elite Technology Team.

JIEDDO The Joint Improvised Explosive Device Defeat Organization was renamed in 2015 to Joint Improvised-Threat Defeat Agency. JIEDDO's mission was to defeat IEDs and IED networks.

MRAP Mine-Resistant Ambush Protected

MRE Meals Ready to Eat

NATO North Atlantic Treaty Organization

NCOIC Noncommissioned Officer In Charge. In this story, the second in command after the JETT officer.

NGA National Geospatial-Intelligence Agency

NPIC National Photographic Interpretation Center

NSA National Security Agency, headquartered at Fort Meade in Maryland.

PDB President's Daily Briefing.

PT Physical Training

PSYOP Psychological operations. PSYOP soldiers specialize in unconventional capabilities, cultural expertise, language proficiency, military deception and advanced communications techniques. Their mission is to influence a targeted group's emotions, motives, and objective reasoning.

R&R Rest & relaxation. Military word for vacation time.

Taliban A Sunni Islamic fundamentalist political movement and military organization in Afghanistan. In 1999, the United Nations Security Council adopts Resolution 1267 linking Al Qaeda and the Taliban as terrorist organizations.

UAV Unmanned Aerial Vehicle

Locations

Ahmed Khel Town northeast of Gardez, near the Pakistan border.

Bagram Largest military base in Afghanistan. North of Kabul.

Baraki Barak Town between Gardez and Kabul. Former capital of Logar Province.

Camp Eggers US base in Kabul, closed in 2014.

Gardez Capital of Paktia Province.

ISAF Headquarters Close to the US Embassy.

Fort Meade Located in Maryland. The National Security Agency and the United States Cyber Command are located on this U.S. Army installation. Commonly called Fort Meade, the official name is Fort George G. Meade.

Jalalabad Town near the Pakistan border. FOB Fenty is located in this town.

J-Bad Slang for FOB Fenty.

Kabul Capital of Afghanistan.

Lake Accotink Park located in Springfield, Virginia.

Shirley Highway I-295. Local name for highway that connects Northern Virginia beltway and Washington D.C.

Shirlington The Village of Shirlington in Arlington. Popular and upscale.

Surobi Town on the Kabul-Nangarhar Highway and halfway between Kabul and Jalalabad.

Tagab Village halfway between Bagram Air Force Base and Surobi.

Final Note by the Author

I retired as a government employee with the National Geospatial-Intelligence Agency (NGA). Like society, the federal government and agencies evolved in their stance on the LGBTQ community and are still changing, hopefully for the better. I'm sure many people are familiar with the general facts of the policy "Don't Ask Don't Tell" (DADT). In that policy, a U.S. military member could lose their career if it were revealed they were gay. There were horrible episodes that some people suffered. DADT was instituted by the Clinton Administration on February 28, 1994, and officially ended on September 20, 2011 by the Obama Administration.

What many people don't know is that President Bill Clinton also signed two Executive Orders. EO 12968 in 1995 and EO 13087 in 1998 provided some protection for gay federal employees (civilians). It's complicated, but it boiled down to a murky gray area where some organizations were more lenient to their civilian employees, and others were strict and unforgiving.

Believe it or not, the CIA was more progressive and implemented positive change way before other agencies. While writing this book, I ran across an article by the Daily Beast. They interviewed Tracey Ballard in 2015; www.thedailybeast.com /how-the-cia-came-out-of-the-closet. The article described Tracey as the co-founder of the Agency's Network of Gay, Lesbian, Bisexual, and Transgender Employees and Allies (ANGLE) in 1996.

About eight years before ANGLE, Tracey came out to the CIA during her "lifestyle" polygraph and was honest about her relationship with her partner, who was in the military. As a result, she was forced to appear before a panel of CIA officers—all men. They pried into her personal life and relationship to "assess whether her sexuality made her a risk to national security." She didn't lose her clearance. Of course, the CIA was not subordinate to the Department of Defense.

I'm sure there are many heroes out there, but Tracey's story rocks my world. I met Tracey in a technical training class sometime around the late 1980s, probably around the same time she was undergoing scrutiny by the male CIA officers. I will forever remember how kind she was.

During that class, I was inexplicably drawn to Tracey and struck up chitchat during lunch. I'm not referring to a physical attraction, but rather a sense that she was different like me—a lesbian. I was drawn to how she dressed, casual and comfortable in slacks, and had an air of independence and confidence.

We discussed the class, movies, music, the weather...anything but why I felt comfortable around her. My intuition told me I could relax even though neither of us mentioned sexuality or politics. Years later, I ran into her and her partner at an LGBTQ event. By then, I was out socially, but still not at work.

When I look back on that class, I now understand a little more about myself. Back then, I was deep in the closet to myself and the world. Okay, I was scared shitless. I feared someone would label me, and I'd lose my job. It didn't help that I was taught as a young kid that "those people are bad and immoral." So, every time I thought about myself being a lesbian, I denied it to be true and buried myself in work. Sound familiar?

Unlike Tracey, I did not come out during my first CIA "lifestyle" polygraph. I was an employee under the Department of Defense rules, and it was illegal for me to hold a clearance and be gay. This was ten years before President Clinton signed those executive orders. I had to take the CIA version because anyone working with them had to take their "lifestyle" polygraph and their counter-intelligence polygraph.

It wasn't until 2006 that I came out to friends. And it was in 2008 that I came out to security in my polygraph. You've read the book now. In real life, I was a complete puddle of tears and snot in my last poly. Unlike the book, it took more than a half-day to bounce back. And yes, the man I grew up with was an alcoholic and abusive. So, that chapter mirrored my life more than any other section of the book. In fact, I kept debating in my own head about how real to make that chapter. I must have changed it a million times.

Coming out is a personal affair, and no two people are alike. It's not unusual in 2019 for a teenager to come out. Some folks don't come out until later years. Other people just are themselves and feel no need to put a label around their neck. There is no wrong or right way to come out or to live or to become your authentic self.

Sadly, despite all of our progress, it is still unsafe for some people to reveal any personal information. LGBTQ history is riddled with three steps forward and at least one or two steps back. A friend said, "Why are you so worried? There's same-sex marriage. This country has made progress." My reply then was, "Yes, but we have a long way to go." I was shocked at her generalization of American society. Cultural differences, biases, and awareness of others are different wherever you go. One cannot make blanket assumptions, even in the United States.

Job and housing discrimination still exist. Married on Sunday and fired on Monday is a reality for some people. How about all the crazy religious freedom laws and regulations that some states and municipalities are trying to pass?

When the case in Oregon about the baker refusing to bake a cake first hit the news, the same friend said, "I don't understand. It's just a cake." I politely pointed out why it was more than just a cake.

We all have a variety of family and friends. Some that we fear turn out to be allies. Other's not so much. A few, like the friend mentioned above, don't understand the precarious situation that the LGBTQ community faces. Yes, my friend loves and accepts me, but she really struggles to understand.

As the saying goes, "History has a way of repeating itself." Civil rights in this country have been trampled on and can still be trampled on. As a member of the LGBTQ community, rights earned yesterday can be taken away tomorrow.

We can't take things for granted. I love this country, but we are not perfect. We can always improve. Improvement is not taking away someone's dignity and rights. There is more work to be done. We cannot go backward.

Those that want us to go backward keep pounding away in the hopes that everyone will just get tired, tune out, and go in their own little corner. I say take coffee and chocolate into your own little nirvana, but don't forget to tune in occasionally. And for heaven's sake, please vote. Vote for love, human dignity, civil rights. Vote to keep us together and not tear us apart.

Sincerely,
Addison M. Conley

About the Author

Addison M. Conley grew up in central Illinois, moved to the east coast in her twenties, and now lives in the eastern panhandle of West Virginia with two fur babies. For many years, her writing was strictly business reports filled with facts, but the yearning to write fiction never left.

Beyond the Checkpoint is her second novel. *Falling for Love: A West Virginia Romance* is the second edition of her first published novel. A third novel (currently untitled), is set in Rehoboth Beach, Delaware, which just happens to be her favorite East Coast beach town.

When not writing, she enjoys playing cards and board games with friends, music, concerts, traveling, photography, reading, and working with stained glass.

Addison would love to hear from you.

Email:
Addison.M.Conley.Author@gmail.com

Facebook:
www.facebook.com/people/Addison-M-Conley/100017653029093 or *www.facebook.com/AddisonMConley.Fiction.Author*

Twitter:
twitter.com/NeoTrinity13. Yeah, Addison's a die-hard fan of the original movie *The Matrix*.

Instagram:
instagram.com/addison.m.conley

Goodreads:
www.goodreads.com/author/show/17138353.Addison_M_Conley

Made in the USA
Las Vegas, NV
20 February 2023

67872816R00225

"Yes!" The screen filled with an email on the Al Qaeda network they were trying to pin down. She made a few notes and forwarded the message to the other JETT members.

"All right, Ace, leftover heaven awaits you."

Ali smiled at the nickname. "About damn time, Henderson. Chow line is only open for another forty-five minutes. Bet they served steak tonight, and you ate it all up. Where's the rest of the team?"

"Stopped at the rec center. Several care packages were in the lobby." He tossed her a tube of hand cream. "I snagged it before it was gone."

Ali rose to high-five him, but the six-foot-one hulk moved his hand high and grinned before lowering it for her to reach.

"Anything interesting happening?" He asked.

Her hands flew up, palm upwards. "Another power outage for about five minutes until generators kicked in and servers rebooted. I had problems with the satellite link, but thank God I didn't have to go on the roof and reset the box. This shit is getting old."

"I heard they've got new generators coming in, which should take care of things."

"I hope so. Someone's going to get hurt if this happens in the middle of a mission." Ali slipped on her jacket. "Oh, I forwarded an email on Al Qaeda number three. I hope we take him down soon. Looks like your genius in signal and electronics intelligence is paying off. Some coordinates also appear to match our other suspect's location."

"I'll check it out. What else are you working on?" He stuck a piece of candy in his mouth. Ali wondered if he ever stopped eating.

"Spatial-temporal analysis—"

"Hold on a minute. In English, please."